Also by Len Deighton

Berlin Game

BERLIN GAME

LEN DEIGHTON

ALFRED A. KNOPF

NEW YORK

1984

THIS IS A BORZOI BOOK
PUBLISHED BY ALFRED A. KNOPF, INC.

Copyright © 1983 by Len Deighton

All rights reserved under International and Pan-American
Copyright Conventions. Published in the United States by Alfred
A. Knopf, Inc., New York. Distributed by Random House, Inc.,
New York. Published in Great Britain by
Hutchinson Books, Ltd, London.

Library of Congress Cataloging in Publication Data

Deighton, Len.   [date]   Berlin game.

I. Title.
PR6054.E37B4   1984   823'.914   83-48104
ISBN 0-394-53407-7

Manufactured in the United States of America

FIRST EDITION

Berlin Game

Chapter 1

How long have we been sitting here?" I said. I picked up the field glasses and studied the bored young American soldier in his glass-sided box.

"Nearly a quarter of a century," said Werner Volkmann. His arms were resting on the steering wheel and his head was slumped on them. "That G.I. wasn't even born when we first sat here waiting for the dogs to bark."

Barking dogs, in their compound behind the remains of the Hotel Adlon, were usually the first sign of something happening on the other side. The dogs sensed any unusual activity long before the handlers came to get them. That's why we kept the windows open; that's why we were frozen nearly to death.

"That American soldier wasn't born, the spy thriller he's reading wasn't written, and we both thought the Wall would be demolished within a few days. We were stupid kids but it was better then, wasn't it, Bernie?"

"It's always better when you're young, Werner," I said.

This side of Checkpoint Charlie had not changed. There never was much there: just one small hut and some signs warning you about leaving the Western Sector. But the East German side had grown far more elaborate. Walls and fences, gates and barriers, endless white lines to mark out the traffic lanes. Most recently they'd built a huge walled compound where the tourist buses were searched and tapped, and scrutinized by gloomy men who pushed wheeled mirrors under every vehicle lest one of their fellow-countrymen was clinging there.

The checkpoint is never silent. The great concentration of lights that illuminate the East German side produces a steady hum like a field of insects on a hot summer's day. Werner raised his head from his arms and shifted his weight. We both had sponge-rubber cushions under us; that was one thing we'd learned in a quarter of a century. That and taping the door switch so that the interior light didn't come on every time the car door opened. "I wish I knew how long Zena will stay in Munich," said Werner.

"Can't stand Munich," I told him. "Can't stand those bloody Bavarians, to tell you the truth."

"I was only there once," said Werner. "It was a rush job for the Americans. One of our people was badly beaten and the local cops were no help at all." Even Werner's English was spoken with the strong Berlin accent that I'd known since we were at school. Now he was forty years old, thickset, with black bushy hair, black mustache, and sleepy eyes that made it possible to mistake him for one of Berlin's Turkish population. He wiped a spyhole of clear glass in the windscreen so that he could see into the glare of fluorescent lighting. Beyond the silhouette of Checkpoint Charlie, Friedrichstrasse in the East Sector shone as bright as day. "No," he said. "I don't like Munich at all."

The night before, Werner after many drinks had confided to me the story of his wife Zena running off with a man who drove a truck for the Coca-Cola company. For the previous three nights, he'd provided me with a place on a lumpy sofa in his smart apartment in Dahlem, right on the edge of Grunewald. But sober we kept up the pretense that his wife was visiting a relative. "There's something coming now," I said.

Werner did not bother to move his head from where it rested on the seatback. "It's a tan-colored Ford. It will come through the checkpoint, park over there while the men inside have a coffee and hot dog, then they'll go back into the East Sector just after midnight."

I watched. As he'd predicted, it was a tan-colored Ford, a panel truck, unmarked, with West Berlin registration.

"We're in the place they usually park," said Werner. "They're Turks who have girlfriends in the East. The regulations say you have to be out before midnight. They go back there again after midnight."

"They must be some girls!" I said.

"A handful of Westmarks goes a long way over there," said Werner. "You know that, Bernie." A police car with two cops in it cruised past very slowly. They recognized Werner's Audi and one of the cops raised a hand in a weary salutation. After the police car moved away, I used my field glasses to see right through the barrier to where an East German border guard was stamping his feet to restore circulation. It was bitterly cold.

Werner said, "Are you sure he'll cross here, rather than at the Bornholmerstrasse or Prinzenstrasse checkpoint?"

"You've asked me that four times, Werner."

"Remember when we first started working for intelligence. Your dad was in charge then—things were very different. Remember old Mr. Gaunt—the fat old man who could sing all those funny Berlin cabaret songs—betting me fifty marks it would never go up . . . the Wall, I mean. I was only eighteen or nineteen, and fifty marks was a lot of money in those days."

"Silas Gaunt, that was. He'd been reading too many of

those 'guidance reports' from London," I said. "For a time he convinced me you were wrong about everything, including the Wall."

"But *you* didn't make any bets," said Werner. He poured some black coffee from his thermos into a paper cup and passed it to me.

"But I volunteered to go over there that night they closed the sector boundaries. I was no brighter than old Silas. It was just that I didn't have fifty marks to spare for betting."

"The cabdrivers were the first to know. About two o'clock in the morning, the radio cabs were complaining about the way they were being stopped and questioned each time they crossed. The dispatcher in the downtown taxi office told his drivers not to take anyone else across to the East Sector, and then he phoned me to tell me about it."

"And you stopped me from going," I said.

"Your dad told me not to take you."

"But you went over there, Werner. And old Silas went with you." So my father had prevented my going over there the night they sealed off the sector. I didn't know it until now.

"We went across about four-thirty that morning. There were Russian trucks, and lots of soldiers dumping rolls of barbed wire outside the Charité Hospital. We came back quite soon. Silas said the Americans would send in tanks and tear the wire down. Your dad said the same thing, didn't he?"

"The people in Washington were too bloody frightened, Werner. The stupid bastards at the top thought the Russkies were going to move this way and take over the Western Sector of the city. They were *relieved* to see a wall going up."

"Maybe they know things we don't know," said Werner.

"You're right," I said. "They know that the service is run by idiots. But the word is leaking out."

Werner permitted himself a slight smile. "And then, about six in the morning, you heard the sound of the heavy trucks and construction cranes. Remember going on the back of my motorcycle to see them stringing the barbed wire across Potsdamerplatz? I knew it would happen eventually. It was the easiest fifty marks I ever earned. I can't think why Mr. Gaunt took my bet."

"He was new to Berlin," I said. "He'd just finished a year at Oxford, lecturing on political science and all that statistical bullshit the new kids start handing out the moment they arrive."

"Maybe you should go and lecture there," said Werner with just a trace of sarcasm. "You didn't go to university did you, Bernie?" It was a rhetorical question. "Neither did I. But you've done well without it." I didn't answer, but Werner was in the mood to talk now. "Do you ever see Mr. Gaunt? What beautiful German he spoke. Not like yours and mine—*Hochdeutsch,* beautiful."

Werner, who seemed to be doing better than I was, with his export loan business, looked at me expecting a reply. "I married his niece," I said.

"I forgot that old Silas Gaunt was related to Fiona. I hear she is very important in the Department nowadays."

"She's done well," I said. "But she works too hard. We don't have enough time together with the kids."

"You must be making a pot of money," said Werner. "Two of you senior staff, with you on field allowances. . . . But Fiona has money of her own, doesn't she? Isn't her father some kind of tycoon? Couldn't he find a nice soft job for you in his office? Better than sitting out here freezing to death in a Berlin side street."

"He's not going to come," I said after watching the barrier descend again and the border guard go back into his hut. The windscreen had misted over again so that the lights of the checkpoint became a fairyland of bright blobs.

Werner didn't answer. I had not confided to him anything about what we were doing in his car at Checkpoint Charlie, with a tape recorder wired into the car battery and a mike taped behind the sun visor and a borrowed revolver making an uncomfortable bulge under my arm. After a few minutes, he reached forward and wiped a clear spot again. "The office doesn't know you're using me," he said.

He was hoping like hell I'd say Berlin Station had forgiven him for his past failings. "They wouldn't mind too much," I lied.

"They have a long memory," complained Werner.

"Give them time," I said. The truth was that Werner was on the computer as "non-critical employment only," a classification that prevented anyone employing him at all. In this job everything was "critical."

"They didn't okay me, then?" Werner said, suddenly guessing at the truth: that I'd come into town without even telling Berlin Station that I'd arrived.

"What do you care?" I said. "You're making good money, aren't you?"

"I could be useful to them, and the Department could help me more. I told you all that."

"I'll talk to the people in London," I said. "I'll see what I can do."

Werner was unmoved by my promise. "They'll just refer it to the Berlin office, and you know what the answer will be."

"Your wife," I said. "Is she a Berliner?"

"She's only twenty-two," said Werner wistfully. "The family was from East Prussia." He reached inside his coat as if searching for cigarettes, but he knew I wouldn't permit it—cigarettes and lighters are too damned conspicuous after dark—and he closed his coat again. "You probably saw her photo on the sideboard—a small, very pretty girl with long black hair."

"So that's her," I said, although in fact I'd not noticed the photo. At least I'd changed the subject. I didn't want Werner quizzing me about the office. He should have known better than that.

Poor Werner. Why does the betrayed husband always cut such a ridiculous figure? Why isn't the unfaithful partner the comical one? It was all so unfair; no wonder Werner pretended his wife was visiting relatives. He was staring ahead, his big black eyebrows lowered as he concentrated on the checkpoint. "I hope he wasn't trying to come through with forged papers. They put everything under the ultraviolet lights nowadays, and they change the markings every week. Even the Americans have given up using forged papers—it's suicide."

"I don't know anything about that," I told him. "My job is just to pick him up and debrief him before the office sends him to wherever he has to go."

Werner turned his head; the bushy black hair and dark skin made his white teeth flash like a toothpaste commercial. "London wouldn't send you over here for that kind of circus, Bernie. For that kind of task they send office boys, people like me."

"We'll go and get something to eat and drink, Werner," I said. "Do you know some quiet restaurant where they have sausage and potatoes and good Berlin beer?"

"I know just the place, Bernie. Straight up Friedrichstrasse, under the railway bridge at the S-Bahn station and it's on the left. On the bank of the Spree: Weinrestaurant Ganymed."

"Very funny," I said. Between us and the Ganymed

there was a Wall, machine guns, barbed wire, and two battalions of gun-toting bureaucrats. "Turn this jalopy around and let's get out of here."

He switched on the ignition and started up. "I'm happier with her away," he said. "Who wants to have a woman waiting at home to ask you where you've been and why you're back so late?"

"You're right, Werner," I said.

"She's too young for me. I should never have married her." He waited a moment while the heater cleared the glass a little. "Try again tomorrow, then?"

"No further contact, Werner. This was the last try for him. I'm going back to London tomorrow. I'll be sleeping in my own bed."

"Your wife . . . Fiona. She was nice to me that time when I had to work inside for a couple of months."

"I remember that," I said. Werner had been thrown out of a window by two East German agents he'd discovered in his apartment. His leg was broken in three places and it took ages for him to recover fully.

"And you tell Mr. Gaunt I remember him. He's long ago retired, I know, but I suppose you still see him from time to time. You tell him anytime he wants another bet on what the Ivans are up to, he calls me up first."

"I'll see him next weekend," I said. "I'll tell him that."

Chapter 2

I THOUGHT you must have missed the plane," said my wife as she switched on the bedside light. She'd not yet got to sleep; her long hair was hardly disarranged and the frilly nightdress was not rumpled. She'd gone to bed early, by the look of it. There was a lighted cigarette on the ashtray. She must have been lying there in the dark, smoking and thinking about her work. On the side table there were thick volumes from the office library and a thin blue *Report from the Select Committee on Science and Technology*, with notebook and pencil and the necessary supply of Benson & Hedges cigarettes, a considerable number of which were now only butts packed tightly into the big cut-glass ashtray she'd brought from the sitting room. She lived a different sort of life when I was away; now it was like going into a different house and a different bedroom, to a different woman.

"Some bloody strike at the airport," I explained. There was a tumbler containing whisky balanced on the clock-radio. I sipped it; the ice cubes had long since melted to make a warm weak mixture. It was typical of her to prepare a treat so carefully—with linen napkin, stirrer, and some cheese straws—and then forget about it.

"London Airport?" She noticed her half-smoked cigarette and stubbed it out and waved away the smoke.

"Where else do they go on strike every day?" I said irritably.

"There was nothing about it on the news."

"Strikes are not news anymore," I said. She obviously thought that I had *not* come directly from the airport, and her failure to commiserate with me over three wasted hours there did not improve my bad temper.

"Did it go all right?"

"Werner sends his best wishes. He told me that story about your Uncle Silas betting him fifty marks about the building of the Wall."

"Not again," said Fiona. "Is he ever going to forget that bloody bet?"

"He likes you," I said. "He sent his best wishes." It wasn't exactly true, but I wanted her to like him as I did. "And his wife has left him."

"Poor Werner," she said. Fiona was very beautiful, especially when she smiled that sort of smile that women save for a man who has lost his woman. "Did she go off with another man?"

"No," I said untruthfully. "She couldn't stand Werner's endless affairs with other women."

"Werner!" said my wife, and laughed. She didn't believe that Werner had affairs with lots of other women. I wondered how she could guess so correctly. Werner seemed an attractive sort of guy to my masculine eyes. I suppose I will never understand women. The trouble is that they all understand me; they understand me too damned well. I took off my coat and put it on a hanger. "Don't put your overcoat in the wardrobe," said Fiona. "It needs cleaning. I'll take it in tomorrow." As casually as she could, she added, "I tried to get you at the Steigerberger Hotel. Then I tried the duty officer at Olympia but no one knew where you were. Billy's throat was swollen. I thought it might be mumps."

"I wasn't there," I said.

"You asked the office to book you there. You said it's the best hotel in Berlin. You said I could leave a message there."

"I stayed with Werner. He's got a spare room now that his wife's gone."

"And shared all those women of his?" said Fiona. She laughed again. "Is it all part of a plan to make me jealous?"

I leaned over and kissed her. "I've missed you, darling. I really have. Is Billy okay?"

"Billy's fine. But that damned man at the garage gave me a bill for sixty pounds!"

"For what?"

"He's written it all down. I told him you'd see about it."

"But he let you have the car?"

"I had to collect Billy from school. He knew that before he did the service on it. So I shouted at him and he let me take it."

"You're a wonderful wife," I said. I undressed and went into the bathroom to wash and to brush my teeth.

"And it went well?" she called.

I looked at myself in the long mirror. It was just as well that I was tall, for I was getting fatter and that Berlin beer hadn't helped matters. "I did what I was told," I said, and finished brushing my teeth.

"Not you, darling," said Fiona. I switched on the Water-Pik and above its chugging sound I heard her add, "You never do what you are told, you know that."

I went back into the bedroom. She'd combed her hair and smoothed the sheet on my side of the bed. She'd put my pajamas on the pillow. They consisted of a plain red jacket and paisley-pattern trousers. "Are these mine?"

"The laundry didn't come back this week. I phoned them. The driver is ill . . . so what can you say?"

"I didn't check into the Berlin office at all, if that's what's eating you," I admitted. "They're all young kids in there, don't know their ass from a hole in the ground. I feel safer with one of the old-timers like Werner."

"Suppose something happened? Suppose there was trouble and the duty officer didn't even know you were in Berlin? Can't you see how silly it is not to give them some sort of perfunctory call?"

"I don't know any of those Olympia Stadion people anymore, darling. It's all changed since Frank Harrington took over. They are youngsters, kids with no field experience and lots and lots of theories from the training school."

"But your man turned up?"

"No."

"You spent three days there for nothing?"

"I suppose I did."

"They'll send you in to get him. You realize that, don't you?"

I got into bed. "Nonsense. They'll use one of the West Berlin people."

"It's the oldest trick in the book, darling. They send you over there to wait . . . for all you know, he wasn't even in contact. Now you'll go back and report a failed contact and you'll be the one they send in to get him. My God, Bernie, you are a fool at times."

I hadn't looked at it like that, but there was more than a grain of truth in Fiona's cynical viewpoint. "Well, they can find someone else," I said angrily. "Let one of the local people go over to get him. My face is too well known there."

"They'll say they're all kids without experience, just what you yourself said."

"It's Brahms Four," I told her.

"Brahms—those network names sound so ridiculous. I liked it better when they had code words like Trojan, Wellington, and Claret."

The way she said it was annoying. "The postwar network names are specially chosen to have no identifiable nationality," I said. "And the number four man in the Brahms network once saved my life. He's the one who got me out of Weimar."

"He's the one who is kept so damned secret. Yes, I know. Why do you think they sent you? And now do you see why they are going to make you go in and get him?" Beside the bed, my photo stared back at me from its silver frame. Bernard Samson, a serious young man with baby face, wavy hair, and horn-rimmed glasses, looked nothing like the wrinkled old fool I shaved every morning.

"I was in a spot. He could have kept going. He didn't have to come back all the way to Weimar." I settled into my pillow. "How long ago was that—eighteen years, maybe twenty?"

"Go to sleep," said Fiona. "I'll phone the office in the morning and say you are not well. It will give you time to think."

"You should see the pile of work on my desk."

"I took Billy and Sally to the Greek restaurant for his birthday. The waiters sang "Happy birthday" and cheered him when he blew the candles out. It was sweet of them. I wish you'd been there."

"I won't go. I'll tell the old man in the morning. I can't do that kind of thing anymore."

"And there was a phone call from Mr. Moore at the bank. He wants to talk with you. He said there's no hurry."

"And we both know what that means," I said. "It means

phone me back immediately or else!" I was close to her now and I could smell perfume. Had she put it on just for me, I wondered.

"Harry Moore isn't like that. At Christmas we were nearly seven hundred overdrawn, and when we saw him at my sister's party he said not to worry."

"Brahms Four took me to the house of a man named Busch—Karl Busch—who had this empty room in Weimar. . . ." It was all coming back to me. "We stayed there three days and afterward Karl Busch went back there. They took Busch up to the security barracks in Leipzig. He was never seen again."

"You're senior staff now, darling," she said sleepily. "You don't have to go anywhere you don't want to."

"I phoned you last night," I said. "It was two o'clock in the morning but there was no reply."

"I was here, asleep," she said. She was awake and alert now. I could tell by the tone of her voice.

"I let it ring for ages," I said. "I tried twice. Finally I got the operator to dial it."

"Then it must be the damned phone acting up again. I tried to phone here for Nanny yesterday afternoon and there was no reply. I'll tell the engineers tomorrow."

Chapter 3

RICHARD CRUYER was the German Stations Controller, the man to whom I reported. He was younger than me by two years and his apologies for this fact gave him opportunities for reminding himself of his fast promotion in a service that was not noted for its fast promotions.

Dicky Cruyer had curly hair and liked to wear open-neck shirts and faded jeans, and be the *Wunderkind* amongst all the dark suits and Eton ties. But under all the trendy jargon and casual airs, he was the most pompous stuffed shirt in the whole Department.

"They think it's a cushy number in here, Bernard," he said while stirring his coffee. "They don't realize the way I have the Deputy Controller (Europe) breathing down my neck and endless meetings with every damned committee in the building."

Even Cruyer's complaints were contrived to show the world how important he was. But he smiled to let me know how well he endured his troubles. He had his coffee served in a fine Spode china cup and saucer, and he stirred it with a silver spoon. On the mahogany tray there was another Spode cup and saucer, a matching sugar bowl, and a silver creamer fashioned in the shape of a cow. It was a valuable antique—Dicky had told me that many times—and at night it was locked in the secure filing cabinet, together with the log and the carbons of the current mail. "They think it's all lunches at the Mirabelle and a *fine* with the boss."

Dicky always said *fine* rather than brandy or cognac. Fiona told me he'd been saying it ever since he was president of the Oxford University Food and Wine Society as an undergraduate. Dicky's image as a gourmet was not easy to reconcile with his figure, for he was a thin man, with thin arms, thin legs, and thin bony hands and fingers, with one of which he continually touched his thin bloodless lips. It was a nervous gesture, provoked, said some people, by the hostility around him. This was nonsense of course, but I did dislike the little creep, I will admit that.

He sipped his coffee and then tasted it carefully, moving his lips while staring at me as if I might have come to sell him the year's crop. "It's just a shade bitter, don't you think, Bernard?"

"Nescafé all tastes the same to me," I said.

"This is pure chagga, ground just before it was brewed." He said it calmly but nodded to acknowledge my little attempt to annoy him.

"Well, he didn't turn up," I said. "We can sit here drinking chagga all the morning and it won't bring Brahms Four over the wire."

Dicky said nothing.

"Has he re-established contact yet?" I asked.

Dicky put his coffee on the desk while he riffed some papers in a file. "Yes. We received a routine report from him. He's safe." Dicky chewed a fingernail.

"Why didn't he turn up?"

"No details on that one." He smiled. He was handsome in the way that foreigners think bowler-hatted English stockbrokers are handsome. His face was hard and bony and the tan from his Christmas in the Bahamas had still not faded. "He'll explain in his own good time. Don't bad-ger the field agents—that has always been my policy. Right, Bernard?"

"It's the only way, Dicky."

"Ye gods! How I'd love to get back into the field just once more! You people have the best of it."

"I've been off the field list for nearly five years, Dicky. I'm a desk man now, like you." Like you have always been is what I should have said, but I let it go. "Captain" Cruyer he'd called himself when he returned from the Army. But he soon realized how ridiculous that title sounded to a Director-General who'd worn a general's uniform. And he realized too that "Captain" Cruyer would be an unlikely candidate for that illustrious post.

He stood up, smoothed his shirt, and then sipped coffee, holding his free hand under the cup to guard against drips. He noticed that I hadn't drunk my chagga. "Would you prefer tea?"

"Is it too early for a gin and tonic?"

He didn't respond to this question. "I think you feel beholden to our friend Bee Four. You still feel grateful about his coming back to Weimar for you." He greeted my look of surprise with a knowing nod. "I read the files, Bernard. I know what's what."

"It was a decent thing to do," I said.

"It was," said Dicky. "It was a truly decent thing to do, but that wasn't why he did it. Not only that."

"You weren't there, Dicky."

"Bee Four panicked, Bernard. He fled. He was near the border, at some godforsaken little place in Thüringerwald, by the time our people intercepted him and told him he wasn't wanted for questioning by the KGB—or anyone else, for that matter."

"It's ancient history," I said.

"We turned him round," said Cruyer. It had become

"we," I noticed. "We gave him some chicken feed and told him to go back and play the outraged innocent. We told him to cooperate with them."

"Chicken feed?"

"Names of people who'd already escaped, safe houses long since abandoned . . . bits and pieces that would make Brahms Four look good to the KGB."

"But they got Busch, the man who was sheltering me."

Unhurriedly, Cruyer finished his coffee and wiped his lips with a linen napkin from the tray. "We got two of you out. I'd say that's not bad for that sort of crisis—two out of three. Busch went back to his house to get his stamp collection. . . . Stamp collection! What can you do with a man like that? They put him in the bag of course."

"The stamp collection was probably his life savings," I said.

"Perhaps it was, and that's how they put him in the bag, Bernard. No second chances with those swine. I know that, you know that, and he knew it too."

"So that's why our field people don't like Brahms Four."

"Yes, that's why they don't like him."

"They think he informed on that Erfurt network."

Cruyer shrugged. "What could we do? We could hardly spread the word that we'd invented that story to make the fellow *persona grata* with the KGB." Cruyer walked across to his drinks cabinet and poured some gin into a large Waterford glass tumbler.

"Plenty of gin, not too much tonic," I said. Cruyer turned to stare blankly at me. "If that's for me," I added. So there had been a blunder. They'd told Brahms Four to reveal old Busch's address; then the poor old sod had gone back for his stamps. And run into the arms of a KGB arrest squad.

Dicky put a little more gin into it, and added ice cubes gently so that they would not splash. He brought it, together with a small bottle of tonic, which I left unused. "No need for you to concern yourself with this one anymore, Bernard. You did your bit in going to Berlin. We'll let one of the others take over now."

"Is he in trouble?"

Cruyer went back to the drinks cabinet and busied himself tidying away the bottle caps and stirrer. Then he closed the cabinet doors and said, "Do you know the sort of material Brahms Four has been supplying?"

"Economics intelligence. He works for an East German bank."

"He is the most carefully protected source we have in Germany. You are one of the few people ever to have seen him face to face."

"And that was almost twenty years ago."

"He works through the mail—always local addresses to avoid the censors and the security—posting his material to various members of the Brahms net. In emergencies he uses a dead-letter drop. But that's all—no microdots, no one-time pads, no codes, no micro transmitters, no secret ink. Very old-fashioned."

"And very safe," I said.

"Very old-fashioned and very safe, so far," agreed Dicky. "Even I don't have access to the Brahms Four file. No one knows anything about him except that he's been getting material from somewhere at the top of the tree. All we can do is guess."

"And you've guessed," I prompted him, knowing that Dicky was going to tell me anyway.

"From Bee Four we are getting important decisions of the Deutsche Investitions Bank. And from the Deutsche Bauern Bank. Those state banks provide long-term credit for industry and for agriculture. Both banks are controlled by the Deutsche Notenbank, through which come all remittances, payments, and clearing for the whole country. Now and again we get good notice of what the Moscow Narodny Bank is doing and regular reports about the COMECON briefings. I think Brahms Four is a secretary or personal assistant to one of the directors of the Deutsche Notenbank."

"Or a director?"

"All banks have an economics intelligence department. Being head of that department is not a job an ambitious banker craves, so they get switched around. Brahms Four has been feeding us this sort of thing too long to be anything but a clerk or assistant."

"You'll miss him. Too bad you have to pull him out," I said.

"Pull him out? I'm not trying to pull him out. I want him to stay right where he is."

"I thought . . ."

"It's his idea that he should come over to the West, not mine! I want him to remain where he is. I can't afford to lose him."

"Is he getting frightened?"

"They all get frightened eventually," said Cruyer. "It's battle fatigue. The strain of it all gets them down. They get older and they get tired and they start looking for that pot of gold and the country house with the roses round the door."

"They start looking for the things we've been promising them for twenty years. That's the truth of it."

"Who knows what makes these crazy bastards do it?" said Cruyer. "I've spent half my life trying to understand their motivation." He looked out the window. Hard sunlight sidelighting the bare lime trees, dark blue sky with just a few smears of cirrus very high. "And I'm still no nearer knowing what makes any of them tick."

"There comes a time when you have to let them go," I said.

He touched his lips; or was he kissing his fingertips, or maybe tasting the gin that he'd spilled on his fingers. "Lord Moran's theory, you mean? I seem to remember he divided men into four classes. Those who were never afraid, those who were afraid but never showed it, those who were afraid and showed it but carried on with their job, and the fourth group—men who were afraid and shirked. Where does Brahms Four fit in there?"

"I don't know," I said. How the hell can you explain to a man like Cruyer what it's like to be afraid day and night, year after year? What had Cruyer ever had to fear, beyond a close scrutiny of his expense accounts?

"Well, he's got to stay there for the time being, and there's an end to it."

"So why was I sent to receive him?"

"He was acting up, Bernard. He threw a little tantrum. You know the way these chaps can be at times. He threatened to walk out on us, but the crisis passed. Threatened to use an old forged U.S. passport and march out through Checkpoint Charlie."

"So I was there to hold him?"

"Couldn't have a hue and cry, could we? Couldn't give his name to the civil police and send teleprinter messages to the boats and airports." He unlocked the window and strained to open it. It had been closed all winter and now it took all Cruyer's strength to unstick it. "Ah, a whiff of London diesel. That's better," he said as there came a movement of chilly air. "But he's still proving difficult. He's not giving us the regular flow of information. He threatens to stop altogether."

"And you . . . what are you threatening?"

"Threats are not my style, Bernard. I'm simply asking him to stay there for two more years and help us get someone else into place. Ye gods! Do you know how much money he's squeezed out of us over the past five years?"

"As long as you don't want me to go," I said. "My face is too well known over there. And I'm getting too bloody short-winded for any strong-arm stuff."

"We've plenty of people available, Bernard. No need for senior staff to take risks. And anyway, if things went really sour on us, we'd need someone from Frankfurt."

"That has a nasty ring to it, Dicky. What kind of someone would we need from Frankfurt?"

Cruyer sniffed. "No need to draw you a diagram, old man. If Bee Four really started thinking of spilling the beans to the Normannenstrasse boys, we'd have to move fast."

"Expedient demise?" I said, keeping my voice level and my face expressionless.

Cruyer became a fraction uncomfortable. "We'd have to move fast. We'd have to do whatever the team on the spot thought necessary. You know how these things go. And XPD can never be ruled out."

"This is one of our own people, Dicky. This is an old man who has served the Department for over twenty years."

"And all we're asking," said Cruyer with exaggerated patience, "is for him to go on serving us in the same way. What happens if he goes off his head and wants to betray us is conjecture—pointless conjecture."

"We earn our living from conjecture," I said. "And it makes me wonder what I would have to do to have someone from Frankfurt come along to get me ready for that big debriefing in the sky."

Cruyer laughed. "You always were a card!" he said. "You wait until I tell the old man that one."

"Any more of that delicious gin?"

He took the glass from my outstretched hand. "Leave Brahms Four to Frank Harrington and the Berlin Field Unit, Bernard. You're not a German, you're not a field agent any longer, and you are far, far too old."

He put a little gin in my glass and added ice, using claw-shaped silver tongs. "Let's talk about something more cheerful," he said over his shoulder.

"In that case, Dicky, what about my new car allowance? The cashier won't do anything without the paperwork."

"Leave it to my secretary."

"I've filled in the forms already," I told him. "I've got them with me, as a matter of fact. They just need your signature . . . two copies." I placed them on the corner of his desk and gave him the pen from his ornate desk set.

"This car will be too big for you," he muttered while pretending the pen was not working properly. "You'll be sorry you didn't opt for something more compact." I gave him my plastic ball-point, and after he'd signed I looked at the signature before putting the forms in my pocket. It was perfect timing, I suppose.

Chapter 4

W E'D ARRANGED to visit Fiona's Uncle Silas for the weekend. Old Silas Gaunt was not really her uncle; he was a distant relative of her mother's. She'd never even met Silas until I took her to see him when I was trying to impress her, just after we'd first met. She'd come down from Oxford with all the expected brilliant results in philosophy, politics, and economics—or "Modern Greats," in the jargon of academe—and done all those things that her contemporaries thought smart: she'd studied Russian at the Sorbonne while perfecting the French accent necessary for upper-class young Englishwomen, done a short cookery course at the Cordon Bleu, worked for an art dealer, crewed for a transatlantic yacht race, and written speeches for a man who'd narrowly failed to become a Liberal Member of Parliament. It was soon after that fiasco that I met her. Old Silas had been captivated by his newly discovered niece right from the start. We saw a lot of him, and my son, Billy, was his godchild.

Silas Gaunt was a formidable figure who'd worked for intelligence back in the days when such service was really secret. Back in the days when reports were done in copperplate handwriting and field agents were paid in sovereigns. When my father was running the Berlin Field Unit, Silas was his boss.

"He's a silly little fart," said Fiona when I related my conversation with Dicky Cruyer. It was Saturday morning and we were driving to Silas's farm in the Cotswold Hills.

"He's a dangerous little fart," I said. "When I think of that idiot making decisions about field people . . ."

"About Brahms Four, you mean," said Fiona.

" 'Bee Four' is Dicky's latest contribution to the terminology. Yes, people like that," I said. "I get the goddamned shivers."

"He won't let the Brahms source go," she said. We were driving through Reading, having left the motorway in search of Elizabeth Arden skin tonic. She was at the wheel of the red Porsche her father had bought her the previous birthday. She was thirty-five and her father said she needed something special to cheer her up. I wondered how he was planning to cheer me up for my fortieth, coming in two weeks' time: I guessed it would be the usual bottle of Rémy Martin, and wondered if I'd again find inside the box the compliments card of some office-supplies firm who'd given it to him.

"The Economics Intelligence Committee lives off that banking stuff that Brahms Four provides," she added after a long silence thinking about it.

"I still say we should have stayed on the motorway. That chemist in the village is sure to have skin tonic," I said. Although in fact I hadn't the faintest idea what skin tonic was, except that it was something my skin had managed without for several decades.

"But not Elizabeth Arden," said Fiona. We were in a traffic jam in the middle of Reading and there was no chemist's shop in sight. The engine was overheating and she switched it off for a moment. "Perhaps you're right," she admitted finally, leaning across to give me a brief kiss. She was just keeping me sweet, because I was going to be the one who leaped out of the car and dashed off for the damned jar of magic ointment while she flirted with the traffic warden.

"Have you got enough space in the back, children?" she asked.

The kids were wedged each side of a suitcase but they didn't complain. Sally grunted and carried on reading her *William* book, and Billy said, "How fast will you go on the motorway?"

"And Dicky is on the committee too," I said.

"Yes, he claims it was his idea."

"I lose count of how many committees he's on. He's never in his bloody office when he's needed. His appointment book looks like the *Good Food Guide*. Lately he's discovered breakfast meetings. Now he gorges and guzzles all day. I don't know how he stays so thin."

The traffic moved again, and she started up and followed closely behind a battered red double-decker bus. The conductor was standing on the platform looking at her and at the car with undisguised admiration. She smiled at him and he smiled back. It was ridiculous, but I couldn't help feeling a pang of jealousy. "I'll have to go," I said.

"To Berlin?"

"Dicky knows I'll have to go. The whole conversation was just Dicky's way of making sure I know."

"What difference can you make?" said Fiona. "Brahms can't be forced to go on. If he's determined to stop working for us, there's not much anyone in the Department can do about it."

"No?" I said. "Well, you might be surprised."

She looked at me. "But Brahms Four is old. He must be due for retirement."

"Dicky was making veiled threats."

"Bluff."

"Probably bluff," I agreed. "Just Dicky's way of saying that if I stand back and let anyone else go, they might get too rough. But you can't be sure with Dicky. Especially when his seniority is on the line."

"You mustn't go, darling."

"My being there is probably going to make no difference at all."

"Well, then . . ."

"But if someone else goes—some kid from the Berlin office—and something bad happens, how will I ever be sure that I couldn't have made it come out okay?"

"Even so, Bernard, I still don't want you to go."

"We'll see," I said.

"You owe Brahms Four nothing," she said.

"I owe him," I said. "I know that, and so does he. That's why he'll trust me in a way he'll trust no one else. He knows I owe him."

"It must be twenty years," she said as if promises, like mortgages, became less burdensome with time.

"What's it matter how long ago it was?"

"And what about what you owe me? And what you owe Billy and Sally?"

"Don't get angry, sweetheart," I said. "It's hard enough already. You think I want to go over there and play Boy Scout again?"

"I don't know," she said. She was angry, and when we got on the motorway she put her foot down so that the needles went right around the dials. We were at Uncle Silas's farm well before he'd even opened the champagne for pre-lunch drinks.

Whitelands was a six-hundred-acre farm in the Cotswolds—the great limestone plateau that divides the Thames Valley from the River Severn—and the farmhouse of ancient honey-colored local stone with mullioned windows and lopsided doorway would have looked too perfect, like the set for a Hollywood film, except that it was wintry and the sky was gray, the lawn brown, and the rosebushes trimmed back and bloomless.

There were other cars parked carelessly alongside the huge stone barn, a horse tethered to the gate, and fresh clots of mud on the metal grating of the porch. The old oak door was unlocked, and Fiona pushed her way into the hall in that proprietorial way that was permitted to members of the family. There were coats hanging on the wall and more draped over the settee.

"Dicky and Daphne Cruyer," said Fiona, recognizing a mink coat.

"And Bret Rensselaer," I said, touching a sleeve of soft camel's hair. "Is it going to be all people from the office?"

Fiona shrugged and turned so that I could help her take off her coat. There were voices and decorous laughter from the back of the house. "Not all from the office," she said. "The Range Rover out front belongs to that retired general who lives in the village. His wife has the riding school— remember? You hated her."

"I wonder if the Cruyers are staying," I said.

"Not if their coats are in the hall," said Fiona.

"You should have been a detective," I said. She grimaced at me. It wasn't the sort of remark that Fiona regarded as a compliment.

This region of England has the prettiest villages and most beautiful countryside in the world, and yet there is something about such contrived perfection that I find disquieting. For the cramped laborer's cottages are occupied by stockbrokers and building speculators, and ye host in ye olde village pub turns out to be an airline pilot between trips. The real villagers live near the main road in ugly brick terraced houses, their front gardens full of broken motorcars.

"If you go down to the river, remember the bank is slippery with mud. And for goodness' sake wipe your shoes

carefully before you come in for lunch." The children responded with whoops of joy. "I wish we had somewhere like
this to go on weekends," Fiona said to me.

"We do have somewhere like this," I said. "We have
this. Your Uncle Silas has said come as often as you like."

"It's not the same," she said.

"You're damn right it's not," I said. "If this was our
place, you'd not be going down the hall for a glass of champagne before lunch. You'd be hurrying along to the kitchen
to scrape the vegetables in cold water."

"Fiona, my darling! And Bernard!" Silas Gaunt came
from the kitchen. "I thought I recognized the children I just
spotted climbing through the shrubbery."

"I'm sorry," said Fiona, but Silas laughed and slapped
me on the back.

"We'll be eating very soon but there's just time to gulp
a glass of something. I think you know everyone. Some
neighbors dropped in, but I haven't been able to get them
to stay for lunch."

SILAS GAUNT was a huge man—tall, with a big belly. He'd
always been fat, but since his wife died he'd grown fatter in
the way that only rich old self-indulgent men grow fat. He
cared nothing about his waistline or that his shirts were so
tight the buttons were under constant strain, or about the
heavy jowls that made him look like a worried bloodhound.
His head was almost bald and his forehead overhung his
eyes in a way that set his features into a constant frown,
which was only dispelled by his loud laughs for which he
threw his head back and opened his mouth at the ceiling.
Uncle Silas presided over his luncheon party like a squire
with his farm workers, but he gave no offense, because it
was so obviously a joke, just as his posture as a farmer was

a joke, despite all the discarded rubber boots in the hall, and the weather-beaten hay rake disposed on the back lawn like some priceless piece of modern sculpture.

"They all come to see me," he said as he poured Château Pétrus '64 for his guests. "Sometimes they want me to recall some bloody fool thing the Department decided back in the sixties, or they want me to use my influence with someone upstairs, or they want me to sell some ghastly little Victorian commode they've inherited." Silas looked around the table to be sure everyone present remembered that he had a partnership in a Bond Street antique shop. The taciturn American Bret Rensselaer was squeezing the arm of the busty blonde he'd brought with him. "But I see them all—believe me I never get lonely." I felt sorry for old Silas; it was the sort of thing that only very lonely people claimed.

Mrs. Porter, his cook-housekeeper, came through the door from the kitchen bearing a roast sirloin. "Good. I like beef," said my small son Billy.

Mrs. Porter smiled in appreciation. She was an elderly woman who had learned the value of a servant who heard nothing, saw nothing, and said very little. "I've no time for stews and pies and all those mixtures," explained Uncle Silas as he opened a second bottle of lemonade for the children. "I like to see a slice of real meat on my plate. I hate all those sauces and purées. The French can keep their cuisine." He poured a little lemonade for my son, and waited while Billy noted its color and bouquet, took a sip, and nodded approval just as Silas had instructed him to do.

Mrs. Porter arranged the meat platter in front of Silas and placed the carving knife and fork to hand before going to get the vegetables. Dicky Cruyer dabbed wine from his lips with a napkin. The host's words seemed to be aimed at him. "I can't stand by and let you defame *la cuisine française* in such a cavalier fashion, Silas." Dicky smiled. "I'd get myself blackballed by Paul Bocuse."

Silas served Billy with a huge portion of rare roast beef and went on carving. "Start eating!" Silas commanded. Dicky's wife, Daphne, passed the plates. She worked in advertising and liked to dress in grandma clothes, complete with black velvet choker, cameo brooch, and small metal-rim eyeglasses. She insisted on a very small portion of beef.

Dicky saw my son spill gravy down his shirt and smiled at me pityingly. The Cruyer boys were at boarding school; their parents only saw them at vacation time. It's the only way to stay sane, Dicky had explained to me more than once.

Silas carved into the meat with skillful concentration. There were ooohs! and ahhs! from the guests. Dicky Cruyer said it was a "sumptuous repast" and addressed Silas as "mine host." Fiona gave me a blank stare as a warning against provoking Dicky into more such comments.

"Cooking," said Silas, "is the art of the possible. The French have been brought up on odds and ends, chopped up and mixed up and disguised with flavored sauces. I don't want that muck if I can afford some proper food. No one in their right mind would choose it."

"Try *la nouvelle cuisine*," said Daphne Cruyer, who was proud of her French accent. "Lightweight dishes and each plate of food designed like a picture."

"I don't want lightweight food," growled Silas, and brandished the knife at her. *"Nouvelle cuisine!"* he said disdainfully. "Big colored plates with tiny scraps of food arranged in the center. When cheap hotel restaurants did it, we called it 'portion control,' but get the public-relations boys on the job and it's *nouvelle cuisine* and they write long articles about it in ladies' magazines. When I pay for good food, I expect the waiter to serve me from a trolley and ask me what I want and how much I want, and I'll tell him where to put the vegetables. I don't want plates of meat and two veg carried from the kitchen by waiters who don't know a herring from a hot-cross bun."

"This beef is done to perfection, Uncle Silas," said Fiona, who was relieved that he'd managed to deliver this passionate address without the usual interjected expletives. "But just a small slice for Sally . . . well-done meat, if that's possible."

"Good God, woman," he said. "Give your daughter something that will put a little blood into her veins. Well-done meat! No wonder she's looking so damned peaky." He placed two slices of rare beef on a warmed plate and cut the meat into bite-size pieces. He always did that for the children.

"What's peaky?" said Billy, who liked underdone beef and was admiring Silas's skill with the razor-sharp carving knife.

"Pinched, white, anemic, and ill-looking," said Silas. He set the rare beef in front of Sally.

"Sally is perfectly fit," said Fiona. There was no quicker way of upsetting her than to suggest the children were in any way deprived. I suspected it was some sort of guilt she shared with all working mothers. "Sally's the best swimmer in her class," said Fiona. "Aren't you, Sally?"

"I was last term," said Sally in a whisper.

"Get some rare roast beef into your belly," Silas told her. "It will make your hair curly."

"Yes, Uncle Silas," she said. He watched her until she took a mouthful and smiled at him.

"You're a tyrant, Uncle Silas," said my wife, but Silas gave no sign of having heard her. He turned to Daphne. "Don't tell me you want it well done," he said ominously.

"*Bleu* for me," she said. "*Avec un petit peu de moutarde anglaise.*"

"Pass Daphne the mustard," said Silas. "And pass her the *pommes de terre*—she could put a bit more weight on. It'll give you something to get hold of," he told Cruyer, waving the carving fork at him.

"I say, steady on," said Cruyer, who didn't like such personal remarks aimed at his wife.

DICKY CRUYER declined the charlotte russe, having had "an elegant sufficiency," so Billy and I shared Dicky's portion. Charlotte russe was one of Mrs. Porter's specialties. When the meal was finished, Silas took the men to the billiards room, telling the ladies, "Walk down to the river, or sit in the conservatory, or there's a big log fire in the drawing room if you're cold. Mrs. Porter will bring you coffee, and brandy too if you fancy it. But men have to swear and belch now and again. And we'll smoke and talk shop and argue about cricket. It will be boring for you. Go and look after the children—that's what nature intended women to do."

They did not depart graciously, at least Daphne and Fiona didn't. Daphne called old Silas a rude pig and Fiona threatened to let the children play in his study—a sanctum forbidden to virtually everyone—but it made no difference; he ushered the men into the billiards room and closed the ladies out.

The gloomy billiards room with its mahogany paneling was unchanged since being furnished to the taste of a nineteenth-century beer baron. Even the antlers and family portraits remained in position. The windows opened onto the lawn, but the sky outside was dark and the room was lit only by the green light reflected from the tabletop. Dicky

Cruyer set up the table and Bret selected a cue for himself while Silas removed his jacket and snapped his bright red braces before passing the drinks and the cigars. "So Brahms Four is acting the goat?" said Silas as he chose a cigar for himself and picked up the matches. "Well, are you all struck dumb?" He shook the matchbox so that the wooden matches rattled.

"Well, I say—" said Cruyer, almost dropping the resin he was applying to the tip of his cue.

"Don't be a bloody fool, Dicky," Silas told him. "The D-G is worried sick at the thought of losing the banking figures. He said you're putting Bernard in to sort it out for you."

Cruyer—who had been very careful not to reveal to me that he'd mentioned me to the Director-General—fiddled with his cue to grant himself an extra moment of thought, then said, "Bernard? His name was put up but I'm against it. Bernard's done his bit, I told him that."

"Never mind the double-talk, Dicky. Save all that for your committee meetings. The D-G asked me to knock your heads together this weekend and try and come up with a few sensible proposals on Monday . . . Tuesday at the latest. This damn business could go pop, you know." He looked at the table and then at his guests. "Now, how shall we do this? Bernard is no earthly good, so he'd better partner me against you two."

Bret said nothing. Dicky Cruyer looked at Silas with renewed respect. Perhaps until that afternoon he'd not fully realized the influence the old man still wielded. Or perhaps he hadn't realized that Silas was just the same unscrupulous old swine that he'd been when he was working inside; just the same ruthless manipulator of people that Cruyer tried to be. And Uncle Silas had always emerged from this sort of crisis smelling of roses and that was something that Dicky Cruyer hadn't always managed.

"I still say Bernard must not go," insisted Cruyer, but with less conviction now. "His face is too well known. Their watchers will be on to him immediately. One false move and we'll find ourselves over at the Home Office trying to figure out who we can swap for him." Like Silas, he kept his voice flat, and contrived the casual offhand tone in which Englishmen prefer to discuss matters of life and death. He was leaning over the table by this time, and there was silence while he put down a ball.

"So who *will* go?" said Silas, tilting his head to look at Cruyer like a schoolmaster asking a backward pupil a very simple question.

"We have short-listed five or six people we deem suitable," said Cruyer.

"People who know Brahms Four? People he'll trust?"

"Brahms Four will trust no one," said Cruyer. "You know how agents become when they start talking of getting out." He stood back while Bret Rensselaer studied the table, then without fuss potted the chosen ball. Bret was Dicky's senior but he was letting Dicky answer the questions as if he were no more than a bystander. That was Bret Rensselaer's style.

"Good shot, Bret," said Silas. "So none of them have ever met him?" He smoked his cigar and blew smoke at Cruyer. "Or have I misunderstood?"

"Bernard's the only one who ever worked with him," admitted Cruyer, taking off his jacket and placing it carefully on the back of an empty chair. "I can't even get a recent photo of him."

"Brahms Four." Silas scratched his belly. "He's almost my age, you know. I knew him back when Berlin was Berlin.

We shared girlfriends and fell down drunk together. I know him the way you only know men you grew up with. Berlin! I loved that town."

"As well we know," said Cruyer with a touch of acid in his voice. He cleared the pocket and rolled the balls back along the table.

"Brahms Four tried to kill me at the end of 1946," said Silas, ignoring Cruyer. "He waited outside a little bar near the Alexanderplatz and took a shot at me as I was framed against the light in the doorway."

"He missed?" said Cruyer with the appropriate amount of concern.

"Yes. You'd think even an indifferent shot would be able to hit a big fellow like me, standing full-square against the light, but the stupid bastard missed. Luckily I was with my driver, a military policeman I'd had with me ever since I'd arrived. I was a civilian in uniform, you see—I needed a proper soldier to help me into my Sam Browne and remind me when to salute. Well, he laid into Brahms Four. I think he would have maimed him had I not been there. The corporal thought he'd aimed at him, you see. He was damned angry about it."

Silas drank a little port, smoked his cigar, and watched my inexpert stroke in silence. Cruyer dutifully asked him what had happened after that. "The Russkies came running. Soldiers, regimental police, four of them, big peasant boys with dirty boots and unshaven chins. Wanted to take poor old Brahms Four away. Of course he wasn't called Brahms Four then, that came later. Alexanderplatz was in their sector even if they hadn't yet built their wall. But I told them he was an English officer who'd had too much to drink."

"And they believed you?" said Cruyer.

"No, but your average Russian has grown used to hearing lies. They didn't believe me but they weren't about to demonstrate a lot of initiative to disprove it. They made a feeble attempt to pull him away, but my driver and I picked him up and carried him out to our car. There was no way the Russians would touch a vehicle with British Army markings. They knew what would happen to anyone meddling with a Russian officer's car without permission. So that's how we brought him back to the West."

"Why did he shoot at you?" I asked.

"You like that brandy, do you," said Silas. "Twenty years in the wood; it's not so easy to get hold of vintage brandy nowadays. Yes—well, he'd been watching me for a couple of days. He'd heard rumors that I was the one who'd put a lot of Gehlen's people in the bag, and his closest friend had got hurt in the roundup. But we talked about old times and he saw sense after a while." I nodded. That vague explanation was Silas's polite way of telling me to mind my own business.

We watched Bret Rensselaer play, pocketing the red ball with a perfectly angled shot that brought the white back to the tip of his cue. He moved his position only slightly to make the next stroke. "And you've been running him since 1946?" I said, looking at Silas.

"No, no, no," said Silas. "I kept him well away from our people in Hermsdorf. I had access to funds and I sent him back into the East Sector with instructions to lie low. He was with the Reichsbank during the war—his father was a stockbroker—and I knew that eventually the regime over there—Communist or not—would desperately need men with top-level banking experience."

"He was your investment?" said Cruyer.

"Or, you might say, I was his investment," said Silas. The game was slower now, each man taking more time to line up his shot as he thought about other things. Cruyer aimed, missed, and cursed softly. Silas continued, "We were both going to be in a position to help each other in the years ahead. That much was obvious. First he got a job with the tax people. Ever wondered how Communist countries first become Communist? It's not the secret police who do the deed, it's the tax collectors. That's how the Communists wiped out private companies: they increased the tax rate steeply according to the number of employees. Only firms with less than a dozen employees had a chance of surviving. When they'd destroyed private enterprise, Brahms Four was moved to the Deutsche Emissions und Girobank at the time of the currency reform."

Dicky smiled triumphantly at me as he said to Silas, "And that later became the Deutsche Notenbank." Good guess, Dicky, I thought.

"How long was he a sleeper?" I asked.

"Long enough," said Silas. He smiled and drank his port. "Good port this," he said, raising his glass to see the color against the light from the window. "But the bloody doctor has cut me back to one bottle a month—one bottle a month, I ask you. Yes, he was a sleeper all through the time when the service was rotten with traitors, when certain colleagues of ours were reporting back to the Kremlin every bloody thing we did. Yes, he was lucky, or clever, or a bit of both. His file was buried where no one could get at it. He survived. But, by God, I activated him once we'd got rid of those bastards. We were in bad shape, and Brahms Four was a prime source."

"Personally?" said Dicky Cruyer. "You ran him *personally?*" He exchanged his cue for another, as if to account for his missed stroke.

"Brahms Four made that a condition," said Silas. "There was a lot of that sort of thing at that time. He reported to me personally. It made him feel safer and it was good for me too."

"And what happened when you were posted away from Berlin?" I asked him.

"I had to hand him over to another Control."

"Who was that?" I asked.

Silas looked at me as if deciding whether to tell me, but he had already decided; everything was already decided by that time. "Bret took over from me." We all turned to look anew at Bret Rensselaer, a dark-suited American in his middle fifties, with fair receding hair and a quick nervous smile. Bret was the sort of American who liked to be mistaken for an Englishman. Recruited into the service while at Oxford on a Rhodes scholarship, he'd become a dedicated Anglophile who'd served in many European stations before taking over as Deputy Controller of the European Economics desk, which later became the Economics Intelligence Committee and was now Bret's private empire. If Brahms Four dried up as a source, Bret Rensselaer's empire would virtually collapse. Little wonder he looked so nervous.

It was Bret's shot again. He balanced his cue as if checking its weight, then reached for the resin. "I ran Brahms Four for years on a personal basis, just as Silas had done before me."

"Did you ever meet him face to face?" I asked.

"No, I never went across to the East, and as far as I know, he never came out. He knew only my code name." He finally finished with the resin and placed it carefully on the ledge of the scoreboard.

"Which you'd taken from Silas?" I said. "What you're saying is that you carried on pretending to be Silas."

"Sure I did," said Bret, as if he'd intended to make this clear from the start. The only thing field men hate more than a Control change is a secret Control change with no name switch. It wasn't something any desk man would boast about. Bret had still not made his shot. He stood facing me calmly but speaking a little more rapidly now that he was on the defensive. "Brahms Four related to Silas in a way no newcomer could hope to do. It was better to let him think his stuff was still coming to Silas." He leaned over the table to make his shot. Characteristically it was faultless and so was his next, but the third went askew.

"Even though Silas had gone," I said, moving aside and letting Silas see the table to choose his shot.

"I wasn't *dead!*" said Silas indignantly over his shoulder as he pushed past. "I kept in touch. A couple of times, Bret came back here to consult with me. Frequently I sent a little parcel of forbidden goodies over to him. We knew he'd recognize the way I chose what he liked, and so on."

"But after last year's big reshuffle he went soggy," Bret Rensselaer added sadly. "He went very patchy. Some great stuff still came from him but it wasn't one hundred percent anymore. He began to ask for more and more money too. No one minded that too much—he was worth everything he got—but we had the feeling he was looking for a chance to get out."

"And now the crunch has come?" I asked.

"Could be," said Bret.

"Or it could simply be the prelude to another demand for money," said Silas.

"It's a pretty fancy one," said Bret. "A pretty damn complicated way of getting a raise in pay. No, I think he wants out. I think he really wants out this time."

"What does he do with all this money?" I asked.

"We've never discovered," said Bret.

"We've never been allowed to try," said Cruyer bitterly. "Each time we prepare a plan, it's vetoed by someone at the top."

"Take it easy, Dicky," said Bret in that kind and conciliatory tone a man can employ when he knows he's the boss.

"No point in upsetting a darn good source just in order to find he's got a mistress stowed away somewhere or that he likes to pile his dough into some numbered account in Switzerland."

It was of course Silas who decided exactly how much it was safe to confide to me. "Let's just say we pay it into a Munich bank to be credited to a publishing house that never publishes anything," said Silas. If I was going over the wire, they'd make sure I knew only what they wanted me to know. That was the normal procedure; we all knew it.

"Hell, he wants a chance to spend his pay," I said. "Nothing wrong with that, is there?"

Silas turned to me with that spiteful look in his eye and said, "Nothing wrong with that, unless you need the stuff he's sending us. Then there's everything wrong with it, Bernard. Everything wrong with it!" He cleared the pocket and sent the ball down the table with such violence that it rebounded all the way back to him. There was a cruel determination in him; I'd glimpsed it more than once.

"Okay, so you're trying to prove that I'm the only one who can go and talk to him," I said. "I guess that's what this friendly little game is all about. Or am I mistaken?" I fixed Silas with my stare and he smiled ruefully.

"You're not the right person," said Bret unconvincingly. No one else spoke. They all knew I was the right person. This damn get-together was designed to show me the decision was unanimous. Dicky Cruyer touched his lips with the wet end of his cigar but did not put it into his mouth. Bret said, "It would be like sending in the massed bands of the Brigade of Guards playing 'Rule, Britannia!' Brahms Four will be terrified, and rightly so. You'll have a tail from the moment you go over."

"I don't agree," said Cruyer. They were talking about me as if I were not present; I had the feeling that this was the sort of discussion that would take place if I went into the bag, or got myself killed. "Bernard knows his way about over there. And he doesn't have to be there very long—just a talk with him so that we know what's on his mind. And show him how important it is for him to stay in position for a couple of years."

"What about you, Bernard?" Silas asked me. "You haven't said much about it."

"It sounds as if someone will have to go," I said. "And someone he knows would have a better chance of getting a straight answer."

"And," said Bret apologetically, "there won't be much time. . . . Is that what you mean?"

Cruyer said, "We sent a courier over by tour bus last month. He took the regular tourist bus over there and came back as easy as falling off a log."

"Do they let the tourists from West Berlin get off the bus nowadays?" said Silas.

"Oh, yes," said Cruyer, smiling cheerfully. "Things have changed since your day, Silas. They all visit the Red Army memorial. They even stop off for cakes and coffee—the D.D.R. desperately needs Westmarks. Another good place for a meeting is the Pergamon Museum. Tour buses from the West go there too."

"What do you think, Bernard?" said Bret. He fidgeted with his signet ring and stared at the table as if interested in nothing but Cruyer's tricky corner shot.

I found their sort of conjecture exasperating. It was the stuff of which long memos are made, the paperwork under which the Department is buried. I said, "What's the use of my guessing? Everything depends upon knowing what he is doing. He's not a peasant, he's a scholarly old man with an important and interesting job. We need to know whether he's still got a happy marriage, with good friends who make speeches at the birth celebrations of his grandchildren. Or has he become a miserable old loner, at odds with the world and needing Western-style medical care. . . . Or maybe he's just discovered what it's like to be in love with a shapely eighteen-year-old nymphomaniac."

Bret gave a short laugh and said, "Two first-class tickets to Rio, and don't spare the champagne."

"Unless the shapely one is working for the KGB," I said.

Bret stared at me impassively. "What would be the best way of 'depositing' someone for this sort of job, Bernard?"

"I certainly wouldn't discuss with you guys the way I'd choose to go over there, except to say I wouldn't want any arrangements made from this end. No documents, no preparations, no emergency link, no local backup—nothing at all. I'd want to do it myself." It was not the sort of private enterprise that the Department liked to encourage. I was expecting vociferous objections to this proposal, but none came.

"Quite right too," said Silas.

"And I haven't agreed to go," I reminded them.

"We leave it to you," said Silas. The others, their faces only dimly seen in the gloom beyond the brightly lit table, nodded. Cruyer's hands, very white in the glare, crawled across the table like two giant spiders. He played the shot and missed. His mind wasn't on the game; neither was mine.

Silas pulled a face at Cruyer's missed stroke and sipped his port. "Bernard," he said suddenly. "I'd better—" He stopped mid-sentence. Mrs. Porter had entered the room quietly. She was still holding a cut-glass tumbler and a cloth. Silas looked up to meet her eyes.

"The phone, sir," she said. "It's the call from London."

She didn't say who was calling from London because she took it for granted that Silas would know. In fact we all knew, or guessed, that it was someone urgently interested in how the discussion had gone. Silas rubbed his face, looked at me, and said, "Bernard . . . help yourself to another brandy if you fancy it."

"Thanks," I said, but I had the feeling that Silas had been about to say something quite different.

Weekends with Uncle Silas always followed the same pattern: an informal Saturday lunch, a game of billiards or bridge until teatime, and a dress-up dinner. There were fourteen people for dinner that Saturday evening: us; the Cruyers; Rensselaer and his girlfriend; Fiona's sister Tessa— her husband away—to partner Uncle Silas; an American couple named Johnson, who were in England buying antique furniture for their shop in Philadelphia; a young trendy architect, who converted cottages into "dream houses" and was making enough money at it to support a noisy new wife and a noisy old Ferrari; and a red-nosed local farmer, who spoke only twice the whole evening, and then only to ask his frizzy-haired wife to pass the wine.

"It was all right for you," said Fiona petulantly when we were in the little garret room preparing for bed that night. "I was sitting next to Dicky Cruyer. He only wants to talk about that beastly boat. He's going to France in it next month, he says."

"Dicky doesn't know a mainsail from a marlinspike. He'll kill himself."

"Don't say that, darling," said Fiona. "My sister Tessa is going too. And so is Ricky, that gorgeous young architect, and Colette, his amusing wife." There was a touch of acid in her voice; she wasn't too keen on them. And she was still angry at being shut out of our conference in the billiards room.

"It must be a bloody big boat," I said.

"It will sleep six . . . eight if you're all very friendly,
Daphne told me. She's not going. She gets seasick."

I looked at her quizzically. "Is your sister having an
affair with Dicky Cruyer?"

"How clever you are," said Fiona in a voice from which
any trace of admiration had been carefully eliminated. "But
you are behind the times, darling. She's fallen for someone
much older, she told me."

"She's a bitch."

"Most men find her attractive," said Fiona. For some
reason, Fiona got a secret satisfaction from hearing me con-
demn her sister, and was keen to provoke more of the same.

"I thought she was reconciled with her own husband."

"It was a trial," said Fiona.

"I'll bet it was," I agreed. "Especially for George."

"You were sitting next to the antique lady—was she
amusing?"

"A lady in the antiques business," I corrected her description, and she smiled. "She told me to beware of fancy
dressers, they are likely to have modern tops and antique
bottoms."

"How bizarre!" said Fiona. She giggled. "Where can I
find one?"

"Right here," I said, and jumped into bed with her.
"Give me that damned hot-water bottle."

"There's no hot-water bottle. That's me! Oh, your hands
are freezing."

I WAS AWAKENED by one of the farm dogs barking, and then
from somewhere across the river there came the echoing
response of some other dog on some other farm. I opened
my eyes to see the time and found the bedside light on. It

was four o'clock in the morning. Fiona was in her dressing gown drinking tea. "I'm sorry," she said.

"It was the dog."

"I can never sleep properly away from home. I went downstairs and made tea. I brought up an extra cup—would you like some?"

"Just half a cup. Have you been awake long?"

"I thought I heard someone go downstairs. It's a creepy old house, isn't it? There's a biscuit if you want it." I took just the tea and sipped some. Fiona said, "Did you promise to go? Berlin—did you promise?" It was as if she felt my decision would reveal how important she was to me compared to my job.

I shook my head.

"But that's what your billiards game was all about? I guessed so. Silas was so adamant about not having any of us in there. Sometimes I wonder if he realizes that I'm senior staff now."

"They're all worried about the Brahms Four business."

"But why send you? What reason did they give?"

"Who else could go? Silas?" I told her the essence of the conversation that had taken place in the billiards room. The dogs began barking again. From downstairs I heard a door closing and then Silas trying to quiet the dogs. His voice was hoarse and he spoke to them in the same way he spoke to Billy and Sally.

"I saw the memo that Rensselaer sent to the D-G," Fiona said, speaking more quietly now as if frightened that we might be overheard. "Five pages. I took it back to my office and read it through." I looked at her with surprise. Fiona was not the sort of person who disobeyed the regulations so flagrantly. "I had to know," she added.

I drank my tea and said nothing. I wasn't even sure I

wanted to know what Rensselaer and Dicky Cruyer had in store for me.

"Brahms Four might have gone crazy," she said finally. "Bret and Dicky both suggest that as a real possibility." She waited while the words took effect. "They think he might have had some kind of mental breakdown. That's why they are worried. There's simply no telling what he might do."

"Is that what it said in the memo?" I laughed. "That's just Bret and Dicky covering their asses."

"Dicky suggested that they let some high-powered medical people attempt a diagnosis on the basis of Brahms Four's reports but Bret squashed that."

"It sounds just like one of Cruyer's bright ideas," I said. "Let the headshrinkers into a meeting and we'll be the front page of next week's Sunday newspaper's review section, complete with misquotes, misspellings, and bits written 'by our own correspondents.' Thank Christ Bret killed that one. What form does the Brahms Four madness take?"

"The usual sort of paranoia: enemies round every corner, no one he can trust. Can he have a full list of everyone with access to his reports? Do we know there are top-level leaks of everything he sends us? The usual sort of loony stuff that people imagine when they're going round the bend."

I nodded. Fiona didn't have the faintest idea of what an agent's life was like. Dicky and Bret had no idea either. None of these desk bastards knew. My father used to say, "Eternal paranoia is the price of liberty. Vigilance is not enough."

"Maybe Brahms Four is right," I said. "Maybe there *are* enemies round every corner over there." I remembered Cruyer telling me the way the Department helped Brahms Four to ingratiate himself with the regime. He must have made a lot of enemies. "Maybe he's not so loony."

"And top-level security leaks too?" Fiona said.

"It wouldn't be the first time, would it?"

"Brahms Four asked for you. Did they tell you that?"

"No." I concealed my surprise. So that was at the back of all their anxiety in the billiards room.

"He doesn't want any more contact with his regular Control. He's told them he'll deal with no one but you."

"I'll bet that finally convinced the D-G that he was crazy." I put the empty teacup on the side table and switched out my bedside light. "I've got to get some sleep," I told her. "I wish I could manage on five hours a night like you, but I need a lot of sack time."

"You won't go, will you? Promise you won't."

I grunted and buried my face in the pillow. I always sleep face downward; it stays dark longer that way.

Chapter 5

On Monday afternoon I was in Bret Rensselaer's office. It was on the top floor not far from the suite the D-G occupied. All the top-floor offices were decorated to the personal taste of the occupants; it was one of the perks of seniority. Bret's room was "modern," with glass and chrome and gray carpet. It was hard, austere, and colorless, a habitat just right for Bret, with his dark worsted Savile Row suit and the crisp white shirt and club tie, and his fair hair that was going white, and the smile that seemed shy and fleeting but was really the reflex action that marked his indifference.

The nod, the smile, and the finger pointed at the black leather chesterfield did not interrupt the conversation he was having on his white phone. I sat down and waited for him to finish telling a caller that there was no chance of their meeting for lunch that day, next day, or any other day in the future.

"Are you a poker player, Bernard?" he said even while he was putting the phone down.

"Only for matchsticks," I replied cautiously.

"Ever wonder what will happen to you when you retire?"

"No," I said.

"No plans to buy a bar in Málaga, or a market garden in Sussex?"

"Is that what you're planning?" I said.

Bret smiled. He was rich, very rich. The idea of him working a market garden in Sussex was hilarious. As for Málaga and its plebeian diversions, he'd divert the plane rather than enter its air space. "I guess your wife has money," said Rensselaer. He paused. "But I'd say you're the type of inverted snob who wouldn't want to use any of it."

"Would that make me an inverted snob?"

"If you were smart enough to invest her dough and double it, you'd do no one any harm. Right?"

"In the evenings, you mean? Or would that be instead of working here?"

"Every time I ask you questions, I find you asking me questions."

"I didn't know I was being questioned," I said. "Am I being vetted?"

"In this business it does no harm to flip the pages of someone's bank account from time to time," said Rensselaer.

"You'll find only moths in mine," I said.

"No family money?"

"Family money? I was thirty years old before I got a nanny."

"People like you who've worked in the field always have money and securities stashed away. I'll bet you've got numbered bank accounts in a dozen towns."

"What would I put into them, luncheon vouchers?"

"Goodwill," he said. "Goodwill. Until the time comes." He picked up the short memo I'd sent him about Werner Volkmann's import-export business. So that was it. He was wondering if I was sharing the profits in Werner's business.

"Volkmann is not making enough dough to pay handsome kickbacks, if that's what you're thinking," I said.

"But you want the Department to bankroll him?" He was still standing behind his desk; he liked being on his feet, moving about like a boxer, shifting his weight and twisting his body as if avoiding imaginary blows.

"You'd better get yourself some new bifocals," I said. "There's no suggestion that the Department give him a penny."

Bret smiled. When he got tired of playing the shy Mr. Nice Guy, he'd suddenly go for confrontation, accusation, and insult. But at least he was unlikely to go behind your back. "Maybe I read it hurriedly. What the hell is 'forfaiting' anyway?"

Bret was like those High Court judges who lean over and ask what is a male chauvinist, or a mainframe computer. They know what they think these things are, but they want them defined by mutual agreement and written into the court record.

"Volkmann raises cash for West German companies so they can be paid promptly after exporting goods to East Germany."

"How does he do that?" said Bret, looking down and fiddling with some papers on his desk.

"There's a hell of a lot of complicated paperwork," I said. "But the essential part of it is that they send details of the shipment and the prices to an East German bank. They sign them and rubber-stamp them and agree that it's all okay with the East German importers. They also agree on the dates of the payments. Volkmann goes to a bank, or a syndicate of banks, or any other source of cash in the West, and uses that 'aval' to discount the cash that pays for the goods."

"It's like factoring?"

"It's more complicated, because you're dealing with a lot of people, most of them bureaucrats."

"And your pal Volkmann gets a margin on each deal. That's sweet."

"It's a tough business, Bret," I said. "There are a lot of people offering to cut a fraction of a percentage off the next one, to get the business."

"But Volkmann has no banking background. He's a hustler."

I breathed in slowly. "You don't have to be a banker to get into it," I said patiently. "Werner Volkmann has been doing these forfaiting deals for several years now. He has good contacts in the East. He moves in and out of the Eastern Sector with minimum fuss. They like him because they know he tries to do tie-in deals with East German exports—"

Bret held up his hand. "What tie-in deals?"

"A lot of the banks just want to handle cash. Werner is prepared to shop around for a customer in the West who'll take some East German exports. In that way he can save them some hard currency or maybe even swing a deal where the export price equals the money due for the imports."

"Is that so," said Bret reflectively.

"Volkmann could be very useful for us, Bret," I said.

"How?"

"Moving money, moving goods, moving people."

"We do that already."

"But how many people do we have who can go back and forth without question?"

"So what's Volkmann's problem?"

"You know what Frank Harrington is like. He doesn't get along with Werner, and never has."

"And anyone Frank doesn't like, Berlin never uses."

"Frank *is* Berlin," I said. "It's a small staff there now, Bret. Frank has to approve every damned thing."

"And you want me to tell Frank how to run his Berlin office?"

"Do you ever read anything I send you, Bret? It says

there that I just want the Department to approve a rollover guarantee of funds from one of our own merchant banks."

"And that's money," said Bret triumphantly.

"We're simply talking about one of our own banking outfits, using their own expertise to give Werner normal facilities at current bank rates."

"So why can't he get that already?"

"Because the sort of banks which best back these forfaiting deals want to know who Werner Volkmann is. And this Department has an old-fashioned rule that onetime field agents shouldn't go around giving the D-G as reference, or saying that the way they got to learn about the forfaiting business was by running agents across the Wall since they were eighteen years old."

"So tell me how Volkmann has stayed in business."

"By going outside the regular banking network, by raising money from the money market. But that means trimming his agent's fee. It's making life tough for him. If he gives up the forfaiting business, we'll lose a good opportunity and a useful contact."

"Suppose he fouls up on one of these deals and the bank doesn't get its money."

"Oh, for Christ's sake, Bret. The boys in the bank are big enough to change their own nappies."

"And they'll squeal bloody murder."

"What do we have those lousy banks for, unless it's for this kind of job?"

"What kind of dough are we talking about?"

"A million Deutschemark rolling over would be about right."

"Are you out of your tiny mind?" said Bret. "A million D-mark? For that no good son of a bitch? No, sir." He scratched the side of his nose. "Did Volkmann put you up to all this?"

"Not a word. He likes to show me what a big success he is."

"So how do you know he's strapped for cash?"

"In this business," I said, "it does no harm to flip the pages of someone's bank account from time to time."

"One of these days you'll come unstuck doing one of your unofficial investigations into something that doesn't concern you. What would you do if the bells started ringing?"

"I'd just swear it was an *official* investigation," I said.

"The hell you would," said Rensselaer.

I started to leave the room. "Before you go," he said, "what would you say if I told you that Brahms Four asked for you? Suppose I said he won't trust anyone else in the Department? What would you say about that?"

"I'd say he sounds like a good judge of character."

"Okay, smart ass. Now let's have an answer for the record."

"It could simply mean he trusts me. He doesn't know many Department people on personal terms."

"Very diplomatic, Bernard. Well, downstairs in Evaluation they are beginning to think Brahms Four has been turned. Most people I've spoken with downstairs are now saying Brahms Four might have been a senior KGB man from the time Silas Gaunt first encountered him at that bar."

"And most people downstairs," I said patiently, "wouldn't recognize a senior bloody KGB officer if he walked up to them waving a red flag."

Rensselaer nodded as if considering this aspect of his staff for the first time. "Could be you're right, Bernard." He always said Bernard with the accent on the second syllable; it was the most American thing about him.

It was at that moment that Sir Henry Clevemore came into the room. He was a tall aloof figure, slightly unkempt, with that well-worn appearance that the British upper class cultivate to show they are not nouveau riche.

"I'm most awfully sorry, Bret," said the Director-General as he caught sight of me. "I had no idea you were in conference." He frowned as he looked at me and tried to remember my name. "Good to see you, Samson," he said eventually. "I hear you spent the weekend with Silas. Did you have a good time? What has he got down there, fishing?"

"Billiards," I said. "Mostly billiards."

The D-G gave a little smile and said, "Yes, that sounds more like Silas." He turned away to look at Bret's desk top. "I've mislaid my spectacles," he said. "Did I leave them in here?"

"No, sir. You haven't been in here this morning," said Bret. "But I seem to remember that you keep spare reading glasses in the top drawer of your secretary's desk. Shall I get them for you?"

"Of course, you're right," said the D-G. "The top drawer, I remember now. My secretary's off sick this morning. I'm afraid I simply can't manage when she's away." He smiled at Bret, and then at me, to make it perfectly clear that this was a joke born out of his natural humility and goodwill.

"The old man's got a lot on his plate right now," said Bret loyally after Sir Henry had ambled off along the corridor muttering apologies about interrupting our "conference."

"Does anyone know who'll take over when he goes?" I asked Bret. Goes ga-ga, I almost said.

"There's no date fixed. But could be the old man will get back into his stride again, and go on for the full three years." I looked at Bret and he looked back at me, and finally he said, "Better the devil you know than the devil you don't know, Bernard."

Chapter 6

THE TWO SISTERS were not much alike. My wife, Fiona, was dark with a wide face and a mouth that smiled easily. Tessa, the younger one, was light-haired, almost blonde, with blue eyes and a serious expression that made her look like a small child. Her hair was straight and long enough to touch her shoulders, and she sometimes flicked it back behind her, or let it fall forward across her face so that she looked through it.

It was no surprise to find Tessa in my drawing room when I got back from the office. The two of them were very close—the result perhaps of having suffered together the childhood miseries that their pompous autocratic father thought "character forming"—and Fiona had been working hard over the past year to patch together Tessa's marriage to George, a wealthy car-dealer.

There was an open bottle of champagne in the ice bucket, and already the level was down as far as the label. "Are we celebrating something?" I asked as I took off my coat and hung it in the hall.

"Don't be so bloody bourgeois," said Tessa, handing me a champagne flute filled right to the brim. That was one of the problems of marrying into wealth; there were no luxuries.

"Dinner at eight-thirty," said Fiona, embracing me decorously, her champagne held aloft so that she would spill none of it while giving me a kiss. "Mrs. Dias has kindly stayed late."

Mrs. Dias, our Portuguese cook, housekeeper, and general factotum, was always staying late to cook the dinner. I wondered how much her labor was costing us. The cost, like so many other household expenses, would end up buried somewhere deep in the accounts and paid for out of Fiona's trust-fund income. She knew I didn't like it, but I suppose she disliked cooking even more than arguing with me about it. I sat down on the sofa and tasted the champagne. "Delicious," I said.

"Tess brought it with her," explained Fiona.

"A gift from an admirer," said Tessa archly.

"Am I permitted to ask his name?" I said. I saw Fiona glaring at me but I pretended not to be aware of it.

"All in good time, darling," said Tessa. "For the moment he remains incognito."

"In flagrante delicto, did you say?"

"You sod!" she said, and laughed.

"And how's George?" I said.

"We live our own lives," said Tessa.

"Don't upset Tessa," Fiona told me.

"He's not upsetting me," Tessa said, tossing her hair back with her bejeweled white hand. "I like George and I always will like him. We're simply not able to live together without quarreling."

"Does that mean you're getting a divorce?" I asked, drinking a little more of the champagne.

"George doesn't want a divorce," she explained. "It suits him to use the house like a hotel during the week, and he has the cottage to take his fancy ladies to."

"Does George have fancy ladies?" I said with no more than perfunctory interest.

"It has been known," said Tessa. "But he's making so

much money these days, I don't think he has much time for anything but his business."

"Lucky man," I said. "Everyone else I know is going broke."

"Well, that's where George is so clever," Tessa explained. "He got the dealerships for smaller, cheaper cars years ago when no one seemed to want them." She said it proudly. Even wives who quarrel with their husbands take pride in their achievements.

Fiona reached for the champagne. She wrapped it in a cloth and poured the rest of it into our glasses with the dexterity of a sommelier. She took care not to touch the bottle to the glass, and the cloth was crossed so as to leave the label still visible as she served. Such professional niceties came naturally to someone who'd grown up in a house with domestic servants. As she poured mine, she said, "Tess wants me to help her find a flat."

"And furnish it and do it up," said Tessa. "I'm no earthly good at anything like that. Look at the mess I made of the place I'm living in now. George never liked it there. Sometimes I think that was where our marriage began to go all wrong."

"But it's a lovely house," said Fiona loyally. "It's just too big for the two of you."

"It's old and dark," said Tessa. "It's a bit of a dump, really. I can understand why George hates it. He only agreed to buying it because he wanted to have an address in Hampstead. It was a step up from Islington. But now he says we can afford Mayfair."

"And this new place," I inquired. "Is George going to like that?"

"Give over!" said Tessa, employing the jocular cockney accent that she thought particularly apt when talking to me. "I haven't found a place yet—that's what I want help with.

I go and see places but I can never make up my mind on my own. I listen to what these sharp real-estate agents tell me and I believe it—that's my trouble."

Whatever kind of trouble Tessa had suffered in her life, it was not on account of her believing anything any man told her, but I did not contradict her. I nodded and finished my drink. It was almost time for dinner. The ever-cheerful Mrs. Dias was an adequate cook but I wasn't sure I could face another plate of her feijoada.

"You wouldn't mind, darling, would you?" said Fiona.

"Mind what?" I said. "Oh, you helping Tessa find a flat. No, of course not."

"You're a sweetie," Tessa told me, and to Fiona she said, "You're lucky to have got your hands on Bernard before I saw him. I've always said he was a wonderful husband."

I said nothing. Only Tessa could make being a wonderful husband sound like being a carrier of pestilence.

Tessa leaned back on the sofa. She was wearing a smoky gray silk button-through dress that was shiny on the curves. One hand held her champagne and the other was toying with a real pearl necklace. Nervously she crossed and re-crossed her legs and twisted the pearls tight against her white neck.

"Tessa wants to tell you something," Fiona said.

"Any more of that champagne, darling?" I said.

"Tessa's Dom Pérignon is all finished," said Fiona. "You'll have to have Sainsbury's from the fridge."

"Sainsbury's from the fridge sounds delicious," I said, passing my empty glass to her. "What do you want to ask me, Tessa?"

"Do you know a man named Giles Trent?" she said.

"Works for the F.O. Tall man, gray wavy hair, low voice, upper-crust accent. Older than me, and not nearly so handsome."

"Not exactly for the Foreign Office," said Tessa archly. "His office is in the F.O., but he's a part of your organization."

"Did he tell you that?" I said.

"Yes," said Tessa.

"He shouldn't have," I said.

"I know," said Tessa. "I was talking to Fiona about him, and she says that Giles Trent was working with your lot in Berlin back in 1978. She says he's quite important."

Fiona came in with the champagne and poured a glass for me. I said, "Well, if that's what Fiona says . . ."

Fiona said, "Tessa is my sister, darling. She's not going to go blurting out all your secrets to the Russians. Are you, Tess?"

"Not until the right Russian comes my way. Even then . . . I mean did you ever see those photos of Russian ladies?" She held the pearl necklace in her mouth; it was a babyish gesture; she liked being a baby.

"What about Giles Trent?" I said.

Tessa toyed with the necklace again. "I got to know him last summer. I met him at a dinner party given by some people who live down the road from us. He had tickets for Covent Garden—Mozart. I forget the name of the opera, but everyone was saying how difficult it was to get tickets, and Giles could get them. Well, it was heavenly. I'm not awfully keen on opera but we had a box and a bottle of champagne in the interval . . ."

"And you had an affair with him," I finished it for her.

"He's a handsome brute, Bernie. And George was away watching the Japanese making motorcars."

"Why not go with him?" I said.

"If you'd ever been on one of those trips that car manufacturers provide for the dealers, you wouldn't ask. Wives are superfluous, darling. There are hot and cold running girls in every bedroom."

Fiona poured champagne for herself and Tessa, and said, "Tess wants to tell you about Giles Trent. She doesn't want your advice on her marriage." This admonition, like all such wifely admonitions, was delivered with a smile and a laugh.

"So tell me about Giles Trent," I said.

"You were joking just now, I know. But Giles is older than you, Bernie, quite a bit older. He's a bachelor, very set in his ways. I thought he was queer at first. He's so neat and tidy and fussy about what he wears and what he eats and all that. In the kitchen—he has a divine house off the King's Road—all his chopping knives and saucepans are placed side by side, smallest on the left and biggest on the right. And it's so orderly that I was frightened to boil an egg and slice a loaf in case I spilled crumbs on the spotless tiled floor or marked the chopping board."

"Tell me how you first discovered he wasn't queer," I said.

"I said he wouldn't listen to me," Tessa complained to Fiona. "I said he'd just make sarcastic remarks all the time, and I was right."

"It's serious, Bernard," said my wife. She only called me Bernard when things were serious.

"You mean it's wedding bells for Tessa and Giles?"

"I mean Giles Trent is passing intelligence material to someone from the Russian Embassy."

There was a long silence until finally I said, "Shit."

"Giles Trent has been in the service a long time," said Fiona.

"Longer than I have," I said. "Giles Trent was lecturing at the training school by the time I got there."

"In Berlin he was in Signals at one time," said Fiona.

"Yes," I said. "And he compiled that training report for interrogators. I don't like the sound of that. Giles Trent, eh?"

"Giles Trent doesn't seem the type," said Fiona. All the ladies had a soft spot for the elegant and gentlemanly Giles Trent. He raised his hat to them and always had a clean shirt.

"They never are the type," I said.

"But no contact with field agents," said Fiona.

"Well, let's be thankful for that at least," I said. I looked at Tessa. "Have you mentioned all this to anyone?"

"Only to Daddy," said Tessa. "He said forget all about it."

"Good old Daddy," I said. "Always there when you need him."

Mrs. Dias came in bearing a large platter of shrimp fried in batter. "Don't eat too many, sir," she said in her shrill accent. "Make you very fat." The Portuguese are a lugubrious breed, and yet Mrs. Dias was always smiling. I had the feeling that we were paying her too much.

"You're wonderful, Mrs. Dias," said my wife, smiling, although the smile faded when she recognized the shrimps as those she'd set aside in the kitchen to thaw for next day's lunch.

"She's a treasure," said Tessa, taking a sample of the fried shrimp and burning her mouth so that she had to spit pieces of shrimp into her paper napkin. "My God, it's hot," she said, pulling a face.

Fiona, who hated anything fried in batter, waved a hand as I offered her the plate. I took one, blew on it, and ate it. It wasn't bad.

"We'll manage now, Mrs. Dias," said Fiona airily. I twisted around to see Mrs. Dias standing at the door watching us with a big smile. She disappeared into the kitchen again. There was a cloud of smoke and a loud crash, which we all pretended not to hear.

I said to Tessa, "How do you know he's passing stuff to the Russians?"

"He told me," she said.

"Just like that?"

"We'd started off in the middle of the afternoon drinking at some funny little club in Soho while Giles was watching the horses on TV. He won some money on one of the races and we went to the Ritz. We'd met a few friends by then, and Giles wanted to impress everyone by giving them dinner. I suggested Annabel's—George is a member. We stayed there late and Giles turned out to be a super dancer. . . ."

"Is this all leading up to something he told you in bed?" I said wearily.

"Well, yes. We went back to this dear little place he has off the King's Road. And I'd had a few drinks, and to tell you the truth I thought of George with all those Oriental popsies and I thought, What the hell. And I let Giles talk me into staying there."

"What exactly did he say, Tessa? Because it's nearly half past eight and I'm getting hungry."

"He woke me up in the middle of the night. It was absolutely ghastly. He sat up in bed and howled. It was positively orgasmic, darling. You've no idea. He howled for help or something. It was a nightmare. I mean I've had nightmares and I've seen other people having nightmares—at school half the girls in the dorm had nightmares every night, didn't they, Fi?—but not like this. He was bathed in sweat and trembling like a leaf."

"Giles Trent?" I said.

"Yes, I know. It's hard to imagine, isn't it? I mean he's so damned stiff-upper-lip and Grenadier Guards. But there he was shouting and having this nightmare. I had to shake him for ages before he awoke."

Fiona said, "Tell Bernie what he was shouting."

"He shouted, 'Help me!' 'They made me do it,' and 'Please please please.' Then I went and got him a big drink of Perrier water. He said that was what he wanted. He pulled himself together and seemed all right again. And then he suddenly asked me what I'd say if he told me he was a spy for the Russians. I said I'd laugh. And he nodded and said, well, it was true anyway. So I said, "For money, do you do it for money?" I was joking because I thought he was joking, you see."

"So what did he say about money?" I asked.

"I knew he wasn't short of money," said Tessa. "He was at Eton and he knows anyone who's anyone. He has the same tailor as Daddy, and he's not cheap. And Giles is a member of so many clubs and you know how much club subscriptions cost nowadays. George is always on about that, but he has to take business people out, of course. But Giles never complains about money. His father bought him the freehold of this place where he lives and gave him an allowance that is enough to keep body and soul together."

"And he has his salary," I said.

"Well, that doesn't go far, Bernie," said Tessa. "How do you imagine you and Fiona would manage if all she had was your salary?"

"Other people manage," I said.

"But not people like us," said Tessa in a voice of sweet reasonableness. "Poor Fiona has to buy Sainsbury's champagne because she knows you'll grumble if she gets the sort of champers Daddy drinks."

Hurriedly Fiona said, "Tell Bernie what Giles said about meeting the Russian."

"He told me about meeting this fellow from the Trade Delegation. Giles was in a pub somewhere near the Portobello Road one night. He likes finding new pubs that no one knows about except the locals. It was closing time. He asked the publican for another drink and they wouldn't serve him. Then a man standing at the counter offered to take him to a chess club in Soho—Kar's Club in Gerrard Street. There's a members' bar there which serves drinks until three in the morning. This Russian was a member and offered to put Giles up for membership and Giles joined. It's not much of a place, from what I can gather—arty people and writers, and so on. He plays chess rather well, and it began to be a habit that he went there regularly and played the Russian, or just watched someone else playing."

"When was the night of this nightmare?" I said.

"I don't remember exactly, but a little while ago."

"And he's told you about the Russians on several occasions. Or just that once in the middle of the night?"

"I brought it up again," said Tessa. "I was curious. I wanted to find out if it was a joke or not. Giles Trent remembered your name, and he knows Fiona too, so I guessed that he was on secret work of some kind. Last Friday, we got back to his place very late and he was showing me this electronic chess-playing machine he'd just bought. I said that he wouldn't have to go to that chess club anymore. He said he liked going there. I asked him if he wasn't frightened that someone would see him with this Russian and suspect him of spying. Giles collapsed onto the bed and muttered something about they might be right if that's what they suspected. He had been drinking a lot that night—mostly brandy, and I'd noticed before that it affects him in a way other drinks don't."

By now Tessa had become very quiet and serious. It was a new sort of Tessa. I'd only known her in her role of uninhibited adventuress. "Go on," I prompted her.

Tessa said, "Well, I still thought he was joking, and I was just making a gag out of it. But he wasn't joking. 'I wish to God I could get out of it,' he said. 'But they've got me now and I'll never be free of them. I will end up at the Old Bailey sentenced to thirty years.' I said couldn't he escape. Couldn't he get on a plane and go somewhere?"

"What did he say?"

" 'And end up in Moscow? I'd sooner be in an English prison listening to English voices cursing me than spend the rest of my life in Moscow. Can you imagine what it must be like?' he said. And he went on all about the sort of life that Kim Philby and those other two had in Moscow. I realized then that he must have been reading up all about it and worrying himself to death."

Tessa sipped her champagne.

Fiona said, "What will happen now, Bernie?"

"We can't leave it like this," I said. "I'll have to make it official."

"I don't want Tessa's name brought into it," said Fiona.

Tessa was looking at me. "How can I promise that?" I said.

"I'd sooner let it drop," said Tessa.

"Let it drop?" I said. "This is not some camper who's trampled through your dad's barley field, and you being asked if you want to press charges for trespass. This is espionage. If I don't report what you've told me, I could be in the dock at the Old Bailey with him, and so could you and Fiona."

"Is that right?" said Tessa. It was typical of her that she asked her sister rather than me. There was a simple directness about everything Tessa said and did, and it was difficult to remain angry with her for long. She confirmed all those theories about the second child. Tessa was sincere but shallow; she was loving but mercurial; she was an exhibitionist without enough confidence to be an actor. While Fiona displayed all the characteristics of eldest children:

stability, confidence, intellect in abundance, and that cold reserve with which to judge all the shortcomings of the world.

"Yes, Tess. What Bernie says is right."

"I'll see what I can do," I said. "I can't promise anything. But I'll tell you this: if I am able to keep your name out of it and you let me down by breathing a word of this conversation to anyone at all, including that father of yours, I'll make sure you and he and anyone else covering up are charged under the appropriate sections of the Act."

"Thank you, Bernie," said Tessa. "It would be so rotten for George."

"He's the only one I'm thinking of," I said.

"You're not so tough," she said. "You're a sweetie at heart. Do you know that?"

"You ever say that again," I told Tessa, "and I'll punch you right in the nose."

She laughed. "You're so funny," she said.

Fiona went out of the room to get a progress report on the cooking. Tessa moved along the sofa to be closer to where I was sitting at the other end of it. "Is he in bad trouble? Giles—is he in bad trouble?" There was a note of anxiety in her voice. It was uncharacteristically deferent to me, the sort of voice one uses to a physician about to make a prognosis.

"If he cooperates with us, he'll be all right." It wasn't true of course, but I didn't want to alarm her.

"I'm sure he'll cooperate," she said, sipping her drink and then looking at me with a smile that said she didn't believe a word of it.

"How long since he met this Russian?" I asked.

"Quite a time. You could find out from when he joined the chess club, couldn't you?" Tessa shook her glass and watched the bubbles rise. She was using some of the skills she'd learned at drama school the year before she'd met

George and married him instead of becoming a film star. She leaned her head to one side and looked at me meaningfully. "There's nothing bad in Giles, but sometimes he can be a fool."

"I'll have to speak to you again, Tessa. You'll probably have to repeat it all to an investigating officer and write it out and sign it."

She placed a finger on the rim of her glass and ran it around a couple of times. "I'll help you on condition you go easy on Giles."

"I'll go easy," I promised. Hell, what else could I say?

DINNER WAS SERVED on the Minton china and the table set with wedding presents: antique silver cutlery from Fiona's parents and a cut-glass vase that my father had discovered in one of the Berlin junk markets he visited regularly on Saturday mornings. The circular dining table was very big for three people, so we seated ourselves side by side, with Tessa between us. The main course was some sort of chicken stew, the quantity of it far too small for the serving dish in which it came to the table. Mrs. Dias had a big gravy mark on her white apron and she was no longer smiling. After Mrs. Dias had returned to the kitchen, Fiona whispered that Mrs. Dias had broken the small serving dish and half the chicken stew had gone onto the kitchen floor.

"Why the hell are we whispering?" I said.

"I knew you'd start shouting," said Fiona.

"I'm not shouting," I said. "I'm simply asking . . ."

"We all heard you," said Fiona. "And if you upset Mrs. Dias and we lose her . . ." She left it unsaid.

"But why are you trying to make *me* feel guilty?" I said.

"He's always like this when something gets broken," said Fiona. "Unless, of course, he did it himself."

I shared out what little there was of the chicken. I took plenty of boiled rice. Fiona had opened one of the few good clarets left in the cupboard, and I poured it gratefully.

"Would you like to come and stay with me while Bernard's away?" Fiona asked her sister.

"Where are you going?" Tessa asked me.

"It's not settled yet," I said. "I'm not sure I'm going anywhere."

"Berlin," said Fiona. "I hate being here alone."

"I'd love to, darling," Tessa said. "When?"

"I've told you, it's not arranged yet," I said. "I might not go."

"Soon," said Fiona. "Next week, or the week following."

Mrs. Dias came in to remove the plates and solicit praise and gratitude for her cookery; these were provided in abundance by Fiona, with Tessa echoing her every superlative.

"Senhor Sam?" To her I was always Senhor Sam; she never said Senhor Samson. "Senhor Sam . . . he like it?" She asked Fiona this question rather than addressing it to me. It was rather like hearing Uncle Silas and Bret Rensselaer and Dicky Cruyer discussing my chances of escaping from Berlin alive.

"Look at his plate," said Fiona cheerfully. "Not a scrap left, Mrs. Dias."

There was nothing left because my share was one lousy drumstick and a wishbone. The greater part of the chicken stew was now spread out on kitchen foil in the garden, being devoured by the neighborhood's cat population. I could hear them arguing and knocking over the empty milk bottles outside the back door. "It was delicious, Mrs. Dias," I said, and Fiona rewarded me with a beaming smile that vanished as the kitchen door closed. "Do you have to be so bloody ironic?" said Fiona.

"It was delicious. I told her it was delicious."

"Next time, you can interview the women the agency send round. Maybe then you'd realize how lucky you are."

Tessa hugged me. "Don't be hard on him, Fiona darling. You should have heard George when the au pair dropped his wretched video recorder."

"Oh, that reminds me," Fiona said, leaning forward to catch my attention. "You wanted to record that W. C. Fields film tonight."

"Right!" I said. "What time was it on?"

"Eight o'clock," said Fiona. "You've missed it, I'm afraid."

Tessa reached up to put her hand over my mouth before I spoke.

Mrs. Dias came in with some cheese and biscuits. "I told him to set the timer," said Fiona, "but he wouldn't listen."

"Men are like that," said Tessa. "You should have said *don't* set the timer, then he would have set it. I'm always having to do that sort of thing with George."

Tessa left early. She had arranged to see "an old school friend" at the Savoy Hotel bar. "That must be some school!" I said to Fiona when she came back into the drawing room after seeing her sister to the door. I always let her see her sister to the door. There were always sisterly little confidences exchanged at the time of departure.

"She'll never change," said Fiona.

"Poor George," I said.

Fiona came and sat next to me and gave me a kiss. "Was I awful tonight?" she asked.

"*Asinus asino, et sus sui pulcher*—an ass is beautiful to an ass, so is a pig to a pig."

Fiona laughed. "You were always using Latin tags when I first met you. Now you don't do that anymore."

"I've grown up," I said.

"Don't grow up too much," she said. "I love you as you are."

I responded by kissing her for a long time.

"Poor Tess. It had to happen to her, didn't it. She's so muddleheaded. She can't remember her own birthday, let alone the dates she met Giles. I'm so glad you didn't start shouting at her or want to list it all in chronological order."

"Someone will eventually," I said.

"Did you have a terrible day?" she asked.

"Bret Rensselaer won't let Werner use the bank."

"Did you have a row with him?" said Fiona.

"He had to show me how tough you get after sitting behind a desk for fifteen years."

"What did he say?"

I told her.

"I've seen you punch people for less than that," said Fiona, having listened to my account of Rensselaer's tough-guy act.

"He was just sounding me out," I said. "I don't take any of that crap seriously."

"None of it?"

"Rensselaer and Cruyer don't think that Brahms Four has been turned—neither does the D-G, you can bet on that. If they thought he was working for the KGB, we wouldn't be debating which member of the London staff goes over there to put his neck in a noose. If they really thought Brahms Four was a senior KGB man, they'd be burying that 'Berlin System' file now, not passing it around to get 'Immediate Action' tags. They'd be preparing the excuses and half-truths they'd need to explain their incompetence. They'd be getting ready to stonewall the questions that come when the story hits the fan." I took the wine that Tessa had abandoned and added it to my own. "And they don't have any worries about me either, or they wouldn't let me within a mile of the office while this was on the agenda."

"They've *got* to deal with you. Brahms Four insists. I told you that."

"What they really think is that Brahms Four is the best damned source they've had in the last decade. As usual, they only came to this conclusion when it looked like they were losing him."

"And what do you make of this ghastly business with Trent?"

I hesitated. I was guessing now, and I looked at her so that she'd know this was just a guess. "The approach to Trent might be a KGB effort to penetrate the Department."

"My God!" said Fiona in genuine alarm. "A Russian move to access the Brahms Four intelligence at this end?"

"To find out where it's coming from. Brahms Four is one of the best-protected agents we have. And that's only because he did a deal with old Silas, and Silas stuck to his word. The only way they would be able to trace him would be by seeing the material we're receiving in London."

"That's unthinkable," said Fiona.

"Why?" I said.

"Because Giles could never get his hands on the Brahms Four material—that's all triple A. Even I have never seen it, and you only get the odds and ends you need to know."

"But the Russians might not know that Giles couldn't get hold of it. To them he's senior enough to see anything he asks for."

Fiona stared into my eyes trying to see what was in my mind. "Do you think that Brahms Four might have got word of a KGB effort to trace him?"

"Yes," I said. "That's exactly what I think. Brahms

Four's demand for retirement is just his way of negotiating for a complete change in the contact chain."

"It gets more and more frightening," said Fiona. "I really don't think you should go there. This is not just a simple little day-trip. This is a big operation with lots at stake for both sides."

"I can't think of anyone else they can send," I said.

Fiona became suddenly angry. "You bloody well want to go!" she shouted. "You're just like all the others. You miss it, don't you? You really like all that bloody macho business!"

"I don't like it," I said. It was true but she didn't believe me. I put my arms around her and pulled her close. "Don't worry," I said. "I'm too old and too frightened to do anything dangerous."

"You don't have to do anything dangerous in this business to get hurt."

I didn't tell her that Werner had phoned me and asked me how soon I'd go back there. That would have complicated everything. I just told her I loved her, and that was the truth.

Chapter 7

I T WAS COLD—damned cold: when the hell would summer come? With my hands in my pockets and my collar turned up, I walked through Soho. It was early evening but most of the shops were closed, their entrances piled high with garbage awaiting next morning's collection. It had become a desolate place, its charm long lost behind a pox of porn shops and shabby little "adult" cinemas. I welcomed the smoky warmth of Kar's Club, and I welcomed the chance of one of the hot spiced rum drinks that were a specialty of the place no less than the chess.

Kar's Club was not the sort of place that Tessa would have liked. It was below ground level in Gerrard Street, Soho, a basement that had provided storage space for a wine company before an incendiary bomb burned out the upper stories in one of the heavy German air raids of April 1941. It was three large interconnecting cellars with hardboard ceilings and noisy central heating, its old brickwork painted white to reflect the lights carefully placed over each table to illuminate the chessboards.

Jan Kar was a Polish ex-serviceman who'd started his little club when, after coming out of the Army at war's end, he realized he'd never return to his homeland again. By now he was an old man with a great mop of fine white hair and a magnificent drinker's nose. Nowadays his son Arkady was usually behind the counter, but the members were still largely Poles with a selection of other East European émigrés.

There was no one there I recognized, except two young champions in the second room whose game had already attracted half a dozen spectators. Less serious players, like me, kept to the room where the food and drink were dispensed. It was already half full. They were mostly elderly men, with beards, dark-ringed eyes, and large curly pipes. In the far corner, under the clock, two silent men in ill-fitting suits glowered at their game and at each other. They played impatiently, taking every enemy in sight, as children play draughts. I was seated in the corner positioned so that I could look up from the chessboard, my book of chess problems, and my drink, to see everyone who entered as they signed the members' book.

Giles Trent came in early. I studied him with new interest. He was younger-looking than I remembered him. He took off his brown narrow-brimmed felt hat in a quick and nervous gesture, like a schoolboy entering the headmaster's study. His gray wavy hair was long enough to hide the tops of his ears. He was so tall that the club's low ceiling caused him to lower his head as he passed under the pink tasseled lampshades. He put his riding mac on the bentwood hanger and ran his fingers through his hair as if it might have become disarranged. He was wearing a Glen Urquhart check suit of the sort favored by wealthy bookmakers. It came complete with matching waistcoat and gold watch chain.

"Hello, Kar," Trent said to the old man seated near the radiator, nursing his usual whisky and water. Most of the members called him Kar. Only some of the older Poles who'd served with him in Italy knew that Kar was his family name.

Trent stayed at the counter where young Arkady dispensed cold snacks, the inimitable rum punch that his father was said to have invented under battle conditions in Italy, good coffee, warm beer, iced vodka, poor advice about chess, and unpalatable tea. Trent took rum punch.

"Mr. Chlestakov hasn't been in tonight," the youth told Trent.

Trent grunted and turned to look around the room. I stared down at my chess problem. By resting my chin in my hand, I was able to conceal my face from him.

Trent's Russian arrived about ten minutes later. He was wearing an expensive camel's-hair coat and handmade shoes. He only came up to Trent's shoulder, a potbellied man with big peasant hands and a jolly face. When he took his hat off, he revealed dark hair brilliantined and carefully parted high on the crown of his head. He smiled when he saw Trent and slapped him on the shoulder, asked him how he was, and called him "tovarich."

I recognized the type; he was the sort of Soviet official who liked to show the happy friendly side of life in the U.S.S.R. The kind of man who never arrived at a party without a couple of bottles of vodka, and winked to let you know he was an incorrigible rogue who'd break any rule for the sake of friendship.

Trent must have asked him what he wanted to drink. I heard the Russian say loudly, "Vodka. I only come here to drink my Polish friend's fine buffalo-grass vodka." He spoke the smooth English that is the legacy of the teaching machine but lacked the rhythms that can only come from hearing it spoken.

They sat down at the table Trent had selected. The Russian drank several vodkas, laughed a lot at whatever Trent was telling him, and ate pickled herring with black bread.

There was a chessboard and a box of well-worn chess pieces on every table. Trent opened the board and set up the chess pieces. He did it in the measured preoccupied way that people do things when they are worrying about something else.

The Russian gave no sign of being worried. He bit into his fish hungrily and chewed the bread with obvious delight. And every now and again he would call across the room to ask old Jan Kar what the weather forecast was, the rate of exchange for the dollar, or the result of some sporting event.

Old Jan had been in a Russian prison camp from 1939 until he was released to go into General Anders's Polish Corps. He did not like Russians, and the answers he gave were polite but minimal. Trent's Russian companion showed no sign of recognizing this latent hostility. He smiled broadly at each answer and nodded sympathetically to acknowledge old Jan's flat-toned negative answers.

I got up from my seat and went over to the counter to get another drink—coffee, this time—and from there, keeping my back toward them, I was able to hear what Trent was saying.

"Everything is slow," said Trent. "Everything takes time."

"This is just a crazy idea that comes now into my head," said the Russian. "Take everything you have down to the photocopying shop in Baker Street, the same place you got the previous lot done."

The Russian had spoken quite loudly and, although I didn't look around, I had the feeling that Trent had touched his sleeve in an effort to quieten him. Trent's voice was softer. "Leave it with me," he said. "Leave it with me." The words came in the anxious tones of someone who wants to change the subject.

"Giles, my friend," said the Russian, his voice slurred as if by the effects of the vodka. "Of course I leave it with you."

I took the coffee that Jan's son poured and went back to my table. This time I sat on another chair to keep my back turned to Trent and the Russian, but I could see them reflected faintly in a fly-specked portrait of General Pilsudski.

I continued to work my way through one of Capablanca's games against Alekhine in the 1927 championships, although I did not understand the half of it. But by the time Capablanca won, Trent and the Russian had disappeared up the stairs and out into the street.

"Can I join you, Bernard?" said old Jan Kar as I tipped my chess pieces into their box and folded my board. "I haven't seen you for years."

"I'm married now, Jan," I said. "And I never was much of a chess player."

"I heard about your dad. I'm sorry. He was a fine man."

"It's a long time ago now," I said.

He nodded. He offered me a drink, but I told him I would have to leave very soon. He looked around the room. It was empty. Everyone was in the room next door watching a game that had developed into a duel. "Working, are you? It was that Russian, wasn't it?"

"What Russian?" I said.

"Insolent bastard," said Jan Kar. "You'd think they wouldn't go where they're not welcome."

"That would seriously limit their movements."

"I'll keep it to myself, of course. And so will my son."

"I wish you would, Jan," I said. "It's very delicate, very delicate."

"I hate Russians," said old Jan.

GILES TRENT'S HOUSE was one of a terrace of narrow-fronted Georgian-style dwellings erected by speculative builders when the Great Exhibition of 1851 made Chelsea a respectable address for senior clerks and shopkeepers. Near the front door—paneled and black, with a brass lion's-head knocker—stood Julian MacKenzie, a flippant youth who'd been with the Department no more than six months. I'd chosen him to keep an eye on Trent because I knew he wouldn't dare ask me too many questions about it or expect any paperwork.

"He arrived home in a cab about half an hour ago," MacKenzie told me. "There's no one inside with him."

"Lights?"

"Just on the ground floor—and I think I saw some lights come on at the back. He probably went into the kitchen to make himself a cup of cocoa."

"You can go off duty now," I told MacKenzie.

"You wouldn't like me to come in with you?"

"Who said I'm going in?"

MacKenzie grinned. "Well, good luck, Bernie," he said cheerfully, and gave a mock salute.

"When you've been with the Department for over twenty years and the probationers are calling you Bernie," I said, "you start thinking that maybe you're not going to end up as Director-General."

"Sorry, sir," said MacKenzie. "No offense intended."

"Buzz off," I said.

I had to knock and ring three times before I could get Giles Trent to open the door to me. "What the devil is it?" he said before the door was even half open.

"Mr. Trent?" I said deferentially.

"What is it?" He looked at me as if I were a complete stranger to him.

"It would be better if I came inside," I said. "It's not something we can talk about on the doorstep."

"No, no, no. It's midnight," he protested.

"It's Bernard Samson, from Operations," I said. Why the hell had I been worrying about Giles Trent recognizing me in the club? Here I was on his doorstep and he was treating me like a vacuum-cleaner salesman. "I work on the German desk with Dicky Cruyer."

I'd hoped that this revelation would bring about a drastic change of mood, but he just grunted and stood back, muttering something about being sure it could wait until morning.

The narrow hall, with Regency striped wallpaper and framed engravings by Dutch artists I'd never heard of, gave on to a narrow staircase, and through an open door I could see a well-equipped kitchen. The house was in a state of perfect order: no nicks in the paintwork, no scuffs on the wallpaper, no marks on the carpet. Everything was in that condition that is the mark of those who are rich, fastidious, and childless.

The hall opened on to the "divine" living room that Tessa had promised. There was white carpet and white walls and gleaming white leather armchairs with brass buttons. There was even an almost colorless abstract painting over the white baby-grand piano. I could not believe it was an example of Giles Trent's taste; it was the sort of interior that is designed at great expense by energetic divorcées who don't take checks.

"It had better be important," said Trent. He was staring at me. He didn't offer me a drink. He didn't even invite me to sit down. Perhaps my sort of trench coat didn't look good on white.

"It is important," I said. Trent had taken off the tie he'd been wearing at Kar's Club, and now wore a silk scarf inside his open shirt. He'd replaced his jacket with a cashmere cardigan and his shoes with a pair of gray velvet slippers. I wondered if he always dressed with such trouble between coming home and going to bed, or whether his informal attire accounted for the delay before he opened the door to me. Or was he expecting a visit from Tessa?

"I remember you now," he said suddenly. "You're the one who married Fiona Kimber-Hutchinson."

"Were you at Kar's Club tonight?" I said.

"Yes."

"Talking to a member of the Russian Embassy staff?"

"It's a chess club," said Trent. He went across to the chair where he'd been sitting, placed a marker in a paperback of Zola's *Germinal*, and put it on the shelf alongside hardback copies of Agatha Christie and other detective stories. "I speak to many people there. I play chess with anyone available. I don't know what they do for a living."

"The man you were with is described in the Diplomatic List as a first secretary but I think he's a KGB man, don't you?"

"I didn't think about it, one way or the other."

"Didn't you? You didn't think about it? Okay if I quote you on that one?"

"Don't threaten me," said Trent. He opened a silver box on the table where the book had been and took a cigarette and lit it, blowing smoke in a gesture that might have been repressed anger. "I'm senior in rank and service to you, Mr. Samson. Don't come into my home trying the bullyboy tactics that work so well with people of your own sort."

"You can't believe that being senior in service and rank gives you the unquestioned right to have regular meetings with KGB agents and discuss the merits of various photocopying services."

Trent went red in the face. He turned away from me, but that of course only drew attention to his discomfiture. "Photocopying? What the hell are you talking about?"

"I hope you're not going to say that you were only going

to photocopy chess problems. Or that you were meeting that KGB man on the orders of the D-G. Or that you were engaged on a secret assignment for a person whose name you are not permitted to tell me."

Trent turned and came toward me. "All I'm going to tell you," he said, tapping my chest with his finger, "is to leave my house right away. Any further conversation will be done through my lawyer."

"I wouldn't advise you to consult a lawyer," I said in the friendliest tone I could manage.

"Get out," he said.

"Aren't you going to tell me that you'll make sure I'm fired from the Department?" I said.

"Get out," he said again. "And you tell whoever sent you that I intend to take legal action to safeguard my rights."

"You've got no rights," I said. "You sign the Act regularly. Have you ever bothered to read what it says on that piece of paper?"

"It certainly doesn't say I'm not entitled to consult a lawyer when I have some little upstart force his way into my house and accuse me of treason, or whatever it is you're accusing me of."

"I'm not accusing you of anything, Trent. I'm just asking you some simple questions to which you are supplying very complicated answers. If you start dragging lawyers into this dialogue, our masters are going to regard it as a very unfriendly reaction. They are going to see it as a confrontation, Trent. And it's the sort of confrontation you can't win."

"I'll win."

"Grow up, Trent. Even if you went to law and did the impossible and got a verdict against the Crown so that you were awarded damages and costs, do you think they'd give you your job back? And where would you go to find another job? No, Trent, you've got to put up with being quizzed by menials like me, because it's all part of the job, your job. Your one and only job."

"Wait a minute, wait a minute. There are a couple of things I want to get straight," he said. "Who says I've been in regular contact with this Russian diplomat?"

"We've got this funny system in interrogation—you wrote one of the training books, so you'll know about this—that it's the interrogator that asks the questions and the man being investigated that answers them."

"Am I being investigated?"

"Yes, you are," I said. "And I think you are as guilty as hell. I think you're an agent working for the Russians."

Trent touched the silk scarf at his neck, loosening it with his fingers as if he were too hot. He was frightened now, frightened in the way that such a man could never be by physical violence. Trent enjoyed physical exertion, discomfort, and even hardship. He'd learned to deal with such things at his public school. He was frightened of something quite different: he was terrified that damage was going to be done to some grand illusory image he had of himself. It was part of my job to guess what frightened a man, and then not to dwell on it but rather let him pick at it himself while I talked of other, tedious things, giving him plenty of opportunity to peel back the scab of fear and expose the tender wound beneath.

So I didn't tell Trent about the misery and disgrace that would be waiting for him. Instead I told him how simple it would be for me to drop this investigation, and destroy my notes and papers, in exchange for his walking into my office the next morning and making a voluntary statement. In that way there would be no investigation; Trent would re-port an overture made to him from a Russian diplomat and we would brief him on how to react.

"And would the Department allow that? Would they agree to it being something that starts with a report from me?"

There was, of course, no report to change or destroy. I hadn't mentioned my conversation with Tessa to anyone at all. I nodded sagely. "Use your imagination, Trent. What do you think the D-G would prefer? If we discover you in contact with the Russians, we've got a disaster on our hands. But if you can be described as one of our people feeding stuff to the Russians, we've got a minor triumph."

"I suppose you're right."

"Of course I'm right. I know how these things work."

"You'd want me to continue my meetings with him?"

"Exactly. You'd be working for us. You'd be making a fool of him."

Trent smiled; he liked that.

After I'd been through my piece a couple of times, Trent became friendly enough to press a couple of drinks on me and thank me for my kindness and consideration. He repeated my instructions earnestly and thankfully, and he looked up to wait for my nod of approval. For by now—in about an hour of conversation—I had established the role of father-confessor, protector, and perhaps savior too. "That's right," I said, this time letting the merest trace of warmth into my voice. "You do it our way and you'll be fine. Everything will be fine. This could even mean a step up the promotion ladder for you."

Chapter 8

WHAT WIFE, at some time or other, has not suspected her husband of infidelity? And how many husbands have not felt a pang of uncertainty at some unexplained absence, some careless remark or late arrival of his spouse? There was nothing definite in my fears. There was nothing more than confused suspicion. Fiona's embraces were as lusty as ever; she laughed at my jokes and her eyes were bright when she looked at me. Too bright, perhaps, for sometimes I thought I could detect in her that profound compassion that women show only for men who have lost them.

I'd been trying to read other people's minds for most of my life. It could be a dangerous task. Just as a physician might succumb to hypochondria, a policeman to graft, or a priest to materialism, so I knew that I studied too closely the behavior of those close to me. Suspicion went with the job, the endemic disease of the spy. For friendships and for marriages it sometimes proved fatal.

I'd returned home very late after my visit to Giles Trent and that night I slept heavily. By seven o'clock next morning, Fiona's place alongside me in bed was empty. Balanced upon the clock-radio there was buttered toast and a cup of coffee, by now quite cold. She must have left very early.

In the kitchen I could hear the children and their young

nanny. I looked in on them and took some orange juice while standing up. I tried to join in the game they were playing but they yelled derision at my efforts, for I'd not understood that all answers must be given in Red Indian dialect. I blew them kisses that they didn't acknowledge and, wrapped into my sheepskin car coat, went down into the street to spend fifteen minutes getting the car to start.

Sleet was falling as I reached the worst traffic jams, and Dicky Cruyer had parked his big Jag carelessly enough to make it a tight squeeze to get into my allotted space in the underground garage. Don't complain, Samson, you're lucky to have a space at all; Dicky—not having fully mastered the technique of steering—really needs two.

I spent half an hour on the phone asking when my new car was going to be delivered, but got no clear answer beyond the fact that delivery dates were unreliable. I looked at the clock and decided to call Fiona's extension. Her secretary said, "Mrs. Samson had an out-of-town meeting this morning."

"Oh, yes—she mentioned it, I think," I said.

Her secretary knew I was trying to save face; secretaries always guess right about that kind of thing. Her voice became especially friendly as if to compensate for Fiona's oversight. "Mrs. Samson said she'd be late back. But she'll phone me sometime this morning for messages. She always does that. I'll tell her you called. Was there any message, Mr. Samson?"

Was her secretary a party to whatever was going on, I wondered. Was it one of those affairs that women liked to discuss very seriously or was it recounted with laughter as Fiona had recounted to me some of her teenage romances? Or was Fiona the sort of delinquent wife who confided in no one? That would be her style, I decided. No one would ever own Fiona; she was fond of saying that. There was always a part of her that was kept secret from all the world.

"Can I give your wife a message, Mr. Samson?" her secretary asked again.

"No," I said. "Just tell her I called."

BRET RENSSELAER liked to describe himself as a "work-aholic." That this description was a tired old cliché didn't deter him from using it. He liked clichés. They were, he said, the best way to get simple ideas into the heads of idiots. But his description of himself was accurate enough; he liked work. He'd inherited a house in the Virgin Islands and a portfolio of stock that would keep him idling in the sun for the rest of his days, if that was his inclination. But he was always at his desk by eight-thirty and had never been known to have a day off for sickness. A day off for other reasons was not unusual; Easter at Le Touquet, Whitsun at Deauville, the Royal Enclosure in June, and the Dublin Horse Show in August were appointments marked in red pencil on Bret's year-planner.

Needless to say, Rensselaer had never served as a field agent. His only service experience was a couple of years in the U.S. Navy in the days when his father was still hoping he'd take over the family-owned bank.

Bret had spent his life in swivel chairs, arguing with dictating machines and smiling for committees. His muscles had come from lifting barbells, and jogging around the lawn of his Thames-side mansion. And one look at him would suggest that it was a good way to get them, for Bret had grown old gracefully. His face was tanned in that very even way that comes from sun reflected off the *Pulverschnee* that only falls on very expensive ski resorts. His fair hair was changing almost imperceptibly to white. And the eyeglasses that he now required for reading were styled like those that California highway patrolmen hang in their pocket flap while writing you a ticket.

"Bad news, Bret," I told him as soon as he could fit me into his schedule. "Giles Trent is coming in this morning to tell us just what he's been spilling to the Russians."

Bret didn't jump up and start doing press-ups as he was said to have done when Dicky brought him the news that his wife had walked out on him. "Tell me more," he said calmly.

I told him about my visit to Kar's Club and overhearing the conversation, and that I'd suggested that Trent report it all to us. I didn't say why I'd visited Kar's Club or mention anything about Tessa.

He listened to my story without interrupting me, but he got to his feet and spent a little time checking through his paper-clip collection while he listened.

"Three Russians. Where were the other two?"

"Sitting in the corner, playing chess with two fingers, and saying nothing to anyone."

"Sure they were part of it?"

"A KGB hit team," I said. "They weren't difficult to spot—cheap Moscow suits and square-toed shoes, sitting silent because their English isn't good enough for anything more than buying a cup of coffee. They were there in case the flashy one needed them. They work in threes."

"Is there a Chlestakov on the Diplomatic List?"

"No, I invented that part of my story for Trent. But this one was a KGB man—expensive clothes but no rings. Did you ever notice the way those KGB people never buy rings in the West? Rings leave marks on the fingers that might have to be explained when they are called back home, you see."

"But you said that in the club-members' book they are all described as Hungarians. Are you sure they are Russians?"

"They didn't do a Cossack dance or play balalaikas," I said, "but that's only because they didn't think of it. This fat little guy Chlestakov—a phony name, of course—was calling Trent 'tovarich.' Tovarich! Jesus, I haven't heard anyone say that since the TV reruns of those old Garbo films."

Bret Rensselaer took off his eyeglasses and fiddled with them. "The Russian guy said, 'This is just a crazy idea that comes into my head. Take everything down to the photocopying shop in Baker Street . . .' "

I finished it for him: " '. . . the same place you got the previous lot done.' Yes, that's what he said, Bret."

"He must be crazy saying that in a place where he could be overheard."

"That's it, Bret," I said, trying not to be too sarcastic. "Like the man said, he's a KGB man who acts upon a crazy idea as soon as it comes into his head."

Bret was toying with his spectacles as if encountering the technology of the hinge for the first time. "What's eating you?" he said without looking up at me.

"Come on, Bret," I said. "Did you ever hear of a Russian making a snap decision about anything? Did you ever hear of a KGB man acting on a crazy idea that just came into his head?"

Bret smiled uneasily but didn't answer.

"All the KGB people I ever encounter have certain well-ingrained Russian characteristics, Bret. They are very slow, very devious, and very very thorough."

Bret put his wire-frame eyeglasses into their case and leaned back to take a good look at me. "You want to tell me what the hell you're getting at?"

"They did everything except sing the 'Internationale,'

Bret," I said. "And it wasn't Trent who did anything indiscreet. He played it close to the chest. It was the KGB man who came on like he was auditioning for Chekhov."

"You're not telling me that these three guys were just pretending to be Russians?"

"No," I said. "My imagination doesn't stretch to the idea of anybody who is not Russian wishing to be mistaken for a Russian."

"So you think these guys staged the whole thing for your benefit? You think they just did it to discredit Giles Trent?"

I didn't answer.

"So why the hell would Giles Trent confess when you confronted him?" said Bret, rubbing salt into it.

"I don't know," I admitted.

"Just four beats to the bar, feller. Okay? Don't get too complicated. Save all that for Coordination. Those guys get paid to fit the loose ends together."

"Sure," I said. "But meanwhile we'd better send someone along to turn Trent's place over. Not just a quick glance under the bed and a flashlight to see around the attic. A proper search."

"Agreed. Tell my secretary to do the paperwork and I'll get it signed. Meanwhile assign someone to it—someone you can rely on. And by the way, Bernard, it's beginning to look as though we might have to ask you to go to Berlin, after all."

"I'm not sure I could do that, Bret," I said with matching charm.

"It's your decision," he said, and smiled to show how friendly he could be. Most of the time he was Mr. Nice Guy. He opened doors for you, stood back to let you into the lift, laughed at your jokes, agreed with your conclusions, and asked your advice. But when all the pleasantries were over he made sure you did exactly what he wanted.

I WAS STILL THINKING about Bret Rensselaer when I finished work that evening. He was different from any of the other department heads I had to deal with. Despite those moments of brash hostility, he was more approachable than the D-G and more reliable than Dicky Cruyer. And Bret had that sort of laid-back self-confidence that you have to be both rich and American to possess. He was the only one to defy the Departmental tradition that only the D-G could have a really big car, while the rest of the senior staff managed with Jaguars, Mercedes, and Volvos. Bret had a bloody great Bentley limousine and a full-time uniformed chauffeur to go with it.

I saw Bret's gleaming black Bentley in the garage when I got out of the lift in the basement. The interior lights were on and I could hear Mozart from the stereo. Bret's driver was sitting in the back seat tapping his cigarette ash into a paper bag and swaying in time to the music.

The driver, Albert Bingham, was a sixty-year-old ex-Scots Guardsman whose enforced silence while driving resulted in a compulsive garrulity when off duty. "Hello, Mr. Samson," he called to me. "Am I parked in the way?"

"No," I said. But Albert was out of his car and all ready for one of his chats.

"I wondered if you would be taking your wife's car," he said. "But on the other hand I guessed she'd be coming back here to collect it herself. I know how much she likes driving that Porsche, Mr. Samson. We were having a chat about it only last week. I told her I could have it tuned up by a fellow I know at the place I get the Bentley serviced. He's a wizard, and he has a Porsche himself. A secondhand one, of course, not the latest model like that one of your wife's."

"I'm going home in this elderly Ford," I said, tapping the glass of it with my keys.

"I hear you're getting a Volvo," he said. "Just the right car for a family man."

"We're too squeezed in my wife's Porsche," I said.

"You'll be pleased with the Volvo," said Albert in that tone of voice that marks the Bentley driver. "It's a solid car, as good as the Mercedes any day, and you can quote me on that."

"I might quote you on that," I said, "if I ever try trading it in for a Mercedes."

Albert smiled and took a puff at his cigarette. He knew when he was being joshed and he knew how to show me he didn't mind. "Your wife wanted to drive Mr. Rensselaer in her Porsche, but he insisted on the Bentley. He doesn't like fast sports cars, Mr. Rensselaer. He likes to be able to stretch his legs out. He was injured in the war—did you know he was injured?"

I wondered what Albert could be talking about. Fiona had arranged to go to Tessa's and sort through some house agents' offers. "Injured? I didn't know."

"He was in submarines. He broke his kneecap falling down a companionway—that's a sort of ladder on a ship— and it was reset while they were at sea. A sub doesn't return from patrol for a little matter of an ensign hurting his leg." Albert laughed at the irony of it all.

Where had Rensselaer gone with my wife? "So you nearly got an evening off, Albert."

Gratified to see I hadn't climbed into the driving seat and fled from him, as most of the staff did when he started chatting, Albert took a deep breath and said, "I don't mind, Mr. Samson. I can use the overtime, to tell you the honest truth. And what do I care whether I'm sitting at home in my poky little bed-sitter or laying back in that real leather.

It's Mozart, Mr. Samson, and I'd just as soon listen to Mozart here in an underground garage as anywhere in the world. That stereo is a beautiful job. Come over and listen to it if you don't believe me."

They couldn't have gone far, or Albert would not have brought the Bentley back to the garage to wait for them. "Much traffic in town tonight, Albert? I have to go through the West End."

"It's terrible, Mr. Samson. One of these days, it's going to lock up solid." This was one of Albert's standard phrases; he said it automatically while he worked out an answer to my question. "Piccadilly is bad at this time. It's the theatres."

"I never know how to avoid Piccadilly when I'm going home."

Albert inhaled on his cigarette. I had given him the perfect opening on his favorite topic: shortcuts in Central London. "Well—"

"Take your journey tonight," I interrupted him. "How did you tackle it? You knew there would be heavy traffic . . . when did you leave—seven?"

"Seven-fifteen. Well, they went for a drink in the White Elephant Club in Curzon Street first. They could have walked from there to the Connaught, I know, but it might have started to rain and there'd be no cabs in Curzon Street at that time. The table at the Connaught Hotel Grill Room was for eight o'clock. No place for a big car like mine in Curzon Street. They're double-parked there by seven on some evenings at this time of year. I got there via Birdcage Walk, past Buckingham Palace and Hyde Park Corner . . . a long way round, you say. But when you've spent as many years driving in London as I have, you . . ."

I let Albert's voice drone on as I asked myself why my wife had told me she was spending the evening with Tessa when really she was having dinner in a hotel with Bret

Rensselaer. "Is that the time," I said, looking at my watch while Albert was in full flow. "I must go. Nice talking to you, Albert. You're a mine of information."

Albert smiled. I could still hear *Così fan Tutte* from the Bentley's stereo when I was driving up the exit ramp.

I WATCHED HER as she took off her rain-specked headscarf. She wore a silk square only when she wanted to protect a very special new hairdo. She shook her head and flicked at her hair with her fingertips. Her eyes sparkled and her skin was pale and perfect. She smiled; how beautiful she seemed, and how far away.

"Did you eat out?" she said. She noticed the dining table with the unused place setting that Mrs. Dias had left for me.

"I had a cheese roll in a pub."

"That's the worst thing you could choose," she said. "Fat and carbohydrates: that's not good for you. There was cold chicken and salad prepared."

"So did Tessa find another house?"

Alerted perhaps by my tone of voice, or by the way I stood facing her, she looked into my face for a moment before taking off her raincoat. "I couldn't get to Tessa to-night. Something came up." She shook the raincoat and the raindrops flashed in the light.

"Work, you mean?"

She looked at me steadily before nodding. We had a tacit agreement not to ask questions about work. "Something Rensselaer wanted," she said, and kept looking at me as if challenging me to pursue it.

"I saw your car in the car park when I left but Security said you'd already gone."

She walked past me to hang her coat in the hall. When

she'd done that, she looked in the hall mirror and combed her hair as she spoke: "There was a lot of stuff in the diplomatic bag this afternoon. Some of it needed translation and Bret's secretary has only A-level German. I went across the road and worked there."

Claiming to be in the Foreign Office as an explanation of absence was the oldest joke in the Department. No one could ever be found in that dark labyrinth. "You had dinner with Rensselaer," I said, unable to control my anger any longer.

She stopped combing her hair, opened her handbag, and dropped the comb into it. Then she smiled and said, "Well, you don't expect me to starve, darling. Do you?"

"Don't give me all that crap," I said. "You left the building with Rensselaer at seven-fifteen. You were in his Bentley when he drove out of the garage. Then I discovered he'd left the reception desk at the Connaught as his contact number for the night duty officer."

"You haven't lost your touch, darling," she said with ice in every syllable. "Once a field man, always a field man—isn't that what they say?"

"It's what people like Cruyer and Rensselaer say. It's what people say when they are trying to put down the people who do the real work."

"Well, now it's paid off for you," she said. "Now all your old expertise has enabled you to discover that I had dinner at the Connaught with Bret Rensselaer."

"So why do you have to lie to me?"

"What lies? I told you I had to do some work for Rensselaer. We had dinner—a good dinner, with wine—but we were talking shop."

"About what?"

She pushed past me into the front room and through into the dining room that opened from it in what designers call "open plan." She picked up the clean plates and cutlery that had been left for me. "You know better than to ask me that."

I followed behind her as she put the plates on a shelf in the dresser. "Because it's so secret?"

"It's confidential," she said. "Don't you have work that is too confidential to talk to me about?"

"Not in the Grill Room of the Connaught, I don't."

"So you even know which room we were in. You've done your homework tonight, haven't you."

"What was I supposed to do while you're having dinner with the boss? Am I supposed to eat cold chicken and watch TV?"

"You were supposed to be having a beer with a friend, and then collecting the children from their visit to my parents' house."

Oh, my God! I forgot. "I clean forgot about the children," I admitted.

"I phoned Mother. I guessed you'd forget. She gave them supper and brought them here in a minicab. It's all right."

"Good old Mum-in-law," I said.

"You don't have to be bloody sarcastic about my mother," said Fiona. "It's bad enough trying to have an argument about Bret."

"Let's drop it," I said.

"Do what you like," said Fiona. "I've had enough talk for one night." She switched off the light in the dining room, went into the kitchen, opened the door of the dishwasher, closed it again, and turned it on. The sprays of the dishwasher beat on its steel interior like a Wagnerian drumroll. The noise made conversation impossible.

When I came from the bathroom, I expected to see Fiona tucked into the pillow and feigning sleep; she did that sometimes after we'd had a row. But this time she was sitting up in bed, reading some large tome with the distinctive cheap binding of the Department's library. She wanted to remind me that she was a dedicated wage slave.

As I undressed, I tried a fresh, friendly tone of voice: "What did Bret want?"

"I wish you wouldn't keep on about it."

"There's nothing between you, is there?"

She laughed. It was a derisory laugh. "You suspect me . . . with Bret Rensselaer? He's nearly as old as my father."

"He was probably older than the father of that cipher clerk—Jennie something—who left just before Christmas."

Fiona raised her eyes from her book; this was the sort of thing that interested her. "You don't think she . . . with Bret, you mean?"

"Internal Security sent someone to find out why she'd left without giving proper notice. She said she'd been having an affair with Bret. He'd told her they were through."

"Good grief," said Fiona. "Poor Bret. I suppose the D-G had to be told."

"The D-G was pleased to hear the girl had proper security clearance, and that was that."

"How broad-minded of the old man. I'd have thought he would have been furious. Still, Bret isn't married. His wife left him, didn't she?"

"The suggestion was that Bret had sinned before."

"And always with someone with proper security clearance. Well, good for Bret. So that's why you thought . . ." She laughed again. It was a genuine laugh this time. She closed her book but kept a finger in the page. "He's going through the regular routine about the danger of security lapses."

"I told him about Giles Trent," I said. "I kept Tessa out of it."

"Bret has decided to talk to everyone personally," said Fiona.

"Surely Bret doesn't suspect *you?*"

Fiona smiled. "No, darling. Bret didn't take me to the Connaught to interrogate me over the bones of the last of this season's woodcock. He spent the evening talking about you."

"About me?"

"And in due course of time he will take you aside and ask about me. You know how it works, darling. You've been at this business longer than I have." She put a marker in her book before laying it aside.

"Oh, for Christ's sake."

"If you don't believe me, darling, ask Bret."

"I might do that," I said. She waited until I got into bed, and then switched out the lights. "I thought there was protein in cheese," I said. She didn't answer.

Chapter 9

Dicky Cruyer was in Bret Rensselaer's office when they sent for me on Wednesday. Cruyer had his thumbs stuck in the back pockets of his jeans and his curly head was tilted to one side as if he were listening for some distant sound.

Rensselaer was in his swivel chair, arms folded and feet resting on a leather stool. These relaxed postures were studied, and I guessed that the two of them had taken up their positions when they heard me at the door. It was a bad sign. Rensselaer's folded arms and Cruyer's akimbo stance had that sort of aggression I'd seen in interrogating teams.

"Bernard!" said Dicky Cruyer in a tone of pleasant surprise as if I'd just dropped in for tea, rather than kept them waiting for thirty minutes in response to the third of his calls. Rensselaer watched us dispassionately, as a passing taxicab passenger might watch two men at a bus stop. "Looks like another jaunt to Big B," said Dicky.

"Is that so?" I said without enthusiasm. Bret was jacketless. This slim figure in white shirt, bow tie, and waistcoat looked like the sort of Mississippi riverboat gambler who broke into song for the final reel.

"Not through the wire, or anything tricky," said Cruyer. "Just a call into our office. An East German has just knocked on Frank Harrington's door with a bagful of papers and demands to be sent to London. Won't talk to our Berlin people, Frank tells me." Dicky Cruyer ran his finger through his curls before nodding seriously at Rensselaer.

"Another crank," I said.

"Is that what you think, Bernard?" said Rensselaer with that earnest sincerity I'd learned to disregard.

"What kind of papers?" I asked Dicky.

"Right," said Cruyer. But he didn't answer my question.

Rensselaer took his time about describing the papers. "Interesting stuff," he stated cautiously. "Most of it from here. The minutes of a meeting the D-G had with some Foreign Office senior staff, an appraisal of our success in tapping diplomatic lines out of London, part of a report on our use of U.S. enciphering machines . . . A mixed bag but it's worth attention. Right?"

"*Well* worth our attention, Bret," I said.

"What's that supposed to mean?" said Cruyer.

"For anyone who believes in Santa Claus," I added.

"You mean it's a KGB stunt," said Rensselaer. "Yes, that's probably it." Cruyer looked at him, disconcerted at Bret's change of attitude. "On the other hand," said Rensselaer, "it's something we ignore at our peril. Wouldn't you agree, Bernard?"

I didn't answer.

Dicky Cruyer moved his hands to grip the large brass buckle of his leather cowboy belt. "Berlin Resident is worried—damned worried."

"Old Frank is always worried," I said. "He can be an old woman, we all know that."

"Frank's had a lot to worry about since he took over," said Rensselaer, to put his loyalty to his subordinates on record. But he didn't deny that Frank Harrington, our senior man in Berlin, could be an old woman.

"All stuff from here?" I said. "Identifiably from here? Verbatim? Copies of our documents? From here how?"

"It's no good asking Frank that," said Dicky Cruyer quickly before anyone blamed him for not finding out.

"It's no good asking Frank anything," I said. "So why doesn't he send everything over here?"

"I wouldn't want that," said Rensselaer, his arms still crossed, his eyes staring at the *Who's Who* on his bookshelf. "If this is just the KGB trying to stir a little trouble for us, I don't want to get their man over here for interrogation. It would give them something to gloat over. Given that sort of encouragement, they'll try again, and again. No, we'll take it easy. We'll have Bernard go over there and sort through this stuff and talk to their guy, and tell us what he thinks. But let's not overreact." He snapped a desk drawer shut with enough force to make a sound like a pistol shot.

"It will be a waste of time," I said.

Bret Rensselaer kicked his foot to swivel his chair and faced me. He uncrossed his arms for a moment, snapped his starched cuffs at me, and smiled. "That's exactly the way I want it handled, Bernard. You go and look it over with that jaundiced eye of yours. No good sending Dicky." He looked at Dicky and smiled. "He'd wind up talking to the D-G on the hot line."

Dicky Cruyer thrust his hands deep into the pockets of his jeans, scowled, and hunched his shoulders. He didn't like Rensselaer saying he was excitable. Cruyer wanted to be a cool and imperturbable sort of whiz kid.

Rensselaer looked at me and smiled. He knew he'd upset Cruyer and he wanted me to share the fun. "Go through the Berlin telex and make a note of what references they quote. Then go and see the originals: read through the minutes of that meeting at the F.O., and dig out that memo about the cipher machines, and so on. That way you'll be able to judge for yourself when you get there." He glanced at Dicky, who was looking out the window sulking, and then at me. "Whatever conclusion you come to, you'll tell Frank Harrington it's *Spielzeug*—garbage."

"Of course," I said.

"Take tomorrow's R.A.F. flight and have a chat with Frank and calm him down. See this little German guy and sort through this junk he's peddling."

"Okay," I said. I knew Bret would find a way of getting me to what Dicky called "Big B."

"And what's the score with Giles Trent?" I asked.

"He's being taken care of, Bernard," said Rensselaer. "We'll talk about it when you return." He smiled. He was handsome and could turn on the charm like a film star. Of course, Fiona could fall for him. I felt like spitting in his eye.

I CAUGHT the military flight to Berlin next day. The plane was empty except for me, two medical orderlies who'd brought a sick soldier over the day before, and a brigadier with an amazing amount of baggage.

The brigadier borrowed my newspaper and wanted to talk about fly fishing. He was an affable man, young-looking compared to most brigadiers I'd ever met, but that was not much of a sampling. It wasn't his fault that he bore a superficial resemblance to my father-in-law, but I found it a definite barrier. I put my seat into the recline position and mumbled something about having had a late night. Then I stared down out the window until thin wisps of cloud, like paint-starved brush-strokes, defaced the hard regular patterns of agricultural land that was unmistakably German.

The brigadier began chatting to one of the medical orderlies. He asked him how long he'd been in the Army and if he had a family and where they lived. The private replied in an abrupt way that should have been enough to indicate that he'd prefer to talk football with his chum. But the brigadier droned on. His voice too was like that of Fiona's father. He even had the same little "huh?" with which Fiona's father finished each piece of reckless bigotry.

I remembered the first time I met Fiona's parents. They'd invited me to stay the weekend. They had a huge mansion of uncertain age near Leith Hill in Surrey. The house was surrounded by trees—straggly firs and pines, for the most part. Around the house there were tree-covered hillsides so that Fiona's father—David Timothy Kimber-Hutchinson, Fellow of the Royal Society of Arts, wealthy businessman and farm owner, and prize-winning amateur watercolor painter—could proudly say that he owned all the land seen from the window of his study.

There is surely a lack of natural human compassion in a host who clears away Sunday breakfast at ten-thirty. Fiona's father did not think so. "I've been up helping to feed the horses since six-thirty this morning. I was exercising my best hunter before breakfast."

He was wearing riding breeches, polished boots, yellow cashmere roll-neck, and a checked hacking jacket that fitted his slightly plump figure to perfection. I noticed his attire because he'd caught me in the breakfast room getting the last dry scrapings of scrambled egg from a dish on the electric hot plate while I was barefoot and clad in an ancient dressing gown and pajamas. "You're not thinking of taking that plate of oddments"—he came closer to see the two shriveled rashers and four wrinkled mushrooms that were under the flakes of egg—"up to the bedroom."

"As a matter of fact, I am," I told him.

"No, no, no." He said it with the sort of finality that doubtless ended all boardroom discussion. "My good wife will never have food in the bedrooms."

Plate in hand, I continued to the door. "I'm not taking it up there for your wife," I said. "It's for me."

That very early encounter with Mr. Kimber-Hutchinson blighted any filial bond that might otherwise have blossomed. But at that time the idea of marrying Fiona had not formed in my mind and the prospect of seeing Mr. David Kimber-Hutchinson ever again seemed mercifully remote.

"My God, man. You've not even shaved!" he shouted after me as I went upstairs with my breakfast.

"You provoke him," Fiona said when I told her about my encounter. She was in my bed, having put on her frilly nightdress, waiting to share the booty from the breakfast table.

"How can you say that?" I argued. "I speak only when he speaks to me, and then only to make polite conversation."

"You hypocrite! You know very well that you deliberately provoke him. You ask him all those wide-eyed innocent questions about making profits from cheap labor."

"Only because he keeps saying he's a socialist," I said. "And don't take that second piece of bacon: one each."

"You beast. You know I hate mushrooms." She licked her fingers. "You're no better, darling. What do you ever do that makes you more of a socialist than Daddy?"

"I'm not a socialist," I said. "I'm a fascist. I keep telling you that but you never listen."

"Daddy has his own sort of socialist ideas," said Fiona.

"He refuses to do business with the French, loathes the Americans, never employs Jews, thinks all Arabs are crooked, and the only Russian he likes is Tchaikovsky. Where is the brotherhood of man?"

"A lot of that tirade was directed at me," said Fiona. "Daddy's been angry ever since I got a reference from old Silas Gaunt. That's Mother's side of the family and Daddy's feuding with them."

"I see."

"When I hear my father going on as he did last night at dinner, I feel like joining the Communist Party, don't you?"

"No. I feel like suggesting your father join it."

"No, seriously, darling."

"The Communist Party?"

"You know what I mean: workers of the world unite, and all that. Daddy pays lip service to the idea of socialism but he never does anything about it."

"You wouldn't escape him by joining the C.P.," I said. "Your father would write out a check and buy it. And then he'd sell off its sports field as office sites."

"Come back to bed," said Fiona. "Now that we've missed breakfast, there's nothing to get up for."

Fiona rarely mentioned her father's politics—and was vague about her own beliefs. Political conversation at the dinner table usually had her staring vacantly into space, or prompted her to start a conversation about children or sewing or hairdressers. Sometimes I wondered if she was really interested in her job in the Department or if she just stayed there to keep an eye on me.

"We're about to land, old boy," said the brigadier. "Make sure your seat belt is fastened."

The plane was over Berlin now. I could see the jagged shape of the Wall as the pilot turned on to finals for the approach to R.A.F. Gatow, the onetime Luftwaffe training college. Its runway ends abruptly at the Wall, except that here the "Wall" is a wire-mesh fence and a sandy patch that intelligence reports say has been left without mines and obstacles in case the day should come when units from the adjoining Russian Army's tank depot would roll through it to take Berlin-Gatow with its runways intact and electronics undamaged.

Chapter 10

Did you ever say hello to a girl you'd almost married long ago? Did she smile the same captivating smile, and give your arm a hug in a gesture you'd almost forgotten? Did the wrinkles as she smiled make you wonder what marvelous times you'd missed? That's how I felt about Berlin every time I went back there.

Lisl Hennig's hotel, just off Kantstrasse, in the Western Sector, was unchanged. No one had tried to repair or repaint the façade pockmarked by Red Army shell splinters in 1945. The imposing doorway, alongside an optician's shop, opened onto the same grandiose marble staircase. The patched carpet, its red now a faded brown, led up to the "salon" where Lisl was always to be found. Lisl's mother had chosen the heavy oak furniture from Wertheim's department store at Alexanderplatz in the days before Hitler. And long before the grand old house became this shabby hotel.

"Hello, darling," said Lisl as though I'd seen her only yesterday. She was old, a huge woman who overflowed from the armchair, her red silk dress emphasizing every bulge so that she looked like molten lava pouring down a steep hillside. "You look tired, darling. You're working too hard."

There had been few changes made in this salon since

Lisl was a child in a house with five servants. There were photos on every side: sepia family groups in ebony frames, faded celebrities of the thirties. Actresses with long cigarette holders, writers under big-brimmed hats, glossy film stars from the UFA studios, carefully retouched prima donnas of the State Opera, artists of the Dada movement, trapeze performers from the Wintergarten, and nightclub singers from long-vanished clip joints. All of them signed with the sort of florid guarantees of enduring love that are the ephemera of show business.

Lisl's late husband was there, dressed in the white-tie outfit he wore to play Beethoven's Fifth Piano Concerto with the Berlin Philharmonic the night the Führer was in the audience. There were no photos of the bent little cripple who ended his days playing for *Trinkgeld* in a broken-down bar in Rankestrasse.

Some of these photos were of family friends: those who came to Lisl's salon in the thirties and the forties when it was a place to meet the rich and famous, and those who came in the fifties to meet men with tinned food and work permits. There were modern pictures too, of long-term residents who endured the trials and tribulations: uncertain hot water and the noise of the central heating, and the phone messages that were forgotten and letters that were never delivered, and the bathroom lights that did not work. Such loyal clients were invited into Lisl's cramped little office for a glass of sherry when they settled the bill. And their photos were enshrined there over the cash box.

"You look terrible, darling," she said.

"I'm fine, Tante Lisl," I said. "Can you find a room for me?"

She switched on another light. A large plant in an art-nouveau pot cast a sudden spiky shadow on the ugly brown wallpaper. She turned to see me better, and part of her pearl necklace disappeared into a roll of fatty muscle. "There will always be a room for you, *Liebchen*. Give me a kiss."

But I had already leaned over to give her a kiss. It was a necessary ritual. She had been calling me *Liebchen* and demanding kisses since before I could walk. "So nothing changes, Lisl," I said.

"Nothing changes! Everything changes, you mean. Look at me. Look at my ugly face and this infirm body. Life is cruel, Bernd, my sweetheart," she said, using the name I'd been known by as a boy. "You will discover it too: life is cruel." Only Berliners can mock their own self-pity to produce a laugh. Lisl was one of life's most successful survivors and we both knew it. She roared with laughter and I had to laugh too.

She let her *Stuttgarter Zeitung* slide onto the carpet. She spent her life reading newspapers and talking about what she discovered in them. "What has brought you to our wonderful city?" she asked. She rubbed her knee and sighed. Now that arthritis had affected her legs, she seldom went out except to the bank.

"Still selling tablets?" she asked. I'd always said that I worked for a pharmaceutical manufacturer that exported medicines to East and West. She didn't wait for a reply; in any case she'd never believed my story. "And did you bring photos of your lovely wife and those beautiful children? Is everything all right at home?"

"Yes," I said. "Is the top room empty?"

"Of course it is," she said. "Who else but you would want to sleep there when I have rooms with balcony and bathroom en suite?"

"I'll go up and have a wash," I said. The attic room had been my room when my father, a major in the Intelligence Corps, was billeted here. The place was full of memories.

"I hope you're not going over to the other side," Lisl said. "They have all the medicine they need over there in the East. They are getting very rough with medicine sellers."

I smiled dutifully at her little joke. "I'm not going any-where, Lisl," I said. "This is just a little holiday."

"Is everything all right at home, darling? It's not that sort of holiday, is it?"

FRANK HARRINGTON, head of Berlin Station, arrived at Lisl's exactly on the dot of four. "You got fed up with sleeping on that sofa at Werner's place, did you?"

I looked at him without replying.

"We are slow," said Frank, "but eventually we hear all the news."

"You brought it?"

"I brought everything." He put an expensive-looking black leather document case on the table and opened it. "I even brought that A-to-Z street guide I borrowed from you in London. Sorry to have had it so long."

"That's okay, Frank," I said, throwing the London street guide into my open suitcase so that I wouldn't forget it. "And where is the man who delivered this stuff?"

"He went back."

"I thought he was staying so I could debrief him. That's what London wanted."

Harrington sighed. "He's gone back," he said. "You know how people are in situations like this. He got nervous yesterday and finally slipped off back over there."

"That's a pity," I said.

"I saw a lovely-looking girl downstairs talking to Lisl. Blonde. Couldn't have been more than about eighteen. Is she staying here?"

Frank Harrington was a thin sixty-year-old. His face

was pale, with gray eyes and a bony nose and the sort of black blunt-ended stubble mustache that soldiers affect. His question was an attempt to change the subject, but Frank had always had an eye for the ladies.

"I couldn't tell you, Frank," I said.

I began to sort through the papers he'd brought. Some of them were verbatim accounts of meetings that had taken place at the Foreign Office when our Secret Intelligence Service people went over there for special briefings. None of the material was of vital importance, but that it had got back to East German intelligence was worrying. Very worrying.

Frank Harrington sat by the tiny garret window from which I used to launch my paper airplanes, and smoked his foul-smelling pipe. "You don't remember the time your father organized a birthday party for Frau Hennig?" Frank Harrington was the only person I knew who called Lisl, Frau Hennig. "He had a six-piece dance band downstairs in the salon and every black marketeer in Potsdamerplatz contributed food. I've never seen such a spread."

I looked up from the papers.

He waved his pipe at me in a gesture of placation. "Don't misunderstand me, Bernard. Your father had no dealings with the black market. The contributors were all Frau Hennig's friends." He laughed at some thought passing through his mind. "Your father was the last man to have dealings with the black market. Your father was a prude, so prim and proper that he made lesser mortals, like me, sometimes feel inadequate. He was a self-made man, your father. They are all like that—a bit unforgiving, unyielding, and inclined to go by the book." He waved his pipe again. "Don't take offense, Bernard. Your dad and I were very close. You know that."

"Yes, I know, Frank."

"No proper education, your father. Left school when he was fourteen. Spent his evenings in the public library. Retired a colonel, and ended up running the Berlin office, didn't he? Damned good going for a self-educated man."

I turned over the next lot of papers to get to the memo on cipher machines. "Is that what I'm like?" I asked him. "Unforgiving, unyielding, and inclined to go by the book?"

"Oh, come along, Bernard. You're not going to tell me you wish you'd been to university. You're *berlinerisch*, Bernard. You grew up in this funny old town. You were cycling through the streets and alleys before they built the Wall. You speak Berlin German as well as anyone I've ever met here. You go to ground like a native. That's why we can't bloody well find you when you decide you can't be bothered with us."

"*Ich bin ein Berliner*," I said. It was a joke. A *Berliner* is a doughnut. The day after President Kennedy made his famous proclamation, Berlin cartoonists had a field day with talking doughnuts.

"You think your father should have sent you back to England so that you could read politics and modern languages? You think it would have been better to have listened to Oxford academics telling you where Bismarck went wrong, and to some young tutor explaining which prepositions govern the dative case?"

I said nothing. The truth was I didn't know the answer.

"Bloody hell, laddie, you know more about this part of the world than any Oxbridge graduate can learn in a lifetime."

"Would you put that in writing, Frank?"

"You're still annoyed about young Dicky Cruyer getting the desk? Well, why wouldn't you be angry? I made my position clear from this end. That you can be sure of."

"I know you did, Frank," I said as I tapped the papers together to make them fit back into the brown paper envelope. "But the fact is that you don't just learn about history and grammar at Oxford and Cambridge, you learn about the people you meet there. And in later life you depend upon those judgments. Knowing the streets and alleys of this dirty old town doesn't count for much when there is a desk falling vacant."

Frank Harrington puffed at his pipe. "And Cruyer was junior to you in service as well as younger."

"Don't rub it in, Frank," I said.

He laughed. I felt guilty about describing him as an old woman, but it would make no difference to his career whatever I said about him, because Frank was due to retire any time, and being pulled out of Berlin would be no hardship for him. He hated Berlin and made no secret of it. "Let me write to the D-G," said Frank as if suddenly inspired with a brilliant idea. "The old man was a trainee with me back in the war."

"For God's sake, no!" That was the trouble with Frank; just like Lisl, he always wanted to treat me as if I were a nineteen-year-old going after his first job. He wasn't so much an old woman as a well-meaning old aunty.

"So what do you make of all that wastepaper?" he said, poking a match into the bowl of his pipe as if searching for something.

"Garbage," I said. "It's just a lot of guesswork someone in Moscow has dreamed up to get us worried."

Frank nodded without looking up at me. "I thought you'd say that. You'd have to say that, Bernard. Whatever it was like, you'd have to say it was rubbish."

"Can I buy you a drink?" I said.

"I'd better get back to the office and put that stuff into the shredder."

"Okay," I said. He'd guessed that London wanted it destroyed. Frank knew how their minds worked. Maybe he'd been here too long.

"You'll be wanting to go round town and see some of your playmates, I suppose."

"Not me, Frank."

He smiled and puffed his pipe. "You were always like that, Bernard. You never could bear letting anyone know what you were up to." It was just the sort of thing I remember him saying to me when I was a child. "Well, I'll look forward to seeing you for dinner tomorrow night. Just wear anything, it's only potluck."

After he'd left, I went to my suitcase to get a fresh shirt. A folded piece of envelope, used as a bookmark, had fallen out of the street guide Frank had returned to me. It was addressed to Frau Harrington, but the address was no more than a postbox number followed by a post-code. It was a damned weird way to get a letter to Frank's wife. I put it into my wallet.

THE RUSSIANS got the State Opera, the Royal Palace, the government buildings, and some of the worst slums; the Western Powers got the Zoo, the parks, the department stores, the nightclubs, and the villas of the rich in Grunewald. And spiked through both sectors, like a skewer through a shish kebab, there is the "East-West Axis."

The Bendlerblock, from where the High Command sent the German Army to conquer Europe, has now been converted to offices for a cosmetic manufacturer. The Bendlerstrasse has been renamed. Nothing here is what it seems, and that appeals to me. The Anhalter Bahnhof, a yellow brick façade with three great doors, was once the station for the luxury express trains to Vienna and all of southeast

Germany. It is no longer a busy terminus. The great edifice stands upon a piece of waste ground long since abandoned to weeds and wild flowers. Werner Volkmann chose it as a meeting place as he had sometimes done before. It was usually a sign that he was feeling especially paranoid. He was carrying a small document case and wearing a big black overcoat with an astrakhan collar. On someone else it might have suggested an impresario or a nobleman, but it simply made Werner look like someone who bought his clothes at the flea market in the disused S-Bahn station on Tauentzienstrasse.

It was getting dark. Werner stopped and looked up the street. From over the high graffiti-covered Wall there was the reflected glare of bluish-green light that in any other city would have marked the position of a large stadium lit for an evening's football. But beyond this Wall there was the large open space of the Potsdamerplatz. Once the busiest traffic intersection in Europe, it had now become a brightly lit *Todesstreifen*, a death strip, silent and still, with a maze of barbed wire, mines, and fixed guns.

Werner loitered on the corner for a moment, turning to watch a dozen or more youngsters as they passed him and continued toward Hallesches Tor. They were attired in a weird combination of clothes: tight leotards, high boots, and Afghan coats on the girls; studded leather sleeveless jackets and Afrika Korps caps on the men. Some of them had their hair dyed in streaks of primary colors. Werner was no more surprised by this sample of Berlin youth than I was. Berlin residents are exempt from military service, and there is a tendency among the young to celebrate it. But Werner continued to watch them, and waited, still staring, until a yellow double-decker bus stopped and took aboard everyone waiting at the bus stop. Only then did he feel safe. He turned abruptly and crossed the street at the traffic lights. I followed as if to catch the green.

He went into Café Leuschner and, after putting his hat on the rack, chose a seat at the rear. His document case he placed carefully on the seat next to him. I waved as if catching sight of him for the first time and went over to his table. Werner called to the waiter for two coffees. I sat down with a sigh. Werner had arrived late, an unforgivable sin in my business.

"It was one of Frank Harrington's people," said Werner. "I had to be sure I'd got rid of him."

"Why would Frank have someone following you?"

"London has been kicking Frank's ass," said Werner. "There is talk of replacing him immediately."

"What have you got to do with that? Why follow *you?*"

"Is there some kind of leak in London?" said Werner. Knowing it was unlikely that I'd answer him, he said, "It's only fair you tell me. You ask me to go over the wire for you, it's only fair you tell me what's going on in London."

"No leak," I said. I might have added that no one had yet asked him to go "over the wire" and that his regular visits to the East were a damned good reason for him knowing as little as possible about what was happening in London.

"And the money? Will London help me with the bank?"

"No money either," I said.

Werner hunched lower over the table and nodded sorrowfully. I looked around the café. It was a roomy place, its gilt-framed mirrors supported by plaster cherubs and its plastic-topped tables fashioned to look like marble. There was a fine old counter that ran the whole length of the room. I'd known it when the Leuschners' father was serving behind it. Berlin kids could get genuine American ice cream here until Leuschner's daughter married her soldier and went to live in Arkansas.

The coffee arrived: two small electroplated pots, together with tiny jugs of cream, sugar wrapped in colored paper advertising tea, and the usual floral cups and saucers. Floral-patterned cups and saucers: they reminded me of my childhood breakfasts when my father used to correct my mother's inadequate German: " *'Es geht um die Wurst,'* 'It depends on the sausage,' means 'Everything depends on it.' But *'Mir ist alles Wurst,'* or 'It's all sausage to me,' means 'I really don't care.' " My mother just smiled and poured more coffee into the floral-patterned cups. She had intended to say that there might not be enough sausage for all of us that evening. But my father was inclined to make everything more complicated than it need be. That too was a characteristic of the self-made man.

I said, "Why did we go through all that business of meeting without being observed? I could just have met you in here."

"And then we would have both been sitting here with Frank's watcher."

"Have it your way, Werner," I said.

"Frank Harrington is worried," said Werner.

"What about?" I said, no longer entirely concealing my irritation. "I thought Frank wouldn't let you near his office."

Werner smiled one of the special Oriental smiles that he thought made him appear inscrutable. "I don't have to go into the office to hear the latest news from there. Frank is getting a lot of trouble from London. Rumors say there's a leak. Frank is frightened he'll be the scapegoat. He's frightened they'll get rid of him and find some way of not paying his pension."

"Balls!"

"If Frank was recalled, do you think the Berlin office would start to use me again?"

"There is no leak of information."

"Good," said Werner, looking at me and nodding. There was nothing quite so disconcerting as Werner trying to be sincere. "Max Binder went back. He had a wife and three kids, and he couldn't get a job. Finally he went back to the East."

Max Binder was at school with us, a studious kid who sang the solo part in "Silent Night" every Christmas and had a secret hoard of forbidden Nazi badges that we all coveted. I'd always liked him. "Max is one of the best," I said. "His wife was from the East, wasn't she?"

"They got one of those 'wedding cake' apartments on Stalinallee." Werner still called the street by its old name. "Nowadays people realize that those apartments are not so bad. At least they have high ceilings and lots of cupboards and storage space. The new places out at Marzahn are really jammed tight together. They've got families of four living in the space of Max's broom cupboard."

"You've been across recently? You've seen Max?"

"I see Max from time to time. He has a good job now. He's in the customs service—chief clerk."

There was something in Werner's voice that caught my attention. "Are you in some racket with Max?"

"With Max?" Nervously he poured himself more coffee.

"I know you, Werner, and I know Max. What are you up to?"

"It's Max's office that handles the paperwork for some of my forfait deals, that's all."

"The avalizing, you mean. The guarantee that the money will be paid. So that's it."

Werner made no attempt to deny that there was some sort of fiddle going on. "Look, Bernard. I saw Zena last week. She's promised to come back to me."

He wanted my congratulations. "That's good, Werner."

"She was in Berlin . . . just a quick visit. We had lunch together. She wanted to know how I was."

"And how were you?"

"I want her back, Bernie. I can't manage without her. I told her that."

"And?"

"I told her I'd have more money. Money was always the problem with us. If I make a bit more money, she'd come back to me. She more or less promised."

"I'll try again to get London to approve the money, Werner. Forget this mad idea of forging the avals or whatever it is you're doing. If you get into trouble in the East, they'll toss you into the cooler and throw away the key. It'll be 'defrauding the people' or some such all-embracing charge, and they'll hammer you to make sure no one else pulls the same trick."

Werner nodded. "I'm just going to do it a couple of times so I have enough cash not to have to go crawling to the banks anymore. Those money-market bastards are squeezing me, Bernie. They take the cream off every deal I do."

"I said forget it, Werner."

"I promised to take Zena to Spain for a really good holiday. Ever been to Marbella? It's wonderful. One day I'll buy a little place there and settle down. Zena needs some sunshine and a rest. So do I. Something like that would give us a new start. Maybe South America, even. It's worth taking a chance for a new start in life."

Werner had finished two cups of black coffee and now he was holding the pot and shaking the last few drops from the spout. I said, "Does Frank know about your import and export racket?"

"Frank Harrington? Good God, no. He goes out of his

way to avoid me. Last month I was in that change office in Zoo station cashing traveler's checks. Frank was there already. When he caught sight of me, he left the line and walked out. Frank Harrington is avoiding me. No. Hell, he's the last person I'd discuss it with." He picked up the second coffeepot, swirling it to find out if there was coffee in it. "Can I have the rest?"

I nodded. "Why not tell Frank?"

This time Werner put cream into his coffee. He had the compulsive desire to drink and nibble that is often a sign of nervousness. "I don't want him to know I'm going over there frequently."

"There's something you're not telling me."

He became very concerned with his coffee, unwrapping another sugar cube, breaking it, and putting half into his cup. Then he put the unused half in his mouth and chewed it noisily while he smoothed the wrapper flat with the edge of his hand. "Don't mother me, Bernie. We grew up together. We both know what's what."

"You're not playing footsie with those people in the East?" I persisted. "You haven't come to some damned-fool arrangement with them?"

"So I can give away all your secrets, you mean?" He folded the sugar wrapper carefully and neatly to make a tiny paper dart. He flew it toward the salt and pepper in a test flight. "What could I tell them? That Frank cuts me dead in the change office, that you come into town and stay at Lisl's? Shall I tell them that rumors say that London's chosen you to take over Berlin from Frank but Frank won't approve you as his successor?"

I looked at his paper dart. "You could be useful to them, Werner. You've got an ear to the ground." I picked up the dart and threw it back at him, but it didn't fly for me.

"Can't you understand," he said in a low voice. "No one

gives me work anymore. Frank has put the boot in. I used to get jobs from the Americans and your military intelligence people were always having something come up they couldn't handle. Now I don't get any of those jobs anymore. I don't know enough to be a double, Bernie. I'm out of it. Your jobs are the only ones I get these days, and you only give me those for old times' sake—I know it and so do you."

I didn't remind Werner that only a few minutes earlier he'd been insisting that it was "only fair" to tell him everything I knew about the leaks in London. "So they're saying that I'm to get Berlin? Maybe they are even saying who will get my job when I move."

Werner picked up the dart. It flew well for him but only because he took his time refolding the wings and adjusting everything for optimum aerodynamics. "You know what it's like in this town, people are always gossiping. I don't want you to think I believe any of that stuff."

"Come on, Werner. You've got my attention now. You might as well tell me what you've heard. I'm not going to break down and weep about it."

Those words appeared to have more meaning for him than I ever intended. We were speaking German and it is in the nature of German syntax that you have to compose the sentence in your mind before you start to say it. You can't start each sentence with a vague idea and change your mind halfway through, as people brought up to speak English do. So once Werner began he had to say it. "There are rumors that your wife is taking over your job from you in London."

"Now that's a neat twist," I said. I still didn't guess what poor old Werner was trying to tell me.

He held the dart up to his face so that he could see it properly in the poor light of the café. He gave all his attention to it as he spoke rather hurriedly: "They say you're splitting up, you and your wife. They say she . . . They say that Rensselaer and your wife are . . ." He launched the dart, but this time it spiraled down into his saucer and the wings went brown with spilled coffee.

"Bret Rensselaer," I said. "He's nearly old enough to be her father. I can't imagine Fiona falling for Rensselaer."

The expression on Werner's face let it be known that the failure of imagination was entirely mine. "If Rensselaer felt guilty about giving Cruyer the German desk and taking your wife from you, he'd be smart to get Berlin for you. It would get you out of his way. The money is good and the unaccountable expenses are the best in the business. It's a job you'd dearly like, and be damned good at. You'd never turn it down, Bernie, you know that."

I thought about it. It made me feel sick, but I was determined not to reveal that. "And I wouldn't stand in Fiona's way if she got the chance of a senior post in Operations. She'd be the only woman on staff level there." I smiled. "It's neat, Werner. Like all good rumors, it's neater than the truth. The fact is that Fiona can't stand Rensselaer, and the old man would never allow a woman in there, and no one's going to offer me Berlin when Frank goes." I smiled, but my smile got stuck and he looked away.

"How can you be sure?" said Werner. "I never thought my wife would go off to Munich with that Coca-Cola driver. I met him a couple of times. She told me he was the brother of a girl at her office. She said he sometimes gave her a lift home. He was in the apartment when I got back home one evening. He was having a beer with her. I never suspected a thing. I was like you are now. She said he was a bit stupid. That's all it took to convince me there was nothing between them. It was just like you said just now. I thought she couldn't stand the guy, like you say your wife can't stand Rensselaer." He unwrapped another sugar cube and began to fold himself another flying dart. "Maybe the fact is that *you* can't stand him—just like I couldn't stand that truck driver—and so you can't imagine your wife going for him either." He abandoned his half-made dart and drifted it into the ashtray. "I've given up smoking," he said mournfully, "but I fidget a lot with my hands."

"You didn't get me over here just to tell me all this stuff about Rensselaer having an affair with Fiona, did you, Werner?"

"No. I wanted to ask you about the office. You're the only person I know who sees Frank Harrington to talk to him on equal terms."

"I don't see him on equal terms," I said. "Frank treats me like I'm a twelve-year-old child."

"Frank is very patronizing," said Werner. "In Frank's day, they were all Cambridge pansies or Greek scholars, like Frank, who thought a little job in the intelligence service would be a good way to earn money while they wrote sonnets. Frank likes you, Bernard. He likes you very much. But he could never reconcile himself to the idea that a tough little Berlin street kid like you could take over the job he's doing. He's friendly with you, I know. But how do you think he really feels about taking orders from someone without a classical education?"

"I don't give him orders," I said, to correct the record.

"You know what I mean," said Werner. "I just want to know what Frank has got against me. If I've done something to make him annoyed, okay. But if it's a misunderstanding, I want a chance to clear it up."

"What do you care about clearing it up?" I said. "You've got some racket going that's going to give you a villa in Marbella and Rioja and roses for the rest of your days. What

the hell do you care about this clearing up misunderstand-
ings with Frank?"

"Don't be *dumm*, Bernie," he said. "Frank could make a
lot of trouble for me."

"You're imagining things, Werner."

"He hates me, Bernie, and he's frightened of you."

"Frightened?"

"He's frightened at the idea of you taking over from him.
You know too much—you'd ask too many questions, awkward questions. And all Frank cares about these days is
keeping himself pure for his index-linked pension. He'll do
nothing to prejudice that, never mind all that stuff he gives
you about how friendly he was with your father."

"Frank is tired," I said. "Frank has got the 'Berlin blues.'
He doesn't hate anyone. He doesn't even hate the Communists anymore. That's why he wants to go."

"Didn't you hear me tell you that Frank Harrington has
blocked your appointment here?"

"And didn't you hear me tell you that that was all bloody
rubbish? I'll tell you why they don't use you anymore, Werner. You've become a gossip, and that's the worst thing that
can happen to anyone in this business. You tell me stupid
rumors about this and about that, and you tell me that no
one likes you and you can't understand why. You need to
pull yourself together, Werner, because otherwise you'll have
to add me to that long list of people who don't understand
you."

Werner was hunched over the table, the bulky overcoat
and fur collar making him look even bigger than he really
was. When he nodded, his chin almost touched the table.
"I understand," he said. "When I first realized my wife had
betrayed me, I couldn't say a civil word to anyone."

"I'll call you, Werner," I said, getting to my feet. "Thanks
for the coffee."

"Sit down," said Werner. His voice was soft, but there was an urgency that transcended our bickering. I sat down. Two men had entered the café. The younger Leuschner had been checking the levels of the bottles of drink arrayed under the big mirror. He turned around and smiled the sort of smile that is the legacy of ten years behind a bar. "What's it to be?" Nervously he wiped the pitted marble counter, which was one of the very few things that had survived the war as well as the Leuschner brothers. "Would you like to eat? I can give you *Bratwurst* with red cabbage, or roast chicken with *Spätzle*."

The men were thirty-year-old heavyweights, with robust shoes, double-breasted raincoats, and hats with brims big enough to keep rain from dripping down the neck. I caught Werner's eye. He nodded; they obviously were policemen. One of them picked up the plastic-faced menu that had been put before them. Young Leuschner twirled the end of the big Kaiser Wilhelm mustache that he'd grown to make himself look older. Now, with his balding head, he didn't need it anymore. "Or a drink?"

"Chocolate ice cream," said one of the men in a voice that dared anyone to be surprised.

"*Schnaps*," said the other.

Leuschner chose from one of the half-dozen varieties of strong clear liquor and poured a generous measure. Then he put two scoops of ice cream into a dented serving dish and supplied napkin and spoon. "And a glass of water," mumbled the man, who'd already begun to gobble the ice cream. His companion turned to rest his back against the edge of the counter and look casually around the room as he sipped his drink. Neither man sat down.

I poured cream into my cup, in order to provide myself with something to do, and stirred it with care. The man eating the ice cream finished it in record time. The other muttered something inaudible, and both men came across to the table where I was sitting with Werner.

"You live near here?" said the chocolate ice cream.

"Dahlem," said Werner. He smiled, trying to hide his resentment.

"That's a nice place to live," said the ice-cream cop. It was difficult to decide how much was pleasantry and how much was sarcasm.

"Let's see your papers," said the second man. He was leaning all his weight on the back of my chair and I could smell the *Schnaps* on his breath.

Werner hesitated for a moment, trying to decide whether anything was to be gained by making them prove they were policemen. Then he brought out his wallet.

"Open up the case," said the ice cream, pointing to the document case Werner had placed on the seat beside him.

"That's mine," I said.

"I don't care if it belongs to Herbert von Karajan," said the cop.

"But I do," I said. This time I spoke in English.

He glanced at my face and at my English clothes. I didn't have to spell it out that I was an officer of the "protecting powers." "Identification?"

I passed to him the Army officer's card that identified me as a Major Bishop of the Royal Engineers. He gave me a bleak smile and said, "This identification expired two months ago."

"And what do you think might have happened since then?" I said. "You think I've changed into someone else?"

He gave me a hard stare. "I'd get your identification brought up to date if I was you, Major Bishop," he said. "You might find the next policeman you encounter suspects you of being a deserter or a spy or something."

"Then the next policeman I encounter will make a fool

of himself," I said. But by that time both men were moving off across the room. The ice cream dropped a couple of coins onto the counter as he passed.

"Bloody Nazis," said Werner. "They picked me because I'm a Jew."

"Don't be a fool, Werner."

"Then why?"

"There could be a million reasons why a cop asks for papers. There could be some local crime . . . a recognized car nearby . . . someone with a description like you."

"They'll get the military police. They'll come back and make us open the case. They'll do it just to show us who's the boss."

"No, they won't, Werner. They'll go down the street to the next café or bar and try again."

"I wish you weren't so damned obstinate."

"About what?"

"Frank Harrington. This is the way he keeps the pressure up."

"Have you ever stopped to think how much it costs to keep a man under surveillance? Four men and two cars on eight-hour shifts working a five-day week. We're talking about a minimum of six men and three cars. The cars must be radio-equipped to our wavelength, so that rules out rented ones. The men must be trained and vetted. Allowing for insurance and special pensions and medical schemes all Department employees have, each man would cost well over a thousand Deutschemark. The cars cost at least another thousand each. Add another thousand for the cost of backup and we're talking about Frank spending ten thousand marks a week on you. He'd have to hate you an awful lot, Werner."

"Ask him," said Werner sullenly. I had the feeling that he didn't want to be disillusioned about Frank's vendetta lest he have to face the fact that maybe Frank sacked him because he wasn't doing the job the way they wanted it done.

I raised my hands in supplication. "I'll talk to him, Werner. But meanwhile you cut it out. Forget all this stuff about Frank persecuting you. Will you do that?"

"You don't understand," said Werner.

I looked at the document case that I'd pretended was mine. "And, just to satisfy my curiosity, what is in 'my' case, Werner?"

He reached out to touch it. "Would you believe nearly half a million Swiss francs in new paper?"

I looked at him but he didn't smile. "Take care, Werner," I said. Even when we'd been kids together, I'd never known when he was fooling.

Chapter 11

I REMEMBERED Frank Harrington's parties back in the days when my father took me along to the big house in Grunewald wearing my first dinner jacket. Things had changed since then, but the house was still the same, and came complete with a gardener, cook, housekeeper, maid, and the valet who had been with Frank during the war.

I shared Frank's "just wear anything, it's only potluck" evening with a dozen of Berlin's richest and most influential citizens. At dinner I was placed next to a girl named Poppy, recently divorced from a man who owned two breweries and an aspirin factory. Around the table there was a man from the Bundesbank and his wife; a director of West Berlin's Deutsche Oper, accompanied by its most beautiful mezzo-soprano; a lady museum director said to be a world author-ity on ancient Mesopotamian pottery; a Berlin Polizei-präsidium official who was introduced simply as ". . . from Tempelhofer Damm"; and Joe Brody, a quiet-spoken American who preferred to be described as an employee of Siemen's electrical factory. Frank Harrington's wife was there, a formidable lady of about sixty, with a toothy smile and the sort of compressed permanent wave that fitted like a rubber swimming hat. The Harringtons' son, a British Airways first officer on the Berlin route, was also present. He was an amiable young man with a thin blond mustache and a complexion so pink it looked as if his mother had scrubbed him clean before letting him come down to the dining room.

They were all dressed to the nines, of course. The ladies wore long dresses and the mezzo-soprano had jewelry in her hair. The wife of the man from the central bank had diversified into gold and the lady museum director wore Pucci. The men were in dark suits with the sort of buttonhole ribbons and striped ties that provided all the information needed, to anyone entitled to know.

Over dinner the talk was of money and culture.

"There's seldom any friction between Frankfurt and Bonn," said the man from the Bundesbank.

"Not while you are pouring your profits back to the government. Ten billion Deutschemark—is that what you're giving to the politicians again this year?" said Frank. Of course they must have guessed who Frank Harrington was, or had some idea of what he did for a living.

The Bundesbank man smiled but didn't confirm it.

The lady museum director joined in and said, "Suppose you and Bonn both run short of money at the same time?"

"It's not the role of the Bundesbank to support the government, or to help with the economy, get back to full employment, or balance trade. The Bundesbank's primary role is to keep monetary stability."

"Maybe that's the way you see it," said the mezzo-soprano, "but it only requires a parliamentary majority in Bonn to make the role of the central bank anything the politicians want it to be."

The Bundesbank official cut himself another chunk of the very smelly double-cream Limburger, and took a slice of black bread before answering. "We're convinced that the independence of the Bundesbank is now regarded as a constitutional necessity. No government would affront public opinion by attempting to take us over by means of a parliamentary majority."

Frank Harrington's son, who'd read history at Cambridge, said, "Reichsbank officials were no doubt saying the same thing right up to the time that Hitler changed the law to let him print as much paper money as he needed."

"As you do in Britain?" said the Bundesbank official politely.

Mrs. Harrington hurriedly turned to the mezzo-soprano and said, "What have you heard about the new *Parsifal* production?"

"Du siehst, mein Sohn, zum Raum wird hier die Zeit." These words, "You see, my son, time here turns into space," provided Mrs. Harrington, the mezzo-soprano, and the ancient-pottery expert with an opportunity to pick the plot of *Parsifal* over for philosophical allusions and symbols. It was a rich source of material for after-dinner conversation, but I wearied of listening to it and found it more amusing to argue with Poppy about the relative merits of *alcool blanc* and whether *poire, framboise, Quetsche,* or *mirabelle* was the most delicious. It was an argument that dedicated experiment with Frank Harrington's sideboard array had left unresolved by the time Poppy got to her feet and said, "The ladies are withdrawing. Come with me."

The desire to flirt with her was all part of the doubts and fears I had about Fiona. I wanted to prove to myself that I could play the field too, and Poppy would have been an ideal conquest. But I was sober enough to realize that this was not the right time, and Frank Harrington's house was certainly not the place.

"Poppy dearest," I said, my veins fired by a surfeit of mixed *eaux de vie,* "you can't leave me now. I will never get to my feet unaided." I pretended to be very drunk. The truth was that, like all field agents who'd survived, I'd forgotten what it was like to be truly drunk.

"*Poire* is the best," she said, picking up the bottle. "And a raspberry for you, my friend." She banged the bottle of *framboise* onto the table in front of me.

She departed clutching the half-full bottle of pear spirits, her empty glass, and discarded shoes to her bosom. I watched her regretfully. Poppy was my sort of woman. I drank two cups of black coffee and went across the room to corner Frank. "I saw Werner last night," I told him.

"Poor you," said Frank. "Let me top up your brandy if you are going to start on that one." He stepped away far enough to get the brandy, but I put a hand over my glass. "What an idiot I am," said Frank. "You're drinking that stuff the ladies are having."

I ignored this barb and said, "He thinks you've got it in for him."

Frank poured some brandy for himself and furrowed his brow as if thinking hard. He put the bottle down on a side table before he answered. "We have an instruction on his file. You know, Bernard, you've seen it."

"Yes, I checked it out," I said. "It's been there nearly five years. Isn't it time we let him try again?"

"Something not very sensitive, you mean. Umm."

"He feels out of things."

"And so he might," said Frank. "The Americans don't use him and he's never done anything much for anyone else here."

I looked at Frank and nodded to let him know what a stupid answer that was: the Americans got copies of the sheet that said we were not using Werner. They would not use him without some very good reason. "He thinks you have a personal grudge against him."

"Did he say why?"

"He said he can't understand why."

Frank looked around the room. The police official was talking to Poppy; he caught Frank's eye and smiled. Frank's son was listening to the mezzo-soprano, and Mrs. Harrington was telling the maid—uniformed in the sort of white cap and apron that I'd seen otherwise only in old photos—to bring the semisweet champagne that would be so refreshing. Frank turned back to me as if regretting that nothing else demanded his immediate attention. "Perhaps I should have told you about Werner before this," he said. "But I try to keep these things on a 'need to know' basis."

"Sure," I said. Poppy was laughing at something the policeman told her. How could she find him so amusing?

"I put Werner in charge of the communications room security one night back in September 1978. There was a lot of signals traffic. The Baader-Meinhof gang had hijacked a Lufthansa Boeing, and Bonn was convinced they were flying it to Prague. . . . You ask your wife about it, she'll remember that night. No one got a wink of sleep." He sipped some of his brandy. "About three o'clock in the morning, a cipher clerk came in with an intercept from the Russian Army transmitter at Karlshorst. It was a message from the commanding general requesting that some military airfield in southwest Czechoslovakia be kept operational on a twenty-four-hour basis until further notice. I knew what that message referred to because of other signals I'd seen, and I knew it wasn't anything to do with the Baader-Meinhof people, so I put a hold on that message. My interception unit was the only one to file that signal that night, and I've checked that one through NATO."

"I'm not sure what you're getting at, Frank," I said.

"That damned message went back through Karlshorst

with 'intercepted traffic' warnings on it. Werner was the only person who knew about it."

"Not the only person, Frank. What about the cipher clerk, the operator, the clerk who filed the signal after you'd stopped it, your secretary, your assistant . . . lots of people."

Artfully, Frank steered the conversation another way. "So you were talking to dear old Werner last night. Where did this reunion take place—Anhalter station?"

The surprise showed on my face.

Frank said, "Come along, Bernard. You used that old military identification card I let you have, and you were too damned idle to hand it back when it expired. You know those bogus cards have numbers that insure we get a phone call when one turns up in a police report. I okayed it, of course. I guessed it was you. Who else would be in Leuschner's café at that time of night except drug pushers, pimps, whores, and vagabonds, and that incurable romantic Bernard Samson?"

Joe Brody, the American "from Siemen's," drifted over to us. "What kind of caper are you two hatching?" he said.

"We were talking about Anhalter station," said Frank.

Joe Brody sighed. "Before the war, that was the center of the universe. Even now old-time Berliners walk out there to look at that slab of broken masonry and fancy they can hear the trains."

"Joe was here in 'thirty-nine and 'forty," said Frank. "He saw Berlin when the Nazis were riding high."

"And came back with the U.S. Army. And shall I tell you something else about Anhalter Bahnhof? When we got copies of Stalin's order to his Belorussian Front and his Ukraine Front for a converging attack that would take Berlin and end the war, the point at which those great armies would meet was specified as Anhalter Bahnhof."

Frank nodded and said, "Joe, tell Bernard what we did about that Karlshorst signal . . . the one about the airfield remaining open for the Russian commanding general. Do you remember?"

Joe Brody was a bright-eyed bald American who held his nose while he was thinking, like a man about to jump into deep water. "What do you want to know, Mr. Samson?"

Frank Harrington answered on my behalf. "Tell him how we discovered who had divulged that interception."

"You've got to realize that this wasn't a big deal," Brody said slowly. "But Frank thought it was important enough to suspend the clearance of everyone on duty that night until we got a lead on it."

"We checked everyone who handled the message," said Frank. "I had nothing against Werner. I suspected the cipher clerk, as a matter of fact, but he came out clean."

"Was Giles Trent handling signals traffic at that time?"

"Giles Trent? Yes, he was here then."

"No, no," said Brody. "No chance you can pin this on Giles Trent. The way I understand it, he had no access to signals traffic."

"Can you remember so well?" I said.

Brody's gold-rimmed glasses flashed as he turned his head to be sure he wasn't overheard. "Frank gave me a free hand. He told me to dig as deep as I wanted. I guess Frank wanted me to go back to my people and tell them you Brits weren't about to paper over the cracks in the future." Frank wet his lips and smiled to show he was still listening even if he had heard the story before. "So I dug," said Joe Brody. "It was your guy Werner something . . ."

"Werner Volkmann," I supplied.

"Volkmann. That's right!" said Brody. "We eliminated the others, one by one. This other guy—Trent, Giles Trent—took a little extra time because London got sticky about letting us read his file. But he was in the clear." He grabbed his nose again. "Volkmann was the leak, believe me. I've done hundreds of these investigations."

"And never made a mistake?" I asked.

"Not that kind of mistake," said Brody. "I don't go around ripping away a security clearance just to make myself feel six feet tall. This was Volkmann. Not Trent, nor any of the others—unless everyone was telling me lies. So you can tell your people in London the file is closed on that one."

"Suppose I told you Trent is now an orange file?" I said.

"Holy cow!" said Brody without too much emotion. "Is this going to become another one of those?"

"It looks as if it's nipped in the bud," I said. "But I would take a lot of convincing that Trent wasn't in on your problem too."

"I know the feeling, young man," said Brody. "Research and investigation are no damn use if they don't support those prejudiced judgments we've already worked so hard on."

"Anyone except Werner—that's it, isn't it?" said Frank.

"No!" I said too loudly. "It's not that."

"Bernard was at school with Werner," Frank explained to Brody.

"Your loyalty does you credit, kid," said Brody. "Jesus, I know guys in your position who'd be trying to pin it on their wife."

Frank Harrington laughed and so did Brody.

THE NEXT MORNING, I had breakfast with Lisl. We sat in the room she called her study. It had a tiny balcony that looked out on the traffic of Kantstrasse.

It was a wonderful room and I remembered it from the

time I was small, and permitted inside when my father came to settle his monthly account. Apart from the walls covered with small framed photos, there were a thousand other wonders for a child's eye. There were small tables littered with ivory snuffboxes, a brass ashtray fashioned from a section of World War I shell-casing, the words A PRESENT FROM LEMBERG hammered into the brass and Russian buttons soldered around its edge. There were two fans, open to reveal Japanese landscapes; and a small china zeppelin with BERLIN-STAAKEN on its side; opera glasses made of yellowing ivory; and a silver carriage clock that didn't work. Most dazzling of all to the small boy I once was, a Prussian medal awarded to Lisl's grandfather, a magnificent piece of military jewelry suitably mounted on faded red velvet in a silver frame that Lisl's maids kept gleaming bright.

Breakfast was set on a small table against the window, which was open enough to move the lace curtain but not enough to move the starched linen tablecloth. Lisl was seated in the high dining chair from which she could get up without assistance. I arrived exactly on time; I knew that nothing dooms a meeting with a German more completely than tardiness. *"Mein Liebchen,"* said Lisl. "Give me a kiss. I can't jump up and down—it's this damned arthritis."

I bent over and kissed her, careful to avoid the heavily applied rouge, powder, and lipstick. I wondered how early she must have risen to have prepared her hair and makeup. "Don't ever change it," I said. "Your glamorous room is still as enchanting as ever."

She smiled. *"Nein, nein."* That unmistakable Berlin accent: ny-yen, ny-yen. I knew I was home when I heard it.

"It's still the same as when my father was alive," I said.

She liked to be complimented on the room. "It's still exactly as it was when *my* father was alive," she said. She looked around to be sure she was telling the truth. "For a

few years, we had a photo of the Führer over the fireplace—
a signed photo—but it was a relief to put Kaiser Wilhelm
back there."

"Even if it's not signed," I said.

"Naughty!" Lisl admonished, but she permitted herself
a small smile. "So, your work is complete and now you go
home to your gorgeous wife and your dear children. When
are you going to bring them to see me, darling?"

"Soon," I said, helping myself to coffee.

"It had better be," she said, and chuckled. "Or your
Tante Lisl will be pushing up the daisies." She tore a piece
from her bread roll and said, "Werner says we Germans
have too many words for death. Is that true?"

"In English we say 'dead shot,' 'dead letter,' a 'dead
fire,' 'dead calm,' and so on. German is more precise, and
has a different word for each meaning."

"Werner says the Germans have a thousand different
words for death, just as the Eskimos are said to have so
many different words for snow. And the Jews have so many
different words for idiot."

"Do they?"

" 'Schmo,' 'schlemiel,' 'schnook,' 'schmuck.' " She
laughed.

"Do you see a lot of Werner?"

"He's a good boy. I get lonely now I'm unable to get
about on my feet, and Werner pops in to see me whenever
he's passing. He's about the same age as you, you know."

"He's a bit older, but we were in the same class at school."

"I remember the night he was born. It was the first of
March, 1943. It was a bad air raid—fires in Bachstrasse
and the Sigismundhof. Unter den Linden suffered and the
passage through to the Friedrichstrasse was ruined. There
were unexploded bombs in the grounds of the Italian Embassy and the house of the Richthofen family. A bomb stopped

the church clock on Ku-damm and it's stayed at seven-thirty ever since. Sometimes I say to him, 'You stopped that clock the night you were born.' Werner's mother was the cook for us. She lived with her husband in an attic just four doors along from here. I went and got her just before her contractions began. Werner was born in this house, did you know that? Of course you did. I must have told you a thousand times."

"Werner," I said. "What kind of name is that for a nice Jewish boy?"

"One name for the world, another name for the family," said Lisl. "That's always the way it is for them."

"Did you hide all the family, Lisl? What about his father?"

"His father was a big strong man—Werner inherited his build—and he worked as a gravedigger at the Jewish cemetery at Weissensee all through the war."

"And was never arrested?"

She smiled the sort of smile I'd seen on other German faces, a look reserved for those who would never understand. "So that the Nazis would have to assign Aryans to look after Jewish graves and bury Jewish dead? No, the workers at Weissensee cemetery were never arrested. When the Russians got here in 'forty-five, there was still a rabbi walking free. He was working there as a gravedigger with Werner's papa." She laughed but I didn't. Only people who'd been here when the Russians arrived were permitted to laugh about it.

"It was after the war that Werner's father died. He died of not getting enough to eat for year after year."

"Werner was lucky," I said. "Five-year-old orphans did not have much chance."

"Is he in some sort of trouble?" said Lisl. She'd caught some careless inflection of my voice.

I hesitated. "Werner can be headstrong," I said.

"I've given him half my savings, *Liebchen*."

"He wouldn't swindle you, Lisl."

Her mascaraed eyelashes fluttered. "I can't afford to lose it," she said. "I had it invested, but Werner said he could make more for me. I have it all in writing. I'm easy to handle, Werner knows that." It was typical of her that she used the fashionable word *"pflegeleicht,"* usually applied to no-iron clothes. But Lisl was not *pflegeleicht*: she was old-fashioned linen, with lots of starch.

"He won't swindle you, Tante Lisl. Werner owes you more than he can ever repay, and he knows it. But if he loses your money, there is nothing in writing that will get it back for you."

"It's something to do with exports," said Lisl as if a measure of confession would persuade me to help her.

"I have to come back here," I said. "I'll talk to him on my next visit. But you should be more careful with your money, Lisl."

She blew air through her teeth in a gesture of contempt. "Careful? We have some of the oldest, biggest, richest corporations in Germany facing bankruptcy and you tell me to be careful. Where am I to invest my savings?"

"I'll do what I can, Lisl."

"A woman on her own is helpless in these matters, darling."

"I know, Lisl, I know." I found myself thinking about Fiona again. I remembered phoning her from Berlin on the previous trip. I'd phoned her three or four times in the middle of the night and got no reply. She said the phone was out of order, but I went on wondering.

Watery sunshine trickled over the Persian carpet and made a golden buttress in the dusty air. Lisl stopped talking to chew her bread roll; the phone rang. It was for me: Frank Harrington. "Bernard? I'm glad I caught you. I'm sending a car to take you to the airport this afternoon. What time do you want to leave Frau Hennig's? Do you want to stop off anywhere?"

"I've fixed up a car, Frank. Thanks all the same."

"No, no, no. I insist."

"I can't cancel it now, Frank."

There was a pause at the other end before Frank said, "It was like old times, seeing you again last night."

"I should have thanked you," I said, although I had already arranged for Mrs. Harrington to receive a bunch of flowers.

"That conversation we had . . . about you know whom . . . I hope you won't be putting any of that in writing in London."

So that was it. "I'll be discreet, Frank," I said.

"I know you will, old boy. Well, if you won't let me arrange a car . . ."

I knew "the car" would turn out to be Frank, who would "just happen to be going out that way" and would bend my ear until takeoff time. So I made regret noises and rang off.

"Frank Harrington?" said Lisl. "Wanting some favor, no doubt."

"Frank's always been a worrier. You know that."

"He's not trying to borrow money, is he?"

"I can't imagine him being short of it."

"He keeps a big house in England and his spectacular place here. He's always entertaining."

"That's part of the job, Lisl," I said. I was long since accustomed to Lisl's complaints about the wasteful ways of government servants.

"And the little popsie he's got tucked away in Lübars—

is she part of the job too?" Lisl's laugh was more like a splutter of indignation.

"Frank?"

"I get to hear everything, darling. People think I am just a stupid old woman safely locked away up here in my little room, rubbing embrocation on my knees, but I get to hear everything."

"Frank was in the Army with my father. He must be sixty years old."

"That's the dangerous age, darling. Didn't you know that? You've got the dangerous sixties to look forward to, *Liebchen*." She spilled coffee trying to get it to her mouth without laughing.

"You've been listening to Werner," I said.

Her lashes trembled and she fixed me with her steely eyes. "You think you can get me to tell you where I heard it. I know your little tricks, Bernard." A waggling finger. "But it wasn't Werner. And I know all about Frank Harrington, who comes in here looking as if butter wouldn't melt in his mouth." She used the equivalent Berlin expression about looking as if he wouldn't dirty a stream, and it seemed so apt for the impeccable Frank and his scrubbed-looking son. "His wife spends too much time in England, and Frank has found other amusements here in town."

"You're a fund of information, Tante Lisl," I said. I kept my voice level to show her that I was not convinced about Frank's double life, and would not be too concerned even if I was convinced.

"A man in his line of business should know better. A man with a mistress in an expensive little house in Lübars is a security risk."

"I suppose so."

I thought she was going to change the subject, but she

couldn't resist adding, "And Lübars is so near the Wall. . . . You're damned near the Russkies right up there."

"I know where Lübars is, Lisl," I said grumpily.

"Happy birthday, darling," she said as I reached the door.

"Thanks, Lisl," I said. She never missed my birthday.

Chapter 12

FROM THE TOP of the brightly colored apartment blocks of Märkisches Viertel, where sixty thousand West Berliners live in what the architects call a "planned community" and its inhabitants call a "concrete jungle," you can see across the nearby border, and well into the Eastern Sector.

"Some of them like it here," said Axel Mauser. "At least they say they do." Axel had aged a lot over the last few years. He was three months younger than I was, but his pinched white face and large bald patch, and the way his years at desk and filing cabinet had bowed his head, made him look nearer to fifty than forty. "They say they like having the shops and the church and the swimming pool and restaurants all built as part of the complex."

I sipped a little beer and looked around the room. It was a barren place; no books, no pictures, no music, no carpet. Just a TV, a sofa, two armchairs, and a coffee table with a vase of plastic flowers. In the corner, newspaper was laid out to protect the floor against oil. On it were the pieces of a dismantled racing bicycle that was being repaired to make a birthday present for his teenage son. "But you don't?"

"Finish your beer and have another. No, I hate it. We've got twelve schools and fifteen kindergartens here in this complex. Twelve schools! It makes me feel like a damned

termite. Some of these kids have never been downtown—
they've never seen the Berlin we grew up in."

"Maybe they are better off without it," I said.

There was a snap and hiss as he opened a can of Export
Pils. "You're right, Bernd," he said. "What will kids find
down there in the middle of the city except crime and dope
and misery?" He poured half the can for himself and the
other half for me. Axel was like that; he was a sharer.

"Well, you've got a view to beat anything."

"It's amazing how far you can see on a really clear day.
But I'd happily trade the view to be back in that old slum
my grandfather had. I keep hearing about the 'German
miracle,' but I don't see any of it. My father gave me a new
bicycle for my twelfth birthday. What can I afford to give
my eldest son? That damned secondhand one."

"Kids don't think like that, Axel," I said. "Even I can
see it's a special racing model. He'll like it all the more
because you've worked so hard to get it ready for him."

Axel Mauser had been one of the brightest kids in the
school; top of the class in chemistry and mathematics, and
so keen on languages that he used to lend me his bicycle in
exchange for English conversation practice. Now he was
working in the Polizeipräsidium records office as a senior
clerk, and living in this cramped apartment with three children and a wife, who—even on Saturdays—worked in the
nearby AEG factory to keep their secondhand BMW running and give them their regular package holiday in Ibiza.
"But where can I afford to move to? Do you know what
rents people are paying in Berlin nowadays?"

"Your dad went back to live in the East."

Axel smiled grimly. "All because of that bloody fool
Binder—Max Binder, remember that *Spieler*?"

Spieler: did he mean actor or gambler, I wondered. Max
was a bit of both. "I always liked Max," I said.

Axel paused as if about to argue with me but then he went on: "Max kept writing to Dad saying how much he was enjoying life over there. My dad believed it all. You know what Dad's like. He kept complaining about how it was over thirty years since he'd strolled down Unter den Linden. He'd wonder if he'd meet old friends on the Alexanderplatz—he was always on about that damned 'Alex'— and he wanted to see the restoration job that's been done on the cathedral. And he'd get talking to Tante Lisl in that bar of hers when there were no customers in, and they'd be wallowing in nostalgia about seeing President Hindenburg in the Bristol and Lotte Lenya at the Wintergarten. . . ."

"And talking to Joseph Goebbels at the bar of the Kaiserhof," I said. "Yes, I've heard all those stories. I couldn't get enough of your dad's yarns when I was young. I saw a lot of him in those days when he was behind the bar at Lisl's." From the next apartment there came the incessant sound of police sirens, shooting, and the joyful shouts of children watching TV. Axel went across to the wall and thumped on it with the flat of his hand. This had no effect other than to make some of the plastic flowers quiver.

Axel shrugged at the continuing noise. "And working for your dad too. Suppose they find out that he used to do those jobs for your dad? They'd throw him straight into prison."

"Don't baby him, Axel. Rolf's a tough old bastard. He can look after himself."

Axel nodded. "So I said, 'If you think you'll recapture your youth by going across the city, Dad, you go. And take Tante Lisl with you. . . .' When my mother was alive, she wouldn't listen to all those stories of his. She'd just tell him to shut up."

"Well, he found a ready audience at that bar."

"He was always complaining about working for Tante Lisl, wasn't he? But he loved standing behind the bar talking about 'the real Berlin,' in the days when there was a respect for Christian values—*eine christliche Weltanschauung.* And after a few customers had bought him drinks, he'd be talking about the *Kaiserzeit* as if he'd been a general in the first war instead of an artillery captain in the second." Axel drank some beer. "There's no fool like an old fool," he said with unexpected vehemence, and looked at his beer so that I could not see his eyes. "I'd hate anything to happen to him, Bernd."

"I know," I said. "But don't worry about him. He's over sixty-five, so he is permitted to visit the West."

"He sees Werner sometimes." He looked at me. "They're in some kind of racket together."

It was more a question than a statement. "Are they?"

"Are you still with the Army intelligence people?"

I nodded. It was my cover story for Berliners such as Axel who remembered my father and had seen me coming and going, and had given me the use of their sofas and their motorcars from time to time. It was not the sort of cover story that earned respect from Germans. Germany is the only country in the world where a job in any sort of intelligence-gathering organization is considered little better than pimping. It is a product of the postwar years when informers were everywhere.

"You're not after Dad?"

"Stop worrying about him, Axel," I said. "Rolf came right through the war, and then survived through the years that followed the war. I'm sure he's doing fine. In fact, I might be able to look him up next time I go into the East Sector. I'll take him something, if you like."

"So what's it all about, Bernd?" said Axel. He got up and went to the window, staring eastward to where the spike of the East German TV tower rose out of the Alexanderplatz. Once it was the heart of the city, where pedestrians dodged bikes, bikes dodged cars, and cars dodged the trams that came through a five-way intersection at frightening speeds. Now the traffic had vanished and the "Alex" was just an orderly concrete expanse, with red flags, flower boxes, and slogans. "You might as well come clean with it," said Axel, still staring out the window.

"With what?"

"It's nice to see you again, Bernd. But you work out of London nowadays, you say. With only a couple of days in the city and lots of old friends to visit, you didn't come to my little place to talk about how well I did in my chemistry exams, and have a can of beer—which I notice you drink very very slowly, as policemen do when they are on duty— and be interrupted by the shouting of the kids next door, and sit close to the heating because I can't afford to turn it up any higher. You must have had a reason to come here, and I think you are going to ask me a favor."

"Remember a couple of years ago when I was looking for that kid who'd stolen a briefcase from an office near the Zoo station?"

"You asked me to look up a post-office box number and tell you who rented it. But that was an official request. That came through the British Army."

"This one is more delicate, Axel." I took from my pocket the envelope that Frank Harrington had left in my street guide. Axel took it reluctantly; even then he didn't immediately look at it. "It's urgent, I suppose? These things are always urgent." He read the address.

"It is, Axel. Otherwise I could have gone through the post office."

He laughed scornfully. "Have you tried getting anything out of our wonderful post office lately? Last week it took them four days to deliver a letter from a postbox in Tiergarten, and then it was nearly torn in two. And the price for a letter now . . ." He read the numbers that were the address. "One thousand is Berlin and twenty-eight is Lübars."

"You said Polizeipräsidium kept copies of the forms the box renters sign. Could you get the name and address of the person who rents that box at Lübars post office? Could you get it even on a Saturday?"

"I'll phone from the bedroom."

"Thanks, Axel."

"It depends who's on duty this morning. I can't order anyone to do it. It's strictly forbidden . . . it's a criminal offense."

"If I could clear up the inquiry immediately, I could go home."

"We all thought you'd grow up to become a gangster," said Axel. "Did I ever tell you that?"

"Yes, Axel. You've told me that many times."

"We asked Herrn Storch, the mathematics teacher, but he said all the English were like you."

"Some of them are worse, Axel," I said.

He didn't laugh; he nodded. He wanted me to know how much he disliked it. He wanted me to think twice before I asked him more such favors. When he went into the bedroom to phone, he turned the key in the door. He wanted to be sure that I could not get close enough to hear him.

The call took only five minutes. I suppose the Polizeipräsidium have such records on a computer.

"The addressee, Mrs. Harrington, is the renter of the box. She gave an address in Lübars," said Axel when he returned from the phone. "I know exactly where it is. It's a street of beautiful houses with a view across open farmland. What wouldn't I give to live in such a place."

"How difficult is it to get a postbox in a false name?" I asked.

"It depends who is on duty. But you don't have to provide much to get it in any name you wish. Many people have boxes under a nom de plume or a stage name, and so on."

"I have not been to Lübars since we were kids. Is it still as pretty as it used to be?"

"Lübars village. We're quite close. If this window faced north, I could show you the street. They've preserved everything: the little eighteenth-century village church, the fire station, and the village green with the fine chestnut trees. The farmhouses and the old inn. It's just a stone's throw away but it's like another world."

"I'll get going, Axel," I said. "Thanks for the beer."

"And what if on Monday they fire me? What then? You say how really sorry you are, and I spend the rest of my life trying to support a family on social welfare payments."

I said nothing.

"You're irresponsible, Bernd. You always were."

I WOULD HAVE EXPECTED Frank Harrington to have his mistress hidden away in a small anonymous apartment block somewhere in the French Sector of the city where no one notices what's happening. But the address Axel Mauser had provided was in the northernmost part of the Western Sector, a prong of land sandwiched between the Tegel Forest and the Wall. There were small farms here just a short way from the city center, and tractors were parked on the narrow cobbled lanes among the shiny Porsches and four-liter Mercedes.

The big family houses were designed to look as though they'd been here since Bismarck, but they were too flawless to be anything but reconstructions. I cruised slowly down an elegant tree-lined road following three children on well-groomed ponies. It was neat and tidy and characterless, like those Hollywood back lots designed to look like anywhere old and foreign.

Number 40 was a narrow two-story house, with a front garden big enough for two large trees and with a lot of empty space behind it. There was a sign on the chain fence: BELLEVUE KENNELS, and another that said "Beware of the Dogs" in three languages, including German. Even before I'd read it, the dogs began barking. They sounded like very big dogs.

Once through the inner gate, I could see a wired compound and a brick outbuilding where some dogs were crowding at the gate trying to get out. "Good dog," I said, but I don't think they heard me.

A young woman came from somewhere at the back of the house. She was about twenty-two years old, with soft gray eyes, a tanned sort of complexion, and jet-black hair drawn back into a bun. She was wearing khaki-colored cotton pants, and a matching shirt with shoulder tabs and button-down pockets. It was all tailored to fit very tight. Over it she had a sleeveless sheepskin jacket—fleece inward—with the sort of bright flower-patterned embroidery that used to be a status symbol for hippies.

She looked me up and down long enough to recognize my Burberry trench coat and Professor Higgins hat. "Did you come to buy a dog?" she said in good English.

"Yes," I said immediately.

"We only have German shepherds."

"I like German shepherds." A big specimen of this breed emerged from the house. It came within six feet of us, looked at the woman before hunching its shoulders and growling menacingly at me.

"You didn't come to buy a dog," she said, looking at my face. Whatever she saw there amused her, for she smiled to show perfect white teeth. So did the dog.

"I'm a friend of Frank's," I said.

"Of my Frank?"

"There's only one Frank," I said. She smiled as if that were a joke.

"Has anything—?"

"No, Frank is fine," I said. "In fact, he doesn't even know I've come to see you."

She'd been peering at me with eyes half closed, and now suddenly she opened her mouth and gave a soft shout of surprise. "You're Werner's English friend, aren't you?"

We looked at each other, momentarily silenced by our mutual surprise. "Yes, I am, Mrs. Volkmann," I said. "But I didn't come here to talk about Werner."

She looked around to see if her neighbors were in their garden listening. But her neighbors were all safely behind their double-glazing. "I can't remember your name but you are the Englishman who went to school with Werner. . . . Your German is perfect," she said, and changed into that language. "No need for us to speak English. I'll put Rudolf in the run and then we'll go inside and have coffee. It's made already." Rudolf growled. He did not want to go into the run unless he took me with him.

"During the week, I have a girl to help me," said Mrs. Zena Volkmann while Rudolf submitted meekly to being pushed into the wired compound. "But on the weekend it is impossible to get anyone at any price. They say there is unemployment but people just don't want to work, that's the trouble." Now her accent was more distinct. *Ostelbisch*: Germans from anywhere east of the River Elbe. Everyone agrees it is not pejorative, but I never heard anyone say it except people who came from west of the River Elbe.

We entered the house through a pantry. Arranged in rows upon a purring freezer were twelve colored plastic bowls containing measured amounts of bread and chopped meat.

There was a mop and bucket in the corner, a steel sink unit and shelves with tins of dog food, and choke chains and collars hanging from a row of hooks on the wall. "I can't go out for more than an hour or two because the puppies have to be fed four times a day. Two litters. One lot are only four weeks old and they need constant attention. And I'm waiting for another litter any day now. I wouldn't have started it all if I'd known what it was like."

She went up a step and opened the door into the kitchen. There was the wonderful smell of freshly made coffee. There was no sign of anything connected with the dogs. The kitchen was almost unnaturally clean and tidy, with gleaming racks of saucepans, and glassware sparkling inside a cabinet.

She snapped off the switch of the automatic coffee-maker, grabbed the jug from the hot plate, put an extra cup and saucer on the tray, and tipped some biscuits onto a matching plate. The cup was as big as a bowl and decorated with the inevitable large brightly colored flowers. We went to sit in the back room. The rear part of the house had been altered at some time to incorporate a huge window. It gave a panoramic view of a piece of farmland beyond the dog enclosures. There was a tractor making its way slowly across the field, disturbing a flock of rooks searching for food in the brown tilled earth. Only the gray line of the Wall marred this pastoral scene. "You get used to it," said Mrs. Volkmann, as if in reply to the question that every visitor asked.

"Not everyone does," I said.

She took a packet of cigarettes from the table and lit one and inhaled before replying. "My grandfather had a farm in East Prussia," she said. "He came here once and couldn't stop looking at the Wall. His farm was nearly eight hundred kilometers from here but that was still Germany. Do you know how far from here Poland is now? Less than sixty.

That's what Hitler did for us. He made Germany into the sort of tiny second-rate little country that he so despised."

"Shall I pour out the coffee?" I said. "It smells good."

"My father was a schoolteacher. He made us children learn history. He said it would prevent the same things happening again." She smiled. There was no humor in it; it was a small, polite, modest smile, the sort of smile you see models wearing in advertisements for expensive watches.

"Let's hope so," I said.

"It will not prevent the same things happening. Look at the world. Can't you see Hitlers all around us? There is no difference between Hitler Germany and Andropov Russia. A hammer and sickle can look very like a swastika, especially when it is flying over your head." She picked up the coffee I'd poured for her. I watched her carefully; there was a lot of hostility in her, even if it was hidden under her smiles and hospitality. "Werner wants me back," she said.

"He knows nothing of my coming here," I said.

"But he told you where to find me?"

"Are you frightened of him?" I said.

"I don't want to go back to him."

"He thinks you are living in Munich. He thinks you ran away with a Coca-Cola truck driver."

"That was just a boy I knew."

"He doesn't know you're still here in Berlin," I said. I was trying to reassure her.

"I never go downtown. Anything I need from the big department stores I have delivered. I'm frightened I'll bump into him in the food department of KaDeWe. Does he still go there and eat lunch?"

"Yes, he still goes there."

"Then why did Frank tell you where I was?"

"Frank Harrington didn't tell me."

"You just worked it out?" she said sarcastically.

"That's right," I said. "I worked it out. There's nothing very difficult about finding people these days. There are bank balances, credit cards, charge accounts, car licenses, driving licenses. If Werner had guessed you were living in the city, he would have found you much more quickly than I did. Werner is an expert at finding people."

"I write postcards and have a friend of mine post them from Munich."

I nodded. Could a professional like Werner really fall for such amateur tricks?

I looked around the room. There were a couple of Berliner Ensemble theater posters framed on the wall and a Käthe Kollwitz lithograph. The fluffy carpet was cream and the soft furnishings were covered in natural-finish linen with orange-colored silk cushions. It was flashy but very comfortable—no little plastic bowls or gnawed bones, no sign anywhere of the existence of the dogs. I suppose it would have to be like that for Frank Harrington. He was not the sort of man who would adapt readily to smelly austerity. Through the sliding doors I glimpsed a large mahogany dinner table set with a cut-glass bowl and silver centerpiece. The largest room had been chosen for dining. I wondered who came along here and enjoyed discreet dinners with Frank and his young mistress.

"It's not a permanent arrangement," said Mrs. Volkmann. "Frank and I—we are close, very close. But it's not permanent. When he goes back to London, it will all be over. We both knew that right from the start." She took a biscuit and nibbled at it in a way that would show her perfect white teeth.

"Is Frank going back to London?" I said.

She'd been sitting well forward on the big soft sofa, but now she banged a fist into a silk cushion before putting it

behind her and resting against it. "His wife would like him
to get promoted. She knows that a posting to London would
break up his affair with me. She doesn't care about Frank's
promotion except that it would get him away from Berlin
and away from me."

"Wives are like that," I said.

"But I won't go back to Werner. Frank likes to think I'd
go back to Werner if and when that happens. But I'll never
go back."

"Why does Frank like to think that? Frank hates Werner."

"Frank feels guilty about taking me away from Werner.
At first, he really worried about it. That sort of guilty feeling
often turns into hatred. You know that." She smiled and
smoothed her sleeve with a sensuous gesture, trailing her
fingertips down her arm. She was a very beautiful woman.
"I get so bored on weekends," she said.

"Where's Frank?"

"He's in Cologne. He won't be back until tomorrow
night." She smiled suggestively. "He leaves me alone too
much."

I don't know if that was the invitation to bed that it
sounded like, but I was not in the mood to find out. I was
getting to the age when feelings of rejection linger. So I
drank coffee, smiled, and looked at the gray line of the Wall.
It was still early afternoon but it was getting misty.

"Then what have you come here for? I suppose London
has sent you to buy me off. Do they want to give me money
to leave Frank alone?"

"What kind of books do you read on those long lonely
nights when Frank's not here, Mrs. Volkmann? The days
when people were paid money for *not* providing sexual favors
went out with policemen in top hats."

"Of course," she said. A bigger smile this time. "And
that was fathers, not employers. What a shame. I was hop-

ing you'd give me a chance to jump to my feet and say I'll never give him up, never, never, never."

"Is that what you would have said?"

"Frank is a very attractive man, Mr. . . . ?"

"Samson. Bernard Samson."

"Frank is an inconsiderate swine at times but he's attractive. Frank is a real man."

"Isn't Werner a real man?"

"Oohh, yes, I know. Werner is your friend. I have heard Werner talk of you. You are a mutual admiration society, the two of you. Well, Werner may be a fine friend, but you live with him for a year and you'd find out what he's like. He can't make up his mind about anything at all. He always wanted me to decide things: how, when, what, why. A woman marries a man to get away from all that, doesn't she?"

"Of course," I said, and tried to make it sound as if I knew what she was talking about. The truth was, I wished like hell that I had a few more people in my life wanting to take orders instead of giving them.

"Have some more coffee," she said sweetly. "But then I must insist that you tell me what this is all about. Mysterious strangers can outstay their welcome too, you know."

"You've been very patient with me, Mrs. Volkmann, and I appreciate that. My purpose in seeking you out was to tell you, unofficially, that under the circumstances my masters in London feel that you must be positively vetted."

"A security check?"

"Yes, Mrs. Volkmann. There will have to be a security check. You will be positively vetted."

"This has already been done when I first married Werner."

"Ah, well, this will be quite different. As you know, Frank Harrington is an important British official. We will have to make this what we call a Category Double X clearance. We hope you will understand why this has to be done and co-operate with the people assigned to the job."

"I don't understand. Can't Frank arrange it?"

"If you pause a moment, Mrs. Volkmann, you'll see how important it is that Frank doesn't know about it."

"Frank will not be told?"

"Let Frank keep his private life secret. Frank's gone to a lot of trouble to do all this. . . . " I waved a hand vaguely in the air. "How would he feel if young men from his own office had to compile reports on where you went, who you saw, how much you have in the bank? And how will he feel if he has to read reports about some old relationships that you have half forgotten and can only cause him pain?"

She inhaled on her cigarette, and looked at me through half-closed eyes. "Are you telling me that this is the sort of thing that your investigators will pry into?"

"You're a woman of the world, Mrs. Volkmann. You've obviously guessed that the investigation has already started. None of the agents assigned to you have actually reported to me yet, but you must have spotted my men following you during the past three or four weeks. We don't assign our most experienced people to these vetting jobs of course, and I'm not surprised that you realized what is in progress."

I waited for her reaction, but she sat well back on the sofa and looked me in the eyes. She smoked but said nothing.

I said, "I should have come to tell you about all this a month ago, but so much work piled up on my desk that I found it impossible to get away."

"You bastard," she said. There was no smile this time. I had the feeling that this was the real Zena Volkmann.

"I'm just carrying out my orders, Mrs. Volkmann," I said.

"So was Eichmann," she said bitterly.

"Yes, well you know more about German history than I

do, Mrs. Volkmann, so I'll have to take your word for that."

I gulped down the last of my coffee and got to my feet. She didn't move but she watched me all the time.

"I won't go out the back way if you don't mind," I said. "I don't want to disturb the dogs."

"You're frightened that the dogs will tear you to pieces," she said.

"Well, that's another reason," I admitted. "No need to show me to the door."

"Frank will get you kicked out of the service for this," she promised.

I stopped. "I wouldn't mention any of this to Frank if I were you, Mrs. Volkmann," I said. "This is a London decision, a decision made by Frank's friends. If it all became official, Frank would have to face a board of inquiry. He'd have a lot of explaining to do. The chances are he'd lose his job and his pension too. If that happened, Frank's friends might feel it was all your fault. And Frank has friends in Bonn as well as London—very loyal friends."

"Get out!"

"Unless you've something to hide, there'll be no problem," I said.

"Get out before I set the dogs on you."

I WENT BACK to the car and waited. I decided to give it an hour and a half and see whether my hastily improvised story provoked any comings and goings. At that time on a Saturday afternoon there was not much traffic; something should happen soon, I told myself.

I could see the house from the driver's seat of the car. It was an hour and a quarter later that she came out, carrying a big Gucci suitcase and an overnight bag. She was dressed in a leopard-skin coat with a matching hat. Real skin, of course. She was not the sort of lady who worried too much about leopards. The car arrived even before she closed the garden gate. She got into the front seat beside the driver and the car moved off immediately. I reached forward to turn the ignition key, but I had already recognized the car she climbed into. It was Werner's Audi and Werner was driving it. She was talking to him with much waving of the hands as the car passed mine. I ducked down out of sight but they were too involved in their discussion to notice me. So much for all her lies about Werner. And so much for all Werner's stories about her.

No point in chasing after them. Werner would be sure to see me if I tried to follow. In any case, Berlin is well covered. The security officers at the road checkpoints, the airport, and the crossing places would be able to tell me where they went.

I went back to the house. I opened the pantry window with a wire coat hanger that I found in my car. She had left hurriedly. The colored plastic bowls were piled up unwashed in the pantry sink. Frank wouldn't like that. In fact, he wouldn't like my putting his lady to flight if he found out what I'd done. There were lots of things he wouldn't like.

There was a note on the phone. It said simply that Zena had gone away for a few days because of a family crisis and she'd phone him at the office next week. It went on to say that a neighbor would feed the dogs, and would Frank leave one hundred marks on the hall table.

Whatever kind of racket Werner was in, it looked as if Zena was in it too. I wondered if it depended upon getting information from Frank, and what sort of information it was.

Chapter 13

From Bret Rensselaer's top-floor office there was a view westward that could make you think London was all greenery. The treetops of St. James's Park, Green Park, and the gardens of Buckingham Palace, and beyond that Hyde Park, made a continuous woolly blanket. Now it was all sinking into the gray mist that swallowed London early on such afternoons. The sky overhead was dark, but some final glimmers of sunlight broke through, making streaky patterns on the emerald rectangles that were the squares of Belgravia.

Despite the darkness of the rain clouds, Rensselaer had not yet switched on the room lights. The thin illumination from the windows became razor-sharp reflections in all the chromium fittings and made the glass-top desk shimmer like steel. And the same sort of metallic light was reflected up into Rensselaer's face, so that he looked more cadaverous than ever.

Dicky Cruyer was hovering over the boss, but moving around enough to see his face and be ready with an appropriate answer. Cruyer was well aware of his role; he was there whenever Rensselaer wanted witness, hatchet man, vociferous supporter, or silent audience. But Cruyer was not a mere acolyte; he was a man who knew that "to everything there is a season . . . a time to embrace and a time to refrain from embracing." In other words, Cruyer knew exactly when to argue with the boss. And that was something I never did right. I didn't even know when to argue with my wife.

"You didn't tell Frank that it was all genuine material?" Cruyer asked me for the third time in thirty minutes.

"Frank doesn't give a damn whether it's genuine or not," I said. They both looked at me with pained shock. "As long as it didn't come dribbling out of his Berlin office."

"You're hard on Frank," Bret said, but he didn't argue about it. He took off his jacket and put it on a chairback, carefully arranging it so it wouldn't wrinkle.

"How would you like it wrapped up?" I said. "You want me to tell you that he's sitting at home every night trying on false whiskers and working out new codes and ciphers just to keep in practice?" I suppose I was angry at Werner's rumor about Frank not wanting me to inherit his job. I didn't believe it, but I was angry about it just the same. The friendship between Frank and me had always been ambivalent. We were friends only when I remembered my place; and sometimes I didn't remember my place.

"I don't want an eager beaver in the Berlin office," said Bret Rensselaer, pausing long enough for me to register the personal pronoun that said Bret Rensselaer was the one who decided who got that coveted post. "Frank Harrington"— the surname was used to distance Bret Rensselaer from his subordinate—"went over there to sort out a mess of incompetence, and he did that. He's not a goddamned superstar, and we all knew it. He was a receiver, sent in to preside over a bankruptcy." Bret Rensselaer had appointed Frank Harrington to Berlin and he resented anything said against his appointee.

"Frank did wonders," said Dicky Cruyer. It was a reflex response, and while I was admiring it he added, "You took a chance putting Frank into that job, Bret, and you did it with half the department heads telling you it would be a disaster. Disaster!" Dicky Cruyer devoted a precious moment to making a clicking noise with his mouth that indicated his contempt for those amazingly shortsighted people who had questioned Bret Rensselaer's bold decision. He looked at me while he did it, for among those doubters I was numbered.

Rensselaer said, "Did you notice anything else about the material that this fast-disappearing helper"—a glance at me as the person who'd let the helper slip through our hands—"slammed down on Frank's desk?"

"You want me to answer, Bret?" I said. "Or are we both going to wait for Dicky to say something?"

"Now, what the hell's this?" said Dicky anxiously. "There are quite a few things about that material that I noticed. In fact, I'm in the process of writing a report about it." Being in the process of writing a report about something was the nearest that Dicky ever came to admitting total ignorance.

"Bernard?" said Rensselaer, looking at me.

"That it all came through Giles Trent's office?"

Rensselaer nodded. "Exactly," he said. "Every document that was in that bundle of material leaked to the Russians had, at some stage or other, passed through Trent's hands."

"Well, let me hang this one on you," I said. "A few years ago—I have the dates and details—the Berlin office made an intercept that was reported back to Karlshorst within three days. Giles Trent was on duty there that night."

"Then why the hell wasn't that in his file?" said Dicky Cruyer. I noticed he was wearing his gold medallion inside his dark blue silk shirt. It went with his white denim trousers.

"He was completely cleared," I said. "Berlin decided who was responsible, and took all necessary action."

"But you don't believe it," said Rensselaer.

I raised my hands in the sort of shrug of resignation that would have been over the top for a road-show actor's Shylock.

"But he was in the building," said Rensselaer.

"He was on duty," I said, avoiding the question. "And he did handle everything that arrived in Berlin last week."

"What do you think, Dicky?" said Rensselaer.

"Perhaps we're being *too* sophisticated," said Dicky. "Perhaps we've got a very straightforward case of Trent selling us out, but we insist upon looking for something else." He smiled. "Sometimes life is simple. Sometimes things are what they appear to be." It was a cry from the heart.

I didn't say anything and neither did Rensselaer. He glanced at my face and didn't ask me what I thought. I guess I'm not as inscrutable as Cruyer.

When Rensselaer had finished with us, Dicky Cruyer invited me into his office. It was the sort of invitation I could decline at my peril, as Dicky's voice made clear, but I looked at my watch for long enough to make him open the drinks cabinet.

"All right," he said as he put a big gin and tonic into my hand. "What the hell is this all about?"

"Where do you want to begin?" I asked, and looked at my watch again. My difficulty in dealing with the stubborn and intractable mind of Bret Rensselaer was compounded by the myopic confusion that Dicky Cruyer brought to every meeting.

"Are you now trying to say that Giles Trent is innocent?" he said petulantly.

"No," I said. I drank some of the very weak mixture while Cruyer was fishing around in his glass to scoop a fragment of tonic-bottle label from where it was floating among the ice cubes.

"So he is guilty?"

"Probably," I said.

"Then I fail to understand why you and Bret were going through that rigmarole just now."

"Can I help myself to a bit more gin?"

Cruyer nodded, and watched to see how much of it I poured. "So why don't we just pull Trent in, and have done with it?"

"Bret wants to play him. Bret wants to find out what the Russkies want out of him."

"Want out of him!" said Cruyer scornfully. "Great Scott! They've been running him for all that time, and now Bret wants to give them more time. . . . How long before Bret is going to be quite sure what they want?" He looked up at me and said, "They want to know what we do, say, and think up here on the top floor. That's what they want."

"Well, that's not so worrying. You could get everything important that is done, said, or thought up here written on the back of a postage stamp, and still have room for the Lord's Prayer."

"Never mind the wisecracks," said Cruyer. He was right about Trent. There would be only one use for an agent who is so close to us; they'd use him to provide "a commentary."

"Trent's a Balliol man, like me," said Dicky suddenly.

"Are you boasting, confessing, or complaining?" I asked.

Dicky smiled that little smile with which all Balliol men like him confront the envy of lesser mortals. "I'm simply pointing out that he's no fool. He'll guess what's going on."

"Trent's no longer doing any harm," I said. "He's been debriefed and now we might as well play him for as long as we can."

"I don't go along with all this damned double-agent, triple-agent, quadruple-agent stuff. You get to a point where no one knows what the hell is going on anymore."

"You mean it's confusing," I said.

"Of course it's confusing!" said Cruyer loudly. "Trent

will soon have got to the point where he doesn't know which side he's working for."

"As long as we do know, it's all right," I said. "We're making sure that Trent only gets to hear the things we want Moscow to hear."

Dicky Cruyer didn't resent my talking to him as if he were an eight-year-old; he appreciated it. "Okay, I understand that," he said. "But what about this new leak in Berlin?"

"It's not a new leak. It's an incident dating from years ago."

"But newly discovered."

"No. Frank knew about it at the time. It's new only to us, and that only because he didn't think it was worth passing back here."

"Are you covering for someone?" said Cruyer. However numb his brain, his antennae were alive and well.

"No."

"Are you covering for Frank, or for one of your old Berlin schoolmates?"

"Let it go, Dicky," I advised. "It's for background information only. Frank Harrington has closed the file on this one. You go digging it all up again and someone is going to say you are vindictive."

"Vindictive! My God, I ask for a few details about a security leak in Berlin and you start telling me I'm vindictive."

"I said you'll run the risk of being accused of it. And Frank sees the D-G socially whenever he's in town. Frank is near enough to retirement to scream bloody murder if you do anything to make ripples on his pond." Cruyer's face went a shade paler under his tan and I knew I'd touched a nerve. "Do what you like," I added. "It's just a word to the wise, Dicky."

He shot me a glance to see if I was being sardonic. "I

appreciate it," he said. "You're probably right." He drank some of his gin and pulled a face as if he hated the taste. "Frank lives in style, doesn't he? I was out at his country place last month. What a magnificent house. And he's got all the expense of living in Berlin as well."

Two houses in Berlin, I felt tempted to say, but I sipped my drink and smiled.

Dicky Cruyer ran a finger along the waist of his white denim jeans until he felt the designer's leather label on his back pocket. Thus reassured, he said, "The Harringtons are treated like local gentry in that village, you know. They have his wife presenting prizes at the village fête, judging at the gymkhana, and tasting the sponge cakes at the village hall. No wonder he wants to retire, with all that waiting for him. Have you been there?"

"Well, I've known him a long time," I said, although why the hell I should find myself apologizing to Dicky for the fact that I'd been a regular guest at Frank's house ever since I was a small child, I don't know.

"Yes, I forget. He was a friend of your father's. Frank brought you into the service, didn't he?"

"In a way," I said.

"The D-G recruited me," said Dicky. My heart sank as he settled down into his Charles Eames leather armchair and rested his head back; it was usually the sign of Cruyer in reminiscent mood. "He wasn't D-G then, of course, he was a tutor—not *my* tutor, thank God—and he buttonholed me in the college library one afternoon. We got to talking about Fiona. Your wife," he added, just in case I'd forgotten her name. "He asked me what I thought about the crowd she was running around with. I told him they were absolute dross. They were, too! Trotskyites and Marxists and Maoists who could only argue in slogans and couldn't answer any political argument without checking back with Party Headquarters to see what the official line was at that moment. Of course, it was years afterwards that I discovered Fiona was in the Department. Then of course I realized that she must have been mixing with that Marxist crowd on the D-G's orders all that time ago. What a fool she must have thought me. But I've always wondered why the D-G didn't drop a hint of what was really the score. Did you know Fiona infiltrated the Marxists when she was still only a kid?"

"Thanks for the drink, Dicky," I said, draining my glass and deliberately putting it on his polished rosewood desk top. He jumped out of his chair, grabbed the glass, and polished energetically at the place where it had stood. It never failed as a way of getting him back to earth from his long discursive monologues, but one day he was sure to tumble to it.

Having polished the desk with his handkerchief, and peered at the surface long enough to satisfy himself that it had been restored to its former luster, he turned back to me. "Yes, of course, I mustn't keep you. You haven't seen much of the family for the last few days. Still, you like Berlin. I've heard you say so."

"Yes, I like it."

"I can't think what you see in it. A filthy place bombed to nothing in the war. The few decent buildings that survived were in the Russian Sector and they got bulldozed to fill the city with all those ghastly workers' tenements."

"That's about right," I admitted. "But it's got something. And Berliners are the most wonderful people in the world."

Cruyer smiled. "I never realized that you had a romantic streak in you, Bernard. Is that what made the exquisite and unobtainable Fiona fall in love with you?"

"It wasn't for my money or social position," I said.

Cruyer took my empty glass, the bottle caps, and the

paper napkin I'd left unused and put them onto a plastic tray for the cleaners to remove. "Could Giles Trent be connected to our problems with the Brahms net?"

"I've been wondering that myself," I said.

"Are you going to see them?"

"Probably."

"I'd hate Trent to get wind of your intention," said Cruyer quietly.

"He's a Balliol man, Dicky," I said.

"He could *inadvertently* pass it to his Control. Then you might find a hot reception waiting for you." He finished his drink, wiped his lips, and put his empty glass with the other debris on the tray.

"And Bret would lose his precious source," I said.

"Don't let's worry about that," said Cruyer. "That's strictly Bret's problem."

Chapter 14

I COLLECTED Fiona from her sister's house that evening. She'd left a message asking me to take the car there, so she could bring back a folding bed that she'd lent to Tessa at a time when she'd decided to sleep apart from George. The bed had never been put to use. I always suspected that Tessa had used its presence as a threat. She was like that.

Tessa had prepared dinner. It was the sort of *nouvelle cuisine* extravaganza that Uncle Silas had been complaining of. A thin slice of veal with two tiny puddles of brightly colored sauces, peas arranged inside a scooped-out tomato, and a few wafers of carrot with a mint leaf draped over them. Tessa had learned to prepare it at a cookery school in Hampstead.

"It's delicious," said Fiona.

"He was yummy," said Tessa when she'd finished eating. She never seemed to need more than a spoonful of food at any meal. *Nouvelle cuisine* was invented for people like Tessa, who just wanted to go through the pretense of eating a meal for the sake of the social benefits. "He had these wonderful dark eyes that could see right through your clothes, and when he was demonstrating the cooking he'd put his arm round you and take your hand. 'Like zis, like zis,' he used to say. He was Spanish, I think, but he liked to pretend he was French of course."

Fiona said, "Tessa has cooked the most wonderful things for me while you were away."

"Like zis?" I asked.

"And meals for the children," said Fiona hurriedly, hoping to appeal to my feelings of obligation. "She has given me a gallon of minestrone for the freezer. It will be so useful, Tess darling, and the children just love soup."

"And how was Berlin?" said Tessa. She smiled. We understood each other. She knew I didn't like the tiny ladies' snack she'd prepared, or her supposed antics with the Spanish cookery teacher, but she didn't give a damn. Fiona was the peacemaker, and it amused Tessa to see her sister intercede.

"Berlin was wonderful," I said with spurious enthusiasm.

"German food is more robust than French food," said Tessa. "Like German women, I suppose." It was directed at me and more specifically at the buxom German girl I was with when Tessa first met me, back before I married Fiona.

"You know that German proverb: one is what one eats," I said.

"Feast on cabbage and what do you become?" said Tessa.

"A butterfly?" I said.

"And if you eat dumplings?"

"At least you are no longer hungry," I said.

"Give him some more meat," Fiona told her sister, "or he'll be bad-tempered all evening."

When Tessa returned from the kitchen with my second helping of dinner, the plate no longer exhibited the finer points of *la nouvelle cuisine*. There was a chunky piece of veal and a large spoonful of odd-shaped carrot pieces that showed how tricky it was to slice thin even slices. There was only one kind of sauce this time, and it was poured over the meat. "Where's the mint leaf," I said. Tessa aimed a playful blow at the place between my shoulders, and it landed with enough force to make me cough.

"Did you notice anything different in the hall?" Tessa asked Fiona while I was wolfing the food.

"Yes," said Fiona. "The lovely little table, I was going to ask you about it."

"Giles Trent. He's selling some things that used to belong to his grandmother. He needs the extra room and he has other things for sale. Anyone who could find space enough for a dining table . . . Oh, Fiona, it's such a beautiful mahogany table, with eight chairs. I'd sell my soul for it but it would never fit here and this table belonged to George's mother. I dare not say I'd like to replace it."

"Giles Trent?" I said. "Is he selling up?"

"He's working with you now, isn't he," said Tessa. "He told me he has talked with you and everything is going to be all right. I'm so pleased."

"What else is he selling?"

"Only furniture. He won't part with any of his pictures. I wish he'd decide to let me have one of those little Rembrandt etchings. I'd love one."

"Would George agree?" asked Fiona.

"I'd give it to George for his birthday," said Tessa. "There's nothing a man can do if you buy something you want and say 'Happy birthday' when he first sees it."

"You're quite unscrupulous," said Fiona without bothering to conceal her admiration.

"I'd go carefully on Rembrandt etchings," I told her. "There are lots of plates around, and the dealers just print a few off from time to time, and ease them into the market through suckers like Giles Trent."

"Are they allowed to do that?" Tessa asked.

"What's to stop them?" I said. "It's not forgery or faking."

"But that's like printing money," said Fiona.

"It's better," I said. "It's like using your husband's money and saying 'Happy birthday.' "

"Have you had enough veal?" said Tessa.

"It was delicious," I said. "What's for dessert—Chinese gooseberries?"

"Tess wants to watch the repeat of *Dallas* on TV tonight. We'd best be getting that bed downstairs and go home," said Fiona.

"It's not heavy," said Tessa. "George carried it all by himself, and he's not very strong."

I had the folding bed tied onto the roof rack of the car and we were on our way home by the time Tessa sat down to watch TV. "Drive carefully," said Fiona as we turned out of the entrance to the big apartment block where George and Tessa lived and saw the beginning of the snow. "It's so good to have you home again, darling. I do miss you horribly when you're away." There was an intimacy in the dark interior of the car and it was heightened by the bad weather outside.

"I miss you too," I said.

"But it all went smoothly in Berlin?"

"No problems," I said. "Snow in May . . . my God!"

"But nothing to clear poor Giles?"

"Looks like he's even deeper in, I'm afraid."

"I wish Tessa wouldn't keep seeing him. But there's nothing serious between them. You know that, don't you?"

"Why would he be selling his furniture?" I said.

"Antiques and furniture have been getting good prices lately. It's the recession, I suppose. People want to put their money into things that will ride with inflation."

"Sounds like a good reason for hanging on to them," I

said. "And if he must sell them, why not send them to a saleroom? Why sell them piece by piece?"

"Is there tax to be paid on such things? Is that what you mean?"

"The etchings are small. The lithographs can be rolled up," I said. "But the furniture is bulky and heavy."

"Bernard! You don't think Giles would be idiot enough to run for it."

"It crossed my mind," I said.

"He'd be a fool. And could you imagine poor old Giles in Moscow, lining up to collect his vodka ration?"

"Stranger things have happened, darling. Surprises never end in this business."

I turned onto Finchley Road and headed south. There was a lot of traffic coming the other way, couples who'd had an evening on the town and were now heading for their homes in the northern suburbs. The snow was melting as it touched the ground but the air was full of it, like a TV picture when an electric mixer is working. The flakes drifted past the neon signs and glaring shopwindows like colored confetti. A few dabbed against the windscreen and clung for a moment before melting.

"I was talking to Frank about the old days," I said. "He told me about the time in 1978 when the Baader-Meinhof gang were in the news."

"I remember," said Fiona. "Someone got the idea that there was to be a second kidnap attempt. I was quite nervous, I hadn't seen one of those security alerts before. I was expecting something awful to happen."

"There was a radio intercept from Karlshorst. Something about an airport in Czechoslovakia."

"That's right. I handled it. Frank was in one of his schoolmaster moods. He told me all about the intercept service, and how to recognize the different sort of Russian Army signals traffic by the last but one group in the message."

"Frank never passed that intercept back to London," I said.

"That's very likely," said Fiona. "He always said that the job of the Berlin Resident is to insure that London is not buried under an avalanche of unimportant material. Getting intelligence is easy, Frank said, but sorting it out is what matters." She shivered and tried to turn up the heater of the car, but it was already fully on. "Why? Is Frank having second thoughts? It's a long time ago—too late now for second thoughts."

I wondered if she was thinking of other things: too late perhaps to be having second thoughts about a marriage. "Look at that," I said. A white Jaguar had skidded on the wet road and mounted the pavement so that its rear had swung around and into a shopwindow. There was glass all over the pavement, white like snow, and a woman with blood on her hands and her face. The driver was blowing into a plastic bag held by a blank-faced policeman.

"I'm glad I didn't take the Porsche over to Tessa's tonight. You don't stand a chance with the police if they find you behind the wheel of a red Porsche. When are you getting the new Volvo?"

"The dealer keeps saying next week. He's hoping my nerve will break and I'll take that station wagon he's trying to get rid of."

"Go to some other dealer."

"He's giving me a good trade-in price on this jalopy."

"Why not have the station wagon, then?"

"Too expensive."

"Let me give you the difference in price. Your birthday is coming up soon."

"I'd rather not, darling. But thanks all the same."

"It would be awfully useful for moving beds," she said.

"I'm not going to give your father the satisfaction of using any of his money."

"He'll never know."

"But I will know, and I'm the one who told him where to put his dowry."

"Where to put *my* dowry, darling."

"I love you, Fiona," I said, "even if you do forget my birthdays."

She put her fingertips to her lips and touched my cheek. "Where were you that night in 1978?" she said. "Why weren't you at my side?"

"I was in Gdansk, involved in that meeting with the shipyard workers who never turned up. It was all a KGB entrapment. Remember?"

"I must have repressed the memory of it. Yes, Gdansk, of course. I was so worried."

"So was I. My career has been one fiasco after another, from that time to this."

"But you have always got out safely."

"That's more than I can say for a lot of the others who were with me. We were in good shape in 1978 but there's not much left now."

"You were always away on some job or other. I hated being in Berlin on my own. I hated the dark streets and the narrow alleys. I don't know what I would have done without dear old Giles to take me home each night and cheer me up with phone calls and books about Germany that he thought I should read to improve myself. Dear old Giles. That's why I feel so sorry for him now he's in trouble."

"He took you home?"

"It didn't matter what time I finished work—even in

the middle of the night when the panic was on—Giles would come up to Operations and have a cigarette and a laugh and take me home."

I carried on driving, swearing at someone who overtook us and splashed filth on the windscreen, and only after a few minutes' pause did I say, "Didn't Giles work over in the other building? I thought he'd need a red pass to come up to Operations."

"Officially he did. But at the end of each shift—unless one of the panjandrums from London was there—people from the annex came into the main building. There was no hot water in the annex, and most of us felt we needed to wash and change after eight hours in that place."

"But there was an inquiry. A man named Joe Brody questioned everyone about a leak that night."

"Well, what are you supposed to say, darling? Do you think anyone is going to let Frank down? I mean, are you going to say that people from the annex come up and steal paper and pencils and take their girlfriends up to that sitting room on the top floor?"

"Well, I didn't know all that was going on."

"Girls talk together, darling. Especially when there are just a few girls in a foreign town. And working in an office with the most disreputable lot of men." She squeezed my arm.

"So everyone told lies to Joe Brody? Giles Trent *did* have access to the signals."

"He was an American, darling. You can't let the old country down, can you?"

"Frank would throw a fit if he knew," I said. It was appalling to think of all Frank's regulations, memorandums, and complicated routines being flouted by everyone, even when he was there in the office. In those days I'd spent most of my working hours off on the sort of assignment that the more artful executives avoid by pleading their German isn't fluent enough. Clever Dicky, stupid Bernard.

"Frank is just a selfish pig," said Fiona. "He likes the money and the prestige but he hates the actual work. What Frank likes is playing host to the jet set while the taxpayer gets the bill."

"There has to be a certain amount of that," I said. "Sometimes I think the D-G only keeps Frank over there to pick up all the gossip. The D-G loves gossip. But Frank understands what is gossip and what is important. Frank has got a talent for anticipating trouble long before it arrives. I could give you a dozen examples of him pulling the coals out of the fire, acting only on gossip and those hunches he has."

"Who will get Berlin when Frank retires?"

"Don't ask me," I said. "I suppose they will go to that computer and see if they can find someone who hates Berlin as much as Frank does, who wastes money as extravagantly as Frank does, who speaks that same *Kaiserliche* German that Frank does, and who looks like an Englishman on a package tour, as Frank manages to look."

"You're cruel. Frank's so proud of his German too."

"He'd get away with it if he didn't try writing out those instructions for the German staff and pinning them on the notice board. The only time I've ever seen Werner laughing, really laughing uncontrollably, was in front of the notice board in the front hall. He was reading Frank's German-language instructions: 'What to do in case of fire.' It became a classic. There was a German security man who used to recite it at the Christmas party. One year Frank watched him and said, 'It's jolly good the way these Jerries are able to laugh at the deficiencies of their own language, what?' I said, 'Yes, Frank, and he's got a voice a bit like yours, did you notice that?' 'Can't say I did,' said Frank. I never was quite sure if Frank understood what the joke was."

"Bret said the D-G mentioned your name for the Berlin office."

"Have you seen Bret much while I was away?"

"Don't start that all over again, darling. There is absolutely no question of a relationship between me and Bret Rensselaer."

"No one's mentioned it to me," I said. "The job, I mean."

"Would you take it?"

"Would you like to go back there?"

"I'd do anything to see you really happy again, Bernard."

"I'm happy enough."

"I wish you'd show it more. I worry about you. Would you like to go to Berlin?"

"It depends," I said cautiously. "If they wanted me to take over Frank's ramshackle organization and keep it that way, I wouldn't touch it at any price. If they let me reshape it to something better suited to the twentieth century . . . then it could be a job well worth doing."

"And I can easily imagine you putting it to the D-G in those very words, darling. Can't you get it into your adorable head that Frank, Dicky, Bret, and the D-G all think they are running a wonderful organization that is the envy of the whole world. They are not going to receive your offer to bring it into the twentieth century with boundless enthusiasm."

"I must remember that," I said.

"And now I've made you angry."

"Only because you're right," I said. "Anyway, it's hardly worth discussing what I'd say if they offered me Frank's job when I know there is not the slightest chance they will."

"We'll see," said Fiona. "You realize you've driven past

our house, don't you? Bernard! Where the hell are we going?"

"There was a parked car . . . two men in it. Opposite our entrance."

"Oh, but Bernard. Really."

"I'll just drive around the block to see if there's any sort of backup. Then I'll go back there on foot."

"Aren't you taking a parked car with two people in it too seriously? It's probably just a couple saying good night."

"I've been taking things too seriously for years," I said. "I'm afraid it makes me a difficult man to live with. But I've stayed alive, sweetheart. And that means a lot to me."

The streets were deserted, no one on foot and no occupied parked cars as far as I could see. I stopped the car. "Give me five minutes. Then drive along the road and into our driveway as if everything was normal."

She looked worried now. "For God's sake, Bernard. Do be careful."

"I'll be okay," I told her as I opened the door of the car. "This is what I do for a living."

I took a pistol from my jacket and stuffed it into a pocket of my raincoat. "You're carrying a gun?" said Fiona in alarm. "What on earth do you want with that?"

"New instructions," I said. "Anyone who regularly carries Category One papers has to have a gun. It's only a peashooter."

"I hate guns," she said.

"Five minutes."

She reached out and gripped my arm. "There's nothing between me and Bret," she said. "There's nothing between me and anyone, darling. I swear it. You're the only one."

"You're only saying that because I've got a gun," I said. It was a rotten joke, but she gave it the best sort of smile she could manage and then slid across to the driver's seat.

It was cold, and flakes of snow hit my face. By now the snowfall was heavy enough to make patterns on the ground, and the air cold enough to keep the flakes frozen so they swirled around in ever-changing shapes.

I turned in to Duke Street, where we lived, from the north end. I wanted to approach the car from behind. It was safer that way; it's damned awkward to twist around in a car seat. The car was not one I recognized as being from the car pool, but on the other hand it wasn't positioned for a hot-rubber getaway. It was an old Lancia coupe with a radiophone antenna on the roof.

The driver must have been looking in his rearview mirror, because the door swung open when I got near. A man got out. He was about thirty, wearing a black leather zip-fronted jacket and the sort of brightly colored knitted Peruvian hat they sell in ski resorts. I was reassured; it would be a bit conspicuous for a KGB hit team.

He let me come closer and kept his hand at his sides, well away from his pockets. "Mr. Samson?" he called.

I stopped. The other occupant of the car hadn't moved. He hadn't even turned in his seat to see me. "Who are you?" I said.

"I've got a message from Mr. Cruyer," he said.

I went closer to him but remained cautious. I was holding the peashooter in the pocket of my coat and I kept it pointing in his direction. "Tell me more," I said.

He looked down at where the gun made a bulge and said, "He told me to wait. You didn't leave a contact number."

He was right about that. Fiona's request to move that damned bed had been waiting for me at home. "Let's have it, then."

"It's Mr. Trent. He's been taken ill. He's in a house near the Oval. Mr. Cruyer is there." He motioned vaguely to the car. "Shall I call him to say you're coming?"

"I'll go in my car."

"Sure," said the man. He pulled the knitted hat down around his ears. "I'll ask Mr. Cruyer to call you and confirm, shall I?" He was careful not to grin but my caution obviously amused him.

"Do that," I said. "You can't be too careful."

"Will do," he said, and gave me a perfunctory salute before opening the car door. "Anything else?"

"Nothing else," I said. I didn't let go of the gun until they'd driven away. Then I went indoors and poured myself a malt whisky while waiting for Cruyer's call. Fiona arrived before the phone rang. She gave me a tight embrace and a kiss from her ice-cold lips.

Cruyer was not explicit about anything except the address and the fact that he'd been trying to get me for nearly an hour, and would I please hurry, hurry, hurry. Not wanting to arrive there complete with folding bed, I lifted it from the roof rack before leaving. The exertion made me short of breath and my hands tremble. Or was that due to the confrontation with the man from the car? I could not be sure.

THE PART of South London that takes its name from the Surrey County cricket ground is not the smart residential district that some tourists might expect. The Oval is a seedy collection of small factories, workers' apartments, and a park that is not recommended for a stroll after dark. And yet, tucked away behind the main thoroughfares, with their diesel fumes, stray cats, and litter, there are enclaves of renovated houses—mostly of Victorian design—occupied by politicians and civil servants who have discovered how conveniently close to Westminster this unfashionable district is. It was in such a house that Cruyer was waiting for me.

Dicky was lounging in the front room reading the *Econo-*

mist. He habitually carried such reading matter rolled up in the side pocket of his reefer jacket that was now beside him on the sofa. He was wearing jeans, jogging shoes, and a white roll-neck sweater in the sort of heavyweight wool that trawlermen require for deck duty in bad weather.

"I'm sorry you couldn't reach me," I said.

"It doesn't matter," said Dicky in a tone that meant it did. "Trent has taken an overdose."

"What did he take? How bad is he?" I asked.

"His sister found him, thank God," said Dicky. "She brought him here. This is her house. Then she called a doctor." Dicky said "doctor" as another man might say "pervert" or "terrorist." "Not one of our people," Dicky went on. "Some bloody quack from the local medical center."

"How bad is he?"

"Trent? He'll survive. But it's probably a sign that his Russian pals are turning the screws a bit. I don't want them tightening the screws to the point where Trent decides they can hurt him more than we can."

"Did he say that? Did he say he's coming under pressure?"

"I think we should assume that he is," said Dicky. "That's why someone will have to tell him the facts of life."

"For instance?"

"Someone is going to have to explain that we can't afford to have him sitting in Moscow answering the questions that a KGB debriefing panel will ask. Losing a few secret papers is one thing. Helping them build a complete diagram of our chain of command and the headquarters structure, and filling in personal details about senior officers for their files, would be intolerable." Dicky held the rolled-up magazine and slapped the open palm of his left hand with it. Ominously he added, "And Trent had better understand that he knows too much to go for trial at the Old Bailey."

"And you want me to explain all that?" I said.

"I thought you'd already explained it to him," said Dicky.

"Did it occur to you that a suicide attempt might indicate that he's already been pressed too hard?"

Dicky became absorbed in the problem of rolling the *Economist* up so tightly that no light could be seen through it. After a long silence he said, "I didn't tell the stupid bastard to sell out his country. You think, because he's a Balliol man I want to go easy on him." He got out his cigarettes and put one in his mouth unlit.

"I never went to college," I said. "I don't know what you're talking about."

He heaved himself off the sofa and went to the mantel-shelf where he rummaged for matches and pulled at a flower petal to see if the daffodils were plastic; they weren't. "You didn't go to college but sometimes you hit the nail on the head, Bernard old friend. I've been thinking of that conversation you had with Bret Rensselaer this afternoon. It was only sitting here tonight that I began to see what you were getting at." I'd never seen Dicky so restless. He found a matchbox on the shelf, but it was empty.

"Is that so?"

"You think everything's coming up too neat and tidy, don't you? You don't like the way in which that material implicating Trent has conveniently come into Frank's hands in Berlin. You're suspicious about his being on duty the night that damned radio intercept was filed. In short, you don't like the way everything points to Giles Trent."

"I don't like it," I admitted. "When I get all my questions answered fully, I know I'm asking the wrong questions."

"Let's cut out all this nebulous talk," he said. He put the matchbox back on the shelf, having decided not to smoke. "Do you think Moscow knows we are on to Trent? Do you think Moscow intends to use him as a scapegoat?" Carefully he put his unlit cigarette back into the packet.

"It would be a good idea for them," I said.

"To make us think every leak we've suffered for the last few years has been the work of Trent."

"Yes, they could wipe the slate clean like that. We put Trent behind bars and heave a sigh of relief and convince ourselves that everything is fine and dandy."

Now Dicky used the magazine to imprint red circles on his hand, examining the result with the sort of close scrutiny fortune-tellers give the palms of wealthy clients.

"There would be only one reason for doing that," said Dicky. He looked up from his hand and stared into my blank face. "They'd have to have someone placed as well as Trent . . . someone who could continue to provide them with the sort of stuff they've been getting from Trent."

"Better," I said. "Much better."

"Why better?"

"Because Moscow Center always like to get their people home. They'll spend money, arrest some poor tourist to use as hostage, or even spring from jail an agent serving a sentence to swap him. But they really try hard to get their people home."

"I could tell you a few people who now find they don't like it at 'home,' " said Dicky.

"That doesn't make any difference," I said. "The motive that Moscow Center play upon is getting them safely back to Russia . . . medals and citations and all that hero bullshit that Moscow does so well."

"And there is no sign yet that they are going to try getting Trent back to Moscow."

"And that will spoil their record," I said. "They'd have to have a really good reason for letting Trent fall off the tightrope. There's only one sort of motive they could have, and that's positioning or making more secure another agent. A better agent."

"But maybe the Russians *don't* know we're on to him."

"And maybe Trent doesn't want to go to Moscow. Yes, I thought of both those possibilities, and either could be true. But I think Trent is going to be deliberately sacrificed. And that would be very unusual."

"This other person," said Dicky. "This other agent that Moscow might already have in position . . . You're talking about someone at the very top? Am I right?"

"Look at the record, Dicky. We haven't run a good double agent in years and we haven't landed any of their important agents either. That adds up to one thing only: someone here is blowing everything we do," I said. "We've had a long string of miserable failures, and some of them were projects that Trent had no access to."

"The record can be a can of worms—we both know that," said Dicky. "If they had someone highly placed, they wouldn't be stupid enough to act on everything he told them. That would leave a trail a mile wide. They are too smart for that."

"Right," I said. "So the chances are that Moscow knows even more than the evidence suggests."

"Do you think it could be me?" said Dicky. He beat a soft but rapid tattoo on his hand.

"It's not you," I said. "Maybe it's not anyone. Maybe there is no pattern of betrayal—just incompetence."

"Why not me?" Dicky persisted. He was indignant at being dismissed so readily as a suspect.

"If you'd been a Moscow agent, you would have handled the office differently. You would have kept your secretary in that anteroom instead of moving her inside where she can see what you are doing all the time. You'd make sure you know all kinds of current matters that you don't bother to find out. You wouldn't leave top-secret documents in the copying machine and cause a hue and cry all round the building the way you did three times last year. A Moscow agent wouldn't draw that kind of attention to himself. And you probably would know enough about photography not to make such a terrible mess of your holiday snapshots the way you do every year. No, you're not a Moscow man, Dicky."

"And neither are you," said Dicky, "or you wouldn't have brought it up in the first place. So let's stick together on this one. You're going to Berlin to contact the Brahms net. Let's keep your reports of that trip confidential verbal ones. And from now on let's keep the wraps on Trent and everything we do, say, or think about him. Between us, we can keep a very tight hold on things."

"You mean, don't tell Bret?"

"I'll handle Bret. He'll be told only what he needs to be told."

"You can't suspect Bret?" Immediately I thought of Fiona. If she was having an affair with Bret, any investigation of Bret would reveal it. Then there would be the very devil of a fuss.

"It can be anyone. You've said that yourself. It could be the D-G."

"Well, I don't know, Dicky," I said.

Dicky became agitated. "Oh, I see what you're thinking. You think this might be a devious method of starving Bret of information. So that I can take over his job."

"No," I said, although that was exactly what had crossed my mind.

"Let's not kick off to a bad start," said Dicky. "We've got to trust each other. What do I have to do to make you trust me?"

"I'd want something in writing, Dicky. Something that I could produce just before they sentence me."

"Then you'll do as I suggest?"

"Yes." Now that Dicky had voiced my fears, I felt un-easy—or, rather, I felt frightened, bloody frightened. A Moscow agent in place endangered all of us, but if he was caught, maybe he'd leave the whole Department discredited and disbanded.

Dicky nodded. "Because you know I'm right. You bloody well know I'm right. There is a Moscow agent sitting right at the top of the Department."

I didn't remind Dicky that he'd started off by saying that it was my conversation with Bret that eventually made him see what I was getting at. It was better that Dicky thought it was all his own idea. Balliol men like to be creative.

There were footsteps and a knock at the door. The doctor came in. "The patient is sleeping now, Mr. Cruyer," he said respectfully. Given the Victorian setting, I had expected a man with muttonchop whiskers and stovepipe hat. But the doctor was young, younger than Dicky, a wide-eyed boy with long wavy hair that reached down to his stiff white collar, and carrying a battered black Gladstone bag that he must have inherited from some venerable predecessor.

"So what's the prognosis, Doc?" said Dicky.

The doctor put his bag down on the floor while he put his overcoat on. "Suicide is no longer the rare tragedy it once was," he said. "In Germany, they have about fourteen thousand a year, and that's more than die there in traffic accidents."

"Never mind the statistics," said Dicky. "Is our friend upstairs likely to try again?"

"Look, Mr. Cruyer, I'm just a G.P., not a soothsayer. But whether you like statistics or not, I can tell you that eight out of ten suicides speak of their intentions before-hand. If someone sympathetic had been available to your friend, he probably wouldn't have taken this desperate step. As to whether he'll try again, if you give him the care and attention he obviously requires, then you will know what he's going to do long before any quack like me gets called in to mop up the mess."

Dicky nodded as if approving the doctor's little speech. "Will he be fit by tomorrow?" said Dicky.

"By the weekend, anyway," said the doctor. "Thanks to Miss Trent." He moved aside to let Giles Trent's unmarried sister push past him into the room. "Her time as a nurse served her well. I couldn't have done a better job myself."

Miss Trent did not respond to the doctor's unctuous manner. She was in her late fifties, a tall thin figure like her brother. Her hair was waved and darkened and her eyeglasses decorated with shiny gems. She wore a cashmere cardigan and a skirt patterned in the Fraser tartan of red, blue, and green. At the collar of her cotton blouse she wore an antique gold brooch. She gave the impression of someone with enough money to satisfy her modest tastes.

The furnishing of the room was like Miss Trent: sober, middle-class, and old-fashioned. The carpets, bureau-bookcase, and skeleton clock were valuable pieces that might have been inherited from her parents, but they did not fit easily here and I wondered if these were things Giles Trent had recently disposed of.

"I used my common sense," she said, and rubbed her hands together briskly. There was a trace of the Highlands in her voice.

The young doctor bade us all good night and departed. Goodness knows what Dicky had told him but, despite his little outburst, his manner was uncommonly respectful.

"And you're the man my brother works for," said Miss Trent.

"Yes, I am," said Dicky. "You can imagine how shocked I was to hear what had happened."

"Yes, I can imagine," she said frostily. I wondered how much she guessed about her brother's work.

"But I wish you hadn't called in your local doctor," said Dicky. He gave her the card listing the Departmental emergency numbers. "Much better to use the private medical service that your brother is entitled to." Dicky smiled at her, and held his smile despite the stern look she gave both to the card and to Dicky. "We'll get your brother into a nice comfortable room with a night nurse and medical attention available on the spot." Again the smile, and again no response. Miss Trent's countenance remained unchanged. "You've done your bit, Miss Trent."

"My brother will stay here," she said.

"I've made all the arrangements now," said Dicky. He was a match for her; Dicky had the thick-skinned determination of a rhino. I was interested to watch the confrontation, but again and again my thoughts went back to Fiona. Morbidly I visualized her with Bret: talking, dancing, laughing, loving.

"Did you not hear what I said?" Miss Trent asked calmly. "My brother needs the rest. You'll not be disturbing him."

"That's a decision that neither of us need concern ourselves with," said Dicky. "Your brother has signed a contract under the terms of which his employers are responsible for his medical care. In situations like this"—Dicky paused long enough to raise an eyebrow—"your brother must be examined by one of our own medical staff. We have to think of the medical insurance people. They can be devils about anything irregular."

"He's sleeping." This represented a slight retrenchment.

"If his insurance was revoked, your brother would lose his pension, Miss Trent. Now I'm sure you wouldn't want to claim that your medical knowledge is better than that of the doctor who examined him."

"I did not hear the doctor say he could be moved."

"He wrote it out for me," said Dicky. He'd put the piece of paper between the pages of his magazine and now he leafed through it. "Yes, here we are." He passed the hand-written document to her. She read it in silence and passed it back.

"He must have written that when he first arrived."

"Yes, indeed," said Dicky.

"That was before he examined my brother. Is that what you were doing all the time before he came upstairs?"

"The ambulance will be here any moment, Miss Trent. Could I trouble you to put your brother's clothes into a case or a bag? I'll see you get it back of course." A big smile. "He'll need his clothes in a day or two, from what I understand."

"I'll go with him," she said.

"I'll phone the office and ask them," said Dicky. "But they almost always say no. That's the trouble with trying to get things done at this time of night. None of the really senior people can be found."

"I thought you were senior," she said.

"Exactly!" said Dicky. "That's what I mean. No one will be senior enough to countermand my decision."

"Poor Giles," said the woman. "That he'd be working for a man such as you."

"For a lot of the time, he was left on his own," said Dicky.

Miss Trent looked up suddenly to see what he meant, but Dicky's face was as blank as hers had been. Angrily she turned to where I was sitting holding a folded newspaper and pencil. "And you," she said. "What are you doing?"

"It's a crossword," I said. "Six letters: the clue is 'Married in opera but not in Seville.' Do you get it?"

"I know nothing of opera. I hate opera, and I know

nothing of Seville," said Miss Trent. "And if you've nothing more important than that to ask me, it's time you took yourself out of my house."

"I've nothing more important than that to ask you, Miss Trent," I said. "Perhaps your brother will be able to solve it."

Jesus, I thought, suppose Bret turned out to be a Moscow man and was trying to recruit Fiona to his cause. That would really be messy.

"It's not a crossword at all," said Miss Trent. "You're making up questions. That's the classified page."

"I'm looking for another job," I explained.

Chapter 15

DICKY HAD TRENT taken out to Berwick House, an eighteenth-century manor named after a natural son of James II and the sister of the Duke of Marlborough. It had been taken over by the War Office in 1940 and, like so many other good things seized temporarily by the government, it was never returned to its former owners.

The seclusion could hardly have been bettered had the place been specially built for us. Seven acres of ground with an ancient fifteen-foot-high wall that was now so overgrown with weeds and ivy that it looked more like a place which had been abandoned than one which was secret.

On the croquet lawn the Army had erected black creosoted Nissen huts, which now provided a dormitory for the armed guards, and two prefabricated structures, which were sometimes used for lectures when there was a conference or a special training course in the main building. But, despite these disfigurements, Berwick House retained much of its original elegance. The moat was the most picturesque feature of the estate and it still had its bulrushes, irises, and lilies. There was no sign of the underwater devices that had been added. Even the little rustic teahouse and gate lodge had been converted to guard posts with enough care to preserve their former appearance. And the infrared beams and sonic warning shields that lined the perimeter were so well hidden in the undergrowth that even the technicians who checked them did not find them of easy access.

"You've got nerve," said Giles Trent. "It's kidnapping, no matter what fancy explanations Dicky gives me."

"Your taking an overdose of sleeping tablets upset him," I said.

"You're a sardonic bastard," said Trent. We were in his cramped second-floor room: cream-painted walls, metal frame bed, and a print of Admiral Nelson dying at Trafalgar.

"You think I should feel sorry for you," I said. "And I don't feel sorry for you. That's why we are at odds."

"You never let up, do you?"

"I'm not an interrogator," I said cheerfully. "And, unlike you, I never have been. You know most of our interrogation staff, Giles. You trained some of them, according to what I saw in your file. Say whom you'd like assigned to you and I'll do everything I can to arrange that you get him."

"Give me a cigarette," said Trent. We both knew that there was no question of Trent's being permitted anywhere near one of the interrogators. Such a confrontation would start rumors everywhere, from Curzon Street to the Kremlin. I passed him a cigarette. "Why can't I have a couple of packets?" said Trent, who was a heavy smoker.

"Berwick House regulations forbid smoking in the bedrooms, and the doctor said it's bad for you."

"I don't know what you wanted to keep me alive for," said Trent in an unconvincing outburst of melancholy. He was too tall for the skimpy cotton dressing gown provided by the housekeepers' department, and he kept tugging at its collar to cover the open front of his buttonless pajama jacket. Perhaps he remembered the interrogation training report in which he'd recommended that detainees should be made to suffer "a loss of both dignity and comfort" while being questioned.

I said, "They're not keeping you fit and well for the Old Bailey, if that's what you mean."

He lit his cigarette with the matches I gave him and then hunched himself in order to take that very deep first breath that the tobacco addict craves. Only when he'd blown smoke did he say, "You think not?"

"And have you center stage for a publicity circus? You know too much, Giles."

"You flatter me. I know only tidbits. When was I a party to any important planning?" I heard in his voice a note of disappointed ambition. Had that played a part in his treachery, I wondered.

"It's tidbits the government really hate, Trent. It's tidbits that are wanted for the papers and the news magazines. That's why you can never get into the Old Bailey through the crowds of reporters. They know their readers don't want to read those long reports about the Soviet economy when they could find out how someone bugged the bedroom of the Hungarian military attaché's favorite mistress."

"If not the Old Bailey, then what—?"

"I keep telling you, Giles. Just keep your friend Chlestakov happy." I sat down on his bed. I wanted to show Trent that I was settling in for a long talk, and I knew that rumpling up his bed would irritate him. Irritation could make a man captious and indiscreet; that too was something I'd read in Trent's training report. I said, "He had a sense of humor, your contact from the Embassy, calling himself Chlestakov. That was the name of the impostor in Gogol's *The Government Inspector*. He's the man who fills his pockets with bribes, seduces the prefect's daughter, lies, cheats, and swindles all the corrupt officials of the town, and then gets away scot free as the curtain falls. He does get away scot free, doesn't he? Or does he get imprisoned at the end?"

"How should I know?"

"Gogol had a sense of humor," I persisted.

"If not the Old Bailey, what?"

"Don't shout, Giles. Well, it's obvious, isn't it? Either they will feel you've cooperated and you'll be put out to grass, and finish your days with the senior citizens of some seaside resort on the south coast . . . or you refuse to cooperate, and you will end up in the ambulance with the flashing lights that doesn't get to the emergency ward in time."

"Are you threatening me?"

"Well, I hope so," I said. "I'm trying like hell to get some sense into your brainless head."

"Chlestakov, or whatever his real name is, suspects nothing. But if you keep me locked up in this place you'll certainly change that. Where are we, by the way? How long was I unconscious?"

"Don't keep asking the same thing, Giles. You know I can't answer. The immediate question is, When are you going to start telling us the truth?" There was no reaction from him except to examine his cigarette to see how many more puffs he had left. "Let's go right back to that first interrogation. I was reading it this morning. . . ." He looked up. "Oh, yes. I keep at it, Giles. I'm afflicted with the work ethic of the lower class. In that first interrogation you said you regularly went to the opera with your sister and Chlestakov, to pass photocopied documents to him. I was interested to notice that you used the word *Treff*." I paused deliberately, wanting to see if my mention of his sister and the visits to the opera had any effect upon him. Now I watched him carefully as I prattled on. "It's a spy word, *Treff*. I can't say I remember ever using it myself, but I've often heard it used in films on TV. It has those romantic overtones that spying has for some people. *Treff:* German for 'meet,' but also for 'strike' or 'hit.' And it has those irresistible military connotations: 'battle,' 'combat,' or 'action.' It means 'line of battle' too. Did you know that, Giles?"

His vigorous puffing had already burned the cigarette down and now he was nursing it, holding it to his lips and trying to make it last. "I never thought about it."

"That's probably why Chlestakov used it on you. It made you both feel more daring, more rakish, more like men who change history. I once asked one of the KGB people why they gave their agents all those gadgets of the sort they gave you. The camera that looks like a cigarette lighter, the radio transmitter disguised as a video recorder, and the one-time pads and all that. Chlestakov never asked you to use any of that junk—the KGB almost never does. Why would they bother, when all they have to do in a free society is have one of their hoodlums take a cab across town and have a chat or spend a couple of minutes in a photocopy shop. And this KGB man told me that it gave their agents confidence. Is that what it did for you, Giles? Did it make you feel more sure of yourself to have all that paraphernalia? It was fatal, of course. When we found all that stuff under the floor-boards, you were sunk. Silly place, under the floorboards. Floorboards and attics—always the first place the searchers look. Was that Chlestakov's suggestion?"

"As a matter of fact, it was," said Trent. He got to his feet and, pulling the belt of his dressing gown tighter, went to the door. He opened it and looked along the corridor. When he came back again, he muttered something about wanting a cup of tea. He said he thought he'd heard the nurse coming, but I knew I had him worried.

"To get back to the point, Giles. You said that you got opera tickets for Chlestakov and your sister, so that the three of you would look"—I paused—"less conspicuous. That was a funny thing to say, Giles. I was thinking about that last night when I couldn't get to sleep. Less conspicuous than what, I thought. Less conspicuous than two men? It didn't make sense to me. Why would you take your sister along to the opera when you wanted to keep your meetings with Chlestakov as secret as possible? So I got up and started reading your transcript again. I found your descriptions of those visits to the opera. You quote your sister as saying that 'Mr. Chlestakov was a pleasant man, considering he was a Russian.' I suppose you said that to emphasize the fact that your sister had no particular liking for Russians."

"That's right," said Trent.

"Or even that she was prejudiced against Russians."

"Yes."

"Whatever your sister's feelings about Chlestakov and his comrades, it certainly seems from your transcript that she was aware of his name and his nationality. Am I right?"

"Yes." Trent had stopped pacing now. He stood by the little electric fire built into the fireplace and rubbed his hands together nervously. "She loved the opera. Having her with us provided a reason for the meeting."

"Your sister hasn't been entirely honest with you, Giles," I said. "Last night I invented a question that even the worst-informed opera buff in the world would have been able to answer. Your sister told me she didn't like opera. She said it vociferously. She said it as if she had some special reason for hating it."

"I don't know what you're getting at."

"Are you cold, Giles? You're shivering."

"I'm all right."

"We know the way it really happened, don't we, Giles? They got to you by means of your sister. Did Chlestakov, a nice gentleman of about the right age, go into that little wool shop your sister owns and ask help in choosing wool? For his mother? For his sister? For his daughter? Not for his wife—what had happened to her? Was he a widower? That's what they usually say. And then when the relationship had flowered—they're never in a hurry, the KGB, and I do admire that; we are always in a rush and the Americans even more so—eventually your sister suggests that you join their outings. And you say yes."

"You make it sound so carefully planned." He was angry, but his anger was not directed at me. It was not directed at anyone. It exploded with a plop, like a bullet thrown onto the fire.

"And you still want to believe it wasn't, eh? Well, I don't blame you. It must make a man angry to find he's performed his prescribed role in a play written in Moscow."

"She nursed my father for ten years. She turned down good proposals of marriage. Was I supposed to crush her little chance of happiness?"

I shook my head in disbelief. "Are you telling me that you thought it was all true? You thought Prince Charming had walked through the door of the wool shop, and your sister's foot just happened to fit the glass slipper? You thought it might be just a coincidence that he worked for the KGB and you worked for the Secret Intelligence Service?"

"He worked for the Soviet Trade Delegation," growled Trent.

"Don't make jokes like that, Giles," I said. "You'll have me fall over laughing."

"I wanted to believe it."

"I know," I said. "Just like me and Santa Claus, but one day you have to ask yourself how he gets those bloody reindeer down the chimney."

"What's the difference whether I went to the opera with them, or she came to the opera with us?"

"Now that's a question I can answer," I said. "The

D-G wouldn't want to put you into the dock, for reasons we've already discussed. But there would be no such inhibitions about putting your sister there."

"My sister?"

"With you as unnamed witness. You know how these things are done. You've read newspaper accounts of spy trials. In your circumstance, I'd have thought you'd read them with great care and attention."

"She has nothing to do with this business."

"You'd be silly to imagine that would be enough to keep her out of prison," I said.

"You swine!"

"Think it over," I said.

"I'll kill myself," he said desperately. "I'll make a good job of it next time."

"And leave your sister to face the music alone? I don't think you will," I said.

He looked so miserable that I gave him a couple of cigarettes and promised to have his clothes sent up to him. "Have your regular medical check and take your tablets or whatever it is the nurse wants. Have lunch and then we'll have a stroll in the garden."

"Garden? It's more like a jungle."

"Be ready at two o'clock."

"Be ready for what?"

"Be ready to come clean on your pal Chlestakov, and straighten out a few of the inconsistencies I've come across in your transcript."

"What inconsistencies?"

"That would be telling, wouldn't it?"

THERE WERE GAPS of blue sky, but the clouds were darkening to nimbostratus and there was rain in the air. Trent wore a short car coat with a fur collar, which he turned up around his ears. On his head was a rather smart peaked cap that had come from an expensive hatter.

He seemed ill at ease in the country, and smoked another cigarette instead of breathing the fresh air. "When will they let me out of here?" he asked. Having disposed of his cigarette, he picked up a twig, broke it into pieces, and tossed them into the stagnant-looking moat.

"You go home tomorrow."

"Is there someone here who will cash a check for me?"

"See the cashier," I told him. We walked alongside the moat until we came to a small wooden bridge and crossed it to where the shrubbery became neglected woodland. "There was a postcard from Chlestakov," I told him.

"At my home?"

"Where would you expect it to arrive?"

"He wants a meeting?"

"It says someone named Geof is having a fishing weekend. He caught four big fish of unspecified type and hopes to be back at work by two p.m. on the sixteenth of this month. I trust that means something to you."

"It means nothing to you, then?"

"It means only that the Moscow spy machine creaks along using the same antiquated ideas that have proved cumbersome for two decades or more."

"It seems to work," said Trent defiantly.

"When a huge police state devotes so much time, money, and personnel to infiltrate the open society we have in the West, it gets results."

"I don't like the Russians any more than you do," said Trent. "I was forced to work with them."

"Because they threatened to report you to our security people. Yes, you told me all that."

"You can sneer—you've no idea of what it's like."

"But you knew how to handle it, didn't you? You did more and more spying. You groveled before your pal Chlestakov and got him anything he wanted. For a man who doesn't like the Russians, you set an example of kindness and cooperation."

"I knew that it wouldn't last forever, that's why. I did many of the things they asked me but I took my time, and sometimes I said no. Sometimes I told Chlestakov that something wasn't possible. I played for time. I knew that eventually they would let me off the hook."

"Why did you believe them? Why would any intelligence service let a well-placed agent off the hook?"

"Chlestakov guaranteed that, from the start." Trent looked me in the eyes. "And I believed him. It was just to be a temporary measure—three years. He promised me that. I imposed other conditions too. He promised never to ask me about things that would endanger our own agents. He wanted general background information."

"And a few little extra specifics," I added.

"There were day-to-day things that Chlestakov needed for his official reports. He asked me about office routines and how the staff was rostered for duty. How old was Rensselaer, and did Cruyer own his house or have a mortgage? Many of his questions I couldn't answer, and some I didn't want to answer. But he told me that he had to have some such items that would impress Moscow."

"He played on your sympathy, did he?" I asked sarcastically. "If you didn't help poor old Chlestakov, he'd be moved to another assignment in some other town. And your sister wanted Chlestakov in London."

"It may sound silly—"

"It sounds squalid," I said. "It sounds stupid and ar-

rogant. Didn't you ever wonder if your treachery was worthwhile? Didn't you think your country was paying a high
price for your sister's sex life?"

"Damn you."

"Didn't you worry about being caught?"

"No."

"Did Chlestakov not discuss with you the procedures
he'd adopt if you came under suspicion? Didn't he tell you
that he'd get you out of Britain if things went sour? Didn't
he give you a number to phone if you had some security
bloodhound asking you tricky questions?"

"I've told you all that before. We never talked about the
possibility of my being caught."

"And you've told me a pack of lies, Trent. Now I want
some straight talking or you'll find yourself in another one
of our country houses, one where there won't be any walks
in the garden or cigarettes with your lunch. Do I make
myself clear?"

"You make yourself clear," said Trent. My threats
produced no real signs of fear in him—just suppressed anger. I could see a physical strength in him that matched his
mental toughness. It was not the strength of the athlete but
just the natural power of a man who'd grown up tall and
strong. It was odd to think of Trent attempting suicide, still
stranger to think of him failing to do it once his mind was
made up, but I did not pursue the subject. We picked our
way through the brambles and the bracken. There was the
crack of twigs underfoot and the squelch of mud. Once a
rabbit sprang out of the undergrowth and startled both of
us.

It was Trent who spoke. "I told them I could never go
to Moscow. I'd sooner be in prison in England than go to
Russia and die an exile. Chlestakov said that was all right.
He said it would suit them. He said it was better that I'd

told them that right from the start, because then he could make sure that I never got any information that could embarrass the KGB if said in court."

"Embarrass the KGB! Is that the word he used? They put sane dissidents into lunatic asylums, consign thousands to their labor camps, they assassinate exiles and blackmail opponents. They must surely be the most ruthless, the most unscrupulous, and the most powerful instrument of tyranny that the world has ever known. But dear old Chlestakov is frightened you might embarrass them."

"The past is past," said Trent defensively. "Tell me what you want of me now and I'll do it."

"What does the postcard mean?"

"I'm to meet Chlestakov next Tuesday evening. I must phone Monday afternoon at three to be told the details."

"I think it would be better if you cut through that one. Get hold of him and tell him it's an emergency. Tell him you were brought here and questioned after taking an overdose. Keep as near the true facts as you can."

"Shall I say you questioned me?"

"Yes," I said. "Tell him you're frightened. Tell him the game's up. Tell him you're scared, really scared."

Trent nodded.

"He'll ask you if anyone else has been questioned, and you'll say that everyone is being questioned. He'll ask you if we had any evidence, and you'll think about that and reluctantly admit that there was none."

"None at all?"

"He'll tell you that it was the overdose that made us take you into custody, and you'll admit that that's probably true. I want it so that Chlestakov is reassuring you. So you keep whining. He'll ask you who is in charge of the investigation, and you'll give him my name. He'll tell you that I'm not senior enough to make this a really important investigation.

And he'll tell you that for something on the scale that you two are doing we'd bring investigators in from outside. Got all that?"

"You've made it quite clear."

"And when the dust has settled on that exchange, you'll tell Chlestakov what a pity it is that you were silly enough to take that overdose, because you're now in a position to get something really big. Tell him you were going to write a report on the Berlin System—all the Berlin networks, every damn thing we are doing over there. That should make his mouth water."

"I've never heard of the Berlin System."

"He will have heard of it."

"But now I won't be able to get it? Is that what I tell him?"

"Softly, softly. It will take time now. You want to be quite sure you're no longer under any sort of suspicion. But this is really big stuff, tell him. This file contains all the facts and figures back for ten years and there will be all the CIA contacts and exchanges too."

"And eventually you'll give me material to pass to him?" asked Trent. "It's better if I know right at the start."

"We won't let you down, Giles. We'll give you something that will make him happy and keep comrade Chlestakov where he can get his slippers warmed."

"Keep my sister out of this."

"Okay. I'll keep her out of it. But you'd better give me two hundred percent."

"I will," he said.

We came back through the shrubbery and onto the little humpbacked bridge. Trent stopped to light another cigarette, ducking into his coat collar to shelter the flame. I said, "There's something I want to ask you. It's not important to the debriefing, I'm just curious."

His head emerged in a cloud of blue smoke. He tossed the spent matchstick into the moat. Two ducks swam quickly toward it but, discovering it wasn't edible, moved away sedately. "What then?" He was looking at the moat, with the dead leaves moving slowly on the current and the patches of weed swaying to the movement of the ducks.

"One night in September 1978—"

"In 1978 I was in Berlin," he said, as if that would mean the end of the question.

"We all were," I said. "Fiona was there, Frank was there, I was there. Dicky was working in Frankfurt and he used to come to Berlin whenever he got the chance. Bret too. I want to ask you about a radio intercept that Signals got one night during the Baader-Meinhof panic. Remember?"

"The airliner hijack—I remember that clearly enough. Frank Harrington seemed to think it had all been done to discredit him." Trent smiled. It was as near as he came to making a joke.

"There was a special inquiry about this Russian Army signal."

Trent turned to look at me. "Yes, I remember that. Frank let an American do the questioning. It was a fiasco."

"A fiasco?"

Trent shrugged but said nothing.

"You went into the main building," I said, "and into Operations at the end of your duty shift. You saw the signal ... maybe on Fiona's desk."

"The night of the big panic? Who said I was in Operations?"

"Fiona. You went up to collect her and take her home."

"Not that night, I didn't."

"Are you sure? You're not telling me you weren't permitted in Operations?"

"Well, officially I wasn't, but anyone who wore a badge

could get into the main building. I'm not denying I gate-crashed Operations regularly. But I didn't do it when I knew Frank was up there holding court and laying down the law. Hell, you know what Frank is like. I've seen him blast a senior man because he'd moved a fire extinguisher out of his office."

"Frank's a bit obsessed about fire precautions," I said. "We all know that."

"Well, he's obsessed about a few other things, including people from the annex going into Operations without an Ops pass. No, I didn't go up there that night. The word went round that Frank was throwing a fit because Bonn thought the mayor of Berlin was going to be kidnapped, and we all stayed well away from him."

"It was just a signal intercept from Karlshorst. . . ."

He nodded. "News of which got back to Karlshorst within three days, and they changed codes and wavelengths. Yes, I know all about it. That American fellow . . . Joe something—'Just call me Joe,' he kept saying—"

"Joe Brody."

"Joe Brody. He explained the whole thing."

"Let's make it off the record," I said.

"Off the record, on the record—it makes no difference. I didn't go up there that night."

"Fiona told me you did."

"Then Fiona is not telling you the truth."

"Why should she lie about it?" I said.

"That's something you'll have to ask Fiona."

"Did you get the information by some other means? I'm determined to press this point, Giles. You may as well come clean."

"Because your pal Werner Volkmann did it? And you'd like to clear him?"

"How did Werner get into Operations that night? He's

never worked in Operations. He's always been a street man."

"Werner Volkmann wasn't up there. He was Signals Security One. He brought it from Signals to Ciphers that night."

"That's all? But Werner would have to be some wizard to decipher a message while he's traveling five blocks in the back of a car."

Trent smoked reflectively. "The theory was that Werner Volkmann was hanging around the cipher room that night. He could have seen the deciphered message. Anyway, he didn't have to decipher it in order to tell the Russians that their traffic was being intercepted. He only had to recognize the heading or the footing codes and the time and the Karlshorst army transmitter identification. The Russians would know exactly what had been intercepted without Werner ever knowing what the message was."

"Do you believe it was Werner?"

"Brody is a very careful investigator. He gave everyone a chance to speak their piece. Even Fiona was interrogated. She handled the message. I never saw the report, of course, but it concluded that Volkmann was the most likely person of those who could have done it."

"I said, Did you believe Volkmann did it."

"No," said Trent. "Werner's too lazy to be a double agent—too lazy to be a single agent, from what I saw of him."

"So who could have done it?" I said.

"Frank hates Werner, you know. He'd been looking for a chance to get rid of him for ages."

"But someone still has to have done it. Unless you think Frank leaked his own intercept just as a way of putting the blame on Werner."

"It's possible."

"You can't be serious," I said.

"Why not?"

I said, "Because if Frank wants to get rid of Werner, he's only got to fire him. He doesn't have to go to all the trouble of leaking an intercept to the Russians."

"It wasn't a vitally important piece of intelligence," said Trent. "We've seen more important things than that used as *Spielzeug* just to boost the reputation of a double agent."

"If Frank wanted to fire him, he could have fired him," I repeated.

"But what if Frank wanted him discredited?"

I stared at Trent and thought about it. "I suppose you're right," I said.

"Werner Volkmann spread stories about Frank."

"Stories?"

"You've heard Werner when he's had a few beers. Werner is always able to see scandal where none exists. He had stories about Frank fiddling money from the non-account-able funds. And stories about Frank chasing the typists around the filing cabinets. I suppose Frank got fed up with it. You keep telling stories like that and finally people are going to start believing them. Right?"

"I suppose so," I said.

"Someone leaked it," said Trent. "If it wasn't Volkmann or Frank, then Moscow had someone inside Operations that night. And it certainly wasn't me."

"God knows," I said, as if I'd lost interest in the mystery. But now I was sure that the Karlshorst intercept was vitally important, because it was the only real slip Moscow's well-placed man had made.

"What do you think will happen?" said Trent. What was going to happen to him, he meant.

"You've had a long time in this business," I reminded him. "Longer than I have. You know how these things work. Do you know how many people just as guilty as you are

have retired from the service with an unconditional pardon
and a full pension?"

"How many?" said Trent. He knew I couldn't answer
and that amused him.

"Plenty," I said. "People from Five, people from Six, a
couple of Special Branch people, and those three from Chel-
tenham that you helped to interrogate last year."

Trent said nothing. We watched four men as they came
out of the house and went down the gravel path toward the
gate lodge. One of them skipped half a pace in order to get
into step with the others. They were security guards, of
course. Only such men are that anxious to keep in step with
their fellows. "I hate prisons," he said. He said it conversa-
tionally, as a man might remark upon his dislike of dinner
parties or sailing.

"You've never been inside, have you?"

"No."

"It's not like this, believe me. But let's hope it won't
come to that—not for you, not for anyone."

"That's called 'leaving the door open,' " said Trent. It
was a subheading in his training report.

"Don't dismiss it on that account," I said. But we both
knew that Trent had written, "Promise the interviewee anything. Promise him freedom. Promise him the moon. He'll
be in no position to argue with you afterward."

Chapter 16

People made jokes about "the yellow submarine," but Fiona seemed to like going down to the Data Centre, three levels below Whitehall. So did I sometimes, for a brief spell. Down there, where the air was warmed, dehydrated, filtered, and purified and where the sky was always light blue, you had the feeling that life had temporarily halted to give you a chance to catch your breath and think your own unhurried thoughts. That's why the staff down there are so bloody slow. And why if I wanted anything urgently, I went down and got it myself.

The Data Centre can only be entered through the Foreign Office. Since this entrance was used by so many others, it was difficult for enemy agents to identify and target our computer staff. The Centre occupied three underground levels: one for the big computers, one for the software and its servicing staff, and the lowest and most secret level for data.

I went through the security room on the ground floor. I spent the usual three minutes while the uniformed guard got my picture, and a physical description, on his identity-check video screen. He knew me of course, the old man on the desk, but we went through the procedures just the same. The higher your rank, the longer it took to satisfy the security check: the men on the desk were more anxious to impress the senior staff. I'd noticed the way some of the junior employees seemed to get past with no more than a nod or a wink.

He punched a code to tell the computer I was entering the Centre, and smiled. "Here we are, sir." He said it as if he'd been more impatient than I had. "Going to see your wife, sir?"

"It's our anniversary tonight," I told him.

"Then it'll be champagne and roses, I suppose."

"Two lagers and an Indian take-away," I said.

He laughed. He preferred to believe I wore these old suits because I was a spy.

Fiona was on level 3 in Secret Data. It was a very big open room like a well-lit car park. Along one wall, the senior staff had been allotted spaces marked out by means of a tiny rug, a waist-high bookcase, and a visitor's chair for visitors who never came. There was endless metal shelving for spools and, facing that, some disk-drive units. Underfoot was the special anti-static carpet, its silver-gray color reflecting the relentless glare of the fluorescent lighting.

She didn't see me as I came along the glass-sided corridor that ran the length of the Centre. I pushed through the transparent door and looked around. Apart from Fiona there was no one about. But there was a hum of electricity and the constantly whirring disk drives. Then came the sudden whine of a machine going into high speed before modulating into a steady pattern of uneven heartbeats.

Fiona was standing at one of the machines, waiting for it to whine down to a complete standstill. Then she pressed the button, and a drawer purred open. She dropped a cover over the disk and snapped the catches before closing the machine again. It was Fiona's boast that she could stand in for any one of the Data Centre staff. "That way they can't tell you it's a long job, or any of the other fairy stories they invent to get home early."

I went to the nearby terminal, a typewriter keyboard with a swivel display screen and printer. There was a roller-foot typist's chair pulled close to it, and a plastic bin spilling over with the wide, pale green paper of the terminal's printer.

"You remembered," said Fiona. Her face lit up as she saw me. "You remembered. That's wonderful."

"Happy anniversary, darling," I said.

"You know we're going to the school to watch our son run his race?"

"Even that I remembered." It was a convention of our marriage that I was the one who was overworked and forgetful, but Fiona gave more hours to her work than I ever did. She was always making mysterious journeys and having long late meetings with people she did not identify. At one time I'd simply felt proud of having a wife senior enough to be needed so much. Now I was no longer sure of her. I wondered who she was with and what she did on those nights when I was alone in my cold bed.

She kissed me. I held her tight and told her how much I loved her, and how I missed her when we were apart. A girl wheeling a trolley loaded with brown boxes of new magnetic tapes saw us, and thought she'd discovered some illicit romance. I winked at her and she smiled nervously.

Fiona began tidying the papers spread across her metal desk; behind her, shelves of files, books, and operator manuals were packed to capacity. She had to move a pile of papers before she could sit down. She began to speak, but changed her mind and waited as a nearby tape suddenly went into high speed and then ran down to silence. "Did you phone Nanny and tell her to give the children early dinner?"

"She was doing something in the garden. I told Billy to tell her."

"You know how Billy gets everything mixed up. I wish

she would stay with the children. I don't want her doing something in the garden."

"She was probably doing something about the children's clothes."

"We have a perfectly good spin dryer," said Fiona.

Nanny preferred to hang the clothes to dry in the garden, but I decided not to mention this. The dryer was an endless source of disagreement between the two women. "Phone her again if you like," I said.

"Are you going to be long?"

"No. Just one personnel printout," I said.

"If you're going to be here for half an hour or more, there's work I could do."

"Ten minutes," I said. I sat down at the terminal and entered "Open." The machine purred and the screen lit up with "Please type your name, grade, and department." I typed that and the screen went blank while the computer checked my entry against the personnel file. Then "Please insure that no other person can see the screen or the console. Now type your secret access number." I complied with that request and the screen said, "Please type the date and time." I did it. The machine requested, "Today's code number, please." I entered it.

"What time does this sports show begin?" Fiona called across to me. She was hunched over her desk giving all her attention to the task of painting her nails Passion Red.

The screen said, "Program?"; I responded with "Kagob" to enter the KGB section. "Seven-thirty, but I thought we'd have a quick drink in that pub opposite."

The same girl who'd seen us kissing came past carrying a huge bundle of computer output clutched to her bosom. There were plenty of other boxes for secret waste, but she obviously wanted to have a closer look at the lovers.

I typed in the other codes, "Redland Overseas" and the

name "Chlestakov," and the screen asked, "Screen only?" It was a "default query," which meant the material was typed on the printer unless the operator specified otherwise. I pressed START.

The terminal made a loud buzzing noise. It was running background, which meant it was rejecting millions of words that were not about Chlestakov. Then suddenly the printer cleared its throat, hiccuped twice, and rattled off four lines of text before the machine settled into background again. "And don't tug at the printout," Fiona called to me. "The new lot of continuous tracking paper has got something wrong with the sprocket holes. We've had three printouts jam this afternoon."

"I never tug at the printout."

"If it doesn't feed, dial oh-three on the internal for the duty engineer."

"And say goodbye to being anywhere before midnight."

"Don't tug at it and it won't jam," she said. She still hadn't raised her eyes from peering closely at her nails.

The printer suddenly came to life and produced a long section of data on Chlestakov, the daisy-wheel whizzing backward and forward. It always amazed me the way it printed every second line backward. It was a little like Leonardo da Vinci mirror writing. No doubt its designers wanted to make human operators feel inferior. The run ended with a little tattoo of end codes to show that all the relevant data had been searched, and the printer was silent. The red light on the console came on to SYSTEMS BUSY, which is computer language for doing nothing.

Fiona walked from her desk waving her extended fingers at me in a manner I would have regarded as threatening had I not seen her drying her nails before. "You had nice weather for your jaunt to Berwick House. You should have taken the Porsche."

"Everybody expects such big tips when they see a car like that."

"How was poor Giles?"

"Feeling sorry for himself."

"Did he take a lethal dose or was it a cry for help?"

"A cry for help? You've been mixing with sociologists again."

"But was it?"

"Who can tell? The bottle of tablets was empty, but it might have only had a couple of tablets in it. Thanks to his sister's quick action, he vomited before the tablets all dissolved."

"And the doctor didn't say?"

"He was only a kid, and Dicky had obviously filled his head with dark hints about the secret service. I don't think he knew what he was doing. It was Trent's sister who did the medical treatment. She only called in the doctor because nurses—even ex-nurses—are brainwashed to believe that they must have a doctor to nod at them while they make the decisions and do all the work."

"Do you think he'll try again?" said Fiona. She blew on her nails.

"Not if he knows what's good for his sister. I told him I'd make sure she stood trial if he did a bolt in any direction."

"You hate him, don't you? It's a long time since I saw you like this. I'll bet you scared the daylights out of poor Giles."

"I doubt that very much."

"You don't know how frightening you can be. You make all those bad jokes of yours and your face is like a block of stone. That's what made me fall for you, I suppose. You were so damned brutal."

"Me?"

"Don't keep saying, 'Me?' darling. You know what a tough bastard you can be."

"I hate the Giles Trents of this world. And if that's what you call being tough, I wish like hell there were more tough people like me. I hate the Communists and the stupid sods in this country who play their game and think they are just being 'caring, sharing, wonderful people.' I've seen them at close quarters. Never mind the smooth-talking little swine that come over here to visit the Trades Union Congress or give talks on international friendship. I've seen them back where they come from, back where they don't have to wear the plastic smiles or hide the brass knuckles."

"You can't run the Soviet Union as though it were the Chelsea Flower Show, darling."

I grunted. It was her usual reply to my tirades about the KGB. Fiona, for all her talk of social justice and theories about alleviating Third World poverty, was happy to let the end justify the means when it suited her arguments. In that I could recognize the teachings of her father.

"But Trent's not really KGB material, is he?" she said.

"They told Trent that they'd only need him for three years."

"I suppose that was just to make it easier for him."

"Trent believed it."

She laughed. "I can't imagine that Trent's saying he believed it cut much ice with you."

"He's not a complete idiot. I think they meant it."

"Why? How would that make sense?"

"And his KGB contact told him to put that radio under the floorboards. That slipped out when we were talking— I'm sure *that* was true."

"So what?"

"Floorboards? I'd only tell one of my agents that if I was hoping he'd get caught. You might as well take a full page in the local paper as hide a clandestine radio under the floor."

"I'm still not following you."

"They didn't give Trent any goodbye codes," I said.

"What are they?"

"Numbers he can phone if he's being followed, or his home has been burgled, or he finds a security man going through his desk one morning when he arrives a bit early. They didn't even promise to get him away if anything went wrong."

"Can you see Giles Trent living in Moscow? Really, darling!"

"KGB procedures are laid down in Moscow. They don't let any local man decide what he thinks will suit the personality of the agent he runs. You don't understand the bloody Russians. *All* KGB agents have goodbye codes."

"Perhaps they have decided to change things."

"They never change anything."

She touched a painted nail very carefully to be sure it was dry. "I'm ready when you are."

"Okay." I got to my feet and read the Chlestakov data again.

"Don't be tempted to take that computer printout from the building," she warned. "Security will go mad."

"On our wedding anniversary? I wouldn't dare." I fed the computer printout into a shredder and watched the paper worms tumble into the clear plastic bag.

"I'll buy it," said Fiona. "Why no goodbye codes or whatever they are?"

"I think Trent has been prepared as a scapegoat. I think they wanted us to catch him. I think they know everything we're saying to him."

"Why?"

"The lack of any preparations for escape, the mention of

three years, and then having him hide the radio—a radio he didn't need and was never trained to operate—under the floor. I think he was set up."

"What for?"

"The only reason I can think of is to hide the fact that they have someone amongst us already."

I was expecting her to laugh, but she didn't; she frowned. "You're serious, aren't you?"

"Someone at the top."

"Have you told Bret this theory?"

"Dicky thinks we should keep it to ourselves."

"So Dicky's in on it."

"Whatever's wrong with Dicky, no one could believe he might be a double agent. The Russians would never employ a twit like him. So I've agreed to keep everything on Trent confidential."

"Everything?"

"Everything relevant."

She moved her head as if trying to see me in a new light. "You're hiding material from Bret? Why, that means you're hiding it, in effect, from the D-G and the committee."

"In effect, yes."

"You've gone crazy, darling. They have a name for what you're doing. They call it treason."

"It's Dicky's idea."

"Oh, that's different," she said with heavy irony. "If it's Dicky's idea, that's all you need say."

"You think it's that crazy?"

She shook her head as if lost for words. "I can't believe all this is happening. I can't believe I'm standing here and listening to you spout this absolute and ridiculous nonsense."

"Let's go and see our son win the Olympics," I said.

She said, "Poor little Billy, he's convinced he's going to win."

"But you're not," I said.

"He's a sweet child," said Fiona, "but I'm sure he'll finish last."

"You don't have a drinks cabinet on this level, do you?"

"No alcohol in the yellow submarine, by order of the D-G," said Fiona.

"For my next birthday," I said, "a hip flask."

Fiona pretended she hadn't heard.

Chapter 17

WE GOT TO BILLY'S SCHOOL at 7:45 so I went inside without that drink I'd promised myself. It was a typical state school, designed in the sixties by the sort of architect who worked with the radio going. It was a giant shoebox that would have been totally featureless but for the cracks in the hardboard and the rust dribbles down the walls.

This evening of sporting events took place in a huge glass-fronted building adjoining the exercise yard. About three dozen dutiful parents, having purchased programs, were perched on metal folding chairs at the chilliest end of the gymnasium. The young bearded headmaster, wearing the colorful and voluminous scarf of some provincial university, told us to hurry because we were late and reminded us that it was forbidden to walk on the wooden floor without gym shoes. Since I had neglected to equip myself with the right shoes, I walked around the gym while the senior boys performed knee bends to the sound of Pink Floyd on a tape recorder that hissed.

There was no room for us with the other parents, so I helped Fiona onto a vaulting horse and got up there alongside her. The headmaster gave me a disapproving look, as if he had decided I was the sort of man who might walk back across his polished floor.

The first event was the junior relay race. There was a lot of shouting, shoving, and jumping up and down in mock excitement. Fiona put her head close to mine and said, "I was thinking about Giles Trent. Was he expecting his sister to call, that night he took the overdose?"

"They both say no, but maybe they are both lying."

"Why would they lie?"

"Him because he's too public-school-macho to admit that he'd pull a stunt like that."

"Why would the sister lie?"

"If she admitted that Trent was expecting her, she'd have to start wondering whether that 'cry for help' was her brother's way of telling her to lay off."

"A drastic way of telling her, wasn't it? Couldn't he tell her over a cup of tea?"

"His sister is a formidable lady. She is not the sort of woman who would admit that her brother need sell his soul to provide her with a man. She would have grunted and shrugged and ignored whatever he said."

"But by that time serious pressure was coming from the Department and from his Russian contact. Did he think a suicide attempt would make the Russians lay off?"

"Maybe," I said. I watched the race. Good grief, the energy those kids had; it made me feel very old.

"Or did he think the suicide attempt would make the Department lay off?" Fiona had started thinking about the Giles Trent problem now that it had sexual and emotional aspects. I guess all women are like that.

"I don't know, darling," I said. "I'm just guessing."

"Your guesses can be pretty good."

"How many married men get an accolade like that from their wives?"

"I'm just lulling you into a false sense of security," she said.

She looked up to watch the hurdles being positioned for the next race. The bearded headmaster was well in evidence. He had a tape measure. He checked the position of everything and marked his approval or disapproval with nods or headshakes. Fiona watched the children parade until she was quite sure that Billy was not anywhere in these teams. Then she returned to the subject of Trent. "Giles did it for the sake of his sister. He didn't have to get into it at all, did he? You said the Russian targeted him through the sister."

"But don't imagine that they hit him when he was cold. Don't think the KGB would go to all the trouble they went to without being confident he would buy their proposition."

"I didn't think of it like that."

"You think a woman goes after a married man just on the off chance that he's fed up with his wife? No, she checks out her chances of success." I'd almost said Tessa but I'd recovered myself just in time.

"What sort of signs would she look for?"

"Some people find it fascinating to think about doing the worst thing they can think of. What would it be like to murder someone? What would it be like to post this stuff off to the Russians? How would it feel to have a vulgar noisy mistress tucked away in a flat in Bayswater? At first they toy with it because it's so crazy. But one day that impossible idea starts to take shape. How would I start to do it? they ask themselves, and step by step the practical planning begins."

"I take due note of the fact that you haven't told me what signs a woman looks for when she's after a married man."

I smiled and applauded the winning hurdler.

She didn't let the subject drop. "You think Giles got beyond the fantasy stage even before the Russians approached his sister?" she asked.

"Maybe not, but he didn't come running into the security office on the day he discovered exactly what his sister's boyfriend did for a living."

"Because he'd thought about it?"

"Everyone thinks about it," I said.

"Mistresses, or selling secrets?"

"It's only human to think about such things."

"So where did Giles go wrong?" she asked.

"He envisaged himself sinning and found he could live with that image of himself." I took out my cigarettes but the headmaster came over and, smiling, shook his head, so I put them away again.

"And you couldn't live with the image of yourself snuggled up with the noisy girl in Bayswater?"

"You can't have everything," I said. "You can't have the fantasies *and* the reality. You can't have the best of both worlds."

"You've just blown a hole in the Liberal Party election platform."

"No one can serve two masters. You'd think even a bean-brained public-school man like Trent would have known that."

"There was never anything between Bret and me," said Fiona, and touched my hand.

"I know," I said.

"Really know?"

"Yes, really know." I wanted to believe it. It was a failing in me, I suppose.

"I'm so pleased, darling. I couldn't bear the idea of you worrying about me." She turned to look into my eyes. "And Bret, of all people . . . I could never fancy him. When is Billy coming on?"

I looked at the program. "It must be the next but one: the junior obstacle race."

I leaned closer to Fiona and whispered how much I loved her. I could smell the faint perfume of her shampoo as I nuzzled against her hair.

"No one thought it would last," she said. She hugged me. "My mother said I'd leave you within six months. She even had a room ready for me right up until Billy was born. Did you know that?"

"Yes."

"Tessa was the only one who encouraged me to marry you. She could see how much I loved you."

"She could see how you wrapped me around your finger."

"What a lovely thought." She laughed at the idea of it. "I've always been frightened that some clever little lady will come along and find out how to wrap you around her finger, but I've seen no sign of it so far. The truth of it is, darling, that you're unwrappable. You're just not a ladies' man."

"What does a ladies' man have to do?"

"You can't be bothered with women. I never worry about you leading a double life. You'd never go to all the trouble needed to tuck that 'vulgar noisy mistress' away in Bayswater."

"You sound like Giles Trent. The other day he told me that Werner Volkmann could never be a double agent because he was too lazy."

"No one could accuse you of being lazy, my darling, but you certainly don't go out of your way to be nice to women— not to me, not to Tessa, or even your mother."

I found these criticisms unreasonable. "I treat women just as I treat men," I said.

"For goodness' sake, my darling thickheaded husband. Can't you understand that women don't want to be treated just like you treat men? Women like to be fussed over and cherished. When did you ever bring home a bunch of flowers or a surprise gift? It never occurs to you to suggest we have a weekend away."

"We're always having weekends away."

"I don't mean with Uncle Silas and the children—that's just to give Nanny a break. I mean a surprise weekend in Paris or Rome, just the two of us in some lovely little hotel."

I never cease to wonder about what goes on in a woman's brain. "Whenever I've asked you to come along on a trip, you say you've got too much work to do."

"I'm not talking about going with you on one of those damned jobs of yours. You think I want to walk around Berlin while you go off to see some old crony?"

"I'll have to go back there," I said.

"I heard Dicky talking to Bret about it."

"What did they say?"

It was typical of Fiona's caution that she looked around to be quite sure that no one was in earshot. She needn't have bothered. Some of the parents were talking to the head, some were out in the dark windswept yard calling for their children, while the rest remained in their seats stoically watching the races. "The D-G apparently said there was no one else experienced enough to send. Dicky said that they'd soon have to wind up the Brahms net. Bret pretended to agree, but Bret won't survive as Department head without his Brahms Four source. But, for the time being, Dicky and Bret have compromised on the idea that they'll squeeze a couple of more years out of him. They think you're the only person who could persuade the network to keep working a little while longer."

"Keep them working until Bret is retired and Dicky is moved to another desk. Is that what they mean?"

"I daresay it's at the back of their minds. When the Brahms Four material stops, there'll be a big reshuffle. Someone will have to take the blame. Even if it's just a stroke of fate, they'll still want someone to take the blame."

"I'm not convinced the Brahms Four stuff is so bloody earth-shaking," I said. "Now and again he's given us some juicy items but a lot of it is self-evident economic forecasts."

"Well, Bret guards it with his life, so I don't suppose either of us has seen more than a fraction of the stuff he sends."

"Even Bret admits that a lot of his messages are simply corroboration of intelligence we already have from other sources. From Brahms Four we usually have good notice of the Soviet grain deals, but often it arrives after we know the new shipping contracts the Russians have signed. The type of ships they charter always gives us clear notice of how much grain they'll buy from Argentina and how much they'll be shipping via the Gulf of Mexico. We didn't need Brahms Four telling us about the Moscow Narodny Bank buying Argentine peso futures. But what did he tell us about the Russian tanks going into Afghanistan? Not a damned whisper."

"But, darling, you're so unreasonable. The Russians don't need any help from their state bank in order to invade Afghanistan. Brahms Four can only give us banking intelligence."

"You think the Russians weren't pouring money into Kabul for weeks before the soldiers went in? You think they weren't buying intelligence and goodwill in Pakistan? And the sort of people you buy in that part of the world don't take Diners Club cards. The KGB must have used silver and gold coins in the sort of quantity that only a bank can supply." They were placing boxes and rubber tires on the floor for the next race.

"Is this Billy?" said Fiona. "What's all that for?"

"Yes, this is Billy. He's in the obstacle race." Obstacle race! Only a son of mine would choose that.

She said, "Anyway, darling, you and I both know it doesn't matter how good the Brahms material is. That source of information, from somewhere in the Soviet-controlled banking world, is the sort of intelligence work that even a politician can understand. You can't explain to the Minister about electronic intelligence gathering, or show him pictures taken by spy satellites. It's too complicated, and he knows that all that technological hardware belongs to the Americans. But tell the Minister that we have a man inside the Moscow Narodny and on their Economics Intelligence Committee, and he'll get excited. Form a committee to process that intelligence, and the Minister can talk to the Americans on his own terms. We all know Bret has built an empire on the strength of the Brahms source, so don't start saying it's anything less than wonderful. Or you'll become very unpopular."

"That would be a new experience for me."

She smiled that sweet sort of smile that she used only when she was sure I'd ignore her advice, and said, "I mean really unpopular."

"I'll take a chance on that," I said angrily. "And if your friend Bret doesn't like my opinions, he can get stuffed." I overreacted of course. She knew I was still suspicious of her relationship with Bret. It would have been far smarter just to make soft noises and let her think I suspected nothing.

Then I spotted Billy. I waved but he was too shy to wave back; he just smiled. He was marching around the gym with all the other juniors. I suppose even clumsy boys like Billy were allowed in the obstacle race.

It was a relay race and for some unexplained reason Billy was first in his team. He scrambled through two rubber tires, zigzagged around a line of plastic cones, and then climbed on a box before beginning his final sprint back to his number 2. He skidded at speed and went full length.

When he got up, his face was covered with blood, and blood was spattered on his white vest. His teammates were shouting at him and he wasn't quite sure which way he was facing. I knew the feeling very well.

"Oh, my God," said Fiona.

I prevented her jumping down and running to him. "It's just his nose," I said.

"How do you know?" said Fiona.

"I just know," I said. "Leave him alone."

Chapter 18

Rolf Mauser always turned up where and when he was least expected. "Where the hell have you sprung from?" I said, unhappy to be dragged out of bed by a phone call in the early hours of the morning. Unhappy too to be standing ankle-deep in litter, drinking foul-tasting coffee from a machine in London's long-distance bus station at Victoria.

"I couldn't wait until morning, and I knew you lived nearby." I'd known Rolf Mauser since I was a schoolboy and he was an unemployed onetime Wehrmacht captain who scratched a living from the Berlin black market and ran errands for my father. Now he was sixty-six years old but he'd not changed much since the last time we'd met, when he was working as a barman in Lisl Hennig's hotel.

"Your son Axel said you were in East Berlin."

"In a manner of speaking, I still am," said Rolf. "They let us old people out nowadays, you know."

"Yes, I know. Have you seen Axel? He worries about you, Rolf."

"Rolf now, is it? I remember a time when I was called Herr Mauser."

"I can remember a time when you were called Hauptmann Mauser," I reminded him. It was my father who, noting that Mauser's promotion to captain had come only

three weeks before the end of the war, had addressed him as
Hauptmann Mauser. Rolf had glowed with pride.

"Hauptmann Mauser." He smiled dutifully, the sort of
smile that family groups provide for the amateur photogra-
pher. "Yes, your father knew how to play on a young man's
vanity."

"Did he, Rolf?"

He heard the resentment in my voice and didn't reply.
He looked around the bus station as if seeing it for the first
time. He wore a brown leather overcoat of the sort that they
sold on East Berlin's Unter den Linden in the shops where
only rich Western tourists could afford to buy. Like so many
Germans, he liked his clothes tightly fitted. The belted overcoat on this big round-shouldered man, and the pointed
nose that twitched each time he spoke, made him look like
an affluent armadillo standing on its hind legs. His face was
round and he had pale skin and tired eyes: the legacy of
years of dark bars, late hours, tobacco smoke, and alcohol.
There was little sign now of that tough young artillery
officer who won the oak leaves to his Knight's Cross at
Vinnitsa on the River Bug in the Red Army's spring offen-
sive of 1944.

"Going far, Rolf?"

"Did you bring everything?"

"You've got your goddamned nerve, Rolf."

"You owe me a favor, Bernd."

A bus arrived, the sound of its diesel engine amplified
by the low entrance arch. It backed carefully into its desig-
nated position under the signs and half a dozen weary trav-
elers scrambled down to get their luggage, yawning and
scratching as if not yet fully awake. "You'll be conspicuous
in your Loden hat and leather coat once you get into the
British hinterland," I told Mauser. He didn't react to this

advice. The driver of the bus got out and wound the roller to change the destination plate to Cardiff.

"Give me the packet, Bernd. Save the lectures for young Werner." He twitched his nose. "Getting nervous about this sort of thing? I don't remember you getting nervous in the old days."

"What the hell do you want with a gun, Rolf?" I felt like saying that I was only nervous because I didn't trust Rolf to know what he was doing with a gun. In the "old days" Rolf had run messages and told stories of his exploits both in the war and after. God only knows what dark deeds he might once have committed. But for many years he'd done little more than hide letters and packets under his bar counter and give them to strangers who knew the right password.

"Did I ask you what you wanted with the motorcycle that day in Pankow?" he said.

It seemed a silly comparison but Rolf obviously thought it appropriate. Funny that he'd not mentioned some of the other favors he'd done for me. He hadn't risked his life but he'd risked his job for me more than once, and laying down a job for a friend comes high on my friendship scale.

He said, "Do I get the briefcase or are you going to unpack it all here in the middle of the bus station?" As a child, I'd been intimidated by Rolf Mauser's appearance and by the big bushy eyebrows that turned up at the outer ends to give him a fierce demonic appearance. When I'd realized that he brushed his straggly eyebrows upward to keep them out of his eyes, my fears of Rolf Mauser had vanished and I saw in him a lonely old man who liked to wallow in memories of his youth.

"Suppose I told you I had no money?" I said.

Behind us a thin Black wielded a gigantic broom, sweeping fried-chicken bones, ice-cream wrappers, and brightly colored litter before him. Rolf turned and tossed his empty paper cup into the heap as the man brushed it slowly past us. "All British senior staff have five hundred pounds in used notes available at home at all times. That's been the regulations for years now, Bernd. We both know that."

"The briefcase is for you." I passed it to him.

"You were always considerate, Bernd."

"I don't like it, Rolf."

"Why?"

"What do you want with a gun, Rolf?"

"Who taught you to crack a safe?"

"That wasn't a safe, Rolf. That strongbox where they kept the school reports could have been opened with a knife and fork."

"My son Axel said you were a good friend, Bernd."

"Did you need Axel to confirm it, Rolf?"

"We both know you are a good friend."

"Or did you decide I was the only one fool enough to give you money and a gun and ask no questions?"

"Good friend. I appreciate it. We all do."

"Who are 'we all'?"

Rolf Mauser smiled. "We all do, Bernd: me, Axel, Werner, and the others. And now we owe you something."

"Maybe," I said cautiously. Rolf was the sort of man whose favors could get you into a lot of trouble.

He put the briefcase down on the ground and held it upright between his ankles while he undid his magnificent leather coat. When he rebuttoned it, he belted it more tightly as if he hoped that would make him warmer.

"Who is Brahms Four, Bernd? What's his name?"

"I can't tell you, Rolf."

"Is he still in Berlin?"

"No one knows," I said. It wasn't true of course, but it was the nearest I could go.

"Rumors say Brahms Four is not working for you any longer. We want to know if he's left Berlin."

"What does it matter to you?" I asked.

"Because when Brahms Four is kaput you'll pay off the Brahms network and close us down. We need to know in advance. We need to get ready."

I looked at him for a moment without replying. Rolf Mauser's participation in Brahms was—as far as my information went—recent and minimal. Then the penny dropped: "Because of your rackets, you mean? Because London is supplying you with things you need to keep Werner's import-export racket functioning?"

"You haven't reported that, have you, Bernd?"

"I have enough of my own problems without trying to find more," I said. "But London Central aren't here to help you run rackets in East Germany, or anywhere else."

"You didn't always talk that way, Bernd. I remember a time when everyone agreed that Brahms was the best source in Berlin System. The best by far."

"Times change, Rolf."

"And now you'd throw us to the wolves?"

"What are you saying?"

"You think we don't know that you have a KGB spy here in London Central. Brahms net is going to be blown any minute."

"Who says so? Did Werner say it? Werner is not a member of the network. He's not employed by the Department at all. Do you know that?"

"It doesn't matter who said it," replied Rolf.

"So it was Werner. And we both know who told him, don't we, Rolf?"

"I don't know," said Rolf staunchly, although his eyes said differently.

"That bloody wife of his. That bloody Zena," I said. I

cursed Frank Harrington and his womanizing. I knew Frank too well to suspect him of revealing to her anything really important. But I'd seen enough of Zena Volkmann to know that she'd trade on her relationship with Frank. She'd make herself sound important. She'd feed Werner any wild guesses, rumors, and half-truths. And Werner would believe anything he heard from her.

"Zena worries about Werner," said Rolf defensively.

"You must be very stupid, Rolf, if you really believe that Zena worries about anything but herself."

"Perhaps that's because no one else worries about her enough," said Rolf.

"You'll break my bloody heart, Rolf," I said.

I'm afraid we parted on a note of acrimony. When I looked back, he'd still not boarded the bus. I suspected that he had no intention of boarding any bus. Rolf Mauser could be a devious devil.

Chapter 19

SOME OF the most secret conversations I'd ever heard took place not in any of the debugged "silent rooms" under the Department's new offices but in restaurants, St. James's clubs, or even in the backs of taxicabs. So there was nothing surprising about Dicky Cruyer's suggestion that I go to his house about ten "for a confidential chat."

A man repairing the doorbell let me in. Dicky's wife, Daphne, was working at home that morning. A large layout pad occupied most of the corner table in the front room. A jam jar of colored felt-tip pens was balanced on the TV, and scattered across the sofa were scribbled roughs for advertising a new breakfast food. Daphne's art-school training was everywhere evident: brightly painted bits of folk art and crudely woven cushion covers, a primitive painting of Adam and Eve over the fireplace, and a collection of matchbox covers displayed in an antique cabinet. The only personal items in the room were photos: a picture of the Cruyers' two sons amid a hundred other grim-faced, gray-uniformed boys in front of the huge Gothic building that was their boarding school; and, propped on the mantelshelf, a large shiny color photo of Dicky's boat. There was some very quiet Gilbert and Sullivan leaking out of the hi-fi. Dicky was humming.

Through the "dining area" I could see Daphne in the kitchen. She was pouring hot milk into large chinaware mugs.

Looking up, she said *"Ciao!"* with more than her usual cheerfulness. Did she know her husband had been having an affair with my sister-in-law? Her hair was that sort of straggly mess that only comes from frequent visits to very expensive hairdressers. From what little I knew about women, that might have been a sign that she did know about Dicky and Tessa.

"Traffic bad?" said Dicky as I threw my raincoat onto a chair. It was his subtle way of saying I was late. Dicky liked to have everyone on the defensive right from the start. He'd learned such tactics in a book about young tycoons. I secretly borrowed it from his office bookshelf one weekend so that I could read it too.

"No," I lied. "It only took me nine minutes."

He smiled and I wished I'd not got into the game.

Daphne brought cocoa on a dented tin tray advertising Pears soap. My cup celebrated the silver jubilee of King George V. Dicky complimented Daphne on the cocoa and pressed me to have a biscuit, while she gathered up her pens and paper and retreated upstairs. I sometimes wondered how they managed together; secret intelligence was a strange bedfellow for a huckster. It was better to be married to a Departmental employee: I didn't have to ask her to leave the room every time the office came through on the phone.

He waited until he heard his wife go upstairs. "Did I tell you Brahms network was going to fall to pieces?"

It was, of course, a rhetorical question: I was expected to confirm that he'd predicted that very thing with uncanny accuracy a million times or more, but I looked at him straight-faced and said, "You may have done, Dicky. I'm not sure I remember."

"For Christ's sake, Bernard! I told Bret only two days ago."

"So what's happened?"

"The people have scattered. Frank is here."

"Frank is here?"

"Don't just repeat what I say. Yes, dammit, Frank is here."

"In London?"

"He's upstairs taking a bath and cleaning up. He arrived last night and we've been up half the night talking." Dicky was standing at the fireplace with fingers tapping on the mantelshelf and one cowboy boot resting on the brass fender.

"Aren't you going into the office?" I cradled the cocoa in my hands, but it wasn't very hot so I drank it. I hate cold cocoa.

Dicky tugged at the gold medallion hanging around his neck on a fine chain. It was a feminine gesture and so was the artful smile with which he answered my question.

I said, "Bret will know Frank is in London. If you are missing from the office, he'll put two and two together."

"Bret can go to hell," said Dicky.

"Are you going to drink your cocoa?"

"It's real chocolate, actually," said Dicky. "Our neighbors across the road brought it back from Mexico and showed Daphne how the Mexicans make it."

I recognized Dicky's way of saying he didn't like it. "Here's health," I said, and drank his cocoa too. His mug was decorated with rodents named Flopsy, Mopsy, Cottontail, and Peter. It was smaller than mine; I suppose Daphne knew he didn't much like cocoa the way the Mexicans fixed it.

"Yes, Bret can go to hell," repeated Dicky. The gas fire wasn't on. He gently kicked the artificial log with the tip of his boot.

If Dicky was hell-bent on a knock-down-drag-out fight, my money would be on Bret Rensselaer. I didn't say that; I didn't have to. "This is all part of your plan to keep Bret out of things?"

"Our plan," said Dicky. "*Our* plan."

"I still haven't had that confidential memo you promised me."

"For God's sake. I'm not going to let you down." From upstairs there came the sound of the Rolling Stones. "It's Daphne," explained Dicky. "She says she works better to music."

"So what is Frank up to? Why come here to whisper in your ear? Why not report to the office?"

Again came Dicky's artful smile. "We both know that, Bernard. Frank is after my job."

"Frank is a hundred years old and waiting for retirement."

"But retiring from my desk would give him another few thousand a year on his pension. Retiring from my desk, Frank would be sure of a CBE or even a K."

"Have you been encouraging Frank to think he's getting your job? There's not a chance of it at his age."

Dicky frowned. "Well, don't let's rake that over, at least not for the time being. If Frank has unspoken ambitions, it's not for us to make predictions about them. You follow me, don't you?"

"Follow you, I'm way ahead of you. Frank helps you to get rid of Bret Rensselaer. Then you get Bret's job and Frank gets yours—except that Frank won't get yours."

"You've got an evil mind," said Dicky without rancor. "You always think the worst of everyone around you."

"And the distressing thing about that, is the way I'm so often proved right."

"Well, take it easy on Frank. He's shaken."

Dicky was of course exaggerating wildly, both about the disintegration of the Brahms net and about Frank Harrington's morale. Frank came downstairs ten minutes later. He looked no worse than I would have looked after sitting up with Dicky all night. He was freshly shaved, with two tiny cuts where he'd trimmed the edges of his blunt-ended mustache. He wore a chalk-stripe three-piece suit, clean shirt, and oxford shoes polished to a glasslike finish, and he was waving that damned pipe in the air. Frank was tired and hoarse with talking, but he was an expert at making the best of himself and I knew he'd display no sign of weakness in front of Dicky and me.

Frank seemed pleased to see me. "I'm glad you're here, Bernard. Has Dicky put you in the picture?"

"I've told him nothing," said Dicky. "I wanted him to hear it from you. Drinking chocolate, Frank?"

Frank looked quickly at his gold wristwatch. "A small gin and tonic wouldn't go amiss, Dicky, if it's all the same to you."

"It's cocoa, Frank," I said. "Made the way they drink it in Mexico."

"You said you liked it," said Dicky defensively.

"I loved it," I said. "I drank two of them, didn't I."

"If you've got Plymouth gin," said Frank, "I'll have it straight or with bitters." He went over to the fireplace and knocked out his pipe.

When Dicky came back from the drinks wagon and saw the charred tobacco ashes in the hearth, he said, "Christ, Frank! Can't you see that that's a gas fire." He handed Frank the gin and then went down on his knees at the fireplace.

"I'm awfully sorry," said Frank.

"It looks just like a real open fire," said Dicky as he

used one of Daphne's discarded breakfast-food roughs to marshal the pipe dottle into a tiny heap that could be hidden under the artificial log.

"I'm sorry, Dicky. I really am," said Frank as he sat back on the sofa with a yellow oilskin tobacco pouch on his knees. He looked at me and nodded before sipping his gin. Then, in a different sort of voice, he said, "It could become bad, Bernard. If you're going over there, this would be the time to do it."

"How bad?"

Dicky got to his feet and slapped his hands against his legs to get rid of any ash on his fingers. "Bloody bad," said Dicky. "Tell him how you first found out what was going on."

"I'm not sure I know what *is* going on yet," said Frank. "But the first real sign of trouble came when I had a call from the police liaison chap in Bonn. The border guards at Hitzacker in Lower Saxony had fished a fellow out of the Elbe. He'd got over the Wall and across all those damned minefields and border obstacles and into the river. He was just about done in, but he wasn't injured in any way. From the West German police report I gather there'd been no sounds of shooting or anything from the other side. It was as near as you can get to a perfect escape."

"Lucky man," said Dicky.

"Or a well-informed one," said Frank. "The border runs along the northeast bank of the river there, so the East Germans can't put obstacles and mantraps in the water. That's why the D.D.R. keeps bellyaching about the way the border should run along the middle of the Elbe. Meanwhile it's a good place to try an escape."

"A border crossing? Why did Bonn get involved and why did anyone call you?"

"Bonn got interested when the interrogator at the reception center found that the escapee was an East German customs official."

Frank looked at me as if expecting a reaction. When I gave none, he spent a few moments trying to light his pipe. "An East German customs official," he said again, and waved the match in the air to extinguish it. He almost tossed the dead match into the fireplace but remembered in time and placed it on the large Cinzano ashtray that Dicky had put at his elbow. "Max Binder. One of our people. A Brahms network man."

Dicky had had a whole night of Frank's measured storytelling, and now he tried to hurry things along. "When Frank put in the usual 'contact string' for the rest of the Brahms network next morning, he got no response from anyone."

"I didn't say that, Dicky," said Frank pedantically. "I got messages from two of them."

"You didn't get messages," said Dicky even more pedantically. "You got two 'out of contact' signals." Dicky had decided that the failure of the Brahms network was his big chance, and he was determined to write the story his own way.

Frank grunted and sipped his gin.

Dicky said, "Those bastards have been working a racket with the import bank credits, and making a fortune out of it. And Bret's probably been authorizing false papers and the contacts and everything they needed."

"They're always complaining about the false papers," I said.

"That was just to put us off the scent," said Frank. "The false papers were what they needed more than anything else."

"We've had a lot of unofficial complaints from the D.D.R.

about 'antisocial elements given aid and assistance,' " I said.

Frank looked up from his pipe and said sharply, "I resent that, Bernard. You know only too well that those East Germans keep up a regular bombardment of complaints along those lines. How the hell was I to know that this time their cocktail-party diatribes were based on fact?"

Dicky could not restrain a grim smile, and he turned away to hide it. The Brahms network being no more than a criminal gang manipulating the Department for its own profit must surely be enough to bring Bret Rensselaer crashing to the ground. And into the bargain Bret would lose his Brahms Four source. "Frank says he expects the D.D.R. to prefer murder charges against them," Dicky added.

"Who? Where?" I said. I immediately thought of Rolf Mauser and was sufficiently surprised to allow my consternation to show. I'd been worrying about the way I'd urged Bret to okay a rollover bank loan for Werner. Would he suspect that I was a part of this racket? To cover myself, I got up and went over to the drinks wagon. "Okay if I pour myself a drink, Dicky?"

"Has anyone been in touch with you?" Frank asked me. "Rolf Mauser's son thinks he went to Hamburg. My bet would be London."

"Anyone else?" I said, holding up the gin bottle. "No. No one's contacted me up to now."

Frank returned my gaze for a moment before shaking his head. "No," he said, "I only said that murder charges would be the next step if the net's been penetrated. It's a device the D.D.R. uses for fugitives," he explained. "A murder charge automatically makes a fugitive Category One. It gets their descriptions circulated by teleprinter and the call goes out to the armed forces, as well as all the police services and the border guards. And of course there is always more chance of a murderer being reported by the public. These days the man in the East German street has become rather tolerant of black marketeers." Frank looked at me again. "Right, Bernard?"

I sipped a little of the gin I'd poured for myself and wondered to what extent Frank guessed that I'd seen Rolf or one of the network. Dicky wasn't suspicious; he could obviously think of nothing except how to use this new situation for his own advancement, but Frank had known me since I was a child. It was not so easy to fool Frank. "It had to come," said Frank. "Brahms have been no use to us except to channel back material from Brahms Four. They've got into mischief, and now they're in trouble. We've seen it happen before, haven't we?"

"You say they're running, without backup or any support or anything from us?"

"No. That's Dicky's interpretation. They might simply be taking cover for a couple of days," said Frank. "It's what they do when the security forces are having a routine shakeout."

"But no matter how routine the shakeout," I said, "they might be picked up. And Normannenstrasse will give them an offer they can't resist and maybe blow another network or so. Is that what you're thinking, Frank?"

"What kind of offer they can't resist?" said Dicky.

I didn't answer but Frank said, "The Stasis will make them talk, Dicky."

Dicky poured himself a drink. "Poor bastards. Max Binder, old Rolf Mauser—who else?"

"Let's leave the mourning until we know they are in the bag," I said. "Where's Max Binder now?"

"He's still in the reception center in Hamburg. The interrogation people won't let us have him until they are through."

"I don't like that, Frank," said Dicky. "I don't like some

little German interrogator grilling one of our people. Get him out of there right away."

"We can't do that," said Frank. "We have to go through the formalities."

"Our Berlin people don't go into the reception center," said Dicky.

Patiently Frank explained, "Berlin is still under Allied military occupation, so in Berlin we can do things our way. But things that happen in the Federal Republic have to go through the state BfV office and then through Cologne, and these things take time."

"When did you see him, Frank?"

Daphne Cruyer tapped and put her head around the door. "I'm off to the agency now, darling. We're auditioning ten-year-olds for the TV commercial. I can't leave my assistant to face that horde of little monsters on her own." She was wearing a broad-brimmed hat, long blue cloak, and shiny boots. She had changed her image since her visit to Silas in floral pinafore and granny glasses.

"Bye bye, darling," said Dicky, and kissed her dutifully. "I'll phone you at the office if I'm working late again."

Daphne gave me an affectionate kiss too. "You men are always working late," she said archly. Now I was convinced she knew about Dicky and Tessa. I wondered if her amazing outfit was also a reaction to Dicky's infidelity.

Only after we'd all watched Daphne climb into her car and drive away did Frank answer my question.

"The positive identification was enough for me," said Frank. "No sense in me trailing all the way out to some godforsaken hole in Lower Saxony. I wasted all next day trying to contact the rest of them."

"Daphne's forgotten to take her portfolio," said Dicky, picking up a flat leather folder from the table where she'd put it while kissing him. "I'll phone her office and tell them to send a motorcycle messenger." It was the sort of solicitude shown only by unfaithful husbands.

Dicky left the room to make his phone call from the hall. His loud voice was muffled by the frosted glass panel.

"You'd better tell me the real story," I told Frank. "While Dicky's phoning."

"What do you mean?"

"A D.D.R. customs man swimming across the Elbe would excite the police liaison man in Bonn like a plate of cold dumplings. And even if this discovery did get him so animated, why would he think of you as someone who must be told immediately?" Frank didn't respond, so I pushed. "Police liaison in Bonn aren't given any phone numbers for SIS Berlin, Frank. I thought even Dicky would sniff at that one."

"They went to Max Binder's home to arrest him."

"On what charge?"

"We don't know. It must have been something to do with their forfait racket. His wife was home. She got a message to him and he cleared out quickly."

"You got this from Max Binder?"

"I got it from someone who was told by Werner," admitted Frank. "Werner is in no danger. There's no evidence that anyone but Binder was involved. And Max Binder escaped by swimming the Elbe at Hitzacker, just as I described. He's still in the reception center. I want to contact Brahms Four, but no one will tell me how."

From the hall I could still hear Dicky's voice. He had explained in considerable detail what the portfolio contained and from where it had to be collected, but now he was worrying if a motorcycle messenger would be able to carry it. The doorbell rang twice and Dicky shouted to tell the electrician to stop testing it. "You got it from someone who was told by Werner," I repeated. "And who was that, Frank?"

"Zena told me," said Frank, prodding about in the bowl

of his pipe so that he wouldn't have to meet my stare. "She's a captivating creature, and I adore the little thing. She has to see Werner from time to time. She filled in some details of this Max Binder story." He sucked at his pipe but no smoke came.

"I see."

"You know about me and Zena Volkmann, don't you?" He probed into the bowl of his pipe. When he was sure that the tobacco was not alight, he put the pipe into his top pocket and took a swig at his drink.

"Yes, I know, Frank. I guess she gave you that box of papers that I came to Berlin to look at."

"It was genuine," said Frank.

"All too bloody genuine," I agreed. "It was straight from Moscow Center. Top-grade stuff, carefully selected to make it look as if Giles Trent was their only man in London. Where did she get it from?"

"Zena knows a lot of people," said Frank.

"She knows too many people, Frank. Too many of the wrong people."

"It's better that we don't go into all that with Bret, and everyone at London Central."

"Zena is obviously in on this racket that Brahms have been running."

"It's possible," said Frank. He finished his gin and licked his lips.

"It's not *possible*, Frank. It's all too bloody obvious. That girl's been making a fool of you. She's been in league with Werner and all the others all the time."

"You're trying to tell me that your pal Werner was pimping for his own wife?" Frank's voice was harsh; he was determined to forgo his own illusions only by destroying mine too.

"I don't know," I said. "Perhaps the breakup with Werner came first. Then she found herself with something she could sell to the Brahms net and Werner was the only contact with them she had."

"Sell what to the Brahms net?" Frank was uneasy now. He clipped and unclipped the flap of his yellow tobacco pouch and studied the tobacco as if it were of great interest to him.

"Information, Frank."

"You're not suggesting that I told her anything that could become critical?"

"We'd better find out, Frank," I said. "We'd better find out damned soon. We've got field agents who must be warned if Zena Volkmann has been providing your pillow-talk to men who might wind up in Normannenstrasse."

"Don't let's overreact," said Frank. "I get information from her, she gets none from me."

"It won't seem like overreaction to me, Frank," I said. "Because I'm going to be there. I'm going to be on the wrong side of Charlie pulling your chestnuts out of the fire, and trying to dance quickly enough to keep the Stasis a jump or two behind me. So just to make sure Zena doesn't hear about my travel plans, I'm going to keep well clear of you and your extramarital activities, Frank."

"Don't be a fool, Bernard. Do you think any of those clowns you drink with in Steglitz would know how to get you through the wire safely? Do you think any of those kids you were at school with know the town as well as I know it? I've spent most of my life reading about, looking at, and talking to Berliners. I get my information from a million different sources and I study it. That's what I do all day long, Bernard. I know Berlin like a librarian knows his shelves of books, like a dentist knows a patient's mouth, like a ship's engineer knows the bits and pieces of his engine. I know every square inch of that stinking town, from palace to sewer."

"You know the town, Frank. You know it better than anyone, I'll admit that."

Frank looked at me quizzically. "For God's sake!" he said suddenly. "You're not saying you don't trust me." He stood up to face me and banged his chest with a flattened hand. "This is Frank Harrington you're talking to. I've known you since you were a tiny tot."

"Let it go, Frank," I said.

"I won't," said Frank. "I told your father I'd look after you. I told him that when you joined the Department, and I told him it at the very end. I said I'd look after you, and if you're going over the other side, you're going to do it my way."

I'd never seen Frank get so emotional. "Let me think about it," I said.

"I'm serious," said Frank. "You go my way or you're not going." It was a way of avoiding it, and for a moment I felt like taking the opportunity. "My way or I'll veto it."

From the hall I could hear Dicky telling the electrician that he was charging too much to fix the bell. Then Dicky put his head around the door and borrowed a fiver from me. "It's the black economy," explained Dicky as he took the money. "You can only get things done if you pay spot cash."

"Okay, Frank," I said when Dicky had gone. "We'll do it your way."

"Just you and me," said Frank. "I'll get you over there." He didn't promise to get me back again, I noticed.

"Dicky is keeping everything very tight," I said. "Did he tell you that?"

Frank was examining his oilskin pouch again to see how

much tobacco he had left. "You can't go wrong that way," he said.

"Not even Bret," I said.

"It's coming from someone," said Frank. "It's coming from someone with really good access to material."

I didn't say anything. Such a remark from Frank was *lèse majesté* and I could think of nothing to reply.

I looked at the clock over the fireplace and wondered aloud if that was really the time. I told Frank to come and have dinner with us sometime, and he promised to phone if he could fit it in. Then I shouted goodbye to Dicky, who was still on the phone explaining that Daphne's folio of breakfast-food roughs was vitally important. It was a contention that someone on the other end of the phone seemed to doubt.

OF THE DEPARTMENTAL safe houses in which to meet Giles Trent I had chosen the betting shop in Kilburn High Road. The girl behind the counter nodded as I came in. I pushed past three men who were discussing the ancestry of a racehorse, and went through a door marked STAFF ONLY and upstairs to a small front room. Its window overlooked the wide pavement, where a number of secondhand bathtubs and sinks were displayed.

"You're always in time for the coffee," said Trent. He was standing at a wooden bench. Upon it there was a bottle of Jersey milk, a catering-size tin of Sainsbury's powdered coffee, and a bag of sugar from which the handle of a large spoon protruded. Trent was pouring boiling water from an electric kettle into a chipped cup with the name Tiny painted on it in nail varnish. "No matter how long I wait for you, the moment I decide to make coffee, you arrive."

"Something came up," I said vaguely. For the first time,

I could see Trent as the handsome man who was so attractive to Tessa. He was tall, with a leonine head. His hair was long and wavy. It was not graying in that messy mousy way that most men's hair goes gray; it was streaked with silver, so that he looked like the sort of Italian film star who got cast opposite big-titted teenagers.

"I really don't think it's necessary for us to go through this amazing rigmarole of meeting here in this squalid room." His voice was low and resonant.

"Which squalid room would you prefer?" I said, taking a cup from those arranged upside down on the draining board of the sink. I put boiling water, coffee powder, sugar, and milk into it.

"My office is no distance from yours," said Trent. "I come across to that building several times a week in the normal course of my work. Why the devil should I be making myself conspicuous in this filthy betting shop in Kilburn?"

"The thing I don't like about powdered coffee," I said, "is the way it makes little islands of powder. They float. You get one of those in your mouth and it tastes horrible."

"Did you hear what I said?"

"I didn't realize you wanted an answer," I said. "I thought you were just declaiming about the injustice of life."

"If you put the coffee in first, then poured the hot water on it a little at a time, it would dissolve. Then you put the cold milk in."

"I was never much good at cooking," I said. "First of all, you are not nearly as conspicuous going into a broken-down betting shop in Kilburn as you like to think. On race days, that shop downstairs is crowded with men in expensive suits who put more on a horse than you or I earn in a year. As to your point that it would be better security procedure for us to meet in my office or yours, I can only express surprise at your apparent naïveté."

"What do you mean?"

"Security from who?" I said. "Or, as you might put it, from whom? What do you think is secure about meeting in that office of yours, with all those Oxbridge graduates staring at us with wide eyes and open mouths? You think I've forgotten the way I had a procession of chinless crustaceans coming in and out of your office the last time I was over there? Each one staring at me to see if people from SIS wore their six-shooters on the hip or in shoulder harness."

"You imagine things," said Trent.

"I do," I said. "That's what I'm paid to do: imagine things. And I don't need to spend a lot of time imagining what could happen to you if things went sour with Chlestakov. You might be a world authority on making instant coffee but you'll be safer if you leave the security arrangements to me."

"Don't give me that security lecture all over again," he said. "I don't want a twenty-four-hour guard on my home, or special locks on the doors and windows."

"Then you're a bloody fool," I said. We were both standing by the wooden table as we talked. There were only hard little wooden chairs in the room; it was more restful to stand up.

"Chlestakov didn't show," said Trent. He was looking out the window, watching a young woman with a baby in her arms. She was stopping people as they walked past. Most of them walked on with tight embarrassed expressions on their faces. "She's begging," said Trent. "I thought those days had gone forever."

"You spend too much time in Mayfair," I said. "So who came?"

"And no one gives her anything. Do you see that?"

"So who came?"

"To the meeting at Waterloo station? No one came."

"It might mean they will get rough," I told him.

He took this suggestion very calmly. "Would you like to hear what I think?"

"I'd like to hear it very much," I said. I was being sarcastic but Trent didn't notice.

"I think you had Chlestakov picked up."

"Picked up? By Special Branch, you mean?"

"Special Branch or your own duty arresting officer. Or perhaps by some agency or department distanced from you."

"What sort of agency 'distanced' from us could I have used to 'pick up' Chlestakov?"

"The CIA."

"You're talking like an eighteen-year-old anti-nuke demonstrator. You know we'd not let the bloody CIA pick up anyone in this country. And you know very well that there are no agencies distanced from us, or undistanced from us, that could take a Russian national into custody."

"No one ever gets a straight answer from you bully-boys," said Trent.

"Are you drunk, Trent?" I said, going closer to him.

"Of course not."

"Christ, it's not even lunchtime."

"Why the hell shouldn't I have a drink if I fancy one? I'm doing all your dirty work for you, aren't I? Who will get a medal and promotion if we pull the wool over the eyes of old Chlestakov? You will, you and Dicky bloody Cruyer and all that crowd."

I grabbed him by the lapel and shook him until his head rolled. "Listen to me, you creep," I said softly. "The only dirty work you're doing is clearing up your own shit. If you take another drink before I give you my permission, I'll get a custody order and lock you away where you can't put agents' lives at risk."

I didn't answer his question. "They must have thought you were being followed, Trent. That's the only explanation for Chlestakov failing to show up. The Russians always show up at a rendezvous. Tell me again about the previous meeting."

"You're right, a police car's arrived and they're putting her into it." He looked at me and said, "It went very well. I told Chlestakov that I might be able to get my hands on the Berlin System, and he went crazy at the thought of it. He took me to dinner at some fancy club in Curzon Street and insisted that we order a big meal and very expensive claret. I'm not all that fond of fancy French food, but he obviously wanted to keep me sweet. That's why I can't understand why the Embassy have cut me."

"Not the Embassy," I said. "Just the KGB Section of the Embassy. They have a motive—you can be quite sure that the Russians always have a motive for everything they do."

"You said they work out of Moscow for everything."

"Did I? Well, if I said that, I was right. The London Section Chief wouldn't change his underwear until Moscow Center have approved the kind of soap the laundry uses."

"But why would Moscow tell them to cut me? And if they were going to drop me, why not tell me so?"

"I don't know, Giles old friend."

"Don't call me 'Giles old friend' in that sarcastic way."

"You'll have to put up with me calling you Giles old anything in any way I choose for the time being," I said. "Because if Moscow Center have decided to drop you, it might not simply be a matter of leaving you off the list of people invited along for vodka and caviar, and a film show about the hydroelectric plant at Kuibyshev."

"No?"

"They always send someone," I said. "And keep well back from the window. Why do you think we put net curtains up?"

"No one arrived. I did it exactly by the book. I arrived under the big four-faced clock at seven minutes past the hour. And then went back two hours later. Still no one. Then I went to the standby rendezvous."

"Where was that?"

"Selfridge's food department, near the fresh fish counter. I did it exactly as arranged."

"Moscow Center like to stick to the tried and true methods," I said. "We arrested one of their people under that damned clock back in 1975." I went to the window where he stood and watched the woman begging. A man wearing a dark raincoat and gray felt hat was reaching into his inside pocket.

"She's had luck at last," said Trent. "I wondered why she didn't stand outside Barclays Bank, but I suppose a betting shop is better."

"Can't you spot a plainclothes cop when you see one?" I said. "To beg or gather alms in a public place is an offense under the Vagrancy Act of 1824, and by having the baby with her she can be charged under the Children and Young Persons Act too."

"The bastard," said Trent.

"The plainclothes cop is there because this is a safe house," I said. "He doesn't know that, of course, but he knows that this is 'Home Office notified premises.' The woman doesn't beg regularly or she'd have learned to keep clear of betting shops, because betting shops attract crooks and crooks bring cops."

"Are you saying the woman is working for the KGB, and they are keeping this SIS safe house under observation?"

"I'm not drunk," he said. He had in fact sobered up now that I'd shaken his brains back into operation.

"If I lose one agent, I'll kill you, Trent."

He said nothing; he could see I was serious. "They're your friends, aren't they," he said. "They're your Berlin school friends. Ahhh!"

I shouldn't have hit him at all but it was only a little jab in the belly and it helped him to sober up still more.

I picked up the phone and dialed our Federal emergency number. I recognized the voice at the other end. "Peter? This is Bernard. I'm in the Coach and Horses." All our safe houses had pub names. "And I need someone to get a male drunk home and look after him while he sobers up. And I don't want anyone whose heart can be broken by a sob story."

I put the phone down and looked at Trent. He was sitting in one of the hard chairs, holding his belly and crying silently.

"You'll be all right," I told him. "Save your tears for Chlestakov. If he's no longer any use to them, they'll send him home and give him the sort of job that will encourage the ones still here to work harder."

Chapter 20

As usual, Rolf Mauser arrived at a bad time. I was watching a very good BBC documentary on model railways, the children were upstairs playing some kind of jumping game, and Fiona was in the kitchen arguing with the nanny about her wages.

I brought Rolf Mauser into the living room and offered to take his leather overcoat from him but he waved me away testily. "Are you all right, Rolf?" I said.

"Give me a whisky."

He looked pale. I gave him a big scotch and he sat down and stared at the trains on TV with unseeing eyes. Light spilling from the table lamp beside him showed a fresh cut on his ear. Even as I noticed that, his hand went up to touch his head. He winced with pain as he found some tender places.

"You all right, Rolf?" All his self-confidence seemed to have gone; even those demonic eyebrows were sagging a little.

"I'm sixty-six years old, Bernd, and I'm still alive."

"You're a tough old bastard, Rolf." His shoes were scuffed and his leather coat had dirty marks on the front. He took paper tissues from a box on the table and cleaned himself up a bit.

The little trains on TV were making a lot of noise. I

used the remote control to switch the sound off. Rolf Mauser looked around furtively and then pulled a brown paper bag from his pocket. He passed it to me. "You said you'd get rid of it."

I took a bundle from the bag. Unwinding a heavy woolen scarf, I found my revolver inside. I broke it and sniffed at the breech. There was no smell except that of fresh thin oil. It had been scrubbed clean. Rolf must have been a good soldier.

"You said you'd get rid of it," he reminded me. I shook the bag. Inside there were three bullets and three used brass cases.

"What have you been doing, Rolf?"

"Get rid of it, I say."

I put the gun and the scarf into the brown paper bag again. And I locked it into the desk where I kept unpaid bills, Fiona's jewelry, and letters from the bank about my overdraft.

Rolf turned to watch what I was doing. He said, "I'm going back tonight. Could you lend me a car to get to Harwich?"

"I'd better know what it's all about," I said.

"Yes or no," he said.

"There's a blue mini outside. What time do you have to be there?"

"Give me a strong envelope and I'll put the keys in the post to you, and tell you where it's parked."

"You're too late for the Hamburg boat," I said. He looked up at me without replying. I doubt if he had any intention of leaving via the cross-Channel ferry from Harwich. Rolf's way of keeping secrets was to confide endless untruths to anyone who'd listen. "I'll get the keys," I said. "It's the nanny's car, so be careful with it."

"Can you find a hat for me, Bernd?"

I came back with a selection of headgear. He took a cloth cap and tried it on. It fitted him well enough to hide his cuts and shadow his face. "You stole the car," I said as I pulled the hat down lower on his head. "You came to see me, found the keys in the car, and drove away without coming to the door."

"Sure, Bernd, sure."

"No one will believe you, but stick to that story and I'll do the same."

"I said yes," he said irritably.

"What's happening to the Brahms net?"

"Nothing."

"Max Binder swam the Elbe."

"Max lost his nerve," he said.

"Who else lost their nerve?"

"Not me," he said, looking me in the eyes. Confidence or no confidence, he was still as ferocious as ever. "I deal with problems as they come up. I don't go swimming across the Elbe and leaving my wife and kids to face the music."

"The rest of Brahms all in place? London are worried."

"A slight hiccup," he said. "Brahms had that slight hiccup that the economists talk about when their miscalculations have thrown half a million people out of work." It was the sort of bitter joke for which he permitted himself a twisted smile.

"Let's hope the hiccup doesn't become whooping cough."

It was "gasping cough" in German. Rolf Mauser nodded. "We took precautions," he said. "We've long ago learned that London cannot protect us."

I let the criticism go. The Brahms net was old and tired. It should have been dismantled years before. Just as the information from Brahms Four was all that made them worthwhile to London, so this damned import-export racket was their sole reason to continue going through the motions.

It was a marriage of convenience and, like all such marriages, it depended upon the continuing self-interest of both parties.

Rolf helped himself to another drink—a large one. Then he got to his feet, buttoned up his coat, and announced his departure.

"Don't stop and ask a cop which way to go," I advised. "Breathe that booze over him and you'll end up in a police cell."

"I'll take my chances," he said. "I like being on my own, Bernd. I never did like doing things the way it's written in the book. Your father knew that."

"Have you got English money?"

"Go back to your TV," he said. "And tell your wife I'm sorry I couldn't stay."

"She'll understand," I said.

He smiled his twisted little smile again. Even from before I married her, he'd never been able to get along with Fiona.

ROLF HAD BEEN GONE three hours or more by the time the phone rang with the call from Dicky. "Where are you?" he said.

"Where am I? Where the hell do you think I am? I'm at home. I'm sitting in front of the TV trying to decide whether to switch the heating back on and watch the late night movie."

"The way they patch these calls, you can't be sure where anyone is these days," grumbled Dicky vaguely.

"What is it?" I said. The film had already started and I didn't want a long chat with him about my Berlin expenses or the new car.

"Has anyone been in touch with you?" he asked. On the

TV screen the titles gave place to a small steamer chugging across a bright blue lake.

"No one."

"You called someone from Security to take Giles Trent back to his home today."

At the bow of the steamer were three men in white suits leaning over the rail peering into the water. "Trent had been drinking," I said. "He was being abusive and accusing us of arresting Chlestakov, his Embassy contact."

"Who answered the phone?"

"In the security office? That kid with the mustache—Peter. I don't know his last name."

"Did he have any trouble with Trent?"

"Look, Dicky," I said. "I decide when someone with an orange file needs to be picked up and taken home. Trent can complain to the D-G if he wants, but if I get any more flak from that bastard I'll lock him up again. And there's nothing anyone can do about that except take me off it. And that's a development I wouldn't mind at all. I don't enjoy it, you know."

"I know all that," said Dicky.

"And if they move me it will be egg on your face, Dicky."

"Don't get hot under the collar," said Dicky placatingly. "No one is blaming you. You did everything that could be done, everyone is agreed on that."

"What are you talking about, Dicky?"

"This fiasco with Trent. The bloody newspapers will start implying that we did it. You know that. And the only way we can argue with them is by telling them more than we want Moscow to know."

"Would you start again, please?" I said.

"Didn't anyone phone to tell you that Trent's been killed?"

"When? How?"

"Late this afternoon or early evening. Someone climbed

over the garden wall at the back and shinned up the drain-pipe to get into an upstairs window that had been left un-locked. Special Branch let us have someone to write up a preliminary docket."

"Trent is dead?"

"Shot. He was in the shower. The curtain was drawn across to save any chance of blood splashing on the killer, or at least that's what the Special Branch detective says. None of the neighbors heard the shot. With the television showing nothing but cops and robbers, you could use a machine gun nowadays without anyone noticing the noise."

"Any idea who did it?"

Dicky gave a tiny derisive hoot. "Are you joking? The report says the bullets hit the bathroom wall with abnor-mally low velocity. The ballistics boys say the bullets had been specially prepared by experts—they'd had a propor-tion of their powder removed. Well, that sounds like a labo-ratory job, eh? That's our KGB friends, I think. Why do they do that, Bernie?"

"So they don't go through the next two or three houses and spoil the neighbors' television. Who found him?"

"His sister. She let herself in with her own key. She'd come to see if he was okay after that business with the sleeping pills. If it hadn't been for that, we wouldn't have discovered the body until tomorrow morning. I'd always suspected that Trent was queer, didn't you? I mean, him never being married. But giving the sister a key to the house makes that unlikely, wouldn't you say?"

"Anything else, Dicky?"

"What? No. But I thought I should ask you if he was acting normally when he left you this morning."

"I can't help you, Dicky," I said.

"Well, I know you've got an early start in the morning. Frank says wrap up well. It's cold in Berlin."

After I rang off, I returned to my desk. When I un-wrapped the pistol, I found a series of holes in the woolen scarf. Rolf Mauser had wrapped the gun in it before shoot-ing Trent. A revolver can't be silenced any other way. I had to use a magnifying glass for a clear sight of the marks left on the bullet cases by the process of hand-loading. There was no doubt that the bullets had been specially prepared by someone with gunsmith's tools and powder measure.

I sat down and looked at the TV before switching off. The steamer was sinking; the men were drowning. I sup-pose it was some kind of comedy.

Chapter 21

I T WAS VERY VERY DARK and Frank Harrington was being ultra cautious, using the electric lamp only to show me a safety well into which I might fall, or large puddles, or the rails when we had to get across to the other side of the railway track.

There is a curious smell in Berlin's underground railway system. It brings to mind the stories about engineers blasting the locks of the canal between Schöneberger and Möckern bridges in those final hours of the war, so that the tunnels flooded to drown civilians, German soldiers, and Russians alike. Some say there was no flooding—just leaks and water that came through the damaged bulkhead that guards the Friedrichstrasse U-Bahn station from the cold waters of the Spree. But don't deny those nightmares to anyone who has picked his way over the cross-ties in the darkness after the trains have stopped, for he will tell you about the ghosts down there. And the curious smell remains.

Frank moved forward very slowly, talking softly all the while so that I would know where he was. "Half the passengers on the underground trains going from Moritzplatz to Voltastrasse don't even realize that they actually go under East Berlin and back into the West again."

"Are we under the East Sector yet?" I asked.

"On this section of line, they do know of course. The

trains stop at Friedrichstrasse station and the passengers are checked." He stopped and listened, but there was only the sound of dripping water and the distant hum of the electric generators. "You'll see the marks on the tunnel wall when we get that far. There's red paint on the wall to mark the boundary." He flashed his light on the side of the tunnel to show me where the marks would be. There was nothing there except bundles of wires sagging from support to support and blackened with decades of filth. As he switched off his lamp, Frank stumbled into a piece of broken drain and cursed. It was all right for him; he had rubber boots on, and wore old clothes under his railway-engineer overalls. The clothes I wore under my overalls were all I had for my time in East Berlin. And we'd both decided that carrying a case or a parcel in the small hours was asking to be stopped and searched.

We walked slowly along the track for what seemed like hours. Sometimes Frank stopped to listen, but there was only the sudden scratching sounds of rats and the ceaseless hum of electricity.

"We'll wait here for a bit," said Frank. He held his wristwatch close to his face. "Some nights there are East Berlin railway engineers going down the track to check the apparatus at the terminal—what used to be Kaiserhof station. Thälmannplatz, they call it nowadays. The Communists like to name streets and stations after heroes, don't they?" Frank switched on his lamp long enough to show a recessed space in the wall of the tunnel, containing a yellow-painted metal box with a telephone in it. This was one of the places the drivers had to come to if their train stopped between stations. There was a bench there too, and Frank sat down. We were not far below street level and I could feel a cold draft coming down the air shaft.

"Ever wonder why the Berlin Wall follows that absurd

line?" said Frank. "It was decided at a conference at Lancaster House in London while the war was still being fought. They were dividing the city up the way the Allied armies would share it once they got here. Clerks were sent out hotfoot for a map of Berlin but the only thing Whitehall could provide was a 1928 City Directory, so they had to use that. They drew their lines along the administrative borough boundaries as they were in 1928. It was only for the purposes of that temporary wartime agreement, so it didn't seem to matter too much where it cut through gas pipes, sewers, and S-Bahn or these underground trains either. That was in 1944. Now we're still stuck with it." We were sitting in the dark. I knew Frank was dying for a puff at that damned pipe, but he didn't succumb to the temptation. He talked instead.

Frank said, "Years back, when the Communists started building that incredible great satellite city at Marzahn, they wanted it to have its own administration and become a *Stadtbezirk,* a city borough in its own right. But the Communist lawyers sat down with the men from Moscow and went through those old wartime agreements. The outcome was that they were told on no account to create a new *Bezirk.* By breaking the old agreement, they would open the way for the Western Powers to make changes too."

"Lawyers run the world," I said.

"I'm going to let you out into the street at Stadtmitte station," Frank said. He'd told me all about it, shown me a map and photos, but I didn't interrupt him when he told me everything all over again. "Stadtmitte is an intersection. East German trains and West German trains both pass through. On different levels, of course."

"How long now, Frank?"

"Relax. We must wait until we're sure the East Germans are not repairing their track. They're not armed but they sometimes have radios to talk to the men who switch off the juice. They have to be sure the section men won't be electrocuted when they start work."

We waited in the darkness for what seemed an age. Then we walked slowly along the tunnel again. "In 1945, the Red Army—fighting their way into the city—were held up at Stadtmitte U-Bahn station," said Frank. "The station was being used as headquarters by the SS Division Nordland. They were the last German regulars holding out, and they weren't very German. Nordland had become a collection of foreign volunteers, including three hundred Frenchmen who'd been sent from another unit. The Germans were shooting from about where we are standing now and the Russians couldn't get down onto the track. You know that old saying about one man can hold off an army if he fights his battle in a tunnel. Well, the Germans were fighting their final battle and it was in a tunnel."

"What happened?"

"The Russians manhandled a field-artillery piece down the entrance steps, along the platform, and onto the tracks. Then they fired along the tunnel here, and that was the end of the story." Frank stopped suddenly and held his hand outstretched as a warning to be silent.

He must have had superhuman hearing, for it was only after we'd stood there for a moment or two that I could hear the sounds of voices and a muffled hammering. Frank put his head close to mine and whispered, "Sounds travel a long way in these old tunnels. Those men are probably no nearer than the old disused platform at Französischestrasse." He looked around. "This is where you leave me." He pointed up to another air shaft. At the top there was the faintest glimmer of gray light seen through a grating. "But move quietly."

I stripped off the overalls and passed them to Frank;

then I climbed up the narrow air shaft. There were iron rungs set into the brickwork. Some of them were rusted and broken, but I had nothing to carry and I got to the top easily enough. The grating was held in place with rusting bars. It looked immovable.

"Lift it," said Frank from below me. "Lift it until you can see the street is clear. Then choose your moment and go."

I put my hand to the grating and it moved easily enough. It hadn't been cleaned and oiled—Frank was too subtle for anything so obvious—but it had been removed recently and made ready for me to push aside.

"Good luck, Bernard."

I tossed my work gloves back down the shaft, and then went through the manhole as quickly as I could, but I need not have worried. The "Friedrichstadt"—the governmental center of old Berlin—is empty and silent, by Western standards, even during the working day. Now there was no one in sight, just the distant sounds of traffic somewhere to the east of the city. For Stadtbezirk Mitte is a Communist fist punched into the West. It is bordered on three sides by the "anti-Fascist protection barrier," or what the rest of the world calls the Wall. It was close by. Endless batteries of glaring lights kept the open strip of borderland as bright as day, and the scattered light made the darkness overhead gray, like the mist that creeps inland from an ice-cold sea.

Frank had chosen my route with care. The entrance to the air shaft was hidden from passersby. There was a pile of sand and big heaps of rubble, some building equipment, and a small generator trailer belonging to the Electricity Authority. Berlin's cast-iron manhole covers are very heavy, and by the time this one was back in place I was red-faced and out of breath. I paused for a moment before walking up Charlottenstrasse, intending to cut along the back of the State

Opera House parallel to Unter den Linden. I would have to cross the Spree. There was no way of avoiding those bridges, for just as the Wall enclosed this part of Mitte on two sides, the River Spree made up the other two sides of what was virtually a box.

As I got nearer to the State Opera, I saw lights and people. Doors at the back of the building were open and men were carrying huge scenery flats and the statue of a horseman that was recognizably from the last act of *Don Giovanni*. I crossed the street to keep in the shadows but two policemen walking toward me from the direction of the old Reichsbank building—now the offices of the Central Committee—made me change my mind quickly. If only we hadn't had to wait until the underground trains stopped, I could have mingled with the tourists and those groups of Western visitors who go through Checkpoint Charlie just to visit the theaters or the opera houses for the evening. Some of them were dressed in dinner suits and stiff-fronted shirts, or the flamboyant mess kit of a garrisoned regiment. With them came women in long evening dresses and expensive hairdos. Such visitors provided a glimpse of Western decadence for the bored locals. None of those visitors ever gets asked for papers on the street, but such dress would be rather conspicuous amongst the workers where I was going.

There were very few people to be seen anywhere. I walked north and stopped under the arch at Friedrichstrasse station. There were a couple of noisy men arguing about the satirical cabaret across the road, some railway workers waiting for their shift to begin, and some silent African tourists staring at everything. The Weidendamm bridge would be my best bet. It was darker there than on the bridges that went over to the island: too many government buildings being guarded on that side of the city.

There were memories everywhere I looked, and there

was no getting away from the war. The last escapers from the Führerbunker had come this way, crossing the river by the footbridge when all else failed, and leaving Martin Bormann dead by the river.

The Charité Hospital. In the mortuary of that grim building, the Red Army found the bodies of the men who'd tried to overthrow Hitler in the July 1944 plot. Their bodies had been kept in the cold room there on Hitler's personal orders.

A policeman came walking up from the old Brecht theater beside the Spree. He hurried his pace as he saw me. My papers were in order but I realized too late that I didn't know how to talk to a policeman. "Hey, you," the policeman called.

How did East Berliners address a policeman nowadays? This wasn't the U.S.A. Being too familiar would be just as suspicious as being too respectful. I decided to be a little drunk, a shift-worker who'd had a couple of vodkas before heading home. But how many vodkas could a man have these days before he risked being taken to the police station?

"What are you doing here?" The policeman's voice was shrill, and his accent revealed his home to be somewhere in the north: Rostock, Stralsund, or Rügen Island, perhaps. On this side of the Wall there was a theory that out-of-town recruits were more reliable than Berliners.

I kept walking. "Get up," the policeman said. I stopped and turned around. He was talking to a couple of men sitting on the ground in the shadow of the bridge. They didn't get up. The cop said, "Where are you from?"

The elder of the two, a bearded man wearing overalls and a battered leather jacket said, "And where are *you* from, sonny?"

"Let's get you home," said the cop.

"Get me home," said the bearded man. "That's right.

You get me home to Schöneberg." He laughed. "Yorck-strasse, please, right near the railway."

The younger man got to his feet unsteadily. "Come on," he said to his companion.

"Yorckstrasse, Schöneberg," said the bearded man again. "Only two stops from here on the S-Bahn. But you've never heard of it and I'll never see it again." He began to sing tunelessly. *"Das war in Schöneberg im Monat Mai."* His singing voice revealed the extent of his drunkenness in a way that his speech did not.

The policeman was less conciliatory now. "You'll have to get off the street," he said. "Stand up. Show me your papers."

The drunk gave an artful little laugh. His companion said, "Leave him alone—can't you see he's not well," in a voice so slurred that his words were almost incomprehensible.

"If you're not on your way home in two minutes, I'll run you along to the police station."

"Er ist polizeiwidrig dumm," said the bearded man, and laughed. It meant "criminally stupid" and it was a joke that every German policeman had heard.

"Come along with me," said the cop.

The man began singing again, louder this time: *"Das war in Schöneberg im Monat Mai . . ."*

I hurried on lest the policeman call for help with his two difficult drunks. Even when I was a hundred meters or more down the road, I could still hear the drunken old man singing about the little girl who had so often and gladly kissed the boys as they did in Schöneberg so long ago.

At Oranienburger Tor, where the Chausseestrasse leads up to the football stadium, I turned in to the dark labyrinth of side streets. I'd forgotten what it was like to be a newly "deposited" field agent with false papers and a not very convincing cover story. I was too old for it; once I was safely back behind my desk in London, I wouldn't fret to move again.

More than a century old, these grim-looking apartment blocks, five and six stories high, had been built to shelter peasants who came to the city looking for jobs in the factories. They had changed very little. Rolf Mauser lived on the second floor in a rambling, tumbledown apartment building in Prenzlauer Berg. He was bleary-eyed and barefoot when he opened the door, a red silk dressing gown over his pajamas.

"What the hell are you doing here?" he said as he took the chain off the door. It was his turn to be surprised in the middle of the night, and I rather relished it.

He motioned me into the sitting room and I sank down on a soft chair without removing either coat or hat. "A change of plan, Rolf," I said. "I had a feeling that it wasn't good on the street tonight."

"It's never good on the street," he said. "Do you want a bed?"

"Is there room for me?"

"Rooms are all I have in abundance. You can take your choice of three different ones." He put a bottle of Polish vodka on the table alongside me and then opened the white porcelain stove to poke the ashes over. "The rents over this side of the Wall are more or less the same, whether you've got a two-room flat or a huge house. So why move?" The acrid smell of burning coal filled the room.

"I wondered whether you'd be here, Rolf."

"Why not? After what happened in London, this is the safest place, isn't it?"

"How do you figure that, Rolf?" I said.

"The evidence will be in London. That's where they'll be looking for the culprit."

"I hope so, Rolf," I said.

"I had to do it, Bernd. I had to bring him around the

corner, you know. That man in London was going to blow the whole network."

"Let's forget it," I said, but Mauser was determined to have my approval for his deed.

"He'd already told Berlin KGB to have personnel and solitary prison accommodation ready for up to fifty arrests. The Brahms network would have been *kaputt gemacht*. And several other networks too. Now do you understand why I had to do what I did?"

"I understand it, Rolf. I understand it even better than you do." I poured myself a shot of Rolf's fruit-flavored vodka and drank it down. It was too fiery for the fruit flavoring to soften it much.

"I had to execute him, Bernd."

" '*Um die Ecke bringen*'—that's gangster talk, Rolf. Let's face the truth. You murdered him."

"I assassinated him."

"Only public officials can be assassinated, and even then the victims have to be tyrants. Executions are part of a process of law. Face it: you murdered him."

"You play with words. It's easy to be clever now that the danger has been removed."

"He was a weak and foolish man, riven by guilt and fear. He knew nothing of importance. He'd never heard of Berlin System until last week."

"Yes," said Rolf. "Berlin System—that's what he promised them. I asked Werner about it. He said that it was a complete breakdown of all networks and contacts, including emergency contacts and interservice contacts, for the whole Berlin area. We were very worried, Bernd."

"Where did you get Trent's name and address?" I asked. He didn't answer.

"From Werner. Who got it from that bloody Zena. Right?"

"You were asking Frank Harrington questions about some

mix-up in 1978. Frank guessed that this man Trent was being investigated."

"And he told Zena?"

"You know Zena. She got it out of him."

"How many times do I have to tell you that Werner is not employed by the Department. Why didn't you get in touch with Olympia Stadion?"

"Not enough time, Bernd. And Werner is more reliable than your people at Olympia. That's why you use him, isn't it?"

"Why didn't you tell me what you were going to do that night in London?"

"We didn't want London Central to know," said Rolf. He poured himself a shot of vodka. He was beginning to sweat, and it wasn't with the heat from the stove.

"Why not?"

"So where was this man Trent getting his Berlin System from? Answer me that. He was going to get it from someone in London, Bernd."

"Damn right," I said angrily. "He was going to get it from *me*." I looked at him, wondering how much to confide to him.

"From you, Bernd? Never."

"It was all part of a play, you fool. I told him to promise it to Moscow. I promised him the System because I wanted to keep him on the hook while I reeled him in."

"It was an official play, you mean?"

"You bloody fool, Rolf."

"I killed the poor bastard for nothing?"

"You messed up my plan, Rolf."

"Oh, my God, Bernd."

"You'd better show me where I'm to sleep, Rolf. I have a busy day tomorrow."

He stood up and mopped the sweat from his brow with

a red handkerchief. "I won't get to sleep, Bernd. It's a terrible thing I have done. How can I sleep with that on my conscience?"

"Think of all the poor bastards you killed in those artillery bombardments, Rolf, and add one."

Chapter 22

THE NEXT MORNING was very sunny. Even Prenzlauer Berg looked good. But Rolf Mauser's second-floor apartment faced out onto a cobbled courtyard almost entirely filled by a large soot-caked chestnut tree. The greenish reflected light from its young leaves made it seem as if the whole place were under water.

Only a few stunted bushes grew in the yard. But there were bicycles there by the dozen and prams double-parked. Rows of rubbish bins too, their contents distributed far and wide by hungry cats that woke me in the night with their angry screeches. The narrow peeling stucco walls of the courtyard, which had brought the chestnut into early bud, echoed every sound. Everyone could hear the admonitions, arguments, and shouted greetings of two women who were throwing pailfuls of water onto the mess and scrubbing energetically with stiff brooms.

"It's not exactly the Kaiserhof in its heyday," said Rolf, serving himself from a dented pot of coffee and leaving me to do the same. He had the bluff manner of a soldier, the self-centered ways of a man who'd lived alone too long. "Those damned cats kept me awake."

"Cobbler's boys," I said, picking up one of the triangular wholemeal rolls that Berliners eat at breakfast time. "I slept very well. Thanks for the bed, Rolf. I'll push on today."

"It's difficult to get them now," said Rolf. "All bread prices are controlled. None of these lazy swine of bakers want the extra work of making anything but ordinary bread." He'd recovered from his self-doubts of the night before, as all soldiers must renew their conscience with every dawn.

"It's the same everywhere," I said.

"Stay a week if you want to. I get a bit fed up being here alone. The couple who let me share it are away visiting their married daughter." He took his cup of coffee from the tray he'd brought, put milk into it, and sat down on the bed while I finished shaving. "But you'll have to take your turn carrying coal from the cellar."

"I hope I won't need a week, Rolf."

"You're going to see Brahms Four?"

"Probably."

"Is there really a person called Brahms Four?"

"I hope so, Rolf."

"I always thought it was the code name for a syndicate. Why else would the Brahms Four material always be kept separate from everything else we sent?"

"Nothing so unusual about that."

"Officially he's in the Brahms network." He paused to let me know he was about to say something significant. "But no one in the Brahms network has ever seen him."

"How do you know that?" I said sharply. "Damn it, Rolf, you should know better than to discuss named agents with third parties."

"Even if the third parties are also agents?"

"Especially then, because the chances of them being interrogated are that much greater."

"You've been a long time away, Bernd. You've been sitting behind a desk in London too long. Now you talk like one of those memos that Frank Harrington likes to write."

"Save some of that coffee for me, Rolf," I complained.

He stopped filling his cup, and looked up and grinned at me. "Suppose you find he doesn't exist?" he said, pouring the last of the coffee into my cup, dregs and all. "Suppose you find he's just a postbox in the KGB building and you've been made a fool of for years and years?"

"Is that your guess, Rolf?"

He bit off a mouthful of roll and chewed it. "No. I'm just being devil's advocate."

ROLF MAUSER was right: although he wasn't a Department employee, I trusted Werner Volkmann more than anyone Berlin Station could provide. He had a car he used on the East side of the Wall. He was waiting for me at that part of Schönhauserallee where the underground trains come up into the daylight and rattle along the antiquated construction that patterns the whole street with shadows.

I opened the door and got in beside him. Without a word of greeting, he started up and headed north.

"No wonder Brahms Four is getting jumpy," I said. "Too many people are becoming curious about him."

"He'll not go undetected for another six months," said Werner.

"London were hoping to squeeze another two years out of him."

He made a noise that expressed his contempt for London Central and all their plans and ambitions. "With Brahms network channeling his reports?"

"Other ways could be tried," I said.

"Such as VHF radio, just powerful enough to transmit to Olympia Stadion?" said Werner with an unmistakable edge to his voice.

"That was mentioned," I admitted. It had been Dicky's

one and only contribution to a very long meeting the previous month.

"By a fool," said Werner.

"But what's the alternative? Putting him into a different network?"

"It could be done, couldn't it?"

"You've never had the job of introducing an agent into a network," I said. "Most of the nets are run by temperamental prima donnas. I couldn't face all the arguments and anxieties that go with these damned shotgun marriages."

"Put him in contact with another network and you'll slow up the delivery," said Werner. He was guessing, of course; he had no knowledge of what other networks we had with access to Berlin. But in fact his guess was right. There are lots of men like Werner; they just can't stop working, pay or no pay. It was probably Werner who'd held Brahms together so long.

"And you increase the number of people who know he exists," I said.

"Does he exist?" said Werner. "Sometimes I wonder."

"Have you been talking to Rolf Mauser?"

"Of course I have," said Werner. "Do you imagine the network can handle material for years and not wonder where it's coming from? Especially when we get bombarded with priority demands for immediate handling."

"I'm seeing Brahms Four as soon as possible," I said.

Werner looked away from the road for long enough to study my face. "You're sharing secrets today, are you? That's out of character, Bernie. Why would you tell me you're seeing him?"

"Because you've guessed already."

"No, no, no," said Werner. "That's not it."

"Because we might have to get him out of East Berlin fast, Werner."

"I'll take you to wherever you want to go," offered Werner. "Downtown? I have nothing to do."

"I'll need the car, Werner. You've got *plenty* to do. I want you to take the London flight and be back here by evening."

"What for?"

"When it happens, it will happen very fast."

"When what happens?"

"Suppose, Werner . . ." It was hard saying it out loud. "Suppose it's Fiona who's the KGB agent in London."

"Your wife?"

"Well, think about it. Everything fits: the Giles Trent fiasco, and the way she tried to pin the leak of that Karlshorst signal on him. Bret wasn't in Berlin at the times in question. Dicky never saw the signal. Fiona is the only one in the right place at the right time, every time."

"You can't be serious, Bernie."

"I want to be wrong, Werner. But if it is Fiona and she decides to run for it, she'll take the children too." I wanted him to say I was talking nonsense.

"But, Bernie, the duty officer at the airport would probably recognize her. Going out alone, she could say she was working. But with two kids I'd say any airport duty officer would be bound to check back with the office before letting her through."

"So what will she do?" I said.

"If she really is KGB, she'll have them arrange about getting your children out separately. Jesus, Bernie. It's too awful to think about. It couldn't be Fiona, could it?"

"We'll have to trust Dicky," I said. "He'll give you whatever you need. Take the children over to my mother. Make it all sound normal. I don't want Fiona to know I suspect her. But have someone with them all the time— guards, I mean, people who will know what has to be done, not just security men—and arrange things so I can swear I know nothing about it, Werner. Just in case I'm wrong about Fiona."

"I'm sure you're wrong about her, Bernie."

"You'd better get going. I'll drop you at a taxi rank and then take your car. I've got a busy day. See you at Rolf's tonight."

"I'm sure you're wrong about Fiona," said Werner, but every time he said it he sounded less and less convinced that I was wrong.

Chapter 23

I WENT TO SEE Brahms Four at his office in Otto-Grote-wohlstrasse. It used to be Wilhelmstrasse in the old days, and just down the street beyond the Wall it still was. The building too had changed its name, for this was the huge and grandiose Air Ministry block that Hermann Göring had built for his bickering bureaucrats. It was one of the few Nazi government buildings that survived the fighting here in the center of the city.

After filling in the requisite form for the clerk on the reception desk, I was shown upstairs. Here was the man who'd come back from what Dicky described as "some god-forsaken little place in Thüringerwald" to dig me out of my hideout in a narrow alley behind the Goethe Museum in Weimar just minutes before they came to get me. I'd never forget it.

Goodness knows what clerk in London Central had named the network Brahms or by what chance this man had become its number four. But it had been put on his documents decades ago and, for their purposes, it was his name still. His real name was Dr. Walter von Munte but, living in the proletarian state of the German Democratic Republic, he'd long since dropped the "von." He was a tall gloomy man of about sixty, with a lined face, gold-rimmed eyeglasses, and gray closely cropped hair. He was frail-looking despite his size, and his stooped shoulders and old-fashioned good manners made him seem servile by the standards of today's world. The black suit he wore was carefully pressed, but like the stiff collar and black tie, it was well worn. And he wrung his hands like a Dickensian undertaker.

"Bernd," he said. "I can't believe it's you . . . after all these years."

"Is it so long?"

"You were not even married. And now, I hear, you have two children. Or have I got it wrong?"

"You've got it right," I said. He was standing behind his desk watching me as I went over to the window. We were close to the Wall: here I could almost see the remains of Anhalter railway station; perhaps from a higher floor I'd see the Café Leuschner. I carelessly touched the telephone junction box on the windowsill, and glanced up at the light fittings before going back again.

He guessed what I was doing. "Oh, you need not worry about hidden microphones here. This office is regularly searched for such devices." He smiled grimly.

Only when I sat down on the molded plastic chair did he sit down too. "You want to get out?" I said softly.

"There is not much time," he said. He was very calm and matter-of-fact.

"What's the hurry?"

"You know what the hurry is," he said. "One of your people in London is reporting regularly to the KGB. It's only a matter of time . . ."

"But you're special," I said. "You are kept apart from everything else we do."

"They have a good source," he said. "It must be someone at the top in London."

"London want you to stay on," I said. "For two years at least."

"London is Oliver Twist. London always want more. Is that why you came here? To tell me to stay on?"

"It's one of the reasons," I admitted.

"You've wasted your time, Bernd. But it's good to see you, just the same."

"They'll insist."

"Insist?" While he considered the idea of London forcing him to stay on, he carefully tore the edging from a block of postage stamps. "How can they insist on anything? If I ceased to report to them, what could they do about that? If they betrayed me, the word would soon get around and your whole service would suffer."

"There would be no question of London betraying you. You know that."

"So what sanction do they have? How could they insist?" Having made the postage stamps look more tidy, he rolled up the stamp edging to make it into a ball.

I said, "You'd have to give up all thoughts of going to the West. And I think you want to go to the West."

"My wife wants to go. She wants to see her brother's grave. He was killed in Tunisia in the war. They were very close as children. But if it proves impossible, then so be it." He shrugged and unrolled the stamp edging, smoothing it flat again.

"And you want to see your son in São Paulo."

He said nothing for a long time, toying with the stamp edging as if he were thinking of nothing else. "You are still as painstaking as you used to be, Bernd. I should have guessed you'd trace the payments."

"A holding company in Luxembourg that receives money from Bayerische Vereinsbank in Munich, and transfers money to the São Paulo office of the Banco Nacional is not exactly deep cover," I said. "That publishing-company account isn't active enough to fool anyone for long."

"Who else knows that?" He opened the brass flap on his ornate pen stand and looked at the dried-up sediment in the inkwell.

"I have told no one."

"I appreciate that, Bernd."

"You got me out of Weimar," I said.

"You were young. You needed help."

He screwed up the stamp edging a second time and tossed it into the dry inkwell with commendable accuracy before closing the brass flap. "They arrested Busch the very next day."

"That was a long time ago."

"I gave them his address."

"I know."

"Who could have guessed the poor old fellow would go back home again?"

"I would have done the same," I said.

"Not you, Bernd. You're made of harder stuff."

"That's why they sent me to tell you to hang on," I said.

He didn't smile. Without looking up from his desk, he said, "Suppose I could help you find the traitor in London?"

So that was it. So that's what all the messages and the difficulties had been leading up to. I said nothing. Munte knew nothing about London except the identity of Silas, who'd been his friend and run him so long ago. And nowadays Silas had little contact with the day-to-day running of London Central. Surely Silas couldn't be one of them.

He spoke again, still fidgeting with the pen stand. "I couldn't name him, but I could identify him positively to your satisfaction. And provide evidence that would satisfy even a law court, if that's the course that London decided upon."

Giles Trent, perhaps. I had to find out if he was trying

to sell me something I already had. "How would you do that? What sort of evidence?"

"Could you get me out?"

"You alone?"

"Me and my wife. Together. It would have to be the two of us together. We wouldn't be separated."

I felt sure that he was going to tell me about Giles Trent. If the KGB had discovered that we were playing Trent, I'd like to know. But I couldn't pull Munte out just for that.

Perhaps he guessed the sort of thoughts that were running through my mind. "I'm talking about someone with access to London Data Centre," he said, staring at me, knowing that I would be surprised to hear he even knew such a place existed. "Someone with pass codes prefixed 'knee jerk.'"

I sat very still and tried to look impassive. Now there was no longer any way of avoiding the awful truth. The "knee jerk" codes were used only by a handful of specially selected top personnel in London Central. Used in the Data Centre's computer, they accessed the automatic link—hence "knee jerk"—to CIA data files. If they'd seen printout with "knee jerk" marks here in East Berlin, there was no limit to what might have been betrayed. It was not Giles Trent we were talking about; it was someone senior, someone very close to Operations. "How soon could you get this evidence?"

"This evening."

"When would you want to travel?" This development changed everything. If Brahms Four could help identify such a well-placed Soviet agent, London would want him there to give evidence.

"You know what women are like, Bernd. My wife would probably need a few days to think about it."

"Tomorrow. I'll take you back with me. But let me make this clear. Unless you produce irrefutable evidence that enables me to identify the person who is supplying this material, the deal is off."

"I'll bring you four handwritten pages of data. Would that satisfy you?"

"Handwriting? Then it's certainly not genuine. No agent would be that stupid."

"Is that what you think, Bernd? Sometimes—when it's late, and one is tired—it becomes very difficult to take all the necessary precautions. Blame the KGB controller in the London Embassy who forwarded the original instead of making a copy. Or blame the clerks here in Berlin who have left the document in the file, Bernd. I feel sorry for the agent. I know exactly how he felt."

"Handwritten? And no one here remarked on it?"

"Lots of our papers are handwritten. We are not quite so automated as you are in the West. It's a distinctive hand—very neat with curly loops."

"From London?" Fiona's writing. But could it all be a plant?

"We are only a bank. Our security precautions are not very elaborate. It was a very interesting and most secret report about proposed Bank of England support for sterling. I recognized what it was only because I was looking for such things."

"By tonight, you say?"

"I know where the report is."

"Your wife must understand that she can't take anything with her except what she can wear and put in her pockets."

"We have talked about it many times, Bernd."

"No friends or relatives, no small dogs or parrots or albums of family photos."

"She understands," he said.

"It doesn't get easier," I said. "Don't frighten her, but make sure your wife understands that she's risking her life."

"She will not be frightened, Bernd."

"Very well."

"I will see you at nine o'clock tonight, my friend. Can you find the Pioneer House at Wuhlheide near Köpenick? It's a twenty-five-minute ride on the S-Bahn from here. Room G-three-forty-one. I'll have the papers."

"I'll find it."

He stood up and, with both hands on his hips, tilted his head back and sighed like a man awakening from a long sleep. "At last the decision is made," he said. 'Can you think what that means to me, Bernd?"

"I'll need to phone my wife in London," I said. "She gets anxious if I don't keep in contact. Can I direct-dial on a secure phone?"

"Use this one. I call the West several times every day. Dial nine and then the number," he said. "There is no monitoring of calls, but it will be logged. Be discreet, Bernd."

"We have a prearranged code," I explained. "Just domestic chat. I'll mention the handwritten paper. She'll understand what's happened."

Chapter 24

The Pioneer Park is a lavish example of the priority that East Germany gives to sport and leisure. Two square miles of parkland are landscaped into a complex of sports stadiums, running tracks, football and athletic fields, baths, swimming pools, and even a course for trotting races. I found the main building, and inside its gleaming interior I picked my way past well-equipped gyms and huge indoor pools that came complete with everything from diving instructors to rows of buzzing hair-dryers.

I found G-341 on the third floor and looked through the glass panel before entering. It was a small rehearsal room, beautifully paneled in contrasting woods, and occupied by four elderly men playing Schubert's "Death and the Maiden" quartet. Dr. Munte was sitting at a grand piano but he was not playing. His head was cocked and his eyes closed as he listened to the performance. Suddenly he got up and said, "No, gentlemen, no. There is no grace there." He saw me looking through the door but gave no sign of recognition. "Perhaps we've had too much Schubert tonight. Let's see how well you remember the Haydn Seventy-seven C Major." He beckoned me into the room and greeted me with a bow and formal handshake while the players sorted out the parts for the quartet.

"This is only our third attempt," he said apologetically. One of the men dropped his music on the floor and had to go on his knees to gather the sheets together again.

"It's a difficult work," I said.

Munte started them playing, using a delicate movement of both hands; then after watching them with a proprietorial satisfaction, he took me to a room beyond. This second room was larger, its walls lined with neat steel lockers for musical instruments and wooden lockers for clothes.

"You missed 'The Trout,' " he said. "I play the piano part for that."

"Did you get the document?"

He bent his head, still listening to the music coming from the next room. "The first violin is not up to it anymore," he admitted sadly. "He's having heat treatment for his finger joints, but I fear it's not helping him a great deal."

"The document," I said impatiently. "Did you bring it?"

"No," he said. "I didn't."

"Why not?"

Before he could answer, the door from one of the other adjoining rehearsal rooms swung open. A plump man came in dragging a small child and a cello, one in each hand. "Now here's Dr. Munte," said the fat man to his son. "Ask him how long you need every day." He turned to us and said, "Getting the little devil to practice would try the patience of a saint. All he thinks about is American jazz. Talk to him, Dr. Munte. Tell him he's got to practice. Tell him he must play real music, German music."

"If the interest is lacking, the child will never love music, Herr Spengler. Perhaps you should let him do what he wants."

"Yes, that's the modern way, isn't it," said the fat man, not bothering to hide his annoyance at Munte's lack of support. "Well, I don't believe in the modern way. This is not California. . . ." He studied my appearance and seemed to guess that I was not an East Berliner. But, having decided that I was not a foreigner, he continued: "We are Germans, aren't we? This is not California—*yet*. And may the Lord protect us from the sort of things that go on over there in the West. If I say my son is going to practice the cello, he'll do it. Do you hear that, Lothar? You'll practice every night for an hour *before* you go out to play football with your friends."

"Yes, *Väterchen*," said the boy with affection. He held his father's hand tightly until the man unclasped it in order to get keys from his pocket. The boy seemed reassured by his father's dictum.

The fat man put the cello into a locker and closed the door. Then he locked it with a padlock. "You're not strong enough for football," he said loudly as they went out. The little boy grabbed his father's hand again.

"We Germans find reassurance in tyranny," said Munte sadly. "That's always been our downfall."

"The document."

"The file containing the document you want is now with the clerk to the head of the bank's Economics Committee."

"Why?" Was the Berlin KGB office already in action?

"It's a big file, Bernd. There could be many perfectly ordinary reasons for his taking it away."

"Can you get it back from him tomorrow?"

"The normal way is to ask the records office, and wait while they find out where it is. Eventually such files turn up on the desk."

"You're not suggesting that we wait while the slow wheels of Communist bureaucracy turn for us?"

"I'm not suggesting anything," said Munte sharply. He

obviously identified himself with the slow wheels of bureaucracy and was offended.

"Go to wherever it is tomorrow. Remove this damned
handwritten document and bring it to me."

"How will I explain such an action? The files—even the
most ordinary ones—are signed in and out. What would the
head of the Economics Committee say if his clerk tells him
that I've taken the file—or even come into the office to look
at it?"

"For God's sake," I said angrily. I wanted to shout at
him, but I kept my voice low. "What do you care how
extraordinary such actions are? What do you care how suspicious anyone gets? We're talking about one last thing you
do before we get you out of here."

"Yes, you're talking about it," he said. "But suppose you
see this document and decide it's not something you want.
Then you say thank you, and leave me to go back into the
office and face the music, while you return to London and
tell them I had nothing worthwhile to offer."

"Very well," I said. "But I can't give you an absolutely
firm undertaking to get you out until London agrees to my
request. I can't get you out on my own, you know that. I
could tell you a pack of lies but I'm telling you the truth."

"And how long will that take?"

I shrugged.

"The slow wheels of Western bureaucracy?" he asked
sarcastically. He was angry. Fear does that to some people,
especially to such introspective sober-faced old men as Munte.
It was odd to think of him fearlessly enduring all the dangers of spying for years and then getting so frightened at the
idea of living in the West. I'd seen it in other men: the
prospect of facing a highly competitive, noisy, quick-mov-
ing, kaleidoscopic society and braving its dangers—sick-

ness, crime, poverty—could be traumatic. He needed reassurance. And if I did not reassure him quickly and properly he might suddenly decide he didn't want to go to the West after all. Such things had happened before, not once but many times.

"Preparations must be made," I said. "You and your wife will not go to a reception center for refugees. You'll be VIPs, looked after properly, so that you have no worries. You'll go to Gatow, the military airport, and fly directly to London on an R.A.F. plane—no customs or immigration nonsense. But for all that you'll need documentation, and such things take time." I said nothing of the dangers of crossing the Wall.

"I'll get it tomorrow," he said. "Will Silas Gaunt be there?"

"He'll be there, I'm sure."

"We were close friends in the old days. I knew your father too."

"Yes, I know." Next door there was a pause in the music before the slow movement began.

"Haydn speaks an everlasting truth," he said.

"You'll be all right once you're there," I said. "You'll see old friends and there will be a lot to do."

"And I will see my son."

I knew they wouldn't let Munte go to Brazil so readily. There would be long debriefings, and even after six months or so, when trips abroad are sometimes permitted, they wouldn't want him to go to Brazil, with its German colony so infiltrated by East German agents. "We might be able to get your son to London for you," I said.

"One step at a time," he replied. "I'm not even in London yet."

"You'll soon be there." I said it glibly while wondering which route to take back to the center of the city.

"Will I?" said Munte in a voice that made me give him my whole attention. "You've told London that I want to get out. And, guessing the real meanings behind the conversation you had with your wife on my phone, they now know about the evidence I'm providing for you to pinpoint the traitor there."

"Yes?" I said doubtfully. From the next room there came the solemn melodies of the quartet, the first violin wringing a plaintive song from under his stiffening fingers.

"Are you really such a fool? Someone in London is worrying what you will discover here. They will make quite certain that they hear any news you supply to London. They will then take measures to eliminate both of us."

"You worry too much," I said. "There will be no official report of what I told my wife."

"I don't believe you. Someone will have to take responsibility for the task of getting us out."

"My immediate superior. He'll be the only person told. Rest assured that he is not the man we are after."

"I'm not going home tonight."

"Then where are you going?"

"We've got a *Laube*. It's just two tiny rooms and a kitchen but we have electricity, and I won't lie awake all night worrying about policemen knocking on the door. My wife went out there earlier today. She will have some hot soup waiting."

"Where?"

"At Buchholz, behind the church. It's a huge spread of allotments. Hundreds of people go out there on the weekend even at this time of year."

"Tonight? It's a long journey to Buchholz. Do you want a ride? I've got a car."

"You're very kind. It's not such an easy journey by bus and the S-Bahn is quite far away from us."

I realized that Munte had deliberately introduced the

topic with the hope of getting a ride there. "How soon will you be ready?"

"I must wait for the end of the Haydn. I must tell my friend that his fingers are getting better. It's not true, of course, but it's the sort of lie one expects from a good friend." He smiled bleakly. "And I will not see any of my friends again, will I?"

FIRST I TOOK Munte to his home in Erkner, a village surrounded by lakes and forests on the extreme eastern edge of the city. I waited in the car ten minutes or more. He returned carrying a small case.

"Family photos, old letters, and my father's medals," he explained apologetically. "I suddenly realized that I will never return here."

"Don't take too much with you," I cautioned.

"I'll throw most of it away," he promised. "I should have done that years ago but I never seemed to have enough time."

I drove north from Erkner on the autobahn with which Fritz Todt—Hitler's chief engineer—had ringed Berlin. The road was in poor condition and more than once the cars were diverted to single-lane traffic. Near the Blumberg exit we were waved down by an army motorcyclist, and military policemen signaled frantically with their special flashlight-batons and ran about shouting in the imperious way that all military policemen learn at training school. Civilian traffic was halted while a Russian Army convoy passed us. It took ten minutes for the heavy trucks—some carrying tanks and others with missiles—to pick their way around the broken sections of roadway. It was during this delay that Munte told me a joke. He not only told me a joke, he told me it was a joke before he started it.

"There is a joke that East Berliners have about these neglected autobahns," he said. "People say why can't those *verdammten* Nazis come back and keep their *Autobahnen* in good order."

"It's a good joke," I said.

We waited a long time while the Russian trucks splashed through the rain puddles and thumped their suspensions on the potholes. Munte watched them with unseeing eyes. "I was driving along here during the Berlin fighting," he said suddenly. "It was toward the end of April 1945. The reports said that tanks of the First White Russian Front were moving into the northwest part of Charlottenburg and had halted at Bismarckstrasse. And there were unconfirmed reports of Red Army infantry in Moabit. In the car with me I had my young brother and two of his school friends. We were trying to get to my parents' home near Wannsee before the Russians got that far south. What an idiot I must have been! We didn't know the Russians coming from the southwest had already got to Wannsee. They were past Grunewald and fighting in the streets of Friedenau by that time."

He was silent until I finally said, "Did you get there?"

"I was on this same road, this same piece of autobahn. Stopped, just as we're stopped, but by some motorized SS unit. They drained every last drop of gas from my car and pushed it off the road. They were doing that with every car and truck that came along here. I even saw them commandeer two Luftwaffe fuel tankers at gunpoint."

"You walked home?"

"When the SS men got us out of my car, they looked at our papers. I had my Reichsbank pass and they accepted that without comment. But the three children were ordered to join an assorted collection of soldiers who were being pressed into battle. I objected but they shut me up by threatening to send me into the fighting too." He cleared his throat. "I never saw any of those boys again."

"It's nearly forty years ago," I reminded him. "You're not still blaming yourself?"

"I should have stayed with him. He was only fifteen years old."

"You did what you thought was right," I said.

"I did what I was told," said Munte. "I did it because I was frightened. I've never admitted that to anyone else, but I will tell you truthfully I was frightened."

The Russian convoy passed and our lane of cars started moving again. Munte sat back in his seat with his head resting against the window. He did not speak again for the rest of the journey, except to warn me when we were getting near to the autobahn interchange for Pankow.

It was late when we reached Buchholz, a village that has become a suburb. The tramlines end in front of the church in a street that is wide enough to be a village square. It was dark and the only light came from a *Weinstube* where a waiter was sweeping the floor of an empty bar.

Munte told me to turn off at the church. We bumped along a narrow country lane alongside a cemetery. It was dark, but by the headlights' beams I could see that there were trees and bushes on each side of a track that was only just wider than the car. Marking these plots of cultivated land were elaborate little wrought-iron gates, neatly painted fences, and trimmed hedges displaying an individuality of taste that bordered on caricature.

Against a horizon faintly pink with the advertising lights of the Western Sector of the city I could make out the squat shapes of the houses and hutments on each patch of ground. Lovingly fashioned by dedicated owners, this was the only sort of private house ownership permitted in the Democratic Republic. And selling such improved property provided a rare opportunity for officially tolerated capitalism.

Munte held out his hand to show me where to stop. I welcomed the careful directions he gave me about how to get out of this maze of narrow tracks, for there was not space enough to turn the car or even to avoid another on the same path.

I said, "Your material is kept quite separate from everything else, Dr. Munte. Even if there is a traitor in London, you needn't fear that you'll be betrayed." The old man got out of the car with a stiff-limbed difficulty that he'd not shown before. It was almost as if he'd aged during the short car journey.

He bent down to look at me. I leaned over the front passenger seat and wound the window down so that I could hear him. "You have no need to be so devious, Bernd," he said. "I intend to go to my office in the morning. I will get the document for you. I am not afraid."

I said nothing. I noticed that he was wringing his hands again, the way he had in his office earlier that day.

"I never go that way," he added as if he owed me an explanation. "No matter how much longer it takes me or where I want to get to, I never go that way. Until tonight, I haven't been back on that section of autobahn since it happened."

"I'm sorry if it upset you, Dr. Munte."

"I should have done it years ago," he said. "At last I've got rid of those terrible old nightmares."

"That's good," I said, although I knew he'd only exchanged old ones for new.

I WAS TIRED by the time I got back to Rolf Mauser's place in Prenzlauer Berg. But I observed the customary precautions and parked Werner's Wartburg around the corner and sat in it for a few moments scanning the area before locking up.

The streets were empty. The only sounds came from the elevated railway trains on Schönhauserallee and the occasional passing car or bus. There was no parking problem where Rolf Mauser lived.

A glimmer of light in the entrance to the apartment building was provided by a low-power bulb situated too high to be cleaned. It illuminated the broken floral-patterned floor tiles and, on the wall, a dozen or more dented metal boxes for mail. On the left was a wide stone staircase. To the right a long narrow corridor led to a metal-reinforced door that gave on to the courtyard at the rear of the building. At night the metal door was locked to protect the tenants' bicycles, and to prevent anyone disturbing the peace by using the rubbish bins or the ash cans.

I knew there was someone standing there even before I saw the slight movement. And I recognized the sort of movement it was. It was the movement a man made when his long period of waiting is at last near an end.

"Don't do anything," said a whispered voice.

I inched back into the shadow and reached in my pocket for a knife, the only weapon I would risk in a town where stop searches were so common.

"Bernie?" It was Werner, one of the few Germans who called me anything other than Bernd.

"What is it?"

"Did anyone see you come in?"

"No. Why?"

"Rolf's got visitors."

"Who?"

There came the sound of two cars arriving. When two cars arrive together at a residential block in Prenzlauer Berg, it is not likely to be a social call. I followed Werner quickly down the narrow corridor, but he could not get the door to the courtyard open. Two uniformed policemen and two men in leather overcoats came into the entrance and shined their flashlights at the names on the mailboxes.

"Mauser," said the younger of the uniformed cops, directing the beam of his torch on one of the boxes.

"Master detective," growled a leather-coated man in mock admiration. As he turned, the light of the torch showed him to be a man of about thirty-five with a small Lenin-style goatee.

"You said number nineteen," said the young policeman defensively. "I took you to the address you gave me." He was very young, and had the sort of Saxon accent that sounds comical to most German ears.

"The boss ordered me to be here fifteen minutes ago," growled Lenin in the hard accent of working-class Berlin. "I should have walked."

"You still would have ended up at the wrong address," said the cop, his Saxon accent stronger than before.

The leather-coated man turned on him angrily. "Maybe someone told you it's a softer touch being drafted into the police service than into the Army. I don't care that your daddy is a Party big shot. This is Berlin. This is my town. Shut up and do as you're told." Before the young conscript could reply, the leather-coated man started up the stairs. The other three followed him, and his harangue continued: "Wait till this KGB colonel arrives. You'll jump then, boys, you'll jump then."

Werner was still twisting the handle of the door to the yard when he realized that the cops were not going to shine their lights and discover us at the end of the corridor. "That was a close thing," he said.

"What's going on?"

"Two of them: Stasis. Upstairs in Rolf's apartment. They got here about three hours ago. You know what that means."

"They're waiting for someone."

"They're not waiting for *someone*," said Werner grimly. "They're waiting for *you*. Did you leave anything in the apartment?"

"Of course not."

"Let's get out of here," said Werner.

"Do you think they'll have a guard posted outside?"

"Let me go first. My papers are good ones."

"Hold it a minute." I could see a shadow, and then a cop came into view. He moved into the doorway as if he might have heard our voices, and then went outside again.

We waited a few more minutes, and then the four security policemen brought Rolf Mauser downstairs to the car. Rolf was making a lot of noise; his voice came echoing down the stairwell long before he came into sight.

"Let me go. What's all this about? Answer my questions. How dare you handcuff me! This could wait till morning. Let me go!"

Rolf's angry shouting must have been heard in every apartment in the building. But no one came to the door. No one came to see what was happening.

The front door crashed closed and we heard Rolf's voice in the empty street before the sound of the cars' engines swallowed his protests.

Only after the police had departed with their prisoner did the apartment doors upstairs open. There were whispered questions, and even quieter answers, for a few minutes before all went completely quiet.

"That's the way to do it," I said. "A silent prisoner might just as well confess. Rolf's shouting might make them pause to think. That might give us a chance to do something to help him."

"He didn't shout to convince them he was innocent," said Werner. "He was shouting to warn you off."

"I know," I said. "And there's nothing we can do to help him, either." Was Rolf Mauser Fiona's first victim, I wondered. And would I be the next one?

Chapter 25

OFFICIALLY, Werner Volkmann had no accommodation in East Berlin, but his riverside warehouse in Friedrichshain, with an office on the ground floor, contained four upstairs rooms that he had converted into comfortable living quarters, complete with tiny kitchen and a sitting room. It was against government regulations for him to stay overnight there—and no one could let a guest stay the night without police permission—but because Werner was earning foreign exchange nothing was ever said about his little "home."

Werner unlocked the massive warehouse door using three keys. "Refrigerators, color TV sets, real—made in the U.S.A.—blue jeans, Black and Decker drills, all the most sought-after delights of the decadent West are stored here from time to time," he said, explaining the need for the complex locks.

"Black and Decker drills?"

"To improve and enlarge living accommodations. Or, better still, fix up some little weekend place that they are legally permitted to sell." He went up a steep staircase and unlocked another door.

"Plenty of Black and Decker here," I said, looking at the newly decorated hall hung with two well-framed watercol-

ors: a contorted nude and a crippled clown. I bent closer to
see them. German Expressionist painters, of course. There
is something in their tragic quality that touches the soul of
Berliners.

"Nolde and Kirchner," said Werner, taking off his coat
and hanging it on an elaborate mahogany hallstand. "Not
your sort of thing, I know."

"But worth a packet, Werner," I said. I looked around
and saw some fine pieces of antique furniture. Werner had
always been a clever forager. At school he'd been able to get
American candy bars, pieces of broken tanks, military badges,
roller-skate wheels, and all the other treasures that school-
boys wanted then.

"Westmarks will buy anything on this side of the Wall.
And there are still mountains of treasures locked away in
cellars and attics."

I put my hat and coat alongside Werner's and followed
him into the next room. Light came in through the window.
Werner went across the room and looked out. Here was the
River Spree. Bright moonlight fell on a grimy stretch of
riverside land. Drawn against the sky was the complex iron-
work of the elevated railway, chopped off abruptly on its way
to the West, and left to rust. Nearer was a roofless factory
building, derelict and untouched since the fighting stopped
in 1945. To the right I could see along the dark river to the
glaring arc lights of the Oberbaum bridge, one of the border
crossing points, for here the river is the boundary between
the East and West sectors.

Werner closed the curtains abruptly and switched on the
table lamps. "We need a drink," he said. There being no
opposition from me, he produced a bottle of German brandy
and some glasses. Then he got ice and a jug of water from a
refrigerator alongside his big stereo-TV.

"That's a sure sign of a separated man," I said. "A man with ice available in his living room. Married men have to go to the kitchen to get ice in their booze."

"And what about a bachelor?"

"Ice in the bedroom," I said.

"You've always got an answer," said Werner. "That used to irritate me when we were kids."

"I know," I said. "I'm good at irritating people."

"Well, you certainly irritated Zena," he said.

"Why didn't you tell me you knew where she was?"

"And have you think she was having an affair with Frank Harrington?"

"Wasn't she having an affair with Frank Harrington?" I said cautiously. I sipped my brandy without the water that Werner was waving in the air.

"You drink too much. Do you know that?"

"Yes, I know because my wife keeps telling me."

"I'm sorry," said Werner. "I didn't mean to criticize. But right now you can't afford to blunt your mind."

"If that's what it does, give me another," I said.

He poured more brandy into my glass, and said, "No, that place in Lübars is a safe house. Zena was doing an undercover job for Frank Harrington. She's never been unfaithful to me. She would have told me more but she knows how much I've always disliked Frank."

"Is that what she told you? An undercover job."

"I've got her back," said Werner. "She's explained everything to me and we've started afresh. Sometimes there has to be a really bad disagreement before two people understand each other."

"Well, here's to you, Werner," I said.

"It was you who really got us back together again," said Werner. "You frightened her."

"Anytime, Werner," I offered.

He smiled the sort of smile that showed me he was not amused. "I did what you wanted. I went to London today and saw Dicky. It was a rush. I only just caught the flight back."

"All okay? No problems at the checkpoint?"

"Was I followed, you mean? Listen, the East Germans don't give a shit about my going to London and straight back here again. London is now at the center of the forfaiting market. I'm always in and out. How the hell do you think I get their deals for them? None of the West German banks are very keen to go into a syndicate unless I've got some nice juicy London or New York bank in it too."

"That's good."

"The D.D.R. needs Westmarks, Bernie. They're desperate for hard currency. They're squeezed between the Russians and the West. They need oil from Russia, but they also need Western technology. And all the time, the squeeze is getting tighter and tighter. I don't know what's going to happen over here a decade from now. And by the way, I paid Lisl back the money I borrowed—and interest too."

"Don't sound so worried, Werner."

"These people are Germans, Bernie. Of course I'm worried about what happens here."

"Sure," I said.

"Don't give me that look," he complained.

"What look was I giving you?"

"That 'Why do you Jews always have to get so emotional?' look."

"Stop being paranoid," I said. "And why are you being so bloody mean with your brandy? It's not even French."

He pushed the bottle over to me this time. "I saw Dicky Cruyer, just as you said, and he agreed that I put you on tomorrow's truck. Your wife had spoken with you on the phone by then, so Dicky fixed it right away. As soon as you are in the Federal Republic, we'll bring your precious Brahms Four out." Werner smiled. He knew that Dicky had sent me to Berlin to keep Brahms Four active and in place.

"Sounds good," I said.

"I'll feel much easier when you're back in the West," said Werner. "There are too many people who could recognize your face."

"And what if they do?"

"Don't be childish," said Werner. He picked up the brandy, recorked the bottle, and put it back into an antique lacquer cabinet decorated with Chinese mountain scenery.

"Was that cabinet something else you picked up for a pair of Levi's?" I asked, irritated by the way he closed the door of it.

"If some smart little bastard from the Stasis recognizes you, they'll take you in for interrogation. You know too much to be running around loose over here. I don't know why London permitted it."

"Well, you don't know everything, Werner," I said. "There are a couple of things now and again that the D-G doesn't check out with you."

"You don't think that was some kind of routine visit that the Stasis made to Rolf Mauser tonight? They know you're here, Bernie. They're looking for you—it's obvious."

"Let me do the worrying, Werner," I said. "I've had more practice."

Werner got to his feet and said, "Let's go downstairs and I'll show you the truck you'll be hiding in."

I got up and drained the dregs from my glass.

"Drinking makes you bad-tempered," said Werner.

"No," I said. "It's having the bottle taken away that does that."

The warehouse, which Werner leased from the Foreign Trade Ministry, was big. There were two thirty-ton trucks parked downstairs and there was still plenty of room for packing cases and workbenches and the office with two desks, three filing cases, and an ancient Adler typewriter.

"We bolt you in," said Werner, climbing into the back of the trailer. His voice echoed in the confined space. "The first couple of times we did it, we welded that section after the people were inside, but we burned someone's leg doing it, so now we bolt it up and paint it with quick-drying paint. I hope you don't suffer from claustrophobia." He pointed to the place at the front of the cargo compartment where two metal sheets had been opened to reveal a narrow compartment. "Plenty of air holes, but they are not visible because of the baffles. These two brackets hold a small wooden seat, and we'll fix a soft cushion on it because you'll be a long time in here."

"How long?"

"Those bastards at the customs don't work a long hard day," said Werner. "Ten minutes of writing out forms and they have to sit down and recuperate for an hour or so."

"How long altogether?"

"Sometimes the trucks are parked in the compound for two days before the officials even look up and nod. Drivers have been known to go crazy in the waiting room. Maybe that's the idea."

"Three days, maximum?"

"We're talking about a game of chance, Bernie. Relax, and take along something to read. I'll fix a light for you. How about that? It could be they'll wave us through."

"I won't be the one traveling in this metal box," I said.

"I knew that," said Werner in a voice that was more annoyed than self-satisfied.

"What did you know?"

"Right from the start, I thought, That bastard is going to pull some kind of switch. And here it is. So who is going?"

"Brahms Four goes first. He wants to take his wife. You could fit two people in here, couldn't you? It's better they go on the first trip."

"That's not the reason. That's just calculated to break my heart and make me think you're a wonderful fellow."

"I *am* a wonderful fellow," I said.

"You're a devious bastard," said Werner.

"You told Dicky?"

"I did it just the way you wanted. No one knows except Dicky Cruyer . . . and anyone he tells."

"And my kids?" Finally I had to ask the question I'd been avoiding.

"You're worrying unnecessarily, Bernie. It can't be Fiona."

"Twenty-four-hour cover? Three men and two cars each shift?"

"I did it just the way you said. Your kids are watched night and day. I was surprised that Dicky Cruyer okayed it."

"Thanks, Werner," I said.

"Does Fiona know where this place is?" So now even he was truly convinced.

"Not from me, she doesn't."

"She wouldn't let you get arrested, Bernie. You're the father of her kids." He spoke of Fiona apologetically. Why does the betrayed partner always get treated like a leper? It's damned unfair. But it was no different from the way I'd treated Werner all through his sufferings with *his* disloyal wife.

"So you'll put two seats in here?" I said, rapping the metal sheet of the hidden compartment.

"Where do we pick them up?"

"We'll have to think carefully about that, Werner," I said. "Not a good idea to let them come here. You don't want some little creep writing down your address in a debriefing sheet that gets circulated to NATO intelligence officers." Werner shuddered and said nothing. I said, "But we don't want a big truck like this going off the main roads. It would stick out like a sore thumb in some back street in Pankow."

"Müggelheimer Damm," suggested Werner. It was a long, almost straight road through the forest that bordered the Grosser Müggelsee—a big lake just outside the city. "There are no houses all the way from Altstadt to Müggelheim—just the forest road. And it's convenient from here."

"Which way will you go? Through Russian Army HQ Karlshorst? Or past the Red Army memorial at Treptow?" Both places were always well provided with sharp-eyed traffic police and plainclothes security men.

"What does it matter? We'll be clean at that stage of the journey."

"A halted truck on that long forest road?" I said doubtfully.

"It will look as if the driver has gone behind a tree," said Werner.

"Where on the Müggelheimer Damm?"

"Keep driving till you see me," said Werner. "It's better that I choose somewhere I like the look of. You'll find me. There won't be many bright yellow thirty-ton articulated trucks parked along that section of road on a weekday."

"At twelve-thirty," I said. "We'll hope the traffic cops will be having lunch."

"Do you think his wife might be claustrophobic? A lot of women are. There was a case some years ago, I remember, where an escapee started beating on the floor of a car to get out. She just couldn't stand being locked in the luggage compartment. They were all arrested. If I gave Brahms Four a needle, could we rely on him to give her a shot?"

"If necessary."

"I knew you wouldn't go first," said Werner. "I knew you'd want to get Brahms Four out before you went yourself."

"What made you think so, Werner?"

"You wouldn't put yourself into a position where London Central could have a change of mind and you not be able to do much about it."

"Go to the top of the class, Werner," I said.

"*Fait accompli,* that's your style. It always has been." He jumped down from the truck.

"One more thing," I said. "Just to be on the safe side, I want Brahms Four under observation right from the time he gets on the streetcar at Buchholz to go to work tomorrow."

"No problem," said Werner.

"Any divergence from what I've told him to do and we'll scrub the whole thing."

"I like you, Bernie. You're the only man I know who's more suspicious than I am, and that reassures me."

"Any divergence at all," I said.

"You won't tell him about Müggelheimer Damm before he gets there?"

"I won't even answer if he says good morning."

"Even if it is Fiona," said Werner, "she can't act on this day-to-day information without making it obvious that she's the KGB agent."

"Moscow might decide it's worthwhile. Brahms Four is a good source—maybe the only really big leak they haven't been able to plug."

"That's why you want him to go first. Moscow will let the first one through even if they know about it. They'll let it go believing it's you and thinking the second escape will be their only chance of getting Brahms Four. It's a dangerous game, Bernie. If you are right, you'll get caught."

"But maybe I'm wrong," I said.

Chapter 26

D ON'T WORRY, Frau Doktor von Munte," I said. "Your husband will soon be back." I looked out the window. The little gardens of fruit and vegetables stretched in every direction across the flat land, and the curious assortment of hutments and sheds looked even more bizarre by daylight. On every side there were heaps of sand, bags of cement, and piles of bricks, blocks, and timber for more amateur building work.

Now May was here. Fruit trees, climbing flowers, shrubs, and bushes were engulfing the buildings. There was lilac—the smell of it was everywhere—and cherry trees in snowy bloom, tubs of roses and dwarf rhododendrons. But the vegetation was not enough to hide the one-story building that the next-door neighbor had painted bright red, and laboriously drawn wobbly lines of yellow upon, to produce the effect of a medieval castle.

The little house that the Muntes owned was more restrained. Painted dark green, to blend with the surroundings, its wooden window shutters bore old-fashioned flower designs. On the side of it there was a tiny lean-to greenhouse with pots of herbs, boxes of lettuce plants and some carnations, all crowded together to catch the sunshine. The garden too was more in keeping with the elderly couple: everything neat and tidy, like an illustration from a gardening manual.

"Why did you tell him to say he wasn't feeling well?" she asked. Mrs. Munte was a severe-looking woman, in a black dress with a white lacy collar. Her hair was drawn back tight into a bun and her face had the high cheeks and narrowed eyes that marked the German communities of the Baltic States. Blue eyes and reddish-flaxen hair are common in Estonia. "Why did you?" It was an inscrutable face but it was calm too, the sort of face that, apart from a few wrinkles and spots, remains unchanged from early teens to old age.

"So that no one will be surprised when he's away from the office for a couple of days."

"I wish we had stayed at the apartment in Erkner. Here we have no TV. I get so bored here."

"Your neighbor is sunning himself. Why don't you spend half an hour outside?" The owner of the *Schloss* next door had stretched a blanket on his minuscule lawn. Now he was applying lotion to his bare chest and searching the sky for dark clouds, a wary frown upon his face.

"No. He'll chatter to me," said Mrs. Munte. "He's a retired bus driver. He's on his own. Once he starts talking, you can't stop him. He grows tulips. I hate tulips, don't you? They look like plastic." She was standing at the tiny window looking out at her rhododendrons and roses. "Walter has worked so hard on his flowers. He'll miss them when we're somewhere else."

"There'll be other roses and rhododendrons," I said.

"Even this morning he went out to spray the roses. I said it was silly but he insisted on doing it."

"They need it at this time of the year," I said. "Mine have got black spots."

"Will you go with us?"

"I follow on."

"You've done this sort of thing before, I suppose?"

"You'll be quite safe, Frau von Munte. It's uncomfortable but not dangerous."

"Of course you'd say that," she said peevishly. "It's your job to encourage us."

"By the time Dr. von Munte gets back here, it will be time to think about leaving."

"Why do you make him come all the way back here before we leave? Why couldn't we meet him in town?"

"It's the way it's been planned," I said.

She looked at me and shook her head. "It's so that you can look at those papers he's bringing you. It's to give you a chance to cancel everything. Walter told me what you said."

"Why not read your book?" I said. It was an anthology called *More Short Stories from Poland*. Twice or three times she'd started to read it and then put it down. Her mind was on other things. I said, "There is nothing to be gained from letting these thoughts go round and round in your mind."

"How do I know my husband isn't already on his way?"

"To the West?"

"Yes. How do I know he's not already on his way?"

"He wouldn't go anywhere without you, Frau von Munte."

"Perhaps that disappointed you," she said. There was a hard note of satisfaction in her voice. "You wanted Walter to go on his own, didn't you?"

"No," I said.

"Oh, yes, you did. You made the arrangements for just one person. You were going to leave me here."

"Is that what Dr. von Munte told you?"

"He confides in me. That is what our marriage has always been."

"What else has he confided to you?" I asked. I smiled to soften my question.

"I know what he's gone back to his office for, if that's what you mean."

"Tell me, then."

"A paper of some kind, handwritten by a Communist agent. Someone very highly placed in the London intelligence service."

I didn't deny that she was right.

"Yes," she said. "And you'll recognize the handwriting and you'll know who it is."

"I hope so," I said.

"But what will you do then, I wonder. Will you reveal who it is or will you use it for your own purposes?"

"Why do you say that?"

"It's obvious to me," she said. "If you wanted only to reveal the truth, you could have had the papers sent to London. But you want to look at them. You want to be the one who has the power."

"Would you make some more coffee, please?"

"My husband is too nice," she said. "He'd never use the sort of power he has to advance himself. He does what he does because of his beliefs." I nodded. She went to a tiny sink, which could be closed inside the cupboard when not in use, filled the electric kettle, and switched it on. "We bought this *Laube* during the war. Walter said the bombs were less dangerous in the soft earth. We grew potatoes, leeks, and onions. There was no electricity then, of course, and we had to go a long walk to get drinking water." She talked compulsively, her arms akimbo as she stared at the kettle. I noticed her small red hands and her red bony elbows as she rubbed her arms as if she felt cold. She had concealed her nervousness until now; it is often accompanied by such bodily chills. She waited until the kettle came to a full boil before pouring the water into the pot. "Do you have a wife?" she asked. She'd put a felt cover on the coffeepot and now she clasped it with her open hands to feel the warmth of it. "Does she sit at home all day getting bored?"

"She goes to work," I explained. "She works with me."

"Is that how you met? I met Walter at the big house his parents had near Bernau. They are an old important family, you know."

"I met your husband's father once," I said. "He was a remarkable old man. I was only a small child, but he spoke to me as an equal. And a few days later, he sent me a leather-bound copy of *Die schöne Müllerin*. It had come from his library, and had his name embossed in gold on the cover and an engraved bookplate inside. My father told me that only a dozen books from his library had survived the war. I have it still."

"You lived in Berlin as a child. That explains your perfect Berlin accent." She seemed more relaxed now that she knew I'd met old von Munte. "Hundreds of local people went to the old gentleman's funeral. They had it out there at the house where all the rest of the family had been buried. My father was a country physician. He attended the old man right until the end. What did your father do for a living?"

"He started out as a clerk. In the thirties he was unemployed for a long time. Then he went into the Army. The war began and he became an officer. After the war he stayed in the Army."

"I'm Walter's second wife, of course. Ida was killed in one of the very first air raids." She poured coffee for us. "Do you have children?"

"Two: a boy and a girl."

"It's Ida's child, of course—the one he wants to see." She pushed the large cup of black coffee across the table to me in a gesture that contained an element of rejection.

"In São Paulo?"

"There's only the one child. That's why Walter dotes on him so much. I hope and pray he is not disappointed."

"Disappointed how?"

"It's such a long time," she said as if on that account the chances of the two men disappointing each other were self-evident.

"He's sure to be grateful," I said. "Walter has given him so much."

"He's given his son everything," she said. "He's given him every penny he's earned from you. He's given him the life that was rightfully mine." She drank some coffee. Her words were bitter but her face was calm.

"And now his son will be able to thank you both."

"We'll be strangers to him. His son won't want the burden of looking after us. And Walter has no chance of earning any more."

"It will be all right," I promised vaguely.

"Our presence will remind him of his obligation, and he will resent that. Then he'll start feeling guilty about such feelings and associate us with that guilt." She drank more coffee. She'd obviously been thinking about it a great deal. "I'm always a pessimist. Is your wife a pessimist?"

"She had to be an optimist to marry me," I said.

"You haven't told me how you met," said Mrs. Munte.

I mumbled something about meeting her at a party, and went over to look out the window. She'd arrived with two other girls. Dicky Cruyer knew her name, and so I immediately approached her with a bottle of Sancerre and two empty glasses. We'd danced to music from a record player that was wound by a handle and discussed our host, a Foreign Office junior clerk who was celebrating a posting to Singapore.

Fiona was typing letters for a travel company in Oxford

Street. It was a temporary job, due to finish the next week. She asked me if I knew of any really interesting work for someone with a good degree who could type and take shorthand in three languages. I didn't think she was serious at first. Her clothes and jewelry made her look anything but desperate for employment.

"She told me she was out of work," I said.

At the time, Bret Rensselaer was setting up an undercover operation that worked out of an office block in Holborn and processed selected data from the Berlin office. We needed staff and Bret had already decided that we would not go through the normal civil-service recruitment procedure. It took too long and involved too much form-filling and interviewing; to make matters worse, the civil service only sent us applicants that the Foreign Office had already decided were not good enough for them.

"What was she wearing?" said Mrs. Munte.

"Nothing special," I said. It was a tight sweater of angora wool. I remember it because it took two dry cleanings and a lot of brushing to remove the final fluffs of wool from my only good suit. I asked her where she'd learned shorthand and typing and she cracked some silly joke that made it clear that she was an Oxford graduate, and I pretended not to understand such subtlety. Dicky Cruyer tried to cut in on our dancing at that point, but Fiona said couldn't he see that she was dancing with the most handsome man in the room?

"But you saw her again?" said Mrs. Munte.

I had a date with her the very next evening. And I wanted to be able to say I had a job for her. It was an attractive idea to have her in the same office with me. Bret Rensselaer didn't much like the idea of taking on someone we hadn't properly vetted, but when we found out that she was related to Silas Gaunt—who'd become something of a legend in the Department—he gave me a grudging okay. At first it was conditional on her working only out of my office, and not having access to the really sensitive material or any contact with our Berlin people. But in a few years, hard work and long hours gave her a series of promotions that put her in line for an Operations desk.

"I got her a job," I said.

"Perhaps it was the job, rather than you, she was after," said Mrs. Munte, tilting her head to one side to show me it was not a serious suggestion.

"Perhaps it was," I said.

I was watching two men at the far end of the narrow lane that led up from the Buchholz church. They were both in civilian clothes, but unmistakably Stasis. It was government policy that the secret police never wore beards or mustaches, and dressed in plain clothes of a type that made them immediately recognizable to every East German who saw them. Everyone except the most naïve realized that there were other plainclothes policemen who weren't so easy to spot, but where the hell were they? "Frau von Munte," I said matter-of-factly, "there are a couple of policemen coming up the lane checking each of the houses in turn." I kept watching them. Now I could see that there were two more men—one in police uniform—and, behind them, a black Volvo negotiating the narrow lane with great care. Beyond that came a minibus with a light fixed to the roof. "Four policemen," I said. "Perhaps more."

She came over to the window, but had the good sense to stand well back from it. "What kind of policemen?" she asked.

"The kind who get Volvos," I said. With the scarcity of any sort of hard currency, only senior ranks or special squads could get an imported car.

"What do we do?" She gave no sign of fear. Married to

a spy for a couple of decades, I suppose, she'd lived through this nightmare times without number.

"Get two boxes of those seedlings from the greenhouse," I said. "I'll just look around in here before we leave."

"Where are we going?"

"Back to my car."

"We'll have to go past them."

"They'll see us whichever way we go. Better to brazen it out."

She put on an absurd fezlike felt hat and fastened it into her hair with ferocious-looking hatpins. She looked around the room. There were obviously many things she'd planned to take with her, but she grabbed only a fur coat from a box under the bed and put it on. She went out to the greenhouse, came back, and handed me a box of seedlings and kept one for herself. As we went out, I smiled at the neighbor stretched out on a blanket in front of his castle. He shut his eyes and pretended to be asleep. Closing the little garden gate carefully after Mrs. Munte, I followed her down the lane toward the policemen.

They were working systematically, a two-man team on each side of the lane. One man to go into the garden and knock at the door, the other to watch the back. The driver of the car would be ready to take a potshot at anyone trying to run for it. In the back of the Volvo there was another man. It was Lenin, the senior officer of the team that had arrested Rolf Mauser. He was sprawled across the back seat ticking off names and addresses from papers on a clipboard.

"Who are you, where are you going?" said one of the policemen as we got near. It was the young Saxon conscript again. He'd been given the job of plodding along the lane to hold back the bushes that might scratch the paintwork of the car.

"None of your business, young man," said Mrs. Munte.

She made an incongruous figure, standing there in the sunshine holding the plants and wearing her fur coat and *Kaffeeklatsch* hat.

"Do you live here?" He moved out to block the path. I noticed that the flap of his pistol holster was undone. His arms were folded across his body, a gesture that policemen like to think looks friendly.

"Live here?" said Mrs. Munte. "What do you think we are, squatters?"

Even the policemen smiled. Whatever Mrs. Munte looked like, she could not be mistaken for one of the dirty long-haired squatters seen so frequently on TV news from the West Sector. "Do you know anyone here named Munte?"

"I don't know any of these people," she said disdainfully. "I come to this dreadful place only to buy things I can't get elsewhere. My son is helping me with these carnations. It's his day off and he's brought his car here. Ten marks for these few seedlings. It's disgraceful. You should be concerning yourself with the profiteers that are flourishing here."

"We are," said the policeman. He still smiled but didn't move.

She leaned close to him. "What are you doing?" she whispered loudly. "Is it wife swappers you are after? Or have the whores moved in here again?"

He grinned and stood aside. "You're too young to know about that kind of thing, *Mutti*," he said. He turned around and watched us as we staggered along with the boxes of plants. "Make way for the busy gardeners," he called to the policemen behind him. And they stood aside too. The man in the back of the Volvo stared at his papers and said nothing. He probably thought our papers had been checked.

Chapter 27

Y BOX of carnation plants was heavy enough to make
me sweat by the time we got to the church at
Buchholz, but Mrs. Munte was not complaining. Perhaps
she was much stronger than she looked. Or perhaps she'd
chosen a lighter one for herself.

Buchholz marks the end of the number 49 tram route.
In the cobbled village square were the bicycles of commuters
who lived beyond the terminus. There were hundreds of
them, racked, stacked, hanging, and piled; the narrow path-
ways that gave access to them made an intricate maze.
Within this maze a man was standing. He had a newspaper
in his hands and he was reading from it in a preoccupied
way that permitted him to glance around him, and to look
down the street as if waiting for the tram to arrive. It was
Werner Volkmann; there was no mistaking the big bearlike
torso and short legs, and the hat that was planted right on
top of his large head.

He gave no sign of seeing me, but I knew he'd chosen
that spot so he could keep the car in his line of vision. I
unlocked the doors and put the plants into the boot and
Mrs. Munte into the back seat. Only then—when Mrs.
Munte was shut into the car and couldn't hear us—did
Werner cross the road to talk to me.

"I thought you'd be across the other side of town," I said quietly, stifling the impulse to scream at him.

"It's probably okay," said Werner. He turned to look up the street. There was a police car outside the post office, but the driver was showing no interest in us. He was talking to a cop in one of the long white coats that only traffic police wear. "Four plainclothes cops visited your man's office this morning. It was nothing more than a few polite inquiries, but it scared hell out of him."

"The same team who arrested Rolf Mauser are now raking through the *Lauben* and asking if anyone knows him."

"I know. I saw them arrive."

"Thanks, Werner."

"No sense in me rushing in there to get arrested with you," said Werner defensively. "I can be more help to you free."

"So where is he?"

"Brahms Four? He left his office soon after arriving at work. He came into the street holding a small attaché case and wearing a pained look. I didn't know what to do—no phone here to reach you. So I had one of my people grab him. I stayed clear. He doesn't know me. I didn't want him to see the warehouse, so I had someone drive him out to Müggelsee. The truck will go separately. Then I came up here to ask you whether we should still go ahead."

"At least let's make the kind of attempt that will look good on the report," I said. "Let's take this old lady over to Müggelsee and put her in the truck."

"You kept your man well wrapped up," said Werner. "Twenty years at least he's been operating in this town, and I'd never seen him until today."

"Deep cover," I said, imitating the voice of Frank Harrington at his most ponderous.

Werner smiled. He enjoyed any joke against Frank.

Werner got in the driver's side and took the wheel. He started up and turned the car south for Berlinerstrasse and the city center. "For Müggelsee the autobahn will be quicker, Werner," I said.

"That would take us out of the East Sector and into the Zone," said Werner. "I don't like crossing the city boundaries."

"I came that way to get here. It's quicker."

"This is Himmelfahrt—Ascension Day. A lot of people will be taking the day off to swim and sun. It's not an official holiday but there's plenty of absenteeism. That's the only kind of 'ism' that's really popular here. There will be cops on the roads that lead out of town. They'll be taking names and arresting drunks and generally trying to discourage people from having a holiday whenever they feel like goofing off."

"You talked me out of it, Werner."

Mrs. Munte leaned forward between the seats. "Did you say we're going to Müggelsee? That will be crowded. It's popular at this time of year."

"Me and Bernie used to swim out there when we were kids," said Werner. "The Grosser Müggelsee is always the first to warm up in summer and the first to freeze for ice skating. It's shallow water. But you're right, *gnädige Frau*, it will be crowded out there today. I could kick myself for forgetting about the holiday."

"My husband will be there?"

I answered her: "Your husband is there already. We'll join him and you'll be across the border by nightfall."

It was not long before we saw the first revelers. There were a dozen or more men in a brewer's dray. Such horse-drawn vehicles, with pneumatic tires, are still common in Eastern Europe. But this one was garlanded with bunches of leaves and flowers and colored paper. And the fine dap-

ple-gray horses were specially groomed with brightly berib-
boned manes. The men in the dray wore funny hats—many
of them black toppers—and short-sleeved shirts. Some wore
the favorite status symbol of Eastern Europe: blue jeans.
And inevitably there were Western T-shirts, one blazoned
"I love Daytona Beach, Florida" and another "*Der Tag geht
. . . Johnnie Walker kommt.*" The horses were going very slowly
and the men were singing loud songs between swigging beer
and shouting to people in the street and catcalling after
girls. They gave a loud cheer as our car went past them.

There were more such parties as we got to Köpenick.
Groups of men stood under the trees at the edge of the road,
smoking and drinking in silence with a dedication that is
unmistakably German. Other men were laughing and singing; some slept soundly, neatly arranged like logs, while
others were being violently ill.

Werner stopped the car well down the Müggelheimer
Damm. There were no other vehicles in sight. Plantations of
tall fir trees darkened the road. This extensive forest continued to the lakes on each side of the road and far beyond.
There was no sign of Werner's big articulated truck, but
he'd spotted its driver standing at the roadside. He was near
one of the turnoffs, narrow tracks that led up to the edge of
the Müggelsee.

"What is it?" Werner asked him anxiously.

"Everything is in order," said the man. He was a big
beefy red-necked man, wearing bib-and-brace overalls and
a red-and-white woolen hat of the sort worn by British football supporters. "I had the truck here, as we arranged, but
a crowd of these lunatics . . ." He indicated some small
groups of men standing in a car park across the road. "They
began climbing all over it. I had to move it." He had the
strongest Berlin accent I'd ever heard. He sounded like one
of the old-style comedians who can still be heard telling

Berliner jokes in unlicensed cabarets in the back streets of Charlottenburg.

"Where are you now?" said Werner.

"I pulled off the road into one of these firebreaks," said the driver. "The earth's not so firm—all that bloody rain last week. I'm heavy, you know. Get stuck and we're in trouble."

"This is the other one," said Werner, moving his head to indicate Mrs. Munte in the back seat.

"She doesn't look too heavy," said the driver. "What do you weigh, Fräulein? About fifty kilos?" He grinned at her. Mrs. Munte, who obviously weighed twice that, didn't answer. "Don't be shy," said the driver.

"And the man?" said Werner.

"Ah," said the driver, "the Herr Professor." He was the sort of German who called any elderly well-dressed fellow-countryman "Professor." "I sent him up to that lakeside restaurant to get a cup of coffee. I told him someone would come for him when we are ready."

While he was saying that, I saw the black Volvo and the minibus coming down the road from the direction of Müggelheim. They would have made good time on the autobahn, flashing their lights to get priority in the traffic or using their siren to clear the fast lane.

"Get the professor," said Werner to me. "I'll drive the old lady down to where the truck is parked, and come back to meet you here."

As I hurried along the woodland path toward the lake, I could hear a curious noise. It was the regular roaring sound that waves make as they are sucked back through the pebbles of a long stony beach. It got louder as I approached the open-air restaurant, but that did not prepare me for the sight I found there.

The indoor restaurant was closed on weekdays, but there

were hundreds of men milling around the lakeside *Biergarten* in inebriated confusion. They were mostly young workers dressed in bright shirts and denim pants, but some wore pajamas and some had Arab headdress and many of them had brought the black top hat that is traditional for Himmelfahrt. I could see no women, just men. There were long lines of them waiting at a serving hatch marked "*Getränke*" and an equally long line at a hatch marked "Kaffee," where only beer, in half-liter plastic cups, was being served. Tables were crammed with dozens and dozens of empty plastic cups stacked together, and there were more empties scattered in the flower beds and lined up along the low dividing walls.

"*Heiliger bim-bam!*" said a drunk behind me, as surprised as I was at the sight.

The roars of sound were coming from the throats of the men as they watched a rubber ball being kicked high into the air. It went up over their heads and cut an arc in the blue sky before coming down to meet yet another skillfully placed boot that sent it back up again.

It took me a few minutes to spot Munte. By some miracle he'd found a chair and was sitting at a table at the edge of the lake where it was a little less crowded. He seemed to be the only person drinking coffee. I sat down on the low wall next to him. There were no other chairs in sight; prudent staff had no doubt removed them from the danger zone. "Time to go," I said. "Your wife is here. Everything is okay."

"I got it for you," he said.

"Thanks," I said. "I knew you would."

"Half the clerks in my department have taken the day off too. I had no trouble walking into the chief's office, finding the file, and helping myself."

"I'm told you had a visit from the police."

"The office had a visit from the police," he corrected me. "I left before they found me."

"They came out to Buchholz," I said.

"I was trying to think of some way of warning you when a man came up to me in the street and brought me here." He reached into his pocket and produced a brown envelope. He put it on the table. I left it there for a moment. "Aren't you going to open it and look inside?" he asked.

"No," I said. Not far away from us, a six-piece wind band had assembled. Now they were making all those sounds musicians have to make before playing music.

"You want to see the writing. You want to see who is the traitor in London Central."

"I know who it is," I said.

"You've guessed, you mean."

"I know. I've always known."

"I risked my freedom to get it this morning," he said.

"I'm sorry," I said. I picked up the envelope and toyed with it as I reasoned out what to do. Finally I handed it back to him. "Take it to London," I said. "Give it to Richard Cruyer—he's a slim fellow with curly hair and chewed fingernails—make sure no one else gets it. Now we must go. The police seem to have traced us here. They're the same ones who went to Buchholz."

"My wife—is she safe?" He got to his feet in alarm. As he did so, the wind band began playing a drinking song.

"Yes, I told you. But we must hurry." I could see them arriving now. I could see Lenin, with his long brown leather overcoat and his little beard. He was wearing a brown leather cap too, and metal-rimmed eyeglasses. His face was hard and his eyes were hidden behind the bright reflections of his lenses. Alongside him was the young Saxon conscript, white-faced and anxious, like a child lost in a big crowd. It was unusual to have a conscript in such a team. His father's

influence must be considerable, I thought. The four policemen had stopped suddenly at the end of the path, surprised,
just as I had been upon first catching sight of the multitude.

The band music was loud. Too loud to make conversation easy. I grabbed Munte's arm and moved him hurriedly
into a crowd of men who had linked arms and were trying
to dance together. One of them—a muscular fellow with a
curly mustache—was wearing striped pajamas over his
clothes. He grabbed Munte and said, "*Komm, Vater. Tanzen.*"

"I'm not your father," I heard Munte say as I stood on
tiptoe to see the policemen. They had not moved. They
remained on the far side of the beer garden, bewildered at
the task of finding anyone in such a crowd. Lenin tapped
one of the older men and sent him down the line of men
waiting to buy beer. He sent the fourth man back along the
path; no doubt he was going to bring more men from the
minibus.

For the second time, Munte disengaged his arm from
that of the man in pajamas. "*Ich bin vaterlos,*" said the man
sorrowfully. The "fatherless" man pretended to cry. His
friends laughed and swayed in time with the oom-pah-pah
music. I grabbed Munte and pushed through the dancers.
Looking back, I caught sight of the leather-capped Lenin,
who was clambering onto a tub of flowers to see over the
heads of the crowd. Around him the dancing had stopped
and the football went rolling down the steps unheeded.

"Walk that way, through the trees," I told Munte. "You'll
meet a broad-shouldered man, about my age, wearing a coat
with an astrakhan collar. In any case, keep going along the
road until you see a very big truck with a bright yellow
tarpaulin marked '*Unterberg.*' Stop the truck and get in. Your
wife will be there already."

"What about you?"

"I'll try to delay the police."

"That's dangerous, Bernd."

"Get going."

"Thank you, Bernd," said the old man soberly. We both knew that, after Weimar, it was what I had to do for him.

"Walk, don't run," I called as he ambled away. His dark suit insured that he would soon be swallowed up by the gloom of the forest.

I pushed my way along to the edge of the lake. A number of men had walked out on the little pier and climbed into a small sailing boat. Now someone was trying to untie the mooring ropes, but it was proving difficult for the maladroit drunk. One of the restaurant staff was shouting at the men, but they paid no heed.

A very loud cheer brought my attention around to the beer garden again. Three young drunks were walking along the top of a low wall. Each carried a pitcher of beer and wore a black top hat, and each was otherwise naked. Every few paces they stopped, bowed deeply to acknowledge the applause, and then drank from the jugs.

Lenin had his three cohorts at his side as he elbowed his way through the muttering crowd of holiday makers, their exuberance stifled by his presence. Thinking the policemen were there to check absentees from work, and were about to arrest the streakers, the onlookers were resentful. Intoxication emboldened them enough to show their resentment. There were catcalls. The four policemen were jostled and pushed. They were confronted by a particularly big opponent, a bearded man in sweat shirt and jeans, who seemed determined to bar their way. But they were trained to deal with such situations. Like all cops, they knew that quick action, with a nicely judged degree of violence, is what crowd control depends upon. One of the uniformed cops felled the bearded man with a blow of his truncheon. Lenin blew three blasts on his whistle—to suggest that many more policemen were on call—and they plunged on through the crowd, which parted to make way for them.

By now Munte was a hundred yards or more into the forest and out of sight, but Lenin had obviously spotted him for, once through the thickest part of the crush of men, he began running.

I ran too, choosing a path that would converge on the policemen's. I ran alongside them through the springy undergrowth of the dark forest. Lenin looked around to see who was chasing him, saw me, and looked to his front again. "This way!" I shouted, and headed down a path that led back to the lakeside.

For a moment Lenin and his three subordinates continued going the way that Munte had gone. Surely the old man had heard them coming after him by now. "You four!" I shouted with the sort of arrogance that was calculated to convince them of my seniority. "This way, you bloody fools. He's heading for the boat!"

Still the men raced after Lenin, while I continued on the other path. This was my last chance. "Do you hear me, you idiots?" I shouted breathlessly. "This way, I say!"

My desperation must have been the convincing factor, for Lenin changed direction and came thumping across the forest floor, his ammunition boots shaking the earth, his eyeballs dilated, and his face bright red with exertion. "The boat is hidden," I shouted to account for what I guessed would be the complete absence of any boat when they reached the water. I waved the uniformed cops past me and then went back up the path as if I were expecting more policemen who might need guidance.

But by the time I was fifty yards up the track, Lenin had got to the waterfront and found no boats or places along the lake's edge where any could be hidden. He'd sent the young Saxon conscript back to find me.

"Stop, sir," said the cop in that unmistakable accent.

"This way!" I shouted, bluffing to the end.

"Stop, sir," said the cop again. "Stop or I shoot." He had his pistol in his hand. I reasoned that a conscript lad who argued with the leader of his arrest team might well be the type who would pull the trigger. I stopped. "Your identification, please, sir," said the cop.

I could see Lenin plodding back up the path, breathing heavily and wriggling his fingers in anger. The game was up. "I was just trying to help," I said. "I saw him come this way."

"Search him," said Lenin to the Saxon boy. He paused to catch his breath. "Then take him back and lock him up." To the other cop he said, "We'll go to the Müggelheimer Damm, but we've probably lost them. They must have had a car waiting there." He came very close to me and stared me in the eyes. "We'll find out all about it from this one."

Chapter 28

THEY LOCKED ME in an office of the police barracks. It had a barred window and a mortise lock; they figured I wasn't dangerous enough to need a prison cell. In a perverse way I resented that. And I resented the fact that Lenin sent the Saxon kid in to do the first interrogation. "What's your name and who employs you?"—all that sort of crap. And always that accent. I kept trying to guess the exact location of his hometown, but it was a game he wouldn't join. I think he was from some little town in the German backwoods where Poland meets Czechoslovakia. But I got him off guard by talking about his accent and his family. And when I suddenly switched the topic of conversation to the fiasco at Müggelsee, he let slip that the Muntes had got away. I nodded and asked him for something to eat so quickly afterward that I don't think he even noticed what he'd said.

After the Saxon kid had finished, they left a blank-faced young cop sitting in the office with me, but he wouldn't respond to my conversation. He didn't say anything, or even watch me, when I went to look out the window. We were on the top floor of what the international intelligence community calls Normannenstrasse, East Germany's State Security Service block in Berlin-Lichtenberg.

From this side of the building I could look down on

Frankfurter Allee. This wide road is Berlin's main highway eastward and there was a steady stream of heavy traffic. The weather had turned colder now, and the only people on the street were clerical staff from the State Security Ministry filing down the steps into Magdalenenstrasse U-Bahn station at the end of the working day.

Lenin joined in the fun about midnight. They'd taken my wristwatch, of course, along with my money, a packet of French cigarettes, and my Swiss Army knife, but I could hear a church or a municipal clock striking each hour. Lenin was amiable. He even laughed at a joke I made about the coffee. He was older than I had estimated, my age perhaps—no wonder that chase through the forest had made him puff. He wore a brown corduroy suit with button-down top pocket and braided edges to the lapels. I wondered if he'd designed it himself or had picked it up from some old village tailor in a remote part of Hungary or Romania. He liked traveling; he told me that. Then he talked about old American films, the time he'd spent seconded to the security police in Cuba, and his love for English detective stories.

He brought out his tiny cheroots and offered me one; I declined. It was the standard interrogator's ploy.

"I can't smoke them," I told him. "They give me a sore throat."

"Then I suggest that we both smoke the French cigarettes we took from you. Permit?"

I was in no position to object. "Okay," I said. He produced my half-empty packet of Gauloise from his coat and took one before sliding the packet across to me.

"I found those Western cigarettes on the U-Bahn train," I said.

He smiled. "That's what I wrote in the arrest report. You think I don't listen to what you say?" He threw his cigarette lighter to me. It was of Western origin, a disposable one with visible fuel supply. It was very low but it worked. "Now we destroy the evidence by burning, you and me. Right?" He winked conspiratorially.

Lenin, who said his real name was Erich Stinnes, had an encyclopedic memory; he was able to recite endlessly the names of his favorite authors—for they were many and varied—and he seemed to know in bewildering detail every plot they'd written. But he spoke of the fictional characters as if they were alive. "Do you think," he asked me, "that Sherlock Holmes, coming across a criminal of some foreign culture, would find detection more difficult? Is it perhaps true that he is effective only when working against a criminal who shares the creed of the English gentleman?"

"They're just stories," I said. "No one takes them seriously."

"I take them seriously," said Lenin. "Holmes is my mentor."

"Holmes doesn't exist. Holmes never did exist. It's just twaddle."

"How can you be such a philistine," said Lenin. "In *The Sign of Four*, Holmes said that when you have eliminated the impossible, whatever remains, no matter how improbable, must be the truth. Such perception cannot be dismissed lightly."

"But in *A Study in Scarlet* he said almost the opposite," I argued. "He said that when a fact appears opposed to a long train of deductions, it invariably proves to be capable of bearing some other interpretation."

"Ah, so you are a believer," said Lenin. He puffed on the Gauloise. "Anyway, I don't call that a contradiction."

"Look, Erich," I said. "All I know about Sherlock bloody

Holmes is the curious incident of the dog in the night-time."

Lenin waved a hand to silence me, sat back with hands placed fingertips together, and said, "Yes, 'Silver Blaze.' " A frown came as he tried to remember the exact words: "The dog did nothing in the night-time. That was the curious incident."

"Exactly, Erich, old pal," I said. "And, as one Sherlock Holmes fan to another, would you mind explaining to me the equally curious absence of any proper bloody attempt to interrogate me?"

Lenin smiled a tight-lipped little smile, like a parson hearing a risqué joke from a bishop. "And that's just what I would say in your position, Englishman. I told my superior that a senior security man from London will wonder why we are not following the normal procedure. He will begin to hope that he'll get special treatment, I said. He'll think we don't want him to know our interrogation procedure. And he'll think that's because he's going home very soon. And once a prisoner starts thinking along those lines, he closes his mouth very tight. After that it can take weeks to get anything out of him."

"And what did your superior say?" I asked.

"His exact words I am not permitted to reveal." He shrugged apologetically. "But as you can see for yourself, he paid no heed to my advice."

"That I should be interrogated while still warm?"

He half closed his eyes and nodded; again it was the mannerism of a churchman. "It's what should have been done, isn't it? But you can't tell these desk people anything."

"I know," I said.

"Yes. You know what it's like, and so do I," he said. "Both of us work the tough side of the business. I've been West a few times, just as you've come here. But who gets the promotions and the big wages—desk-bound Party bastards. How lucky you are not having the Party system working against you all the time."

"We have got it," I said. "It's called Eton and Oxbridge."

But Lenin was not to be stopped. "Last year my son got marks that qualified him to go to university, but he lost the place to some kid with lower marks. When I complained, I was told that it was official policy to favor the children of working-class parents against those from the professional classes, in which they include me. Shit, I said, you victimize my son because his father was clever enough to pass his exams? What kind of workers' state is that?"

"Are you recording this conversation?"

"So they can put me into prison with you? Do you think I'm crazy?"

"I still want to know why I'm not being interrogated."

"Tell me," he said, suddenly leaning forward, drawing on his cigarette, and blowing smoke reflectively as he formed the question in his mind. "How much per diem do you get?"

"I don't understand."

"I'm not asking you what you do for a living," he said. "All I want to know is how much do they pay you for daily expenses when you are away from home."

"One hundred and twelve pounds sterling per day for food and lodging. Then we get extra expenses, plus travel expenses."

Lenin blew a jet of smoke in a gesture that displayed his indignation. "And they won't even pay us a daily rate. The cashier's office insists upon us writing everything down. We have to account for every penny we've handled."

"That's the sort of little black book I wouldn't like to keep," I said.

"Incriminating. Right. That's it, exactly. I wish I could

get that fact into the heads of the idiots who run this bureau."

"You're not recording any of this?"

"Let me tell you something in confidence," said Lenin. "I was on the phone to Moscow an hour ago. I pleaded with them to let me interrogate you my way. No, they said. The KGB colonel is on his way now, Moscow says—they keep saying that, but he never arrives—you are ordered not to do anything but hold the prisoner in custody. Stupid bastards. That's Moscow for you." He inhaled and blew smoke angrily. "Quite honestly, if you broke down and gave me a complete confession about having an agent in Moscow Central Committee, I'd yawn."

"Let's try you," I said.

He grinned. "What would you do in my place? This KGB colonel will take over your file when he gets here tomorrow morning. Do you think he'll give me any credit for work done before he arrives? Like hell he will. No, sir, I'm not going to dig anything out of you for those Party big shots."

I nodded but I was not beguiled by his behavior. I'd long ago learned that it is only the very devout who toy with heresy. It's only the Jesuit who complains of the Pope, only the devoted parent who ridicules his child, only the super rich who pick up pennies from the gutter. And in East Berlin it is only the truly faithful who speak treason with such self-assurance.

THEY TOOK ME downstairs at seven o'clock the next morning. I'd heard cars arriving shortly before, and men shouting in the way that guard commanders shout when they want to impress some visiting brass.

It was a plush office by East European standards: modern-design Finnish desk and chairs and a sheepskin rug on the floor. A faint aroma of disinfectant mingled with the cheap perfume of the floor polish. This was the smell of Moscow.

Fiona was not sitting behind the desk; she was standing at the side of the room. My friend Lenin was standing stiffly at her side. He'd obviously been briefing her, but Fiona's authority was established by the imperious way in which she dismissed him. "Go to your office and get on with it. I'll call if I want you," she said in that brisk Russian that I'd always admired. So the so-called Erich Stinnes was a Russian—a KGB officer, no doubt. Well, he spoke bloody good Berlin German. Probably he'd grown up here, the son of an occupier, as I was.

Fiona straightened her back as she looked at me. "Well?" she said.

"Hello, Fiona," I said.

"You guessed?" She looked different; harder perhaps, but confident and relaxed. It must have been a relief to be her real self after a lifetime of deception. "Sometimes I was sure you'd guessed the truth."

"What guessing was needed? It was obvious, or should have been."

"So why did you do nothing about it?" Her voice was steel. It was as if she were pushing herself to be as robotic as a weighing machine.

"You know how it is," I said vaguely. "I kept thinking of other explanations. I repressed it. I didn't want to believe it. You didn't make any mistakes, if that's what you mean." It wasn't true of course, and she knew it.

"I should never have handwritten that damned submission. I knew those fools would leave it in the file. They promised . . ."

"Is there anything to drink in this office?" I asked. Now

that I had to face the truth, I found it easier than dealing with the dread of it. Perhaps all fear is worse than reality, just as all hope is better than fulfillment.

"Maybe." She opened the drawers in the desk and found an almost full bottle of vodka. "Will this do?"

"Anything will do," I said, getting a teacup from a shelf and pouring myself a measure of it.

"You should cut down on the drinking," she said impassively.

"You don't make it easy to do," I said. I gulped some and poured more.

She gave me the briefest of smiles. "I wish it hadn't ended like this."

"That sounds like a line from Hollywood," I said.

"You make it hard on yourself."

"That's not the way I like it."

"I always made it a condition that nothing would happen to you. Every mission you did after that business at Gdynia I kept you safe."

"You betrayed every mission I did, that's the truth of it." That was the humiliating part of it, the way she'd protected me.

"You'll go free. You'll go free this morning. It made no difference that Werner demanded it."

"Werner?"

"He met me with a car at Berlin-Tegel when my plane landed. He held me at pistol point. He threatened me and made me promise to release you. Werner is a schoolboy," she said. "He plays schoolboy games and has the same schoolboy loyalties you had when I first met you."

"Maybe that was my loss," I said.

"But not my gain." She came closer to me, for one last look. "It was a good trick to say you'd cross first. It made me think I might get here in time to catch Brahms Four, your precious von Munte."

"Instead you caught me," I said.

"Yes, that was clever, darling. But suppose I hang on to you?"

"You won't do that," I said. "It wouldn't suit you to have me around. In a Soviet prison I'd be an impediment to you. And an imprisoned husband wouldn't suit that social conscience you care so much about."

"You're right."

"At least you're not trying to find excuses," I said.

"Why should I bother? You wouldn't understand," she said. "You just *talk* about the class system and make jokes about the way it works. I do something about it."

"Don't explain," I said. "Leave me something to be mystified about."

"You'll always be the same arrogant swine I met at Freddy Springfield's party."

"I'd like to think I was just a little smarter than the man you made a fool of then."

"You've got nothing to regret. You'll go back to London and get Dicky Cruyer's desk. By the end of the year you'll be running Bret Rensselaer out of his job."

"Will I?"

"I've made you a hero," she said bitterly. "You made me run for cover, and at a time when no one else suspected the truth. Until you phoned that message about the hand-written report, I thought I could keep going forever and ever."

I didn't answer. I kicked myself for not acknowledging the truth years before—that I had been Fiona's greatest asset. Who would believe that Bernard Samson would be married to a foreign agent and not realize it? Her marriage to me had made her life more complicated, but it had kept her safe.

"And you rescued your precious agent. You got Brahms Four home safely enough to make all your other agents breathe easily once more."

I still said nothing. She might be leading me on. Until I was sure that the Muntes were safe, I preferred to play dumb on the subject.

"Oh, yes. You're a professional success story, my darling. It's only your domestic life that is a disaster. No wife, no home, no children."

She was gloating. I knew she wanted to provoke me into an outburst of bad temper. I recognized that tone of voice from other times, other places, and other arguments. It was the tone of voice she sometimes used to criticize Werner, my grammar, my accent, my suits, my old girlfriends.

"Can I go now?"

"The arresting officer—Major Erich Stinnes—is taking you to Checkpoint Charlie at nine o'clock. The arrangements are all made. You'll be all right." She smiled. She was enjoying this chance to show me how much authority she had. She was a KGB colonel; they would treat her well. The KGB looks after their own, they always have done. It's only the rest of the world they treat like dirt.

I turned to go, but women won't let anything end like that. They always have to sit down at the table for a lecture, or write you a long letter, or make sure they have not just the last word but the last thought too.

"The children will go to the best school in Moscow. It was part of the arrangements I made. I might be able to arrange that you have a safe passage to see them now and again, but I can't promise."

"Of course not," I said.

"And I can't send them to England on visits, darling. I just couldn't trust you to send them back, could I?"

"No," I said. "You couldn't. Now can I go?"

"I paid off the overdraft and put six hundred into your account to pay off Nanny. And one hundred for some outstanding bills. I wrote it all down and left the letter with Mr. Moore, the bank manager."

"Okay."

"The D-G will send for you, of course. You can tell him that the official policy at this end will be one of no publicity about my defection. I imagine that will suit him all right, after all the scandals the service has suffered in the past year."

"I'll tell him," I promised.

"Goodbye then, darling. Do I get one final kiss?"

"No," I said. I opened the door; Lenin was waiting on the landing, leather cap in hand. He saw Fiona standing behind me. He didn't smile in the presence of a senior officer. I wondered if he knew she was my wife. She'd probably be working out of Berlin. Poor Erich Stinnes.

When we got to the ground floor, I walked past him and he hurried to catch up with me as I marched to the front door to get out of that foul building. "Is there anything else?" Lenin asked as he signaled for the car.

"For instance?" I said.

I sat in the black Volvo and looked out at the sunny streets: Stalinallee that had become Karl Marx Allee one night when all the street signs were changed before daybreak. The Alex, left onto Unter den Linden, and then left again so that Checkpoint Charlie was to be seen at the bottom of Friedrichstrasse.

"I'll take you right through the checkpoint," said Stinnes. The driver touched the horn. The frontier police recognized the car, put the booms up, and we drove through without stopping.

The American soldier in the glass-sided hut on the Western side gave us no more than a glance. "Far enough," I said. "I'll get one of these cabs." But in fact I'd already caught sight of Werner. He was seated in the car over the road where we always parked when we waited at Checkpoint Charlie. The Volvo turned and stopped. I got out and took a deep breath of that famous *Berliner Luft*. I wanted to run down to the canal and follow it to Lützowplatz and then to Dad's office on Tauentzienstrasse. I would open his desk and take the chocolate bar that was his ration. I'd climb up the mountain of rubble that filled half the street, and slide down the other side in a cloud of dust. I'd run through the carefully swept ruins of the clinic, where cleaned bottles, dusted bricks, and salvaged pieces of charred timber were arranged so proudly. At the shop on the corner I'd ask Mr. Mauser if Axel could come out to play. And we'd go and find Werner and maybe go swimming. It was that sort of day. . . .

"Did it go all right, Werner?"

"I phoned England an hour ago," said Werner. "I knew it would be the first thing you'd ask. There's an armed police guard around your mother's house. Anything the Russians try won't work. The children are safe."

"Thanks, Werner," I said. Thinking about the children made it easier not to think about Fiona. Better still would be not having to think at all.

A Note on the Type

The text of this book was filmset in a type face called Baskerville. The face is a facsimile reproduction of types cast from molds made for John Baskerville (1706–1775) from his designs. The punches for the revived Linotype Baskerville were cut under the supervision of the English printer George W. Jones.

John Baskerville's original face was one of the forerunners of the type style known to printers as "modern face"—a "modern" of the period A.D. 1800.

Composition by Centennial Graphics, Inc.,
Ephrata, Pennsylvania
Printing and Binding by The Haddon Craftsmen, Inc.,
Scranton, Pennsylvania

Typography and binding design by Virginia Tan